A m...
moonlit m...
a danger...

A Bride by Moonlight

He felt every muscle in his body tighten. "By God," he whispered, "I ought to arrest you for murder—*and* for unladylike language."

She had the audacity to push her face into his. "Have at it," she answered, "and see how far it gets you."

Blinded by frustration and something like lust, Napier tightened his grip. She backed up against the bookcase, rattling a vase of white gladioli perched upon the mantelpiece.

Her eyes widened as he thrust one leg between hers, effectively pinning her. "You once offered me something, Miss Ashton, for my cooperation," he whispered, his hot gaze drifting over her face. "Tell me, does that offer still stand? Are you still so bold?"

She pushed back, setting the heels of her hands to his shoulders. "I'm bold enough to do what I must," she answered. "I'm a survivor, Mr. Napier. And no, I'm not a fool. I know what you are. I see behind your gentlemanly façade. Now I ask you again: *What do you want of me?*"

By Liz Carlyle

A BRIDE BY MOONLIGHT
THE BRIDE WORE PEARLS
THE BRIDE WORE SCARLET
ONE TOUCH OF SCANDAL

Coming Soon

IN LOVE WITH A WICKED MAN

AVON

An Imprint of HarperCollins*Publishers*

AVON BOOKS
An Imprint of HarperCollins*Publishers*
195 Broadway
New York, NY 10007

Copyright © 2013 by Susan Woodhouse
ISBN 978-0-06-210028-3
www.avonromance.com

First Avon Books mass market printing: March 2013

Avon Trademark Reg. U.S. Pat. Off. and in Other Countries, Marca Registrada, Hecho en U.S.A.
HarperCollins® is a registered trademark of HarperCollins Publishers.

Printed in the U.S.A.

10 9 8 7 6 5 4

A Bride
by Moonlight

Our Illustrious
Cast of Characters

The Intrepid Hero & Heroine:

Royden Napier: Hard-bitten assistant commissioner of London's Metropolitan Police, Napier always gets his man. Regrettably, he's had less luck with women. Could it be his cold, steely stare?

Elizabeth "Lisette" Colburne: Tragically orphaned, she was sent to America to be raised under the harsh thumb of an uncle, Mr. Ashton. Now she's back in London, fierce, shrewd, and sworn to punish the man she believes ruined her life—Rance Welham.

With Encore Performances by . . .

Rance Welham, Lord Lazonby: A notorious gambler once arrested for murder, he despises Napier. The enmity deepens when they find themselves vying for the same lady.

Lady Anisha Stafford: Once the object of Napier's affections, she has now turned her attention to Lazonby—yet she hasn't completely cast aside her old beau.

Sir Wilfred Leeton: One of Lazonby's old gambling cohorts, Sir Wilfred's appearance is brief. *Very* brief.

On Loan from the British Government:

Sir George Grey, Bt.: Home Secretary and Napier's indirect supervisor, he selflessly served Crown & Country for over two decades. (Yes, really.)

And Introducing Napier's family:

Henry Tarleton, Viscount Duncaster: Napier's estranged grandfather, he rules his dynasty with an iron fist. But the recent deaths of both his brother-in-law and his heir have nearly broken him.

Miss Gwyneth Tarleton: Duncaster's eldest granddaughter. Professional spinster and blue-stocking, she dislikes men on principle, and her upstart cousin Napier in particular.

Anne, Lady Keaton: Gwen's sister, Lady Keaton is happily wed and has reserved judgment with regard to Napier.

Miss Beatrice Tarleton: Gwen and Anne's half-sister, aged eleven. With her father and great-uncle dead within months of one another, Bea fears Grandpapa Duncaster could be next.

Cordelia, Lady Hepplewood: Duncaster's half sister, widowed under mysterious circumstances. Great-aunt to Napier as well as to Gwen, Anne, and Bea, she is an egregious snob and horrified Napier might inherit the title.

Tony, now Lord Hepplewood: Cordelia's son is a charming wastrel who has ignored his mother's commands to find a wife. Could his prodigious gaming debts have something to do with a sudden betrothal?

Miss Diana Jeffers: Lady Hepplewood's companion, Diana was betrothed to Lord Duncaster's heir, Lord Saint-Bryce, but he died before they could marry.

And lastly:

Mr. Bodkins: Former family solicitor to Lisette's late grandfather, the kindly Bodkins still tries to keep Lisette out of trouble—but she doesn't make it easy.

Fanny: Lisette's maid and companion, she always speaks her mind.

Jolley: A professional forger, he reluctantly serves as Napier's valet.

Mrs. Jansen: Impoverished widow and Gwen's old schoolmate, Mrs. Jansen is Bea's governess.

Dr. Underwood: Duncaster's family physician.

Miss Felicity Willet: Tony's new fiancée. Her father is Lady Hepplewood's worst nightmare—a nouveau-riche industrialist.

Sir Philip Keaton: Anne's quiet but kind husband, and a prominent MP.

PROLOGUE

A Vision in Blue

1847
Whitehall

*T*ruth.

This simple word was Royden Napier's stock in trade. The means by which he made his way in the world. The yardstick by which he measured every person who came into his life and into his office.

But truth, like beauty, was often elusive, whereas lies were common as houseflies. Sooner or later, in Napier's experience, everyone lied. Or cheated. Or pilfered. Or worse— sometimes *much* worse. And thus was the whole of the Metropolitan Police employed in the service of Her Majesty the Queen.

Oh, Napier had often been called cynical, but every person who climbed the four flights of stairs that led from Whitehall Place up to his offices inevitably had a tale to tell, from the government toadies who came to bluster and to press their political influence upon him, to the investigators who served under him, all the way down to the criminals occasionally hauled up from Scotland Yard to face him.

Most all of them were willing to sacrifice the truth—or push it bloody near a precipice—in order to get what they wanted. To make things look as they wished them to look, and to achieve something that would bring them influence or revenge or freedom.

And the beautiful woman waiting outside his office was, in Napier's hard-honed estimation, right amongst them. In what way, and to what end, he could not quite make out. Not *yet*.

But she intrigued him all the same.

What tale, he wondered, would such a beautiful woman tell? What self-serving need drew her here to this place of angst and shadows where no one came of their own volition, unless they wanted something quite, quite desperately?

Cocking his head a tad to the left, Napier cut an assessing glance through the crack in his office door and down his long, wood-planked antechamber. The room housed his clerks to one side, and to the other a row of high-backed, notoriously uncomfortable chairs.

Generally speaking, it was his policy to keep visitors squirming, and to dispatch them out again with all haste. Number Four Whitehall was rather like a gristmill, with more work to grind out than wanted weighing, and Napier was booked from now until death with meetings, appointments, and general government arse kissing.

But the long-legged, whippet-thin redhead beyond his door looked ruthlessly determined to wait him out, like some harrier haunting a foxhole.

He let his gaze drift over her, taking her measure. Her gloved hands were fisted hard in her lap, while her chin was lifted almost arrogantly. Perhaps five-and-twenty, he guessed, the lady wore a hat, a small but passé confection of dark blue net and velvet that oddly suited her cloud of wild, fiery hair.

She had not dressed that hair in the insipid loops and ringlets currently in vogue, but instead had twisted it loosely into a soft chignon that had fought its constraints and was winning. Tendrils curled about her face, and let down, he estimated, it would have fallen halfway to the floor like a cascade of red satin. Interestingly, a small, shabby portmanteau sat at her feet.

Napier was especially mistrustful of women—thrice so when they were beautiful.

The redhead, however, was not precisely beautiful.

No, she was . . . *striking.* And furious. He knew enough of human nature to recognize that raw emotion when he saw it.

No matter. He yanked open his door, and prepared to dispatch her back down the stairs with the rest of them.

"Assistant Police Commissioner Napier," he said brusquely, blocking the width of the door with his shoulders. "How may I be of service?"

Her head swiveled toward him, her eyes sharp as shooting stars on a moonless night.

"By doing your job," she said, rising in a rustle of crisp, dark blue silk.

"I beg your pardon," he said coldly, "but I believe I've not the pleasure of a proper introduction."

The lady did not so much as blanch. "You might remember me as Elizabeth Colburne."

It was a common enough name, but one he couldn't place. Still, she was looking at him expectantly, and he felt a curious shiver; a premonition, he was later to think. With a wave of his hand, he stepped back and ushered her in.

"Your servant, ma'am."

Dark, angular brows flew aloft. "Are you indeed?" she

said curtly. "London's newspapers leave one with the impression you are the Earl of Lazonby's servant."

Napier was left in a rare moment of speechlessness.

The lady swished past, the portmanteau in one hand, her skirts lightly lifted in the other, as if she feared his very presence might sully them.

He shut the door rather harder than was his habit. "Understand me, madam," he said rounding on her. "I am no friend of Lord Lazonby's. Besides, the man is edging near his deathbed—cancer, I hear. No friend but God can help him now."

"Oh, what drama!" She gave a disdainful sniff. "The man is a *Welham*, is he not? That vile, vulgar breed is hard to kill—as I believe his son and heir has so aptly—and so repeatedly—demonstrated to you."

"Rance Welham may have thumbed his nose at the law and survived a long life on the run," said Napier grimly. "But I am neither judge, nor jury, nor executioner, ma'am. I'm with the Metropolitan Police. And we've done our job with regard to Lord Lazonby's son. And done it admirably."

"*Admirably?*" she said shrilly. "Good God, you could not even kill the man properly! And now I read he is about to be exonerated and let out of prison again! It is unconscionable!"

Napier planted one hand flat on the corner of his desk and leaned into her. "I beg your pardon," he said coldly, "but the matter is practically settled."

"And if the police had done their jobs the first time, Rance Welham would have long ago rotted in his grave! But it was a travesty. It was a—a bungled mess of bureaucratic humbug! It was grossly, egregiously inadequate! Good God, sir, can you people not even tie a proper knot in a noose?"

Napier forced a tight smile. "You are a master of the adjective, ma'am."

But her eyes had begun to shimmer tellingly. "Bad enough,

sir, you could not even hang him properly," she went on. "But now you mean to let him simply waltz out of Newgate Prison a free man?"

"Waltz?" Napier muttered. "A royal cavalcade, more like."

"No, no," she went on, her voice rising, "*better than* a free man! Why, once that influence-peddling father of his actually *is* dead, Rance Welham will be a peer of the realm—he will *be* Lord Lazonby—and he will enjoy a life of leisure and wealth beyond measure, whilst his victims lie forgotten."

His temper finally slipped a notch. "God's truth, madam," he said coldly, "do you think I'm any better pleased with this turn of events than you are? My own father fought this case to his dying breath—and it was not easy to convict the son of a peer, particularly one so rich as the Earl of Lazonby."

For a moment, the room fell perfectly still save for the clatter of afternoon traffic turning the corner into Whitehall Place, far below his open window. The woman had gone suddenly pale—more pale, that was to say, than she had been upon walking into his office, for her skin had a shimmering ivory translucence that showed her every emotion.

"Yes, that's what it always comes down to, isn't it?" Her voice dropped, oddly tremulous. "Money, money, money—always, and every time—for this is England, and influence is bought by the rich, and the poor be damned. Oh, that much I well remember!"

Thrown by her sudden turn, Napier hesitated.

It was a heartbeat too long. Mrs. Colburne still clutched the portmanteau, and in one smooth motion, she stepped toward him and upended it, sending a cascade of bundled banknotes down upon the burnished surface of his desk in an avalanche.

Napier could only stare. The heap shifted, and one bundle fell to the floor, bursting its string and sending the notes skittering across his floor in the autumn breeze.

"My God," he whispered.

He lifted his gaze from the pile to her eyes, and his mouth went dry.

There was a look of unholy satisfaction in her cool, unblinking gaze.

"Well," she said softly. "There you have it, sir. American dollars, yes, for I came in great haste. Still, I account it some twenty thousand pounds. So tell me, Mr. Napier: How much English justice will *that* buy me?"

"I beg your pardon?"

She waved a hand across his desk. "Take it," she said. "It is all the cash I have in the world, or near it. But my money is as good as Lord Lazonby's. And by my reckoning, twenty thousand pounds ought to be just enough to keep Rance Welham in jail—this time until he's *damned well dead.*"

"Good God, I begin to believe you are mad." He jerked the case from her grip and began methodically shoving the piles of banknotes back into it. "Madam, it is against the law to attempt to bribe a Government employee. Kindly take your money and get out or I swear to God I will arrest you."

"Arrest me?" Any softness vanished. "My heavens, the law of the land must have changed mightily since I last lived in London. It is perfectly acceptable for stone-cold killers to walk free, but my outright bribe is thought an insult?"

"Sit *down*," he ordered, "and *hush*. Yes, I said *arrested*, madam. And do not dare try me."

But she did not sit down—or hush. "Dear me," she murmured, watching him gather the loose bills. "I have badly miscalculated you, Mr. Napier."

Napier rammed the last fistful home, dropped the portmanteau to the floor by her feet, and glowered. "That, madam, is a grievous understatement."

Apparently undaunted, she crossed the office to stand mere inches from him. He could feel the heat of her anger rising and with it her scent; something warm and exotic, like Oriental lilies beneath a hot August sun.

Tugging off her gloves with neat, sharp jerks, she let her gaze drift down him; an assessing, almost artful glance. "Well," she said, her voice gone husky. "If not money, Assistant Commissioner, is there any other way I might . . . just *might* . . . persuade you?"

Tossing aside the gloves, the woman flicked open the first button of her bodice, revealing an inch of tender flesh, pale and rich as cream.

There was a way, yes.

Or for an instant, it felt so. Napier felt lust shiver through him, surging like liquid heat into his loins. A rush of desire pooled in his belly. He wanted what she was apparently offering and was at once appalled that he would even consider it. Still, he was not a saint.

Napier swallowed hard and tried to force his gaze back up. Good Lord, the woman wasn't even his type. Too thin, too tall. Too wild eyed and red haired. Too . . . *intense.*

She stepped another inch closer, and slipped free another button. "Is that interest burning in your eyes, Mr. Napier?" Her breath teased over his cheek. "Come, make me an offer. *Quid pro quo.* I am quite desperate, you see."

Napier willed himself to step back, but it was harder than it should have been. *Everything* was getting harder than it should have been. He fairly itched to set his finger to that seductive hollow below her throat, and then to draw it lower. And lower still.

Acknowledgment flickered in her eyes, then she let her gaze trail down his waistcoat.

He crooked one eyebrow. "By God, madam," he said, "you are a bold piece."

Her lashes fluttered back up. "When I've no choice, yes," she replied. "I want Rance Welham punished—or hanged—

and I'll sell my soul to the devil to get it. Selling myself to you—well, really, would there be any difference?"

Napier cut her off ruthlessly. "Account yourself fortunate, my dear, I don't simply toss up your skirts and take what you're throwing at me, *quid pro quo* be damned." He'd seized her arm and was urging her toward the door. "I'm not known for my gentlemanly restraint."

"Why, Mr. Napier, is the rest of you as firm as that grip?" she said, tossing a hot gaze over her shoulder. "And are you quite, quite sure you cannot be persuaded to bargain?"

Something exploded then—rage or raw lust—he was never quite sure. But he spun her around, intent on tempering the vixen's tart tongue.

And it was then that he saw it; the flash of unmistakable fear in her eyes. Oh, she hid it well, but Napier had a decade's experience spotting cheats, liars, and false bravado. He softened his grip a little.

"Listen to me," he said grimly, "I know trumpery when I see it. You're overwrought, yes, and angry. But surely this isn't the sort of woman you are."

"Do you think not?" Her chin came up again, but the gaze faltered. "I—I could do it. Indeed, you're handsome enough, save for those grim, hard eyes. So will you? Help me, I mean? If I do . . . well, whatever you ask?"

He felt that awful combination of desire and disgust shiver through him again. But the woman's bottom lip was trembling now, and there was no hiding her potent mix of fear and fury.

"My dear," he said quietly, "believe me when I say you are desirable. But you play a dangerous game. What could possibly be worth what you're offering me? Your honor. Your integrity. Would you really taint yourself for mere vengeance?"

At that, something inside her seemed to collapse, her face softening with grief and her shoulders rolling inward as if she might swoon. "*Oh, God*," she whispered, one hand going to her mouth.

Without conscious thought, Napier caught her hard against him. She sagged to his chest on a deep, wretched sob that seemed to have been dredged from a well of despair, her fingers curling into his coat as if clinging to him might keep her from drowning in it. Against all wisdom, he held her to him, one hand set between her shoulder blades.

Damn it all, he thought.

Napier had little experience with crying females, but he was not cruel, he hoped. And her tears were those of true hopelessness, without one whit of artifice. Worse, a traitorous part of him *wanted* to hold her; wanted to draw in her warm, exotic scent and pretend this was not utter madness.

But it *was* madness. She seemed to realize it, too, pushing herself suddenly, almost roughly, from his embrace. She whirled about, turning her back and dashing at her eyes with the backs of her hands.

"Oh, this won't do!" she rasped, sounding angry with herself. "I have *not* come all this way merely to turn craven. I cannot. I *won't*."

Napier felt suddenly awkward—and with his lust diminished, logic was creeping back in. "Ma'am, perhaps you might enlighten me," he said. "I don't entirely grasp your interest in the Welham case."

She turned, her eyes still shimmering with unshed tears. "Have you never even bothered to read your father's files, Mr. Napier?" she asked softly. "I'm the youngest daughter of Sir Arthur Colburne, who was ruined—indeed, practically *killed*—by Mr. Welham."

Napier went still inside.

The horrific mess of a murder case had been his late father's, yes, but at least a dozen years ago. And Sir Arthur hadn't been the victim. Indeed, he'd scarcely been involved.

Still, Napier did vaguely remember a daughter. Ellen? Elinor? She had been the murdered man's fiancée, but she'd died shortly after the trial. Had there been a younger child? Apparently so. And she was a *Miss*, not a Mrs. . . .

Damnation.

"Miss Colburne," he said quietly, "all this happened long before I came to work here. I believe Rance Welham killed your sister's fiancé, yes. But as I understood it, Sir Arthur killed himself."

"Because Welham left him no choice!" Emotion blazed up again, burning her cheeks. "He died of desperation! And what of my poor sister? Sent off to die a penniless orphan, a world away from all the comforts she had known! Her fiancé murdered, her heart broken. And all of it, Mr. Napier—*all of it*—lies at Welham's door."

Napier set his jaw hard. "I am sorry for your loss, ma'am," he said. "But neither your money nor your tears can alter what's to come. Welham has found himself some influential friends—friends close to the Queen. Moreover, his father has persuaded the key witness to recant. And now the Lord Chancellor means to overturn his conviction."

"Overturn it, perhaps, and that's a travesty," she cried. "But that cannot be the end of your prosecution, for you must try again to—"

"Yes, Miss Colburne, that *will* be the end of it," he grimly interjected, "whether either of us likes it or not."

He strode to the door and drew it open. The lady, however, stood pat, her fury returning tenfold. "You, sir, are a dastard and a—a *bully*," she said, her voice quaking. "But make no mistake, I am neither—and I *will* make Welham pay, Mr. Napier—if you will not. Indeed, if you *dare* not."

"I dare to do a great many things, Miss Colburne," he said darkly, "but I have little interest in political suicide. Now kindly go. And in the future, I'd suggest you temper your words. However sympathetic I might feel, the Crown will account what you just said as a threat, and expect me to charge you accordingly."

Eyes blazing, she reached around him and snatched her portmanteau. "Oh, it was not *a threat*, sir," she said, shooting him one last parting glance as she strode out. "It is simply God's own truth—a thing, I daresay, wholly unfamiliar to you."

Napier said no more.

He was not a man who hesitated, or suffered much in the way of uncertainty. And yet, with one hand set high upon his door frame, he stood and watched the woman stalk across his antechamber, and did nothing.

He did nothing because he knew in his heart that she was right.

Elizabeth Colburne had lost everything.

And Rance Welham was a cheat and a killer who deserved to die.

The truth, after all, was Napier's stock in trade.

Angry with himself—and with circumstance—he slammed the door and returned to his desk, looking down in pure frustration.

The woman had left her blasted gloves on his desk. Impossibly delicate bits of kidskin that fastened down the wrist with tiny pearl buttons. They were still warm, the scent of lilies and new leather rising with what was left of her heat.

For an instant, Napier allowed himself to draw in the tantalizing fragrance. Then, on a muttered oath, he yanked open a desk drawer, slapped them inside, and slammed it almost viciously shut.

CHAPTER 1

In Which the Devil
Snatches His Own

1849
Greenwich

There are a few rare men who can run roughshod over the perils of life armed with little more than superior instincts and an innate distrust of the human race. Napier was just such a man, and it had earned him an ugly nickname.

Roughshod Roy.

London's underworld had long ago ginned that one up. But today's call had nothing to do with the underworld, more was the pity.

His hackles up, Napier stepped down from the elegant carriage that had been sent to drag him from his files and his afternoon cup of Darjeeling, now left to go cold upon his desk. Ramming his black leather folio under one arm, he paused amidst the magnificence, his heavy, hooded gaze swiftly sweeping the labyrinth of aristocrats that wound through Sir Wilfred Leeton's rear gardens. Then slowly, he exhaled.

All the elegance in the world could not mask it.

Death.

He could feel it like a tangible thing.

Two uniformed constables followed him down, their boots crunching softly in the pea-gravel. The carriage, emblazoned in gold with the arms of the Earl of Lazonby, clattered away to leave the trio standing alone like grim chunks of flotsam plunked into an ocean of opulence.

Noticing them, a portly, agitated butler hastened from a knot of servants by the kitchen gardens and bowed.

Napier leaned very near. "*Not . . . Sir Wilfred?*" he murmured.

But the servant's eyes were bleak as he nodded. After a brief exchange of whispered words, he pointed at a small stone outbuilding.

The murmuring clusters of ladies and gentlemen fell away from Napier's path, their eyes following him uneasily as he strode up the swath of manicured lawn that led from the mansion's rear gardens toward the little structure, half sunk into the earth.

And even then—despite his ill temper and impatience—it struck him as odd that, of all the eyes upon him, it was the cold, viridian gaze of Elizabeth Ashton he felt most keenly.

It was especially odd since, until that moment, he'd known nothing of Elizabeth Ashton's existence. Well, not *precisely*. But he felt the heat of that gaze—if a cold gaze can be said to give off heat—all the way up the path, though why she would have caught his attention so thoroughly he could not possibly have said. Perhaps—even amidst those first, critical moments—some part of him realized that an old wheel was slowly turning full circle.

Or perhaps it had something to do with the fact that the

lithe, brown-haired lady in gray felt oddly familiar as she stood like a dove amongst the peacocks.

And troublingly, her gloved hand rested upon the arm of the very man who'd dragged him here: Rance Welham, the recently ennobled Earl of Lazonby, a scoundrel so tainted by trickery and deceit his soul could not have been washed clean had it been turned inside out and boiled in lye.

But however genial or villainous a man might be, when death came upon him it was always the same: ugly and graceless. Often brutish. The death inside the stone building had been particularly so, he realized, staring down at it.

Sir Wilfred had an oozing, ashen hole in the middle of his forehead with a small stream of blood trickling from it, now thickening to a dark red trail across the white-tiled floor. Napier felt the hair on his neck prickle again. This wasn't the first murder Sir Wilfred had been involved in, for he'd once been a witness at a salacious trial—Lazonby's, in fact. The coincidence troubled him.

Ignoring the rustle of skirts and the buzz of whispers behind him, Napier stepped from the grass down the stone steps into the cool depths of what had once been a sort of dairy, or perhaps just a springhouse.

Illogically, perhaps because it was expected of him, he squatted down to take the man's nonexistent pulse.

"Ah, Will!" he murmured, rising. "What secrets, I wonder, were you keeping?"

It was a habit of his—and a bad one—this talking to corpses.

Sir Wilfred did not respond; they never did.

Now supine upon the floor, with his bristled, thinning hair, his brown waistcoat drawn taut over a middle-aged paunch, and his surprisingly dainty feet shod in dark leather, Sir Wilfred resembled nothing so much as an overfed woodchuck who'd chosen the wrong moment to dart from his hedgerow.

But no wee forest creature, this. No, Sir Wilfred Leeton

was trouble of the worst sort: the political sort—and given the circumstances of his death and the people involved—Christ Jesus! Before this case was finished, its tentacles would likely spread throughout the whole of the Home Office.

Already Napier was ensnared in those tentacles—just as had been intended, he suspected, by Lord Lazonby. Assistant police commissioners did not handle murder investigations. But he would have to handle this one; no mere minion would do. Because something had just gone very wrong here—something more significant than Sir Wilfred's death. And for the life of him, Napier could not grasp what. Not yet. But he would.

Not too many days past, Napier had been to the opera with a hale and hearty Sir Wilfred—or had met up with him there, at any rate. The fellow had been an old acquaintance of Napier's late father, the previous assistant commissioner. And while Napier had neither liked nor trusted Sir Wilfred, the waste of any human life—even one so pampered and dissolute as this—left him fairly itching for justice.

Suddenly, an inexplicable frisson of awareness ran down his spine. Napier cut a glance at the open window. Even from a distance, he could see the woman in gray still watching him, her clear, cool gaze unwavering. The frisson twisted and shot deep; the strangest, most intimate shiver, like lust long remembered or a yearning he couldn't explain.

Napier caught his breath, shook off the ridiculous notion, and turned away. The lady was none of his concern. *Yet.*

Beyond the little door, he could hear the widow's wracking sobs begin, her stunned incomprehension having at last given over to grief. With a curt gesture, he motioned down the local constable, who hesitated uncertainly just beyond the top step, wringing the hat he clutched in his hands. This being Greenwich rather than London, the fellow looked as different from a Metropolitan Police officer as chalk from cheese.

Oh, yes. This one was *definitely* chalk.

Napier forced a thin smile, and prayed for the well-being of his just-polished boots.

The chap tiptoed across the tiled floor. "Y-yes, Assistant Commissioner?"

"Your first death, is it, Mr. Terry?"

"F-first one shot, aye," the young man managed. "Mostly just get drownings here—though last winter we f-found a sailor knifed."

"Good man." Napier gave the constable a firm, bucking-up thump between the shoulder blades. "You're inured to violent death."

"W-well, that chap, 'e was knifed on Deptford Green, then the corpse dumped here," the lad went on, his eyes following the blood that trailed across the white tile and into the cement spring box, tingeing the water pink.

Napier dipped his head to catch the shorter fellow's gaze. "Mr. Terry?"

He looked up, his wide, pale eyes blinking once. "Y-yes, sir?"

"You aren't going to cast up your accounts on our crime scene, are you?"

Terry's lips thinned as if to press his mouth shut. He gave a feeble shake of his head.

"Relieved to hear it." Napier motioned to a bloody garden spade by the spring box. "Now, what's that about?"

"They're s-saying Sir Wilfred—" The young man swallowed hard, and cut a glance down at the corpse. "That he attacked a lady with it and—"

"What lady?" Napier demanded.

"The Indian lady from the fortune-teller's tent," said Terry, dropping his voice to a whisper. "Reckon he meant to kill her, but they're keeping it mum. Awful, in'it, sir?"

Napier felt a chill run through him. It was true, then, what the butler had said. Lady Anisha Stafford, a woman he greatly esteemed, had been somehow involved.

"How badly was she hurt?" Napier demanded, his voice gone utterly cold.

"She . . . she walked away, I heard. But Lord Lazonby rushed her off at once. To protect her from the scandal."

"Good for him," said Napier darkly. And for once, he meant it.

"But it *is* a frightful lot of blood, sir," Terry went on, "when you add it all up, I mean." This was followed by another heaving grunt. He clapped a hand over his mouth.

"Damn it, man, *get out*." Napier thumbed toward the door.

With a withering look, the fellow fled back up the steps and into the slanting sun.

Napier grimly surveyed the old stone structure and its supine corpse again, his eyes missing little. The garden spade. The blood. An overturned stool. A broken crock, tipped off a marble slab beneath the window.

Damn it all. Violent death was never a good thing, but it was a vast deal worse when the aristocracy was involved. Proving his point, Lazonby remained outside with the lush lady in gray, arrogant as ever and obviously bent on obstructing justice at every turn.

He felt the rage well up in him again, his hand fisting impotently. Lazonby was nothing but a murderous thug in fine wool worsted who'd run circles around Scotland Yard for years, once even eluding the gallows. He was not fit to shine Lady Anisha's shoes, let alone court her. *And now he'd got her hurt.*

But what could have caused such a sequence of harrowing events?

Sir Wilfred and Lazonby had once run in the same dangerous circles. Perhaps it had something to do with Lazonby's past? And after killing Sir Wilfred—or having had him killed—Lazonby had sent for Napier simply to taunt him?

On the bright side, if Napier could prove that theory, the Crown might give him another crack at putting Lazonby back on the gallows.

Napier flipped open his black leather folio, and set to work in earnest.

*F*rom across the broad swath of grass, the Earl of Lazonby watched as Greenwich's green-faced constable hastened back up the dairy stairs, gagging, to bolt for the trees—nauseated by Royden Napier's incessant conceit, no doubt.

To his left, he could hear Sir Wilfred's widow beginning to sob quietly. The sound tore at him. Lazonby was not a heartless monster. He wanted to go to her and say . . .

What? That her husband had been a lying, murderous bastard who deserved something a good deal worse than a bullet between the eyes? And more promptly served up, too. About fifteen years sooner would have suited Lazonby, and saved him two stays in prison with a miserable career in the French Foreign Legion sandwiched between.

He had not known until today how deceitful—how utterly evil—Sir Wilfred had been. Funny how a gun to his head had put the bastard in such a confessional mood.

No, in his present state, it was far better to leave Lady Leeton's consolation to the experts: that bevy of well-bred dowagers who now flitted about her, cooing and dabbing at their hostess's tears. As to her annual charity garden party, next year's subscription sales would surely treble this. Society loved nothing so well as a scandal.

As to the tears more immediate to Lord Lazonby, they had long since dried, though the woman who now called herself

Mrs. Elizabeth Ashton still bore a bit of her weight upon his arm. Nonetheless, much of her color had returned since he'd dragged her from Sir Wilfred's dramatic denouement, and the lady's visage had resumed the proud angles that were so familiar to him.

He was stunned to realize how long it had taken him to recognize her. But now, as his gaze drifted over her face—an unconventional face, to be sure, but interesting all the same—he could so easily make out precisely who she was.

Who she had been all along.

He felt an utter fool. For better than a year, Elizabeth had hounded him—in one guise or another—making his life a greater hell than it already had been. She had blamed him for a murder he had not committed. For causing, indirectly, her father's suicide. And today, at long last, he understood why. Because Sir Wilfred had set him up.

"You have regained yourself, I see, Mrs. Ashton," he said, not unkindly, "if that is indeed your name nowadays?"

A faint blush crept up her face—all the way up to her strong, finely angled cheekbones. "There's nothing nefarious about it. Since I volunteer at Lady Leeton's charity school, I simply decided *Mrs.* sounded more prudent than *Miss.*"

"Ah! So the name *isn't* Ashton?" he asked coolly.

She lightly lifted both brows. "As opposed to Colburne?"

"Oh, let's not talk about your many aliases just now," said Lazonby. "I'm not sure I can count that high. But you *are* clever, my dear. I should have realized how clever back when you started hounding my every step, and insulting my character at every turn—in the newspapers, no less."

Her smile was faint. "Whatever roles I may have been playing, I have never denied that I'm Sir Arthur Colburne's daughter," she said. "But since my aunt and uncle Ashton were compelled to raise me once that monster killed my father—"

"No, no, dear girl!" Lazonby quietly interjected, squeezing her hand where it lay upon his coat sleeve. "Set your every word with care now. My friend Napier there believes he has a murder on his hands. And we all know your father killed *himself.*"

Her strange, blue-green eyes glittered. "After he was ruined, yes."

"Indeed," said Lazonby tightly. "But you wished to believe that was *my* doing. So did the police. Every one of you played right into Sir Wilfred's hands all those years ago. And look what that stubbornness has brought down upon our heads, my dear."

"I am not *your dear,*" she said hotly. "And you are still a scoundrel."

"Aye," said Lazonby dryly, "but an innocent one."

The lady cut a sidelong glance at the dairy's door. "Oh, dear God," she whispered, pressing her fingertips to her mouth. "I keep thinking I'll wake up—that I can go back— but Sir Wilfred really is . . . *dead.*"

"And in the end, neither of us will feel much regret about it," Lazonby predicted, cutting an assessing glance around. "But press that point too loudly, my dear, and you'll be giving yourself a clear motive for murdering him."

She looked suddenly afraid. "But I . . . I need to tell Napier *everything,*" she whispered. "He'll find out, Lazonby. And then I shall be the one in prison, not you."

"Don't you dare," Lazonby grimly ordered. "I can only do so much to protect you."

"I wonder you even trouble yourself," she said bitterly.

"Only because I want something from you," Lazonby returned. "I need my good name cleared. I can't have you accused of murder. Napier is dangerous; he'd have a noose round your neck in an instant—regardless of guilt. Trust me. I know how his father was."

"Trust you!" she murmured. "Dear God."

"Elizabeth, listen to me. You're the only person who heard Sir Wilfred's confession before he died. After all these years of blaming me, now you *know* I'm innocent—and you are going to make Napier believe it. Ruined, you're of no use to me. Moreover, I've *been* to prison, you'll recall. I would not wish it on anyone."

"Yes, he'd see me hanged, wouldn't he?" she whispered, looking away. "You will never let me forget this, will you?"

"Why should I?" he said calmly. "By the way, kindly adjust your shawl. You have a powder burn on your bodice— yes, just there. Thank God you had the presence of mind to wear gray."

"I always have presence of mind," she returned.

"Indeed, I have noticed."

"Though I'll say it again, Lord Lazonby," Miss Ashton interjected, "just in case you failed to grasp it the first time: I did not carry that pistol in my reticule all these months with any intention of shooting Sir Wilfred Leeton."

Lazonby flashed a muted grin. "Lord, no!" he agreed. "I think we all know your intent was to shoot *me*—assuming you couldn't get the noose round my neck again."

But this insightful pronouncement was met by Napier's reappearance from the shadows of the dairy to converse with his constables. A moment later, Napier was striding purposefully toward them.

Lazonby cut his gaze toward her and winked. "Well, curtains up, my dear!" he murmured. "Now, are we ready to tread the boards?"

*W*ith the torch passed and a few simple reminders given for the coroner, Napier went back up the steps and onto the manicured swath of green that stretched to the Leetons' mansion.

"Direct everyone away from here," he ordered to the two officers he'd dragged with him from Scotland Yard, "save for Lazonby and the other witness."

"Aye, sir," said the more senior. "And what of the widow?"

But Napier's gaze—and his breath—had caught on the woman in gray again. "Just see Lady Leeton safely inside," he murmured distractedly, "and I'll speak with her after I'm done with Lazonby and the governess, or whatever the devil she is."

Already Napier had asked the butler to provide him the garden party's guest list; the thing would doubtless read like a page ripped from DeBrett's. But it little mattered. All of them, he'd been told, had been situated by the tea tent on the west lawn. They had merely heard rather than seen the shot that felled their host.

All save for Lady Anisha, and the pair who now regarded him across the swath of grass.

He watched the woman carefully as he approached. Those icy, blue-green eyes flickered again with the faintest hint of discomfiture as he drew up before them, but the tell was quickly veiled, and her pale, luminescent mask thoroughly returned to its place.

The look of her set him on edge. There was something . . . something familiar in the turn of her face. And yet it was wrong somehow.

No. He did not know her.

Did he?

"Lazonby." Napier gave the earl a too-curt nod then introduced himself to the woman.

"Elizabeth Ashton," she returned, her voice husky as if with tears. "I teach grammar at Lady Leeton's charity school."

That took Napier aback. Despite his joke to the constable, there was nothing of the prim schoolmistress in those cool, knowing eyes. And seen up close, her plain gray gown was of an obviously fine quality.

"Won't you have a seat, ma'am?" he suggested, waving a hand at the stone bench Lady Leeton had vacated.

Lord Lazonby, however, did not relinquish her arm, but instead escorted her to the bench and remained standing stiffly beside her like the soldier he'd once been.

Napier jerked his head toward the path. "Walk with me a moment, Lazonby, if you would be so kind?"

"I've nothing to say that cannot be said in front of Miss Ashton," said the earl coolly.

Napier cut the lady another glance. "Very well, then," he said. "What's the meaning of all this? Why send for me?"

Lazonby's smile was faint. "Your old friend's corpse isn't cause enough?"

"Sir Wilfred was barely an acquaint—"

"Oh, he was much more than an acquaintance to your late father, the previous assistant commissioner." Lazonby's voice had a nasty, warning edge to it now. "In fact, Sir Wilfred was explaining—mere moments before his untimely death—precisely *how* close they were."

"What is your point, Lazonby?" Against his will, Napier felt his ire rising, as it always did in the earl's presence. "I'm hardly my father."

"No, but you have his old job," Lazonby countered. "His old office. His old files. *My* old files, in point of fact—the ones documenting my wrongful conviction for murder."

Napier felt his lip curl. "I may be a mere civil servant, my lord, but I'll be damned to hell before I'm accountable to the likes of *you*," he whispered. "Besides, this is Greenwich, not London. I've no jurisdiction here."

"Jurisdiction, perhaps not," said Lazonby. "But influence? Aye, and plenty of it."

"You're wasting my time, Lazonby," said Napier.

Lazonby's eyes flashed. "I sent for you because it is to our mutual benefit that Sir Wilfred's death be handled discreetly."

Napier answered his disdainful smile with one of his own. "Is it indeed?" he murmured. "I cannot think of one other occasion, sir, when our best interests have had so much as a nodding acquaintance with one another."

"Sir Wilfred lies dead in his own dairy," said Lazonby again. "Don't you wish to know how it happened?"

"Admittedly I might be wrong," said Napier snidely, "but I was of the impression the gentleman had been shot in the head."

"Yes, but it was an accident!" the lady interjected. "Sir Wilfred was—he was a madman! He seized the gun and—"

"And it went off inadvertently," Lazonby interjected, settling a hand over the woman's shoulder.

"Oh?" Napier's gaze swung down, pinning the lady's odd eyes. "Did it indeed?"

"Really, Miss Ashton," Lazonby continued. "You are overset. Permit me to explain."

"Oh, I don't know," said Napier. "I might trust the lady's opinion over yours. Moreover, she looks about as cool as an ice pick to me."

At that, Lazonby leaned very near. "You overstep yourself, Assistant Commissioner," he whispered, "and at great peril. Now, I will tell you just what happened here today. And you will take down every word of it in your little black book. And then, sir, you will make this business go away."

But this last Napier scarcely heard. Instead he had tugged out his pocket watch and was staring at it.

"Dear me, old chap," said Lazonby mockingly. "I do hope we aren't keeping you from your afternoon constitutional?"

Napier raised his gaze to meet the earl's. "By God, you sent for me *before* Sir Wilfred was shot!" he said accusingly. "You had to have done. That corpse is still warm. The Leetons' butler says the shot was heard round four o'clock. I was halfway across Westminster Bridge by then."

"Napier, old fellow, do drop your voice." Lazonby laid a hand on his arm. "Yes, I sent for you, because—"

"By God, Lazonby, if you've murdered another innocent man, I vow to see you hanged for it—hanged this time 'til you're bloody well *dead*."

At this, the woman leapt off the bench. "But Lazonby didn't murder anyone!" she insisted. "He *never* did, don't you see? And there was nothing innocent about Wilfred Leeton. *Nothing!* He was an evil, deceitful devil!"

Her vehemence struck Napier as oddly familiar. "Madam, calm yourself."

"No! My God. Can't you see?" Miss Ashton's husky voice was tremulous with rage now, as if something inside her had finally snapped. "This—all of this—is the result of . . . of lies and incompetence!" she went on. "Of vain assumptions and callous greed! Leeton made fools of us all, Mr. Napier—*your sainted father included.*"

"Oh?" Napier's foreboding sense of familiarity was deepening. "So did *you* shoot Sir Wilfred?"

She dragged in a ragged breath. "I—I—"

"Here is what we are going to say," interjected Lazonby, cutting Napier a dark glance. "Her brother shot Sir Wilfred. Accidentally."

Here, the lady shocked Napier by collapsing into the grass, sobbing as though her world had ended, her skirts puddling around her in a pool of shimmering gray silk.

"Ah!" Napier waved a hand around the lawn. "And this mysterious brother, just where might he be?"

"Spooked and ran." Lazonby had knelt to console the sobbing woman. "By the way, he's Jack Coldwater with the *Morning Chronicle*," he said, flicking a cool glance up at Napier. "You'll want to write that down in your interview notes."

"Jack *Coldwater*—? That hot-penned, red-haired radical reporter who keeps churning up your murder conviction in the newspapers? Lazonby, that makes no sense."

"Well, that's how it was," he said as Napier helped him lift the sobbing, shaking woman to her feet. "And just before the shots rang out—as the penny dreadfuls so cleverly put it— Sir Wilfred confessed to stabbing the very chap your father had me sent to Newgate for killing."

"You must be quite mad."

"He—he is *not* mad." Miss Ashton's remarkable eyes had gone soft, tears streaming down her cheeks.

"Indeed, I am perfectly sane—as I have been for all the years since old Hanging Nick Napier managed to get *me* convicted of murder." Lazonby gingerly urged Miss Ashton back onto the bench. "I've told you time and again I'd nothing to do with it. And now here is your proof."

"Proof?" Napier exploded. "There is no proof!"

But Miss Ashton had seemingly gathered herself. "There *is* proof," she said, her voice still low and tremulous. "I overheard Sir Wilfred confess everything. Apparently Lady Anisha had become suspicious of him. I don't know why, exactly. But Sir Wilfred hit her in the head with a garden spade, and dragged her in there to drown her in the spring box."

Napier's gaze narrowed. "And you'd know this . . . *how*?"

"I followed them."

"Indeed? Why?"

"Let's just say she was looking for her brother," Lazonby interjected. "Jack Coldwater had followed them, too."

"Well, that must have been quite a parade!" Napier shook his head, as if it might clear his vision.

"No, it's really quite simple," said Lazonby—and Napier knew it was anything but. "We are going to put it about that Miss Ashton saw her brother in the crowd, and guessed that Coldwater had come looking for Sir Wilfred."

"*We are going to put it about*?" Amidst all the confusion, Lazonby's weasel-words were finally coming clear to Napier. "No, by God, I'll have the truth—from the *both* of you."

"And the truth is, Jack Coldwater was in that dairy because he'd been investigating that old murder case, just like Anisha," Lazonby reminded Napier almost accusingly. "*You* should know. *You* let her into your office to see your father's files. Because of that, she asked one too many questions, and Sir Wilfred feared his house of cards was collapsing."

Napier could only stare at the man. A cold chill was slowly creeping over him. He *had* allowed Lady Anisha into his office—and for selfish reasons, too. And now it was coming horrifically clear just *why* he had been summoned here.

But Lazonby was still speaking—and rather too authoritatively. "So Coldwater was stalking Sir Wilfred when he saw him strike Lady Anisha and drag her in the dairy. Coldwater tried to save her but Sir Wilfred rushed him. A struggle ensued. And Coldwater's pocket pistol went off. Accidentally."

"An interesting story," said Napier snidely. "But then you've always possessed quite an imagination, my lord."

"You have Miss Ashton as a witness," Lazonby barked. "And then there is Anisha herself. But I shall warn you here and now I'll not have her further involved in this mess. So you are going to tidy this up, Napier. *You* are."

"The devil!" swore Napier. "I'll do no such thing."

"Oh, I very much think you ought." Miss Ashton's voice had stopped quavering now. "For it's all true. Moreover, Sir Wilfred said something else, Mr. Napier, just before he died—bragged about it, really."

"Oh?" Napier tried not to sound callous. "And what was that?"

The lady's odd green-blue gaze now held his, unblinking and certain, and Napier was suddenly sure he knew her.

And he realized, too, with his policeman's instincts that she was about to say something he did not wish to hear.

She dragged in a deep, almost ragged breath. "Sir Wilfred bragged that he had bribed the former assistant commissioner of the Metropolitan Police," she said. "He bribed your father, Mr. Napier. To ensure Rance Welham—now Lord Lazonby—was accused and convicted of a murder he did not commit."

Napier could only stare at her. The shiver inside him turned to a surge of blood-chilling uncertainty, like some secret, dammed-up dread too long held back. It roared in his head, threatening to burst free of all constraint.

"No. I . . . I do not believe you," he finally managed.

For what else was there to say?

Nicholas Napier had been known far and wide as the Crown's most resolute, most ruthless man within the Metropolitan Police. And once his officers arrested a man, the chap was as good as hanged; only Lazonby had managed to slip the Newgate knot.

As a boy, Napier had idolized his father; had always imagined him flawless. Above reproach. And if, in later years, there had come the occasional question or inconsistency . . . well, he'd be damned before he'd admit it to the likes of a convicted killer.

If Lazonby was, in fact, a killer . . .

Napier dragged a hand down his face. The significance of it all sunk in on him again, forcing him to will his own breath.

Sir Wilfred—oh, *he* had always been too bloody clever for anyone's good. No one would long mourn him once the shock was past.

And Lazonby, the arrogant bastard—he had suddenly stepped a little away—ever the gentleman!—as if to give Napier the time and space to collect himself.

Miss Ashton merely sighed. "Mr. Napier, you do not remember me, do you?" she said. "It was nearly two years ago. In your office."

Napier could only stare at her. And suddenly, he knew why she was so familiar. Why he felt that strange connection that was so alluring yet so disturbing.

"Elizabeth Colburne!" he growled. "By God, this *cannot* be coincidence."

"It actually is, rather," she said quietly, her slender hands set almost prayerfully together.

It was her eyes, he realized. Those incredible eyes were the clue. And the only clue, too, for her hair was somehow darker, her figure fuller and far more shapely.

"And as to what Lord Lazonby has said," the lady went on, her voice trembling a little, "I fear that you *will* come to believe it. Just as I have done. Though neither of us, I daresay, are going to enjoy having our comfortable, time-worn views so drastically altered."

He held her eyes, waiting on the next shoe to drop. For this day had been so damnable, he knew without doubt there was one.

And then Elizabeth Colburne-Ashton, or whatever her damned name was, sighed again, her viridian gaze settling over him in a way that made his breath catch. She leaned into him, so near he could breathe in her perfume, that exotic combination of sun-warmed lilies and jasmine, unique as the lady herself.

"And now, Mr. Napier," she whispered in her husky voice, "wouldn't it be best for all of us if we just let this awful business drop?"

Napier looked at her blankly, his head swimming from her scent and her proximity. "What do you mean?"

But Lazonby broke the spell by setting a heavy hand on Napier's shoulder. "She means let sleeping dogs lie," he said, giving him a hearty pat. "Embrace it, old chap. Trust me, it will only ruin your father's good name if you go churning up old muck. And Miss Ashton, you will kindly stop talking now."

"The devil!" Napier swore.

But Lazonby, damn him, merely winked.

"Now listen closely, my old friend," he murmured, slipping his arm fully about Napier's shoulders and urging him down the path, away from the lady in gray. "For I am about to tell you a tale which, if I were you, I would not much question."

"Oh, a *tale*, is it?" said Napier. "Coming from you, I oughtn't be surprised."

"Well, let us call it a legend," Lazonby corrected. "The legend of a talented but radical young newspaperman named Jack Coldwater—he's had a long and storied career on two continents, our Jack. And now he is going to save us a vast deal of unpleasantness, and spare your sainted father's reputation in the bargain."

"Is he indeed?" snapped Napier. "I wonder how?"

"Because he's elusive as quicksilver," said Lazonby with a huge grin, "and dashed hard to catch hold of. I tried like the devil to figure him out and failed miserably—as, I fear, will *you*."

CHAPTER 2

A Quiet Coze
in the Two Chairmen

Situated as it was in a quiet Westminster backstreet, the Two Chairmen had long been the turf of civil servants and undersecretaries, drawn there not by its particularly fine ale, but by its food swiftly served. Save perhaps for those rarified few who sat in the House of Lords, the government's business waited for no man, be he hungry or not.

On this particular drizzly day, Sir George Grey fell upon a slab of gammon steak like a man with no time to spare.

Royden Napier, however, had suffered inappetence for days now, and merely rooted his food around on his plate, as if doing so might uncover some truffle of a clue about the mysteries that had so recently come to plague him.

And the conversation—well, that was looming, too, he did not doubt. The home secretary had not invited an underling to dine with him in a common public house just to discuss the weather.

"Wot, din't yer like it?" asked the harried serving girl who snatched the dishes up.

Napier managed a tight smile. "I had a late breakfast."

With a saucy shrug, she swept away, bearing their dirty plates aloft as she edged sideways through the crowd now streaming through the door. At the last moment, however, she spun around to smile at the home secretary.

"'Nother pint, Sir George?"

He held up two fingers, and tilted his head at Napier.

Once she was out of earshot, Sir George leaned back in his chair, his grand, graying mutton-chops seeming to sink as he drew a long-fingered hand down his face. He was not a happy man.

"I cannot like it, Royden," he said, not for the first time. "It's been well over a week now. How can this newspaper chap have simply vanished into thin air?"

"Not air, sir, but water." Napier flashed a rueful smile. "Jack Coldwater's name was found on a passenger log for a Boston-bound freighter. She sailed two days after Sir Wilfred's death."

Napier hated lying—though strictly speaking, it was exactly what he'd *seen*. But that name, he suspected, had been the work of Lord Lazonby, or someone in his service. How hard could it be to bribe a clerk to jot down the name of an imaginary passenger?

"*Hmph!*" said Sir George. "Back to the States, eh? Well, we must find him there. We cannot have killers—even accidental ones—running from the Queen's justice now, can we?"

"No, sir. Of course not."

But this one, he said inwardly, *we are never apt to catch.*

Sir George shook his head. "I greatly respected your father, Royden," he said. "You must know that. But my God, how did he manage to bungle this old murder case so badly?"

Napier was too proud to hang his head. "I do not know, sir," he said again. "I am struggling to come to terms with it myself."

Which was the understatement of the century.

"And now we have Rance Welham—or Lord Lazonby, I should say—exonerated after years of public humiliation and harassment by the newspapers," Sir George complained. "And the real killer, Sir Wilfred Leeton, living a life of luxury—and being knighted for it! Really, it is too much to be borne."

Napier didn't know what to believe.

The case had begun years ago, when two young gentlemen had quarreled over a card game in Sir Wilfred's home. Some had claimed the quarrel was more about a woman than cards, but however it had begun, it had ended with a duke's son accusing Lazonby, then simply Mr. Welham, of cheating. The following day, the duke's son had been found stabbed in his rooms.

But now, if Lazonby was to be believed, Sir Wilfred had been the killer—and he'd been paid a lot of money by some very dangerous men to get rid of Lazonby, whose luck at the card tables had been intolerably good.

The story held just enough credence to make Napier uneasy.

"Recall, sir, if you will, that there was a witness—a porter at the Albany—who identified Lord Lazonby as the killer all those years ago."

"A witness, yes." Sir George stared at him across the scarred wooden table. "One who recanted on his deathbed. One whom Lazonby has long claimed was bribed by someone. And I think we both now know who that someone was."

"Sir Wilfred, it would appear." Napier cleared his throat a little roughly. He felt as if something was caught in it—his integrity, perhaps. "Well," he finally added, "we'll have our friends across the pond on the lookout for Mr. Coldwater.

And I have placated poor Lady Leeton as best I can. I think she still cannot grasp her husband's perfidy."

"Indeed, who can?"

"Indeed. So . . . what further would you have me do, sir?"

They both knew, however, it was a rhetorical question. The Crown's original murder case was so old the files had damn near molded. One man stabbed and another dead by his own hand, and all of it over a card game turned ugly. And now, years later, Sir Wilfred had apparently confessed to the stabbing, and been accidentally shot.

Allegedly accidentally shot.

But in any case, there was nothing further to be done; everyone save Lazonby—and now Sir Arthur's disturbing daughter—was dead or had vanished. And Lazonby had cleverly stymied Napier's further investigative efforts, as he had been doing for years.

But to be fair, had the Crown had left Lazonby with any choice?

Oh, Napier would forever loathe the arrogant devil. It stung to admit, even to himself, he might have been mistaken about the man.

Well, he hadn't been mistaken, damn it. Not entirely.

And neither had his father. In his youth, Lazonby had been a cardsharper of the worst order. More than a few men had thought the scoundrel had got what he deserved.

"And this witness, this Elizabeth Ashton," Sir George went on. "Went off to America and took her aunt's name, eh?"

"It seems Sir Arthur's sister married a Mr. Ashton, owner of a struggling newspaper—the *Boston Examiner,* I think it was—but the Ashtons were childless, so perhaps that's why."

Napier forbore pointing out the lady's tendency to alter her name as it suited her purpose. So far he was up to three, he was fairly well certain, and still counting.

"Well, I pray she isn't a troublemaker like her brother," said Sir George. "Where did Jack Coldwater come from, by the way? I thought Sir Arthur Colburne had only daughters."

Napier lifted one shoulder, and told another of his almost-lies. "A bastard, Lazonby alleges, by some actress whose name no one recalls," he said. "Miss Ashton claims her father acknowledged the child amongst close family. She says she lost touch with Coldwater for a time, then he turned up in Boston and went to work in the Ashtons' newspaper business."

Claims. Alleges. Says.

Christ, he'd sunk all the way down to Lazonby's level. Weasel-words, indeed!

"An illegitimate son," Sir George murmured. "I cannot claim surprise. I knew Sir Arthur Colburne in passing—a charming rakehell, forever on the verge of financial ruin. What is the daughter like?"

Napier was inexplicably reluctant to answer. The truth was, he had tried not to remember, despite the fact it was his job to remember everything. But the lady was a conundrum wrapped in an enigma. Alas, Napier loved nothing better than a mystery.

Perhaps it was that dichotomy—her intelligent, almost ruthless eyes and stubborn mouth, contrasted with that luminous skin and alluring scent—which had so roused his attention. And his suspicion.

What *was* she like? *Ethereal* was the word that came most readily to mind. And yet *ethereal* implied *heavenly*, and there was nothing angelic about Elizabeth Ashton.

"She is a lady," he said reluctantly, "and quite tall and striking in appearance."

"Striking?" Sir George set his head to one side. "In what way?"

Frustrated, Napier shook his head. "Her eyes are a remarkable shade of green," he said. "Or perhaps it's blue. Like . . . a cat. And her face—it is almost luminous—like something out of a Romney portrait. And her hair is quite—"

He jerked to a halt, realizing that he wasn't perfectly sure *what* color her hair was.

"Quite what?" urged Sir George.

"—*lovely*," he finished awkwardly.

Sir George cocked an eyebrow. "My word, Royden. You sound smitten."

Napier opened his mouth to snap out a retort, then remembering his place, shut it again. "Not in the least," he finally managed. "I have my eye on her, that is all."

"Yes?" said Sir George almost hopefully. "To what end?"

Napier's shoulders fell. "To no end, sir, truth be told," he finally answered. "This case is likely never to be resolved. And I think we both know it."

Sir George sighed deeply. "Still, the Home Office must give every impression of taking this matter seriously," he said. "Do . . . *something*, Royden."

"Such as?"

His answering smile was wan. "Interview her again," he said. "Handle it personally—but gently, of course. At least we'll be seen banging on the lady's door."

"She lives out in Hackney," said Napier dryly. "No one's apt to recognize me."

The girl came back with two tankards and set them down with heavy *clunk!*—a sound of true finality.

"So that's it, then." Sir George threw up his hands. "Sir Wilfred was guilty, Lord Lazonby wasn't, our police have been humiliated, and Jack Coldwater has fled, never to be apprehended. Does that about sum up this bloody mess?"

Napier could not bear to answer. The clamor in the pub had risen now—but not loud enough to drown out his guilt.

Finally, Sir George gave him a thin smile. "Well, none of this is your fault."

"It happened on my watch," Napier returned. "And on my father's."

"Ah, yes. Your father. That brings me to another topic." Sir George looked suddenly uncomfortable. "I've had another letter from your grandfather. From Lord Duncaster."

Napier stiffened. His paternal grandfather, Henry Tarleton, sixth Earl of Duncaster, was a bitter old man, long estranged from Napier's father. Indeed, Napier had never even laid eyes on his grandfather until last autumn, when Sir George had sent him to the vast family estate in Wiltshire to investigate a curious letter.

"Meddling again, is he?" Napier grumbled.

Sir George waved his hand as if it were no matter. "He presumes upon our old family friendship. Do you know, I believe I am to this day the only person connected to the Metropolitan Police who was entirely certain of your late father's exalted family connections."

"Which was just as my father wished," said Napier tightly.

Sir George set both hands flat upon the tabletop and cleared his throat.

"Duncaster acknowledges, Royden, that you're now his heir," he finally said. "Lord Saint-Bryce, your father's elder brother, has been dead two months, God rest him, so you're all that's left. And, simply put, Duncaster wishes you to come home."

Napier stiffened. "The only home I have ever known, sir, is London."

"And whose choice was that?" asked Sir George quietly. "I took a particular interest in your father, not because I was close to him, for I wasn't. No one was. He took care to see to that. But our long-standing family friendship—ah, that was one thing your father could not alter. Nicholas might change his surname to Napier. But that Tarleton blood? Oh, blood is immutable—much as you might wish otherwise."

"I've never given it much thought, one way or the other," said Napier.

"I believe you have," said Sir George softly. "You went home last year at Lord Hepplewood's behest."

"*Twice*," said Napier tightly. "I went to *Wiltshire* twice. Once by your order to investigate that strange, rambling letter which he sent to *you*, not me. And yes, I went a few weeks later for his funeral. I . . . I still don't know why I did."

Sir George's face tightened. "Royden, you are wasting yourself here in London. And now your life has a greater purpose."

"Sir, how can you say that?" Napier shoved back his chair with a sharp scrape. "By God, I've given my life to this department and to this city. And how can any purpose be greater than truth and justice?"

But the question rang hollow, even to his own ears. Always Napier had aspired to follow in his father Nicholas's footsteps. And now . . . and now he did not know even the meaning of truth. Or of justice.

Worse, he was beginning to wonder if he'd even known his father.

Napier had always believed that to accept anything Lord Duncaster might offer him would be rejecting all that his father had sacrificed for when he'd left the family and changed his name. Was there not honor in living by one's own wits? Or in wishing to succeed without the support of a rich and powerful family?

But what, precisely, had Nicholas Napier sacrificed?

Surely not his own honor? Surely he had not wished merely to punish Lord Duncaster over a quarrel? Could a man be so prideful—so bent on retaliation—he might sacrifice his own morals for money? That he might take *bribery* and convict an innocent man?

Surely it was not possible.

"I shouldn't have said a greater purpose," Sir George

amended, drawing Napier from his reverie. "Just an unexpected turn. Lord Hepplewood was Duncaster's best friend. And now, within the space of six months, Duncaster has also lost the last of his three sons. To outlive one's children— dear God! That sort of grief is incomprehensible to me. Now your grandfather has no one."

Napier scowled. "He has his widowed sister, Lady Hepplewood, still happily ensconced beneath his very nose," he said, "not that *she* has ever spared my lowly branch of the family a kind word."

Sir George opened both hands expressively. "Look, as I said, I did not know your father Nicholas well."

"No, you did not." Napier's words came out more harshly than he'd intended.

"I did not," said Sir George more gently. "Nicholas Napier was a man who kept his own counsel and did his job with ruthless efficiency. He wanted nothing from his family. But really, was his father Duncaster the ogre he made out? And if he was, can a man not mellow with age?"

"Mellow with age?" echoed Napier. "Duncaster is hardly a bottle of brandy. Besides, the man must have one foot in the grave, and most of his toes."

Sir George leaned a little across the table. "All the more reason to go," he said quietly. "Perhaps your grandfather wishes to make peace? He must be nearly eighty, Royden. You are his only grandson. His heir. And someone . . . someone must see to things."

"I do not see why that someone must be me."

But he had known for a while now that there mightn't *be* anyone else.

Had he somehow imagined he could avoid this?

All three of Duncaster's sons were dead. The eldest had died without children. And now the middle son, who'd sired only daughters, had recently passed on to his great reward— mere weeks before he was to marry again, with every hope of begetting an heir that might saw off Hanging Nick Napier's embarrassing branch of the family tree.

Napier had wished his uncle well in his efforts. He already considered himself sawn off.

But his uncle, Lord Saint-Bryce, had been in his fifties, and the gleeful anticipation of bedding a beautiful woman half his age had apparently done the poor fellow in. Either that or Lady Hepplewood's incessant nagging. From what little Napier had grasped, the old dragon had dogged her nephew's every step, determined to marry the poor devil off again.

Napier thought again of the oddly scribbled plea Hepplewood had written Sir George all those months ago. The old man's rambling notions suggested someone at the vast family estate wished him ill. So Napier had gone, at Sir George's insistence, to see what nefariousness was afoot in Wiltshire.

Except that there had been no nefariousness. Hepplewood had been nearly insensible upon Napier's arrival, and had never really regained himself. He had simply begun to suffer, Lady Hepplewood claimed, of his family's curse, senility.

Another mystery solved.

Napier shook his head. He did not need another.

Sir George extracted a letter, and pushed it across the table.

"I promised Duncaster I'd beg you," he said. "And I do. Beg you, that is. Go, and at least placate him. I'll have your duties here in London seen to until you make up your mind."

"Make up your mind?" Napier looked at him incredulously. "To do what?"

"To stay here and waste your blood and your talent," said Sir George, "or to go home, and take up your duty as Lord Duncaster's heir."

"Heir!" Napier spat out the word. "I'm a bureaucrat's son."

"Nonsense," Sir George admonished. "You have the manners, the education, and all the bearing of a gentleman. Indeed, you are a gentleman born."

Napier shook his head again, and felt his lips thin.

"He is an old man, Royden; likely frail and near death. Don't you wish to hear his side of it?"

No, damn it all, he *didn't*.

Or at least . . . he hadn't.

Not until Lazonby had clouded his life with what Napier so desperately wished to believe were lies about his father. But now he was beginning to question all he'd believed in. That his father was a stoic hero; a relentless crusader for good over evil. That his grandfather was a rich, unreasonable despot surrounded by sycophants and a house full of pompous, parasitic dependents.

As with all things, the truth was likely somewhere in the middle.

He sighed. "Give me the letter," he said, thrusting out a hand.

His index finger set in the center, Sir George pushed the folded paper another inch, then hesitated. "There is one other thing."

"Yes, with that lot, there always is." Napier fell back into his chair. "Well, go on. What is it?"

"Lady Hepplewood—your great-aunt, that is . . ." Sir George looked suddenly sheepish. "She has a companion, or . . . or a sort of ward?"

"Saint-Bryce's intended bride?" Napier looked at him oddly. "Yes, there's some vague family connection. She was Hepplewood's cousin, I think."

Sir George glanced away, never a good sign. "Well, Lady Hepplewood has told Duncaster that the girl has been given every expectation of becoming the next Baroness Saint-Bryce."

"Well, that will be a damned sight more difficult with

Saint-Bryce in the grave," said Napier dryly, "but I wish Lady Hepplewood every success."

"Doubtless she'll be relieved to hear it. Because Royden . . . well, *you* are Saint-Bryce."

"The devil I am."

"Technically, you are," said Sir George.

"No," he countered. "*Technically*, I'm assistant commissioner of the Metropolitan Police—unless you mean to sack me over this Coldwater debacle."

"But Baron Saint-Bryce *is* Viscount Duncaster's secondary title," Sir George pointed out. "The courtesy title traditionally borne by the heir."

"And if he offered it to me," Napier gritted, "I would bloody well refuse it."

Sir George lifted his shoulders lamely. "I fear that he and Lady Hepplewood are already referring to you as such."

"Good God."

"Oh, I doubt your grandfather shares his younger sister's marriage schemes," said Sir George consolingly. "After all, Duncaster's much older than she and—well, he is a *man*, Royden. He'll likely be satisfied with merely your boot across his threshold."

"I fear they are both to be disappointed," said Napier coldly. "Moreover, they are never satisfied. I've already seen that much."

"But Lady Hepplewood—" Here, Sir George leaned forward. "Well, my boy, you spent several days in her company. Does she not intimidate you? I always found her terrifying."

Napier lifted one shoulder. "The lady scarcely spared me a glance," he said honestly.

Sir George fell back. "Well, she will have more than a glance for you now, my boy," he warned. "I have known the lady for years, Napier, and I very much suggest . . ."

"What?"

"That you prepare yourself," he said. "Perhaps . . . perhaps you ought not go alone?"

"How kind of you, sir," said Napier a little acidly. "I shall greatly enjoy your company on the long ride to Wiltshire."

Sir George blanched. "No, no, I meant . . ."

"Yes—?"

"Well, I did happen to see you at the opera recently," he said, "with a strikingly lovely widow on your arm."

Napier could only glower at him. "With Lady Anisha Stafford, do you mean?"

"Indeed, and she appears both graceful and self-possessed." The sheepish smile returned. "Her late husband was one of the Dorset Staffords, you know. Certainly her Scottish roots are noble and ancient."

He was tiptoeing around the fact of Anisha's Rajput mother, Napier noticed. But no matter. "What, sir, is your point?"

"Nothing," said Sir George. "But I'm given to understand that the two of you have been keeping company. That you recently dined in her home, and that she has occasionally visited your office. And I just thought that, if there were anything in it, then now might be the time to announce—"

"There's nothing whatever," Napier gruffly interjected. "The vaguest of friendships. As to Lady Anisha's finer feelings, I believe they are otherwise engaged."

"Oh." Sir George's face fell, and he looked suddenly weary. "Oh, that's unfortunate."

He mightn't think so, thought Napier grimly, had he known of Anisha's involvement in Sir Wilfred's death. Napier felt a stab of guilt for having used his influence to keep her name from the witness list. But he did not doubt Lazonby's threat; the man would have mired the Napier name in mud forever, and ruined his father's legacy.

That, however, had hardly been the deciding factor. Napier truly had no wish to involve Anisha. Oh, he no longer thought of her as anything save a dear friend; the whole of his attention was subsumed by this case.

And by the lady in gray.

Good God. He tried to shove the thought of Elizabeth Ashton away again.

But even now he could feel her cool eyes cutting into him. Could feel the heat of her hand in his as he'd settled her back onto the bench. She was as different from Anisha as the moon from the sun.

"Oh, well," said Sir George worriedly. "It would have been ideal, of course, to take a prospective bride to visit your grandfather."

"A bride?" Napier retorted. "I've rarely time for breakfast, let alone a bride."

"Well, nothing less, I fear, will put Lady Hepplewood off her notion."

"Lady Hepplewood's notions are no concern of mine," said Napier.

"Hmm." Sir George looked worried. "We shall see about that."

But the talk of Lady Hepplewood's scheming had stiffened Napier's resolve. "No, we shan't see," he answered. "I haven't the time to traipse off to Wiltshire to dance attendance on an old man and his whims."

At last irritation sketched over Sir George's face. "Royden, for God's sake, be reasonable," he hissed beneath the clamor of the room. "When Duncaster dies, what then? Do you think for one moment Commissioner Mayne will keep you on at Scotland Yard? Or will even *want* you? And I shan't force him, I tell you. One cannot simply give up estates and titles. One is expected to do one's duty to the Crown."

"I did not ask for this," Napier muttered. "Good God, I never even dreamt it!"

"No one did," said Sir George grimly. "But far better you go now and make something like peace with Duncaster—

and learn a bit of how things go on. For if you wait until he dies, my boy, you'll be viewed as nothing but a neophyte to be taken advantage of by the staff, the estate agents, and that wheedling pack of granddaughters. You'll be utterly ignorant—and you'll be hated in the bargain."

Napier shrugged. "Already they regard me as nothing but a burr under their proverbial saddles."

At that, Sir George's mouth quirked. "Well, then," he said, flicking the letter across the table. "It will be just like a day at the office for you, won't it?"

*C*he rain clouds that had visited Hackney in the wee hours of the morning had apparently taken a long-term lease. By early afternoon, the traffic passing by Elizabeth Ashton's tidy cottage had winnowed away to an occasional carriage clattering past, and a farm cart with an ancient driver wrapped in a damp brown blanket who, hunched miserably as he was, greatly resembled a drowned rat.

With the tip of one finger, she leaned into the parlor's bow window and pulled back the light underdrapes to look out for about the fifth time at her small but sodden front garden. The gutters around the house still rumbled and rain still bounced off the flagstone path like pea-gravel flung from the heavens. Elizabeth dreaded going out into it. And yet she had to resist the almost overwhelming urge to do just that.

To run. No, to *flee*.

To rush headlong into something, anything, that might take her away from here.

Or away from herself, perhaps.

Refusing to wring her hands over her plight, she clenched the ends of her shawl in one fist instead. Wherever she was to go, she could not go today. It had taken the past several days to summon her solicitor and tidy her affairs. Still, she had a little time yet; a very little, perhaps, but Elizabeth had become adept at calculating risk and opportunity.

Dropping the drapery, she turned from the glass and considered ringing for a fire to be built up. But the cold she felt, Elizabeth feared, was a chill no fire would mend; it was a coldness of the soul—and one brought upon herself.

The elderly gentleman scratching out a document deep in the shadows of the parlor stretched forward to dip his pen into his inkwell, the creak of his chair drawing her back to the present. Mr. Bodkins returned to his efforts with utter concentration, as if unaware his client still remained in the room.

Suddenly, light, quick footsteps came down the stairs and Elizabeth's maid Fanny poked her head over the banister, holding a large wicker case by its leather strap.

"Beg pardon, Miss Lisette, but this one for the hats?" she asked. "Or would you rather the boxes?"

Elizabeth blinked, trying to draw her mind back to the pressing tasks at hand. Away from Sir Wilfred's pale corpse. Away from Lord Lazonby's knowing gaze, and the black, soulless eyes of Royden Napier. But all of them had begun to haunt her nights.

"The wicker, I think," she said vaguely.

"And—er—Mr. Coldwater's things have been sorted." Something like sympathy sketched over the maid's face. "Shall I put them in the trunks?"

Elizabeth stilled her hand on the shawl. "We shan't have room," she finally said. "Take them up to St. John's. The Ladies' Parish Committee will know what's best done with them."

Fanny cut an assessing look at their caller. "Those old tabbies might quiz me, miss," she warned.

"Drop Mr. Coldwater's things in the vestry," said Elizabeth flatly. "If anyone asks you why, act as if you've been struck dumb."

At that, Bodkins snapped shut the latch on his rosewood writing box and rose from the parlor table, a worried crease down the middle of his forehead. It had become a permanent fixture over the last twenty years, Elizabeth realized.

"Well, that's that, Lisette," he said, making a creaky bow. "If I could just have your signature?"

She went to the table and hastily scribbled upon the lines as he shuffled papers and pointed them out.

"Very well," he said when she'd laid the pen aside. "Everything has been signed and your accounts brought current. Now, as to the lease on this house—"

"Thank you, Bodkins," Elizabeth preempted, "but I'm quite persuaded to quit Hackney."

Bodkins's crease deepened as he peered at her over his silver spectacles. "But where will you go, my dear, if I may ask?" he said uneasily. "I went to great lengths to obtain this house—and at your insistence. Moreover, Hackney is a quiet, lovely village, and you have the wherewithal to live here in a measure of comfort."

"Thank you," she said, "nonetheless, I insist."

Bodkins shook his head. "But my dear, *where* do you mean to go?" he pressed. "And when?"

"The day after tomorrow," she said crisply. "As to where—" Here, her own forehead creased. "Where did you say that old manor house was located?"

"The one that came to you ten years ago?"

"Was there another?" she asked mordantly. "Heavens, if we were so flush with them, perhaps Papa might have sold one and paid the bailiffs rather than take the grim alternative of shoving a pistol up his nose."

Bodkins paled. "It is no jesting matter, Lisette, your father's failings. And certainly not his death."

She widened her eyes. "Indeed it is not," she agreed, her voice suddenly husky. "Not to me. For I found him, and had to mop up the blood afterward, since Elinor couldn't—she could never bear such things, you know—and the servants simply wouldn't. They'd not been paid, you see. And with no hope of ever being paid, everyone save Nanna left us."

"Oh." Bodkins's face fell. "Oh, I fear you are very bitter, my dear."

"And you are very astute," she replied, "though well intentioned, I'm sure."

"But you *have* become cynical, Lisette. It breaks my heart."

Bodkins held her gaze a moment and then, apparently persuaded no more was forthcoming, went on. "In any case, the manor passed down to you upon your grandmother's death ten years ago, since your mother and sister predeceased you," he said. "As I explained to your father's sister, Mrs. Ashton, it was the one inheritance your maternal grandfather did not control because your grandmother's marriage settlements provided—"

"Yes, thank you," she interjected. "I comprehend marriage settlements. But you . . . you mean to say you wrote to America—to Aunt Ashton—of this inheritance?"

His confusion returned. "Why, I would have been remiss in my duties to your late mother's family, Lisette, had I not," he said. "Until this morning, I thought you knew."

Elizabeth looked at him blankly. "And what did Aunt Ashton say?"

"That I should sell it," he said acerbically, "and send the money to you—well, to Mr. Ashton, really—in Boston. But I flatly refused to do it until you'd reached your majority, and given me your personal instruction. I heard no more, and simply let the rents accumulate, pittance though they are."

Elizabeth waved her hand as if it didn't matter, but she was suddenly, and very deeply, grateful to Bodkins. "Thank you," she said more gently. "Thank you for looking after me, Bodkins. You have been, I think, my only friend in England. Now tell me, where is the manor located?"

"Well, why, it is in Caithness."

"Caithness?" Her eyebrows drew together. "And where is that?"

"Scotland, miss."

"Ah, far from London, then," she murmured. "Excellent."

"The *North* of Scotland, my dear." Bodkins was looking alarmed again. "Indeed, the very, very tip of the wretched place."

"Come now!" Elizabeth forced a smile. "How wretched can it be?"

"My dear girl, they don't even have roads that far!"

"Oh, Bodkins, do not be ridiculous! There are roads everywhere nowadays—trains, too, almost."

"Lisette, my dear, I fear you've been too long in the colonies."

"The United States, Bodkins," she reminded him dryly. "I believe they've not been colonies for quite some decades. And no, they actually *don't* have roads everywhere. Indeed, most of it is an uncivilized hell. But Scotland—why, that is still a part of Britain, unless some vast change has occurred since I left my little schoolroom in London."

"Yes, yes, to be sure," he said. "But you can practically see the Orkneys from Caithness, ma'am. And no, they *do not have roads.*"

But Elizabeth was in deep thought now. The North of Scotland did indeed sound grim. But what was the alternative? Having put herself in this wretched position, she could expect no one save herself to drag her out of it. She had to get away from Lazonby's ultimate vengeance—which she fully deserved—and Napier's more immediate investigation.

Perhaps she deserved that, too. Perhaps she should just give herself up. Explain everything. But how to explain what one scarcely understood? What in God's name had happened to her? Elizabeth turned her head, and fought the urge to burst into tears.

Damn it, *she did not cry.*

And yet her heart felt like one of those hot-air balloons, once magnificently swelled with the fire of righteous indignation, now left limp and directionless. She had reached lofty, almost giddy heights in her search for revenge, her wings borne high by her hatred of Lord Lazonby. And now she had fallen to the earth, and to the crushing reality of her own mistakes.

Her own madness, perhaps.

Perhaps that was the awful cold she felt; insanity creeping into the crevices of her soul.

Oh, she had to escape it all! "How long will it take to get there, Bodkins?"

"Weeks!" he said stridently. "If you *can* get there from here. Which I do sincerely doubt. Moreover, the house itself has been uninhabited for years. Consider what it must look like. Consider the weather. Truly, my dear, it is out of the question."

"But Bodkins—"

He cut her off. "And if my advice seems presumptuous," he interjected, lifting one finger, "recall that I have served Lord Rowend's old and noble family for nearly four decades, and your mother Lady Mary Rowend herself until she wed your father. Your welfare is a serious matter."

Something inside Elizabeth snapped. "You are kind, Bodkins," she said, her hand clenching again, "yet I cannot help but wonder where Lord Rowend's concern was when I was orphaned at twelve, and actually needed it."

The elderly gentleman drew back as if he'd been slapped. "I do beg your pardon."

Elizabeth felt the hot press of tears again. "No, I beg yours, sir," she said more gently. "I . . . I am not myself today. And I realize, of course, it was not your choice I be packed up and sold like a bale of wool. Or that my sister died in the middle of the Atlantic, to be tossed overboard as if she were no better than a piece of old baggage."

"Lisette, my dear!" Bodkins drew back an inch. "Lady Mary's family—they simply were not situated to take on two rambunctious granddaughters. And your father's family, why, they seemed determined to have you in America. Indeed, they begged for you."

"Is that what Lord Rowend told you?" She strolled toward the parlor door, as if to encourage the old man's departure. "That he had not even the smallest nook in that great, grand mansion where his orphaned granddaughters might have lived? Well. I shall not challenge it."

But Bodkins remained steadfast by the table, his jowls trembling a little. "I believe this Coldwater fellow has overset you," he said bitterly. "Such a scandal he's mired you in with this dreadful shooting business! And yes, it is true Lord Rowend disliked your father, and had no wish to be reminded of him, but—"

"And we were naught but reminders?" she interjected. "Elinor and I?"

The old man drew himself up indignantly. "It was a misjudgment, perhaps, to send you to your father's family," he admitted, "yet one could not but feel for your grandfather. Poor Lady Mary was seduced by Sir Arthur and her fortune run through like water. It left Lord Rowend so distraught he disavowed any relation to her husband."

Elizabeth was too emotionally spent to debate the definition of *seduced*.

"Father was charming, 'tis true," she said. "And they both enjoyed fine things. But he always spoke of Mother as if she'd been the great love of his life."

But both her parents had lived far beyond their means, she knew. And as to the great love of Papa's life—well, there had been others aplenty, both before and after. Perhaps even during. She prayed not, but Bodkins was right. Her older, wiser self had become jaded.

As to Lady Mary Colburne, she died so young she likely

never realized the poverty into which her children were being plunged. Elizabeth had only a child's memory of her, but Elinor, her elder sister, had always painted their parents' marriage a grand romance.

Elinor, on the other hand, had been much like Papa. Vivacious and captivating. Eternally optimistic—often to the point of naïveté. And oh, yes—*beautiful*.

"Bodkins," she said in a surprisingly clear voice, "did you not realize my grandfather had *paid* Aunt and Uncle Ashton to take us?"

Bodkins looked suddenly guilty. "A choice I like to think Lord Rowend came to regret," he answered. "After all, he has left you a small trust; enough to lease this cottage and enjoy a decent life and lovely things. Does that account for nothing?"

The old man sounded truly wounded now.

Elizabeth sighed. Was any of this Bodkins's fault, really?

"Oh, do try to understand, sir," she said more plaintively. "I just cannot stay here any longer. I simply cannot!"

He cut her a knowing look. "That devilish Coldwater fellow!" he said grimly. "Had I known of that cad's mere existence, I should have counseled you strongly to cast him off. After all, you cannot really account him family."

"No," said Elizabeth, unable to hold his gaze, "perhaps not."

"Indeed not!" said Bodkins. "And now you're to be driven from your home by this scandal of *his* making. I know, my dear, that is why you are so intent on leaving."

Her home.

Yes, *hers*. Though she'd come here alone and still griefstricken, Elizabeth had nonetheless found a measure of peace in this house. A place of *belonging*—the first since her father's death. Despite all the years she'd spent beneath Aunt Ashton's roof, she'd never felt it her home.

Blinking rapidly, she looked around the large, well-furnished parlor with its broad, age-blackened beams, the pale yellow wallpaper sprinkled with roses, and the delicate pianoforte she'd so enjoyed—on those rare occasions when she'd let her mind relax enough to stray from the mission she'd set for herself.

The ruination of Rance Welham, Lord Lazonby.

The man who had selfishly set in motion everything that had destroyed her family.

Except . . . *he hadn't.*

Dear God. Lazonby hadn't ruined her life. He hadn't stabbed poor Percy, Elinor's rich fiancé—the man who was to have dragged them all from the brink of bankruptcy. He had not driven her father to suicide. Or caused Elinor to die of grief and fever. He had not, in all likelihood, even cheated at cards.

Elizabeth had returned to London in relentless pursuit of retribution—*from the wrong man.*

The cold horror of it ran through her again, and the urge to flee rose up in her breast like a panic, threatening to steal her breath.

Dear heaven, she could not stay here and simply wait for Lazonby to take his revenge.

For better than a year she'd put him through hell, smearing his name in the newspapers and skulking behind him, pillar to post. She'd spied on his friends, bribed his servants, and apparently driven Lady Anisha into asking dangerous questions, in some desperate attempt to prove her lover innocent.

Elizabeth had even gone through Lazonby's rubbish bins in an effort to find something—*anything*—that might send him back to prison.

It was all she'd known *to* do; hate and bitterness had been her only comforts during those long, lonely years in Boston. The burning need to avenge the family she'd lost, and make Lazonby pay for all that he had taken from her. Papa. Elinor. Percy. Her entire existence, really.

And now, suddenly, it was over.

Her entire *raison d'être* had caved in atop her head.

No, Lazonby wasn't apt to let any of this stand—not once he'd had time to think, and had his good name restored. And even if he did, that hawk-nosed, black-eyed police commissioner assuredly would not. Lazonby might be a laughing, devil-may-care scapegrace, but Napier was something else altogether.

Napier was ruthless; it oozed from his pores. And he meant to see that someone, eventually, paid for Sir Wilfred's death . . .

Suddenly, it was as if the parlor floor shimmied a little beneath her feet.

"Lisette?" Bodkins moved as if to catch her arm.

She regained herself, and drew away. "I . . . I am fine, thank you."

He let the hand drop. "Well, do reconsider leaving," he said gently. "I'm sure the scandal will blow over. You must, of course, avoid Lady Leeton. But another school will be glad for your volunteer work."

Elizabeth forced a smile. "I thank you, Bodkins, but you quite waste your worry on me. I've a notion to quit Hackney at once. Mrs. Fenwick will remain behind to shut up the house."

Bodkins sighed. "I see you will not be dissuaded," he said. "But I beg you, not Scotland. Consider . . . Paris, perhaps?"

Elizabeth hesitated. "It doesn't seem all that far away," she said, thinking of Napier's black eyes and long reach.

Bodkins smiled. "The South of France, then, or the Italian coast?" he suggested. "A little house along the *Camin deis Anglés*, perhaps, with a view of the sea?"

"But not another lease," she warned him. "I am done with travel, Mr. Bodkins. I want . . . I want a home. One that is *mine*. One I cannot be turned out of—or sent away from—on anyone else's whim."

The old man sighed. "Give me a few days, Lisette," he said, "and I shall see what can be done."

$\mathscr{A}$t the end of an afternoon wedged with too many appointments and fraught with inner conflict, Royden Napier arrived home in Eaton Square to a blessedly silent front hall and the scent of roasting poultry wafting up from his kitchens. The efficient Mrs. Bourne, of course, for this was the first Thursday of the month, which meant guinea fowl basted with bacon fat and a buttery three-root mash.

The scent was heartening, even absent an appetite.

Indeed, under the gentle hand of Mrs. Bourne, his entire house ran like clockwork. Some might have called it a life of dull predictability, but in his line of work one too often waded through life's chaos and the tragic aftermath. In his private life, he strove for order and unruffled calm, a goal by and large achieved, save for the occasional entrance of a woman into his life.

Lady Anisha Stafford had been just such a woman—or could have been. Napier had met her months ago, and had been immediately struck by her warmth. When she'd eventually asked to see Lazonby's old case file, he had agreed, perhaps foolishly. Yes, he had been attracted to her—and she had not been indifferent to him. That, however, had quickly come to naught, perhaps for the best. She was far above his station.

And yet, she wasn't, was she?

On a soft curse, Napier tossed aside his hat, his attention veering back to his awkward conversation with Sir George. Had he made it known he was the grandson of Viscount Duncaster—and suddenly heir apparent to the title—would Lady Anisha have looked more favorably upon his suit?

Certainly her elder brother Lord Ruthveyn would have.

Yet he had *not* told her. And Napier was not so lacking in self-knowledge as to misconstrue his own motivations. Yes, he had wanted her to desire him for who he was, not what he was. But a part of him had simply not wished to take the time away from his work for the niceties of a proper courtship.

Though on this one occasion, he had been very tempted. Tempted to surrender his unruffled calm for something that had felt, yes, a little like chaos.

But he had dragged his feet, and the lady, it seemed, had cast in her lot with Lazonby.

Ah, well. At the great age of four-and-thirty, Napier was on his way to confirmed bachelorhood and his aunt Hepplewood be damned, unless some plump, pretty widow turned up to warm his bed and then persuaded him to make a fool of himself. Still, it would be no woman of Lady Hepplewood's choosing—of that he was bloody well certain. The Wiltshire branch of his family had not dictated to the London Napiers in going on four decades. He'd be damned if they'd start now.

Yanking Sir Wilfred Leeton's file from his valise, he went into the passageway that opened on each side to his front reception rooms. In an uncharacteristically reflective mood, he paused to look around with new eyes at the gleaming wooden floors, the velvety Wilton carpets swept to within an inch of brand new, and the gleaming porcelain, marble, and hints of gilt that adorned the whole of it.

Did he want more than this?

It was not opulence that surrounded him, no. But it was upper middle-class elegance, at the very least, and since boyhood he had lived here with all the security and certainty that came from a life lived without want.

Yes, whatever Nicholas Napier's failings, his son had lacked for little. And, as Sir George had pointed out, all that security and a fine Belgravia town house had been topped off by an education to rival any gentleman's. All this despite the fact that Nicholas Napier had been, initially, nothing more than a low-level bureaucrat married to a government clerk's daughter.

And suddenly, Napier wondered how he'd afforded it. Not just the house, but their entire way of life. So far as he could remember, his late mother had dressed as finely as any lady. They had dined well—sometimes even lavishly—and even entertained on occasion.

How? How had it been accomplished? In the back of his mind, he had often wondered.

Perhaps he need wonder no longer.

On a flash of irritation, he hurled the file aside and went into the drawing room to pour himself a generous splash of brandy, damning Lazonby to hell.

It was not possible. He would not think of it.

Napier set the decanter back down on the side table with a *thunk!* After tossing the brandy back with rather too much relish, he lifted away his afternoon copy of the *Gazette*, and began to sort meticulously through the post which always lay neatly stacked beneath it.

There was nothing save a couple of routine bills— statements from his haberdasher and his vintner—already slit open and unfolded for his review, along with an invitation to a musicale at the home of a superintendent in the General Register Office, a fellow whose means were far outstripped by his social aspirations.

Such invitations had come more regularly since vague rumors of Napier's family connections had begun to worm their way through Whitehall. His friendship with Lady Anisha had merely added fuel to the fires of speculation, for her brother was a marquess, and a personal favorite of the Queen.

Still, the fact that he might suddenly be in demand made Napier snort with laughter. He pushed the invitation away to see what lay beneath it, and went a little cold.

"*Jolley!*" he shouted.

At once, footsteps came softly up the stairs, and within moments the servant appeared, looking rather like a wraith with his cloud of white hair, wooly white muttonchops, and long white work apron over his stark black suit. It was a deceptive appearance, to be sure. Jolley was utterly of this world.

"Yes, sir?"

"This letter." Napier set a fingertip upon the offending paper. "When did it arrive?"

"Why, with the morning post." Jolley looked mystified.

"And did no one question to whom it was addressed?"

Jolley looked more closely. "Gor blimey!"

Napier looked down at it again. The words taunted him:

Lord Saint-Bryce
22 Eaton Square
London

"You did not open it," Napier remarked.

"No, sir," he said. "It seemed of a personal nature."

Napier took up a nearby penknife, slit the seal, and snapped the letter open. His gaze swept over the crabbed handwriting that listed badly starboard, and used only the topmost third of the page:

My Lord,

I wonder if You oughtn't come home to Burlingame? If we might prevale upon You to do so, it might be for the best. Doubtless London is Great Fun, but things here continue passing strange cince the mysterious Deaths and Some of us remain Most Troubled that some Wickedness is afoot.

Yr. humble servent,
A Concerned Citizen

"A *concerned citizen?*" Napier tossed the letter back down. "*Wickedness*—?"

"May I, sir?"

At Napier's curt nod, Jolley reached past him, and picked it up. "Well," he said after reading it, "at least it's not total rambling nonsense like poor old Hepplewood's piece."

"No, but it's just as full of innuendo," Napier growled.

"And that's a business I still don't like, sir," said Jolley. "Gentlemen like Hepplewood do make enemies."

"But Saint-Bryce had none," Napier pointed out. "He was just like every other country gentleman moldering away in Wiltshire: paunchy, balding, and obsessed with tromping around in wet grass shooting at things. Where's the wickedness in that?"

Jolley's brow furrowed. "No connection between the titles, is there?" he asked. "I mean, otherwise, sir—well, put it like this—you'd be the only one ter gain by Saint-Bryce's death."

"Only you, Jolley, would have the gall to suggest me as a murderer," said Napier evenly. "But no, Hepplewood was merely my grandfather's friend and brother-in-law. His death brought me nothing. And Saint-Bryce's will bring me nothing but grief."

Jolley laid the letter down. "Still, who could have written such a thing?"

Napier took it up again. "Some desperate near-illiterate, one assumes," he grumbled. "It's probably naught but some sort of mischievous forgery. I ought to burn it."

"Not a forgery, sir," Jolley countered. "Without specific

intent to defraud, sir, the law holds there is no such thing. They haven't pretended to be someone they aren't, nor asked you for any money."

"No, not *yet*." Napier scowled down at him. "And spare me your well-honed legal hair-splitting, Jolley. It was that, you know, which put you here."

"Aye, so you say, sir. So you say."

Jolley shuffled off, and began to inspect the wicks for the evening.

Napier returned his attention to the letter, oddly troubled. "No, not an illiterate, perhaps," he murmured. "The sentence structure is fine, and the form is not bad—save for the fact that they cannot spell, and seem confused as to how I prefer to be addressed."

Having accompanied him to Wiltshire during Lord Hepplewood's illness, Jolley understood Napier's family connections. "Still, sir, it does make one think," the servant called over his shoulder, "of Hepplewood's bizarre ramble wot was sent to the home secretary. Shall I compare them?"

It was a good idea.

"Thank you, yes." Napier extracted a small key from his waistcoat. "It is in the second slot of the parlor bureau."

Jolley found the document in short order, and carried it across to the windows. Napier followed, awaiting the expert opinion with more unease than he cared to admit. Why send such a letter? And why to him, of all people?

Because he was the heir?

Or because he was with the police?

"Hmm," said Jolley.

"Key," Napier barked, holding out his hand.

Jolley rolled his eyes, and surrendered it.

Napier tucked it back into his pocket. For all his angelic appearance, in his day Jolley had been the underworld's most infamous screever, a professional forger of documents. He'd also been its most talented. Indeed, Jolley had loved his craft like an art form, forging things even when there was no real need and little profit to be made, just to see if he could get away with it. Wills, bills of exchange, certificates of shares; any manner of legal instrument fell to child's play under Jolley's deft hand.

He also had a barrister's grasp of pertinent case law, often oozing around the technicalities like butter into the cracks of a hot crumpet. A few years past, however, Jolley came up against a charge he was not likely to defeat, for he'd been set up by a newer, rougher class of competitors in the East End. And he was no longer young.

Napier had offered Jolley an amicable alternative to a slow death in Newgate—something like the old adage to keep your friends close and your enemies closer. It worked well. Jolley could eliminate his East End accent at will, and affect all the manners of a gentleman when necessary. He made a perfectly serviceable valet and general servant—provided one kept a close eye on him.

Jolley had extracted an old jeweler's loupe from his pocket and stuck it in his eye. "*Hmm*," he said again. "Paper's been torn from a larger sheet—like a letterhead cut off—then turned upside down and wrote upon."

"And—?" Napier pressed as the servant turned the older document toward the light.

"But no similarity in ink, pen, nor paper," said Jolley, "and certainly not in wording. Still, both look to have been posted from Wiltshire. Marks are true as any I've seen."

Pensive, Napier scrubbed a hand down his jaw. Something was nagging in the back of his mind—something to do with Lord Hepplewood.

In his day, Hepplewood had been a powerful man, a politician to his very core and a mover and shaker of the highest order. He'd held ambassadorships and even served on King William's Privy Council. Such men knew things—oftentimes dangerous things.

But Saint-Bryce had been just a genial country gentleman who'd done nothing more controversial than judge the fruit preserves at the county fair. The phrase *passing strange* did not seem to remotely apply. Hepplewood had been old. Saint-Bryce had been a tad corpulent. Such men died, and that was that.

But Jolley had laid both sheets to the window glass with an expression of confusion on his face. "Now, this new one, sir," he said, squinting through the loupe at it, "is curiously watermarked."

"Watermarked?"

"Aye, it's been made, sir, with a dandy-roll on a continuous papermaking machine."

"I know what a damned watermark is, Jolley," said Napier irritably.

"Well, then, have a look at it, sir." Jolley popped out the loupe and offered it. "It's the Maid of Dort mark."

"Dort? What's Dort?"

"It means Dordrecht, sir. It means the paper weren't made here, but in Holland."

"Not British paper?" Napier slapped the paper to the glass to better see the faint embossing. "I don't need the loupe, thank you. What the devil is she holding? A hat on a stick? And a . . . a creature of some sort?"

"Just so, sir," said Jolley in the tone of one tutoring a child. "That's the Maid of Dort, and she's speared her enemy's helmet. And her lion—see him, just here?—he's got some arrows and a sword. It's like a warning, sir, to Holland's adversaries. And if you find a paper with this mark, then you might know who wrote the letter."

"Interesting," muttered Napier. "It must be a relatively rare paper, mustn't it?"

"Not common, no." Jolley handed Hepplewood's old letter back. "What d'you mean ter do, sir?"

Napier tossed them onto the table and stared at them for

a long moment, still thinking about death—and, if he were honest—about Lazonby's vile accusations against his father. Actually, they had been Miss Ashton's accusations, though he still believed Lazonby was behind it.

It was like circles running around circles. Letters upon letters suggesting this and demanding that.

Damn it all, he did not have time for any of it. With a muttered curse, Napier refilled his brandy, three fingers' worth this time, watching as the liquid gold shimmered in a shaft of fading sunlight.

He set the decanter down, forgetting it was open. The nagging in the back of his mind and that dark, awful doubt would not relent. And frustratingly, the truth to all of it likely lay at Burlingame Court.

"Jolley," he finally said, "would Mrs. Bourne fancy a fortnight's visit to her sister down in Hull, do you reckon?"

"Oh, I should imagine." Jolley reached around to stopper the decanter.

"Well then, old fellow." Napier paused to slowly exhale. "Perhaps you and I ought to take a little trip of our own."

"Ooh, sir, not ter Wiltshire again." Jolley flashed a sidelong wince. "Never much cared for the country, meself."

Napier shrugged. "I fear that's of no consequence," he said picking the offensive letters up again. "You've chosen house arrest—and the choice of which house must be *mine*."

CHAPTER 3

An Accident in Mayfair

$\mathcal{V}$alise in hand, Napier set off the following morning in the general direction of Hackney, intent upon executing Sir George's orders. Although he found himself inexplicably hesitant to call upon Elizabeth Ashton, he wanted it over with.

After that first fateful meeting in his office—nearly two years ago now—Napier had naïvely imagined he need never see Sir Arthur Colburne's daughter again. What a fool he had been. Trouble had practically wafted from her skin like that unusual scent she favored. Even now he could see those long, slender fingers deftly slipping loose the buttons of her bodice, those bewitching eyes locked to his—taunting him—as she suggested just how she might negotiate her position.

She had called herself Elizabeth Colburne then. And she had called herself desperate.

He wondered how desperate she was now. And then he wondered why such a thought had crossed his mind. Good Lord. He had only to call upon her and step through her statement one last time—while trying hard not to drown in those incredible eyes—before beginning his fool's game of waiting for the American authorities to apprehend her ephemeral brother.

No, it was not likely the lady would be slipping loose any buttons for him now.

As if to clear the vision from his mind, Napier drew a deep breath of the cold spring air, noting as he did so that the acrid smell of coal smoke had diminished during the night. Then carefully timing the traffic, he dashed between a cartload of bricks and a westbound mail coach to make his way across Hyde Park Corner.

Napier had always believed his curricle too flashy for a public servant, and there being as yet no trains to Hackney Station—or even a roof over it—he'd thought it best to simply walk up to Oxford Street and catch the green omnibus. But despite these well-laid plans, he found himself taking an oddly indirect route, and halfway up Park Lane, turned onto Upper Grosvenor Street, telling himself he was taking a shortcut through the alleyways of Mayfair.

At Lady Anisha's house, the semicircular drive was empty, the iron gates still shut up. It was, of course, too early to call. Which was a ridiculous notion, when he had not even *meant* to call.

Feeling a trifle foolish, Napier turned up the alleyway alongside the house, intent upon reaching Oxford Street as quickly as possible. But halfway along the lane separating the house from the mews, there came a great splash of water over the fence, right between two shrubs.

He leapt back on a curse, very nearly stumbling into a pile of fresh horse manure.

"Oh!" A colorful scarf poked between the shrubs. "Oh, dear! I'm so frightfully . . . good heavens. *Mr. Napier*—?"

"Indeed, ma'am," he said, glancing down at his shirtfront. "Good morning."

"Oh, I am *so* sorry!" Lady Anisha Stafford peeped out of the greenery at him, her head and shoulders swathed in a bright gossamer scarf, her chocolate eyes wide as saucers. "How awkward I am!"

Napier regained himself, and sketched her a little bow. "Not in the least," he managed. "You are, as always, grace and beauty personified."

"Then either Grace or Beauty has ruined your coat." She rushed down the fence and unlatched a little gate. "Which does not sound especially welcoming to someone I am so glad to see. Oh, come in, *do*. I was just trying to wash out Milo's cage, and—"

"Haven't you servants for that?" he interjected, before thinking better of it.

She flashed an embarrassed smile. "Yes, but Milo likes his things cleaned just so, and then certain herbs cut for him, and his water—oh, but never mind that. Now do come in. I shall have some tea sent out to the conservatory, and make a proper inspection of your coat."

"Thank you," he said, "but I can assure you, in my line of work, I get far worse than water hurled at me."

She set her head stubbornly to one side, and motioned him in. Only then did he see the wire cage sitting in the grass beside the empty bucket. Satchel in hand, he followed her down a flagstone path past the rear entrance. She was dressed this morning for the privacy of her home, her slender form attired in a pair of silk trousers over which she wore a calf-length gown of shimmering blue, the scarf flowing behind.

"Round the corner," she called over her shoulder, "and we'll just pop in the back."

A pair of doors gave onto a lofty space glassed in on three sides where a green bird glided about in the rafters. The persnickety Milo, he assumed.

Napier settled into the rattan chair she offered, and after

ringing for tea, Anisha took one opposite. The bird sailed onto the curved back with a great *whoosh!* and proceeded to peck at the gold embroidery of her headscarf. "Milo!" she chided, tossing back the scarf with a laugh.

Only then did he see the wicked yellow bruise that ran from her temple deep into her hairline. "My God!" he exclaimed, coming half out of his chair. "Anisha!"

The lady threw up her hand. "Mr. Napier, I am quite all right. And as you see, my traditional scarf can be a quite useful wardrobe accessory."

Until that moment, he realized, he had not been entirely sure of Lazonby's wild story. "By God, I could kill Sir Wilfred Leeton myself," he gritted.

"Thankfully, that job has been done for you," she said wryly. "In truth, I expected you before now. I did not think for one moment you would heed Lazonby's threats to stay away from me. You are here for my statement, I daresay?"

He deliberately cocked one eyebrow. "But I was given to understand you remembered nothing."

She eyed him carefully across the tea table. "I took a frightful blow to the head, yes, and was unconscious for a time," she said slowly, as if carefully choosing her words. "But I can remember whatever is necessary to see justice done."

He wasn't sure what she was offering. Or threatening. "And your notion of justice would be?"

"Has anyone been charged with anything?"

"No, the mysterious Jack Coldwater has vanished," he said dryly, "never to be seen again, I'm reasonably confident."

Anisha exhaled on a long sigh. "Good!" she said. "Then we must leave well enough alone. We *will* leave well enough alone, Assistant Commissioner, will we not? None of us, I think, want this scandal reopened?"

He settled back into his chair on a sigh. "I'm man enough to know when I'm beaten," he said. "Yes, I suppose we're done. And I don't wish your statement. Like Lazonby, I wish you fifty miles away from this frightful scandal."

"And that poor girl?" Anisha was still watching him. "Miss . . . Ashton, was it not? What did you think of her, by the way? Unconventional, isn't she? And quite striking, too."

"I was just on my way to see her," he said, ignoring the rest of her question. "I need to review her statement one last time, as I'm leaving town for a while."

At that point, the tea arrived. After pouring, Anisha settled back into her chair, cradling her cup in her palm as she studied him. "And where do you go, Mr. Napier?" she asked. "On holiday, I hope?"

"No, family business."

"Oh, at Burlingame Court?" she enquired lightly.

When he looked at her in surprise, she smiled. "I recall you went some months past," she added. "When Lord Hepplewood died."

"You were aware of that?"

"That you had a death in the family, yes," she said. "Really, Mr. Napier, you must know Lazonby had your every move watched, as you watched his. Though precisely *how* the gentleman was related to you, I never heard."

"Lord Hepplewood married my great-aunt."

"And she was—?" Anisha's smile was coy. "You see, having come so recently from India, Mr. Napier, I have not yet memorized *Burke's Peerage*. If I look closely, might I find your name in it?"

It was the moment of decision, he realized, or something like it.

"I think not," he finally answered, "though I've never looked. In his youth, my father quarreled irrevocably with his family over his choice of bride, and took his wife's name, Napier. I believe it was put about by his family that he'd died."

She drew back an inch, her smile softening. "Mr. Napier, Lazonby once said you had eyes like a pair of kitchen knives," she said. "I do believe you are stabbing me with them now."

He felt his mouth twitch. "What, had he nothing to say of my nose? I have always been rather proud of it."

"That it looked like a hatchet," she added, setting down her tea. "There, I have pried enough, Mr. Napier. And I think you know I'm quite fond of your eyes and your nose. They suit you."

He felt silent for a time then put his teacup on the table. "My last uncle recently died," he said quietly. "There were three sons, you see, my father being youngest. So despite my grandfather's ire, no one believed my father's *marrying down* would do much harm to the family's blue blood."

"Ah," she said quietly. "But now the elder brothers are gone? And gone without sons, dare I surmise?"

"Something like that," he said ruefully. "My grandfather is a miserable old tyrant, and now he demands my return."

"Ha!" she said. "He mustn't know you very well if he imagines *demanding* will do the trick."

"He scarcely knows me at all," said Napier. "So he has written to Sir George Grey instead. Sir George's sire and my grandfather were old friends, I collect."

"Oh, dear." Anisha looked solemn. "Why do I begin to suspect there is an old and noble title involved here? The Grey family is *haute ton*; even I know that much."

"Yes." For an instant, he hesitated. "And my grandfather is Viscount Duncaster, and my uncle was Baron Saint-Bryce by courtesy."

"I fear I know nothing of either gentleman," she said apologetically. "Are they great and noble titles indeed, then? Yes, I can see by the look on your face that they are."

When he said nothing, her face fell. "And you are to have no say in the matter, are you?" she went on. "Sir George will not permit you to go on at work as if nothing has happened. The laws of entail will not permit Duncaster to disinherit you. Oh, Mr. Napier, I know what it is like to be jerked out of one life and thrust into another. Will that be your fate? Are you now Baron Saint-Bryce against your wishes?"

He gave an inward sigh of relief. Only Lady Anisha, he was certain, could have understood such a thing. And the sympathy on her face was real, he thought.

"Yes," he quietly admitted. "I daresay I am."

"Oh, well!" she said, that same face suddenly brightening. "There's nothing else for it; you'll be stuck with power and riches unimaginable. However, I will say, in my own defense, you should have told me you were coming into money. I might have considered your suit more carefully."

He wanted, suddenly, to roar with laughter. "You don't think like that, Anisha. Neither of us even believes you capable of it."

The bird had begun to tug at the dangle on one of her earbobs. "Thank you," she said.

He gave an audible sigh. "Lady Anisha, is it true, what I suspect? Have you agreed to marry Lazonby?"

She dropped her gaze. "I fear he has not officially asked me."

"And if—no, *when* he does—will you say yes?"

She lifted her wide eyes back to his. "Yes," she said quietly. "When he does, I will happily say *yes*. But you are my dear friend, and I'm sorry you don't like him."

"I don't like him," Napier agreed. "But you are no fool. And he will make you happy, I think. He will be too afraid of your brother Ruthveyn not to."

Her mouth twisted. "Oh, Lazonby doesn't have the sense to be afraid, even when he ought," she said. "A character flaw he shares with you. Indeed, it might be the two of you are too like ever to get on. Did you ever consider that?"

"Don't be ridiculous."

"Mr. Napier," she said slyly, "why, exactly, have you come here today?"

He gave a crooked smile. "I didn't think I *was* coming here," he said. "Although, if I'm to be as honest as you, I think in the back of my mind, I had the faintest notion of asking a favor."

"A favor? Of what sort?"

"A great favor," he confessed. "But your expectations of Lord Lazonby have forestalled it. I am . . . glad. I think I could not have asked it anyway."

"But what might the favor be? And how do you know I would refuse it?"

He hesitated a heartbeat. "As I said, I have to go away," he replied. "And I wanted you . . . well, I wanted you to come with me. And worse, under false pretenses."

"Ah. This has something to do with your family at Burlingame, does it not?"

"It does." He shot her a withering look, and sighed. "I needed a woman on my arm—a beautiful—and very eligible—one. An ornament, if you will, to forestall a matchmaking great-aunt—Lady Hepplewood, in fact. Duncaster's sister."

Anisha laughed again. "How you do flatter a lady. But surely the great Royden Napier would not be cowed by *that*?"

"Well, one would hope not," he muttered. "But Sir George warns she'll bedevil me to distraction. It's not precisely a social visit, you see, and I'd as soon Lady Hepplewood not know it, for there've been—"

He couldn't think how to explain it, the gut feeling he'd had all those months ago upon reading the letter Hepplewood had sent Sir George. And again last evening, that curious missive in the post . . .

Still, it made no sense.

"Well, you've had two relations die under vague circumstances," said Anisha tactfully. "So your expression is more daunting than usual, and understandably."

"It's probably nothing," he said. "But I desperately need someone to guard my wicket and keep the old girl from dogging me whilst I poke around a bit."

"Well, to be honest, I'm sorry I can't, for it sounds like quite a lark." She laughed again. "The misbegotten heir and his half-caste bride! Can you imagine the old dear's expression? Still, if Lady Hepplewood is anything like Aunt Pernicia, I fear for you."

"You aren't giving me much comfort here," he muttered.

"Wait, I've an idea—what about simply hiring an actress?"

Napier laughed. "Unlike yourself, Aunt Hepplewood probably sleeps with a copy of *Burke's Peerage* under her pillow—annotated and updated in her own hand."

Anisha's shoulders fell. "Yes, that little ruse would last just long enough for the old girl to write a quizzing letter to one of her London cronies, wouldn't it?"

"Ah, well." Napier set down his teacup. "On to the things I *can* manage. I should be off to Miss Ashton's, I daresay."

For an instant, Anisha snared her lip between her teeth. "Have a care, Napier," she said quietly, "in dealing with Miss Ashton."

This time his laugh was harsh. "I'm not an utter fool, my dear. Do you think I don't know what she is?"

"Oh, I think it quite likely you do not." Anisha did reach for his hand then, turning it palm up to stroke her thumb around the mounds of flesh. "Royden, I . . . I have seen her hand. That day in the fortune-teller's tent. She's deeply tormented; her whole life has been nearly destroyed by her family's death."

Napier narrowed his gaze. "What do you mean, Anisha, *seen her hand*?"

She flicked an impatient look up at him. "It is called *hasta*

samudrika shastra," she said, "and no, don't gape at me.
It's a science, not a parlor trick. And no, I am *not* like my
brother, so please do not start."

He wasn't about to discuss Lord Ruthveyn's dark talents;
they spooked the hell out of him. "So you really *meant* to tell
fortunes in Lady Leeton's tent?" he said, incredulous.

"No, I meant only to entertain." She released his hand
and sighed. "It was supposed to be a charity event. But Miss
Ashton's hand—it shocked me—and I fear I frightened her."

Napier felt a smile twist at his mouth. "Oh, from what
little I've seen, my dear, nothing frightens Miss Ashton."

"Then at the very least, I made her angry." Anisha sat back
onto her seat. "But never mind that. Now, are you perfectly
certain you do not need my statement? Be assured I shall do
my duty as a citizen, whether Lazonby likes it or not."

"Lazonby is using my affection for you against me,"
Napier grumbled. "You know that, do you not?"

"He is hopelessly intractable." She looked at him with a
speculative gleam in her eye. "And your affection for Miss
Ashton?" she added lightly. "What of that?"

"I beg your pardon?"

Anisha made a pretense of straightening the folds of her
tunic. "Well, I cannot but notice that whilst my name has
remained quite out of the newspapers, hers very nearly has,
too. One would almost gather the lady was merely strolling
by when the shooting occurred, and didn't know Mr. Coldwater at all."

He looked at her pointedly—and a little darkly. "I cannot
imagine, Lady Anisha, what you mean to imply."

She had the audacity to smile. "Only that you are kinder
in heart, I think, than you wish people to believe," she said.
"You owe very little to Miss Ashton, and yet someone—
you, I'm sure—has shielded her from the worst of the news
reports."

"*Hmph,*" said Napier. "Perhaps you should thank your

almost-fiancé for that. He has threatened to leave my father's name in tatters."

"Oh, no, my fine fellow!" countered Lady Anisha. "Lazonby doesn't give a fig for Miss Ashton. In fact, he has every reason to wish her . . . ah, but never mind!"

Suddenly uncomfortable, Napier rose. "I fear I have detained you too long."

The jewels on her slippers caught the sun as she leapt up. "Oh, must you go?"

"I fear so," he said, which was entirely true. "I will await news of your happy event, Lady Anisha, before I call again—"

"*Napier!*" she chided.

"—at which time I pledge to set aside my bitterness—oh, for a day or so!—and bring the two of you my best wishes and a case of excellent champagne."

As if delighted, she clasped her hands. "How very kind."

"And then I shall endeavor," he belatedly added, "*not* to hope Lazonby chokes on it."

Perched atop a step stool in her cottage's tidy kitchen, Lisette let her gaze trail over the half-empty shelves. Pots and bowls now littered the kitchen worktable.

"Well, that's the lot of it," she said, wiping her dusty hands on her apron. "The rest came with the letting."

"Not my fine-mesh chinoise." Mrs. Fenwick spoke into the depths of a packing crate. "Here, miss, hand it down and I'll stick it inside me stewpot."

"This battered old thing?"

"Aye, just like meself," said Mrs. Fenwick in a chiding tone. "Can't make a proper puree or even a decent soup without I have it."

"Shall we start wrapping all this in newspaper?" Lisette

passed down the conical contraption. "You must have two months' worth laid back."

Just then, the sound of the knocker dropping rang through the house. The old woman sighed, and shoved her mobcap back into place.

"I'll go." Lisette hopped down and untied her apron. "Perhaps it's Mr. Bodkins with word of a house."

"Aye, well, anyplace but Scotland, miss," warned Mrs. Fenwick.

Despite her words, however, Lisette approached the door with grave trepidation, her gait slowing as logic caught up. It was not Bodkins; it was too soon. Leaning into the parlor's bow window, she glanced through the sheer underdrapes to the sunlit walkway beyond, her stomach sinking.

Assistant Commissioner Napier stood upon her front step, foreboding as Mephistopheles himself, his hand fisted around the handle of a black leather valise with glittering brass hardware.

Satan's emissary was, however, impeccably attired in a tall black hat and a matching frock coat cut to the turn of a slender waist. Beneath it Lisette could make out a cabernet-colored waistcoat and a snowy, starched neck cloth, its knot tightly—and perfectly—centered at his throat. Sheer masculine elegance, freshly turned out by Bond Street, she guessed.

After running her hands over her hair, she crossed into the front hall, yet her fingers froze upon the doorknob. But there was nothing for it; this call was as inevitable as Faust's visit from hell.

After sending up a prayer for strength to a God who likely no longer listened, she threw open the glossy blue door. "Mr. Napier," she said. "How do you do?"

"Well enough, thank you." His voice deep as a gravel pit, the man swept off his hat to reveal his dark, almost-black hair combed harshly back off a high forehead, and a lean, angular face unfashionably clean shaven, though she could still make out the faint shadow of his beard. "Might I have a word?"

She forced a light smile. "Have I any choice?"

Napier did not return the smile. "Regrettably not."

She was not a fool; she knew what his coming here meant. Oh, she had got what she had wanted, albeit inadvertently, in Sir Wilfred Leeton's death. But there was always a price to be paid. And Royden Napier, she very much feared, had just come to collect.

"Well," she said briskly, "one hates to thwart the ever-diligent Scotland Yard." Lisette stepped back, and waited for the next chapter of her life to begin. "Do come in."

CHAPTER 4

Mephistopheles Lays Out His Terms

Napier let his gaze take in Elizabeth Ashton's tidy front hall as he stepped inside. It was an instinctive act on his part, this swift assessment of an unfamiliar space: the doors, the windows, the potential for escape.

Which was ridiculous when the lady had no reason to flee. Lazonby had seen to that—at least for now. And still Napier looked. Wide arches gave off the small room in three directions, and in the large parlor to his right he could see a flight of stairs leading to the floors above. The hall was furnished with a fine drop-leaf table set with a pair of candlesticks that would have equaled a constable's annual salary. A gilt-framed landscape hung above, completing the impression of gentrified comfort, if not outright wealth.

"Hardly the grandeur of Mayfair," she said as if reading his thoughts. "But it's home."

Napier did not rise to the bait—if bait it was. With her, one could never be sure. "Is there a place we might speak in private?" he said instead, returning his gaze to her cool, crystalline eyes. "Sir George Grey wishes me to review your statement."

"How very thorough," she said. "But really, Mr. Napier, there is nothing more I can tell you."

He gave a bark of laughter. "Come now, Miss Ashton. I don't think either of us believes that."

Her smile tightened. There was a brittle look about the corners of her eyes today, he noticed, and faint shadows beneath. The lady had not been sleeping. Perhaps she was not as calculating as she seemed.

"Would you care for coffee?" she asked, leading him into the parlor.

"Thank you," he said, noting a row of baggage alongside the stairs. "Going somewhere, Miss Ashton?"

"I have a home in Scotland," she said vaguely. "Pardon me whilst I go into the kitchen. I don't keep much staff. Do have a seat at the table if it suits you."

She reentered the shadowy entrance hall and turned into the door that gave onto the rear of the house, leaving Napier to wonder if she mightn't simply vanish out the back. But he'd seen no desperation in her eyes. She had faith, it seemed, in Lazonby's ability to protect her. At least for now.

And so the hunted had become . . . what? The huntress's ally? It was an atypical roll for Lazonby, and Miss Ashton did not look like the sort of woman who would ally herself with anyone. There was not one whit of trust in the lady's eyes. But perhaps life had taught her well. No, she would not run. Not yet. The infernal woman was too bold for that.

He set his valise down on the round table. It likely served as a breakfast table, he imagined, for the room was the sort of parlor used for many purposes. A pair of tall bookcases was built to either side of the hearth, an old pianoforte sat along the back wall, and ladies' marquetry writing desk was nestled beneath a side window. Through it he could see a charming garden gate arched over with a climbing rose, now lush and sagging with white blossoms.

Oddly on edge, Napier followed Miss Ashton's trail back into the hall. The door opposite the parlor gave onto a formal withdrawing room hung with blue watered silk and a fine gilt pier glass. The furniture, however, he could not make out for it had been swaddled in holland cloth.

He had guessed rightly, then. Miss Ashton was shutting up the house.

Pondering this, Napier retraced his steps. Atop the marquetry writing desk he noticed an oval silver-framed miniature sitting alongside a pair of heavy crystal inkwells. He picked it up, and looked into the round, cerulean eyes of a young lady attired in a pink ball gown, the cut of which told him the portrait was far from recent.

The lady was an undeniable beauty, with a fine, thin nose and full lips accented by a beauty mark set at one corner. Miss Elinor Colburne, he guessed, for the resemblance to her younger sister was unmistakable.

And yet they looked little alike.

It was very odd, thought Napier, turning it to the light. Elinor's eyes were pretty but of a quite ordinary shade, while her hair was blonde. Elizabeth Ashton's eyes were a rare blue-green and faintly almond-shaped, her skin pale as porcelain and her hair a dull chestnut.

The only similarly, really, was in the shape of their faces; pure, perfect ovals, both of them, with firm, slanting cheekbones that spoke of blue-blooded elegance. *And those mouths.* Lush cupid's bows with full, almost bee-stung bottom lips that made a man think of—

"I see you've found Elinor's picture." The rattle of china sounded behind him.

Jerked back to sanity, Napier put the miniature down a little awkwardly and turned to see that Miss Ashton had carried in a galleried tray, a massive silver affair set with a full coffee service that could not have been light.

"I would gladly have helped you with that," he said, looking at the tray.

She lifted her cool gaze to his, faint distain on her face. "Really, Mr. Napier, have you somehow come away with the impression I'm frail?" she murmured, setting the tray on the table. "If so, you much mistake the matter." Here, she tilted her head toward the desk. "Ellie was the delicate one."

Napier still held his hat, which she had neglected to take from him. "Frailty takes many forms, Miss Ashton," he said quietly. "I see the gamut in my sort of work. But no, I do not doubt your abilities."

She settled into a chair. "Well. Do have a seat, Mr. Napier, and get on with your questions."

But he did not sit, and instead merely put down his hat. "Firstly," he said, staring down at her, "I want you to admit precisely what happened in that dairy on—"

Miss Ashton threw up her hand, palm out. "I have said, sir, all I mean to say on that score. You have my statement. Do you wish to review it or not?"

"*Damn it*," he said under his breath. "I want you to admit, Miss Ashton, that no one named Jack Coldwater came within an inch of Sir Wilfred's estate that day. *That* is the truth, and all the rest of this is a rat's nest of lies."

Miss Ashton merely widened her unusual eyes. "If he did not do it," she said calmly, "then whom do you imagine shot Sir Wilfred? Was it Lazonby? Good luck with that prosecution. Lady Anisha? I confess, she doesn't seem the violent type. But wait—perhaps you think it was I? If it was, then I have the right under law not to incriminate myself, and I'm not fool enough, Mr. Napier, to waive it."

"This is a waste of my time, is it not?" he said, frustrated by her demeanor. "You'll tell me nothing; indeed, you've been well schooled by your friend Lazonby."

Stiff as a duchess, she rose again. "Oh, Lazonby is far from my friend, Mr. Napier," she said. "I wouldn't trust the man as far as I could throw him."

Napier gave a bark of laugher. "In that opinion, madam, we are agreed," he said. "And yet—"

"And yet what?" She swished around the table toward him. "And yet I have unfairly blamed him? And yet I have tormented an innocent man all these months? Oh, come now, Mr. Napier! Even if you could prove it, that cannot be what brings you here. Besides, some would say that rich, titled men like Lazonby are rarely innocent of much."

"Really, Miss Ashton—"

"Oh, for God's sake, just get on with it." She jerked to a halt before him. "Why are you here? Kindly say it—or ask it—and spare me your moralizing."

"I'm not sure I should waste my breath," he retorted, uncertain why he was so angry. Or even what he wanted from her. The truth? Tears? He'd likely get neither. "You and Lazonby look two of a kind to me, both of you willing to twist and bend the truth as it suits you."

"Look here, Napier, your trouble with Lazonby is your own," she snapped. "My business in London is done. If his holding your father's reputation hostage is what frustrates you, then go trouble *him* with your questions."

Without an instant's thought, Napier seized both her shoulders. "Do you think me an utter fool, Miss Ashton?" he exploded, burning to shake sense into her. "Do you think for one moment I don't see what you and Lazonby have conspired to do here? And consider this, since you're so conniving: Lazonby will have a knife in your back the instant he no longer needs you. He'll swear on a pile of Bibles that you killed Sir Wilfred—whether you did or you didn't—just to get even for the hell you've put him through."

She paled at that, but stood her ground. "And I'll swear

it was the *Morning Chronicle*—and Jack—who harassed him."

He did shake her then. "Do you imagine I haven't been down to Fleet Street, Miss Ashton?" he all but shouted. "I've put the fear of God into every man working at the *Chronicle*. I've upended Coldwater's office and his rooms in Shoe Lane, too. So let's just say it out loud—*there is no Jack Coldwater.* And there never was, was there?"

Elizabeth Ashton leaned into him very slowly. "Well, if there isn't, sir, you shall have to prove it," she said softly. "But the *Chronicle*'s staff, I'm guessing, has already told you they worked cheek by jowl with him for better than a year. His landlady has doubtless reported she saw him going in and out regularly. Moreover—"

"Yes, but she also saw—"

"Moreover," she pressed on, "ask that bullyboy who loiters round Lazonby's club just who's been bribing him to watch Lazonby all these months. Jack Coldwater was known to half the thugs in town. And half of *them* were his paid tipsters, which made him a dashed fine reporter in the bargain. Oh, perhaps Jack wasn't around the office much, but the *Chronicle* got what they paid for. And not a one of those men will willingly admit to being taken in by a mere woman. Assuming, of course, that they *were*."

"Balderdash," Napier snarled, "all of it. You're no better than Lazonby, and I grow weary of being run around the facts with prevarications and half-truths. You set out to ruin Lazonby—to hound and harass and to convict him of murder—and you chose the court of public opinion in which to do it. And that's all Jack Coldwater ever was. A weapon. A *chimera*."

Disdain sketched across her face. "Is there a question buried amidst all this high-handed accusation, Mr. Napier?" she replied. "And if so, do you really want me to answer it the way you seem to hope? Because if I should—well, you fancy yourself a gentleman, do you not? There'd be all that gentlemanly honor to wrestle with. All that duty to the Crown. All that right and might and moral obligation needling you like a pin the laundress left in your collar. Well, I long ago ceased to be troubled by truth and honor, Mr. Napier. It never did a damned thing for me or my family. So leave me to bear the guilt, if guilt there be. And let your father's fine reputation rest easy in the grave."

He felt every muscle in his body tighten. "By God," he whispered, "I ought to arrest you for murder—*and* for unladylike language."

She had the audacity to push her face into his. "Have at it," she answered, "and see how far it gets you."

Blinded by frustration and something like lust, Napier tightened his grip. She backed up against the bookcase, rattling a vase of white gladioli perched upon the mantelpiece.

Her eyes widened as he thrust one leg between hers, effectively pinning her. "You once offered me something, Miss Ashton, for my cooperation," he whispered, his hot gaze drifting over her face. "Tell me, does that offer still stand? Are you still so bold?"

She pushed back, setting the heels of her hands to his shoulders. "I'm bold enough to do what I must," she answered. "I'm a survivor, Mr. Napier. And no, I'm not a fool. I know what you are. I see behind your gentlemanly façade— and yes, Lazonby's, too. Now I ask you again: *What do you want of me?*"

"I want you in jail," he gritted. "I want you, by God, where I can keep an eye on you."

And with that, he speared his fingers into her hair. On a small cry, her eyes widened, and she turned her face as if to thwart his kiss, the heels of her hands ramming hard into his shoulders.

But Napier did not kiss her—though the desire, and a good deal more, was thrumming through his loins. Instead, he viciously ripped off her elaborate arrangement of chestnut curls. It came away in a scatter of pins, one of them pinging off the chimneypiece mirror.

Miss Ashton shuddered in his grasp, refusing to turn her face to his.

"Oh, I thought remembered those wild, flaming locks," he said, hurling the chestnut wig aside, "though you haven't much of it left. Still, I never forget a face, Miss Ashton. I never forget height. Eyes. The scent of a woman. *Or her true hair color.*"

"Let me go, you cad," she whispered.

Instead he leaned nearer, his rough breath dragging in her fragrance as he watched her lashes flutter shut like dark, feathery fans over alabaster skin. And all of it designed, he did not doubt, to madden a man. To leave him unable to think straight.

He did not succumb. Not *quite.* "Oh, that dull wig, drab gown, and the stone you've gained may have made me question things in Sir Wilfred's garden," he said gruffly, "but I've sensed all along something about you was not quite right."

She opened her eyes, and for his own sanity, Napier pushed her a little away.

She had regained herself, it seemed.

"Why, how you do flatter a lady, Assistant Commissioner," she said mockingly. "I did not realize I had captured your imagination so thoroughly. But whatever it is you are imagining just now"—here, the little vixen let her gaze drift to his thickening crotch—"just be aware I've servants about."

Disgusted with himself, Napier released his grip on her slender shoulders, and spun away. But her scent, heady and floral, followed him. Good God, this was madness. With this woman he was playing with fire—almost literally.

And the thoughts she stirred up in his head . . .

As he stood there, angry with himself and grappling for

control, he heard the rustle of her silk skirts behind him, and the soft sound of leather sliding across the table.

Miss Ashton appeared before him, her cap of bright red curls springing from their pins to fall almost angelically around her face.

"I wondered," he muttered almost to himself, "just how on earth you tamed that wild mess of hair."

She smiled with feigned sweetness. "I'm told many gentlemen use Macassar oil," she said, dangling his valise from one fingertip, "though I really wouldn't know. Now, on your way out, Mr. Napier, don't forget your bag."

Her confidence caused something in him to snap—his good judgment, apparently—as he sneered down at her. "Oh, I am not leaving, Miss Ashton," he said. "Nor are you."

Her false smile faded, her eyes darting toward the row of baggage by the stairs.

"Very well," she said, letting the valise fall to the floor. "Arrest me—if you think you can make it stick. And if you think you can survive Lazonby's onslaught. He desperately needs my statement regarding Sir Wilfred's confession, you will recall."

"Oh, I'm not afraid of Lazonby, and never have been," said Napier. "You, on the other hand—*you* are dangerous— and about two-thirds deranged, I begin to think."

She gave a sharp laugh. "Well, you know what they say. 'Great wits are sure to madness near allied.'"

"'—and thin partitions do their bounds divide,'" he finished grimly.

Her eyes widened. "Why, you do know your Dryden, Mr. Napier," she said. "Under better circumstances, I'd quite enjoy matching wits with you."

"Aye, well, deal with the circumstances at hand, my dear," Napier warned. "Perhaps you don't deserve to hang—Lord knows Sir Wilfred wanted killing—but there is always a price to be paid for duplicity. And let's face it, my dear: you elevate duplicity to an art form."

Miss Ashton had stepped away, calmly pulling what was left of the loose pins from her short, fiery curls. "And so?" she said, tossing a few onto the table.

"And so I want you, by God, where I can keep an eye on you," he said, "until this business of Sir Wilfred's death dies down."

"Mr. Napier," she said wearily, "if you try to put me in jail, Lazonby will—"

"Not jail," he snapped. "Until he has no further need of you, he'll just lie and get you out again."

Her hand stilled. "Then . . . where?"

"Somewhere else," said Napier, too bloody stupid to bite his tongue. "Somewhere, perhaps, that might make good use of your incorrigible talents."

"Oh, I think not." Her eyes shied warily as she edged away.

But he scarcely heard her, his mind in a whirl. "Aye, it might do, at that," he muttered. "Something in the way of a bargain—a Faustian bargain, or near it."

And Napier knew in that moment that he had truly taken leave of his senses. That he was making the one mistake he was infamous for *never* making—allowing emotion to rule over cold logic.

Miss Ashton apparently concurred. "That's a scheming look in your eyes, Napier," she said warningly. "And I'll tell you straight out, sir, that I'm not doing anything underhanded."

"Oh, *now* you find your moral high ground!" Napier laughed. "Good God, madam, does your audacity know no bounds?"

And yet his sudden notion seemed to make a shocking sort of sense. He was loath to leave the woman; loath to unleash such a fey and clever creature on an unsuspecting society until he was sure she wasn't after someone else—Lazonby again, perhaps, for Miss Ashton was clearly possessed of a mind too sharp for her own good.

Was she dangerous? He thought not.

Well, not now. But a part of him burned to keep an eye on the woman, to discover exactly what she'd done and why. He only hoped it was the part above his waist, and not below.

Miss Ashton, however, had backed even farther away. "You may call it audacity, Napier," she said. "But whatever I may have done, I have always sought justice."

He sharpened his gaze. "Yes, and now you need to leave London rather desperately, don't you?" he said, thinking aloud. "You're wise enough to know Lazonby's restraint will last about as long as it takes him to clear his name in the press and get back in the good graces of polite society— which won't be long. He doesn't want Anisha's name tarnished. So aye, he'll use you. And then he might just throw you to the wolves."

Miss Ashton lifted one shoulder, but she was listening. "And so I'm to make a deal with the devil, am I?" she said lightly. "And then . . . *what*? You'll protect me from Lazonby if he somehow turns on me in order to get back at my brother Jack?"

"Something like that," he said.

She lifted her chin, all of her arrogance restored. "Be *specific*."

He jerked his head at the row of baggage. "Unpack that lot," he said. "You'll need just one trunk; your most elegant things, but suitable for the country—and for a house in mourning. My driver will pick you up on Tuesday at eight o'clock in the morning."

Miss Ashton froze. "To take me where," she said, "do you wildly imagine?"

"To Wiltshire," he said, snatching up his valise. "And I do not imagine it, wildly or otherwise. You *are* going. That, you see, is your penance."

"To Wiltshire? With . . . *you*?" She stared after him. "But why? To do what?"

"To *act*," he said grimly. "God knows you're good at it."

"Good at acting as a drab grammar teacher, certainly," she acknowledged. "But I rather doubt they need another of those in Wiltshire."

"No, but I need an affianced bride," he said, snaring his hat from the table. "Fool that I am, Miss Ashton, I am not without sympathy for what you've lost. But by God, until I know you are neither mad nor dangerous, then I mean to keep an eye on you."

At last, he had rendered the lady speechless. Her eyes turned to saucers and her mouth literally fell open. Dredging up a faint sliver of pity for her, Napier relented.

"Miss Ashton," he said darkly, "it is my theory that for better than a year you've fooled half of London into believing you some radical young newspaper reporter. Surely, for a mere fortnight, you can make my meddling relations believe that you are at least a little in love with me."

Was it his imagination, or did her expression relent?

"And after that, I am free to go where I wish?" she said, her mouth turning up at one corner. "I have your word as a gentleman?"

He cocked his head to one side, studying her. "Well, that will depend," he finally answered, "on whether one accounts me a gentleman. And whether you can behave as a sane, responsible member of society. *And* on how well you do at keeping those meddling relations from . . . well, meddling. I must conduct a sort of enquiry, you see. And it's your job to ensure I do it unhindered."

Miss Ashton crossed her arms. "Then send your man to fetch me, Mr. Napier," she said. "And perhaps I'll be ready to go. Or perhaps I'll be halfway to Scotland."

He smiled. "Oh, you'll not be off to Scotland, my dear."

She smiled back, dazzlingly. "You think not?"

"Oh, I know not," he replied, setting off again toward the door. "For I'll have a half dozen London constables watching every road out of Hackney."

At that, she hastened after him. "But I am not a prisoner," she complained. "You cannot restrain me here."

"Can I not?" he said over his shoulder.

"Napier!" Her eyes burned into the back of his head. "Napier, you are unconscionable."

"Yes, it's often been remarked," he said, turning to make her a pretty bow. "Now, I shall meet you at Paddington under the sign for the Number One platform on Tuesday morning, tickets in hand—or I *will* find a way to arrest you."

"You heartless dog," she whispered. "I can see they call you Roughshod Roy for a reason."

"They do indeed," he said. "So, Tuesday morning. Pray do not be late. Now, have you a maid? If not, hire one."

"Yes. Yes, of course I've a maid." Miss Ashton fisted her hands at her sides. "But perhaps I shan't be there at all. Perhaps I shall be the one person who stands up to your bullying."

"Ah, bridal nerves already, my dear?" Napier forced a munificent smile and set off again. "I shouldn't have thought it of you."

"*Napier*—" she said grimly.

But Napier merely threw open the door. "Now I bid you good day, Miss Ashton," he said with specious cheer, slapping his hat back on. "And I shall count the hours until I can again gaze upon my beloved bride-to-be."

*L*isette watched Royden Napier stride down her flagstone path, barely resisting the urge to hurl one of the massive brass candlesticks after him. But they were very fine candlesticks, and likely wouldn't survive the blow against Napier's rock-hard skull.

Besides, yes, there was always a price to be paid.

At least she now knew what Napier's price was.

Her stomach twisted in knots, Lisette turned and retraced her steps into the parlor. Fanny stood in the shadows, halfway down the staircase, one hand seemingly frozen upon the banister, her expression stricken.

"I'm going with you," said Fanny.

"Oh, Fanny." Lisette cast her an anxious glance. "Were you near enough to hear it, then?"

"Of course." The maid's worry lines had deepened to wrinkles. "I knew t'was trouble when I saw that one come swaggering up the path."

Lisette went to the desk, and fell into the chair, her gaze fixed on Ellie's portrait. "He knows, doesn't he?"

"Aye, he knows." Fanny's expression was grim as she descended. "But he knows, too, t'will be the devil to prove it."

Dragging a hand through her unruly curls, Lisette pondered it as Fanny collected the hairpins scattered around the breakfast table. She had to admit a grudging respect for Royden Napier. He did not like her. But he had not liked Sir Wilfred Leeton very much, either.

Fanny was shaking out the wig. "So you actually mean to go, then?"

Her aplomb returning, Lisette rose. "Why not?" she said, turning from the desk. "I wanted out of London and out of Lazonby's reach. Perhaps . . . perhaps Napier can be managed?"

"Ooh, I don't know about that one, miss." Fanny looked skeptical.

"Well, we must try." Lisette forced a smile. "So let's set to it, then. Kindly go tell Mrs. Fenwick to stop packing, and instead send me all the newspapers we'd collected for the wrapping."

"Aye?" The maid looked at her quizzically. "What for?"

"One must always know one's enemy, Fanny," Lisette replied. "And I intend to know *mine* very well indeed."

CHAPTER 5

In Which Our Intrepid Heroine Commences an Adventure

The clamor around the Great Western's temporary terminus was near deafening by half past nine in the morning. Having been deposited in front of the entrance by Mr. Napier's driver, Lisette hitched her carpetbag onto her wrist, sucked up her courage, and hooked her arm through Fanny's.

Together they picked their way around a pair of waiting hansom cabs, waded inside, and were at once swept up in the rivers of passengers either rushing to catch a train, or flooding forth from one newly arrived. Added to this a maelstrom of porters, servants, and clerks, and the whole of it felt unnerving.

Lisette had taken the train just once in her life, from Liverpool down to London, but in such a state of agitation she scarce remembered it. Indeed, she'd yanked herself up by the roots from Boston so hastily she'd not even shut up the house properly, practically flying across the Atlantic with that old, crumpled copy of the *London Times* still clutched in her fist, having already memorized every word of the front-page article predicting Lazonby's release from prison.

And thinking all the way of Papa, so handsome and so gay. Of Ellie, so beautiful and full of promise. And wondering why she, the awkward one, had been spared.

No, the voyage and the train were but blurs to her. But that article, and her fateful meeting with Royden Napier thereafter—ah, those she still recalled with crystalline clarity.

"Look, there it is, miss." Fanny pointed around the tall top hat of the gentleman blocking their way. "The sign, hanging from a bracket."

"Ah, so it is. Off we go then, Fanny."

Lisette, by far the taller, pushed her way along the platform past makeshift spaces marked *Cloak Room, Ticketing,* and *Telegraph Office* until finally she neared the sign.

The assistant police commissioner stood tall and rigid beneath it, dressed far more elegantly than ever Lisette had seen him. Today Napier wore a black cutaway coat over a gray silk waistcoat and a wide, snowy cravat. As if in deference to mourning, his tall hat was banded in black crepe, while a charcoal cloak lined with pewter silk swung casually from the crook of his elbow.

His mahogany-colored hair fell, heavy and lustrous, at an angle that shadowed his face, and long, faintly hollowed cheeks accentuated the powerful lines of his cheekbones above a jaw that was—like the rest of Napier, she suspected—harsh and squared away.

A large leather portmanteau sat at his feet and his weight was borne ever so slightly onto an elegant, brass-knobbed walking stick. But that grim, relentless gaze was fixed upon the pocket watch in his hand, the gold case flipped open as if he timed her every step.

Drawing up before him, Lisette dropped her carpetbag at his feet and looked up. And fairly far up, too, for though she was tall, Napier seemed to tower over her almost intimidatingly.

Lisette ignored it. "Good morning, my love," she said brightly, presenting her gloved hand for his kiss. "Oh, *how* the hours have dragged since last I gazed upon your handsome face."

Dark, storm-colored eyes leveled to hers, his gaze direct and far too incisive. "Save it for Wiltshire, Sarah Siddons," he said, snapping the case shut and ramming the watch back into his waistcoat. "Did my driver see to your baggage? Ah, here is Jolley! Have you the tickets? Good man."

Lisette let the hand fall.

Jolley, it appeared, was Napier's valet, who informed them that, yes, tickets were in hand, the baggage seen to, and the driver sent on his way. A thin, slightly stooped man of some years, Jolley had a world-weary gaze and an attitude utterly uncowed by his master.

"And I had to take the last two seats," he finished in a put-upon voice, "in *second* class."

"Doubtless you've survived worse." In one smooth, effortless motion, Napier picked up his portmanteau, snaring Lisette's bag in the same hand. "Send your maid with Jolley, Miss Ashton, and follow me."

With no further explanation, Napier set off down the platform, his long strides undeterred by either the baggage or the walking stick, the elegant cloak billowing gently off his elbow as he moved.

After one last squeeze of Fanny's hand, Lisette dashed after him with something less than ladylike grace. Just as she passed the hissing green locomotive, however, the thing let off a horrific blast of steam, very nearly frightening her out of her wits.

She stopped, and clapped a hand to her heart.

Was this what the world was coming to? Everyone dashing madly about like rats flushed from a nest? Just so they might clamber into frightful, hot, clattering contraptions that would whisk them off to another place of haste and confusion?

Napier strode on, oblivious.

With a muttered imprecation, Lisette adjusted her hat and set off again.

Another twenty yards farther along, Napier broke stride to slap a coin into the palm of a waiting porter. The fellow dashed down the platform to throw open the door to a first-class compartment, Napier hurled in the bags, and the porter climbed in to rack them.

When the fellow leapt down, Napier handed Lisette up the slight step. But as he did so, his gaze caught hers and some dark, unsettled emotion seemed to sketch across his face, and for the merest instant, Lisette wished that her hand were ungloved.

Was the man's touch, she wondered, as confident as his eyes? Was that steady arm as powerful as it felt?

But Napier followed her in and set away his stick with a loud *clack!* that severed the odd, fanciful moment. The door slammed shut after him just as a second horrific hiss sounded, and the train lurched. Lisette, still perched crookedly on the edge of her seat, was thrown sideways. She landed awkwardly, but Napier's hand whipped out to steady her, catching her firmly beneath the elbow.

Embarrassed, Lisette clapped a hand onto her hat to secure it. "Well, that was a near-run thing," she grumbled as his hand slid away. "Cutting it close, weren't you?"

He looked at her blandly. "Until Jolley saw you drive up, we weren't ticketed," he said, settling back onto his banquette. "I did not expect you to turn up of your own accord."

Lisette glared at him. "I sent round a note yesterday,"

she said, "accepting your . . . well, let us call it your *kind invitation*."

He made a dismissive motion with his hand. "I assumed it a ruse—something to throw me off guard."

Lisette rolled her eyes. "Alas, poor Napier!' she said. "Such an innate distrust of human nature. I wonder how you live with yourself."

Was it her imagination, or did Napier's mouth twitch?

"I manage," he replied.

He turned that dark glare to the window, staring out at the tall iron columns of Paddington as they slowly slipped past, and the rhythmic ring of metal upon metal came faster and faster. The man sat as if he owned the compartment, she noted irritably, his arm stretched the length of the banquette, his legs set wide, and his fine cloak tossed over the seat beside him.

Lisette regarded him in silence, as if she might will him to speak further. After some five minutes, it worked.

He turned from the window, and fixed her with a stern eye. "You understand, then, that I mean to hold you to your bargain?" he finally said in his low, rumbling voice. "And I warn you, Miss Ashton, I'll brook no opposition to my instructions, nor put up with any of your deceit."

"Why, I would not think of it," she said sweetly. "No deceit at all—or none, that is to say, save that which you've already blackmailed me into."

He cut her a long, assessing look, the first time he'd allowed his eyes to actually linger. They drifted down her face with a studied interest, as if he knew not what to make of her.

She sensed an odd sort of reluctance in him today, and began to wonder if he were regretting his impulsive plan. And impulsive it had been; Lisette had realized that much even as he'd bellowed his orders in her parlor that day. And yet Napier did not seem a man much given to impulse. He seemed cold, and utterly calculating. What would he have done, she suddenly wondered, had she indeed not shown up this morning? Was it possible he might have been secretly relieved, caught the later train, and gone on about his business?

"I think, Mr. Napier, that you are regretting our little bargain," she ventured.

He said nothing for a long moment. "I'm fairly confident I will live to regret it, yes," he finally admitted. "This trip is a delicate business. But like a fool, I let my temper lay my plan."

"And you do not trust me," she added.

"And I do not trust you," he echoed, one corner of his mouth lifting in a grim smile. "Indeed, I feel rather as if I've seized a wolf by the ears."

"Oh, and I have not?"

Then, letting her head fall gracelessly back against the banquette, she gave a deep sigh. "I should have run, shouldn't I?" she went on. "You'd not have caught me—I *think* you would not have. But you'd have hounded me, I daresay, to the hinges of hell out of sheer spite."

"Without question," he admitted.

"But I did turn up, and now we are stuck together," she said, "at least until the next station."

They said no more for a time, but merely sat in the silent shadows of the compartment as the rhythmic *clack-clickity-clack* of the train sped up and the edge of suburban London rolled away.

In gentlemanly fashion, Napier had taken the reverse seat, leaving Lisette to look out upon the approach of Notting Hill. She noted the creep of civilization with bland disinterest until there was nothing but countryside flying past, and nothing but silence within.

She cleared her throat sharply. "Where do we go, precisely," she asked, "and how long have we?"

"Something around three hours," he replied, "to Swindon Junction, where we will make our way into the godforsaken backwaters of Wiltshire."

She tried to give a sarcastic smile but to her horror, it wobbled. "So you don't mean to let me off at the next station?"

Napier was looking out the window again, his brow deeply furrowed.

Could he actually be considering such a thing? And why did the notion leave her with a faint stab of disappointment? She was more than a little afraid of Napier. There was nothing remotely approachable about the man. He distrusted her, understandably. But he also disliked her. Loathed her, perhaps.

Was *that* what troubled her?

Well, that, perhaps, and the fact that her whole life had just fallen apart again.

Inexplicably, Lisette felt tears spring warm and bitter behind her eyes. Better than half her twenty-seven years had been lived with one single, if slowly galvanizing, intent: *vengeance.* And now that she had tasted it, the thing was bitter as ash in her mouth. As if she had emerged from some near-madness like a mole popping its head out into the light of day, only to be blinded by sudden clarity.

Surely, *surely* there was something more to her life than that? And if she did not find it—or find, at the very least, some temporary distraction—she really might go mad. But good Lord, was *Royden Napier* all that was left to her? Did she actually *want* to go to Wiltshire in his company?

At the moment, it seemed so. Such was her desperation to escape herself.

"Look here, Napier," she said, "I may have made a deal with the devil, but—"

"Did you now?" His head jerked around, one dark eyebrow crooking a little dangerously.

Lisette lifted one shoulder in feigned nonchalance. "This moment, yes, it feels like it. But I am here, am I not?"

"And why does that thought little comfort me?" he murmured.

Lisette glowered at him. "Well, with that attitude, we're in for some miserable days."

"Aye," he muttered, "or weeks."

"How utterly delightful," she said mordantly.

"Why, had you a schedule to keep to, Miss Ashton? Someone else to persecute or scam or fleece, perhaps?" Napier's gaze had hardened. "By the way, kindly remove that dreadful wig."

"But—" Lisette stared at him. "But I haven't any hair."

"Yes, you do," he countered. "Moreover, it suits you. The wig does not."

"Short curls went out when Caro Lamb died," Lisette warned, lifting her hands to unpin the wig. "But if you wish your fiancée to appear unconventional, I daresay it's nothing to me."

"Miss Ashton," he said blandly, "there is nothing remotely conventional about you—and no wig will ever hide that fact."

Lisette could not tell if she had been insulted or complimented. But she removed the wig, unfastened the short pin curls Fanny had so carefully wound, then raked her fingers through to loosen them. Across the carriage, Royden Napier watched her hands fixedly, but said not a word.

Lisette did not bother to put her hat back on for it now held the wig and all the pins. Instead she turned her gaze to the window, shutting herself off as he had done earlier. Trees were flying past now; an old orchard lining a low stone fence. Stone as hard as her heart. Trees as warped with age, perhaps, as her bitterness had warped her.

She did not want to let go of that bitterness, and her hard heart had been hard won. She was going to help Napier—for reasons mostly selfish but perhaps . . . just perhaps a tiny bit altruistic?

Still, that didn't change what she'd done. It certainly would not change what Napier was—or what he thought of her. Nothing, she feared, would repair that damage. And nothing was apt to soften that ruthless look in his eyes or that perpetual sneer upon his lips. She told herself she really didn't give a damn, and prayed that it was true.

Lisette turned from the window and fixed him with a hard stare. "Well, then," she said. "If you don't mean to let me go, we'd best get on with it, hadn't we?"

One eye narrowed. "Get on with what?"

"Getting our stories straight," she said. "Heavens, you're a sort of policeman, are you not? How are we to manage this little hoax of yours if we haven't a plan?"

"Yes, of course," he said, his sneer twitching. "I defer to the expert. How shall we begin?"

"Firstly," said Lisette, "I should like to know if you think Lord Saint-Bryce died a natural death."

Suspicion flared in his eyes. "I beg your pardon?"

"And secondly, I should like to know your precise connection to the gentleman."

"Would you?" The suspicion softened but little. "And I should like to know how—"

She threw up a hand, palm out. "Yes, I helped out in my uncle's newspaper business, Mr. Napier," she said. "I have some idea how to dig out facts. You said you were going to see family. In Wiltshire. Specifically, to a house in mourning. And you instructed me to pack my most elegant clothing."

"And so . . . ?"

"And so the facts tell me that there was but one gentleman of great consequence who died in all of Wiltshire these last three months or better, and that was Baron Saint-Bryce, so—"

"Good Lord," he interjected.

"—so one can only conclude you have some relation to him," she pressed on. "And since you seem no more happy than I to be making this journey, and since you have ordered me to confuse and waylay your relations, one must conclude you are investigating something of a criminal nature."

"Good Lord," he said again.

"Yes," said Lisette impatiently, "He is. But He is not apt to help either of *us*, is He? So you may as well cease using His name and just tell me who is who and what is what in Wiltshire."

He shot her a dark look. "You seem to have grasped a vast deal without my having said a word. Why do I not permit you to simply carry on?"

Lisette forced an indulgent smile. "Come now, Napier, I've accepted your bargain. Is there any reason I should do it halfway? Better a good job swiftly done, and all the sooner we'll part ways. That's how I see it."

"Aye, now there's a bit of logic to cling to," he grumbled, "along with my sanity, I pray. But very well. Saint-Bryce was my father's elder brother. And I have no notion what killed him. His death, however, was sudden, and occurred mere weeks before he was to marry again."

Lisette pondered the explanation for a long moment. "But his family name is Tarleton," she finally said. "Are you a bastard?"

"Perhaps. But my parents were married." There was a glint of sardonic humor in his gaze, and for the first time Lisette realized his eyes were not really black, but a dark, lustrous blue. "My father took his wife's name. It's rather a long story."

"And this is rather a long train ride," Lisette responded. "But we'll let that go for the nonce. We're traveling then, I collect, to Burlingame Court?"

"Yes," he said laconically.

"Which was the home of Baron Saint-Bryce and of . . ." Here, she considered it. "His father, who would be your grandfather?"

"Yes."

"So your grandfather, then, is Viscount Duncaster?" she pressed. "Really, Napier, must you make me pull teeth here? I've lived half my life in America. I haven't time to sort through a decade of newsprint along with the society gossip, too."

"What do you wish to know?"

"You must tell me about these people."

Napier tossed his elegant black hat onto the seat beside him, and puffed out his breath through his cheeks. "Very well," he said. "Duncaster had three sons. My father, the Honorable Nicholas Tarleton, was the youngest, but left the family after a quarrel and was disowned."

"Ah," said Lisette. "Money? Or marriage?"

"Marriage," said Napier. "Hence, there was no money. Well, no family money."

"No, there usually isn't," said Lisette dryly. "But your father changed his name. That's . . . impressive—well, it's something, anyway—and it explains how you came to be earning your own crust. How often do you go home?"

"Every evening after work," he said tightly. "But I've been to Burlingame only twice. Last year the Earl of Hepplewood wrote to ask the Home Secretary to—"

"And Hepplewood is married to your great-aunt, I collect?" she interposed. "To Lord Duncaster's sister?"

"A half sister, yes," said Napier. "The issue of a second wife. As to her husband, Hepplewood died at Burlingame after writing a strange letter to the Home Secretary. My great-aunt remains there, dripping crepe and venom."

"At Burlingame? Not at her husband's home?"

"I gather they've always spent a part of each year with Duncaster," said Napier, "then moved in semi-permanently a year or two ago. One gets the impression Hepplewood's seat in Northumberland is a drafty old pile."

"*Northumberland* and *drafty* do not sound ideal together."

Napier shrugged. "And Lady Hepplewood has always been willful, I collect," he said. "She is much younger than her brother, much doted on, and prefers her childhood home. Hepplewood, being a diplomatic man, apparently obliged her."

"Yes, I recall his political career," Lisette remarked. "Was he not briefly the ambassador to the United States?"

"I believe so."

"And such an important man might wish to remain close to London. Who manages his estates?"

"Some distant cousin." Napier gave an offhand gesture. "Though Hepplewood does have a pampered, overweening son knocking about London."

"Who is now Lord Hepplewood," added Lisette.

"Yes. Tony, I think he's called." Napier's gaze turned inward. "Aunt Hepplewood had him late in life and doubtless spoils him. Beyond that, I know little of the fellow save that he's frightfully rich, lives in Clarges Street, and gambles incessantly—but only in the very best places, of course."

"Never dropped by for dinner in Eaton Square, this dashing cousin of yours?" asked Lisette dryly. "I wonder why."

"I daresay he did not fancy dining with a disinherited government drudge," Napier returned, "any more than I fancied dining with a spoilt and arrogant wastrel."

Lisette shrugged. "One imagines Burlingame a crowded place," she remarked. "Saint-Bryce left children, did he not? And dear old Grandpapa Duncaster still breathes?"

Again, Napier's mouth twitched. "Despite certain protestations to the contrary, I expect to find Duncaster quite in the pink," he said. "And yes, Saint-Bryce has a married daughter who's often about. The eldest is an avowed spinster and the third and youngest is still in the schoolroom."

"And Lady Saint-Bryce?"

"There were two. The last died about a year ago after a long illness."

"So both wives left Saint-Bryce with no heir," Lisette murmured. "And he died before he could marry again. Interesting. Whom else I should know about?"

Napier grunted. "That's it, thank God," he said. "No, wait—Hepplewood's cousin, Diana Jeffers. I gather she's a companion to Lady Hepplewood."

"Very well. Let us reprise who is who." Lisette ticked them off on her fingers. "At Burlingame we have your grandfather Duncaster. Then his much-younger sister, Lady Hepplewood, now widowed. We have her son Tony, who resides in London. Her companion, Diana. And Saint-Bryce's three daughters—give or take one. May I know their names?"

"The eldest, the spinster, is called Gwyneth, I think," said Napier. "Anne is married to a balding, put-upon-looking fellow whom I merely glimpsed at the funeral. Bea is the little one."

"Very well," said Lisette. "At least I now have some idea who we're dealing with. And yet you don't mean to tell me precisely why you are going or what it is you suspect?"

"I do not," he replied.

"As you wish." Lisette lifted one shoulder. "I concede it wasn't part of our bargain."

Without further argument, she rose, dragged her carpet-bag off the rack, then rummaged through it for paper and pencil. But just as she handed the bag up again, the train let go a loud whistle and lurched left, braking hard. Caught in mid-reach, Lisette was pitched violently backward.

"Oh!" she cried, tumbling.

But a pair of sure, strong arms caught her around the waist. The train straightened, the whistle faded, and Lisette realized she was staring up into Royden Napier's piercing blue eyes, and splayed crookedly across his lap. One of his arms was lashed around her waist, and the other hand was settled quite snuggly over her right breast.

She swallowed hard, heat flooding her face. "Oh!"

The large, warm hand covering her breast slid away, but in no great hurry. "I beg your pardon," Napier murmured.

Lisette seemed unable to respond, or even to think. They were so close, she could smell his musky, masculine scent and see the hint of black stipple that shadowed his cheeks. A shock of dark hair had tumbled over his forehead, softening the severity of his face but making him look faintly disreputable.

Lisette blinked up at him. "Heavens," she managed. "How awkward—even given our pending marriage."

The tension broke, Napier's eyes glittering oddly. And somehow Lisette found the presence of mind to clamber off his lap, with Napier lifting her away as if she were no more than a feather. But his hands left her almost lazily, hesitating a trifle longer, she thought, than strictly necessary.

Seizing the luggage rack for balance, she shook out her twisted skirts, then sat down with as much grace as she could muster. The train had now *clackity-clacked* its way into a station—a mere shed of a place, from the look of it— and was grinding to a halt.

"Thank you," she said, "for catching me." She took up her pencil and paper, praying her face was not beet red.

"Miss Ashton—" said Napier a little tightly.

She glanced up to see Napier's knuckles had gone white where he gripped the seat. "Yes?"

"That was . . . inappropriate."

Lisette flung the pencil down. "Well, *pardon* me," she said hotly, "but I've little experience with trains. As to inappropriate, sir, that was *your* hand on *my*—well, never mind that."

"That was not what I meant," he returned. "What I meant was . . . that I was . . . or that we—well, we should perhaps not be too often together at Burlingame. It might be for the best. I shall have my job, and you shall have yours."

"Well, yes. I daresay."

"And we should keep our minds on what we're about," he added a little harshly. "We cannot afford to step wrongly here."

"Napier, I did not *step wrongly*." Lisette snatched up the pencil again. "I was flung upon you by this awkward, monstrous beast of a machine you've blackmailed me onto."

But his eyes were still glittering dangerously. "You've quite a fondness for that term *blackmail*."

"Because it's accurate," she retorted. "Moreover, the last useful mechanical contraption invented, to my mind, was the printing press. So once this curst business is over, you may put me on the first mail coach back to London, kissing my heels as I go. And trust me, once I've grasped the details of this awful chore, I will do *my half* of this job faultlessly."

Now Napier looked oddly amused. "I'm very glad to hear it."

Lisette made a sound of exasperation. "Look, just go through all the names and precise titles again," she said. "I must write it all down and memorize it."

"Why should you care," he said without rancor, "when I scarcely do?"

Lisette looked at him impatiently. "You're too entirely accustomed to bludgeoning your way through life, and having the power of the law on your side," she said. "But now you are on your way to visit family, Napier, and under disingenuous circumstances at best."

He lifted one broad shoulder. "And—?"

"—and you mean to present me as your future wife," she finished. "Even if you have no interest in those people, it will appear quite odd to them if I do not. It is the sort of thing women *know*, Napier. It is the sort of thing, to them, that matters greatly."

"Yes, I daresay."

"You daresay?" Lisette looked at him chidingly. "What

if I am an opportunist? Most women are, you know. I am almost certainly marrying you for your family connections."

"And not my overwhelming charm?" said Napier mordantly. "Or my vast wealth?"

"You haven't any charm," she said. "But pray tell me more of this vast wealth. It may kindle my affections."

"A wolf by the ears," he muttered.

Lisette just smiled, pencil held expectantly aloft.

The bustle beyond the window at an end, the train started up again and after dragging a hand down his face, Napier began to recite off every detail of the Tarleton family, practically down to their height and weight. Lisette was not surprised; it was his job to know everything when directing an investigation.

He recited it, however, in a precise but dispassionate way, as if they were someone else's family, his gaze focused unseeingly out the window, with Lisette occasionally glancing up at him as she took notes. The morning sun shone faintly upon his face now as they traveled a stretch of open countryside, casting him half in shadow and half in light—which seemed oddly in keeping with his nature.

Lisette had once suggested it in jest, but Napier was quite a striking man. Not a beautiful one, no, for his face was too strong, his eyes too hard. And he had a harsh blade of a nose that spoke of Roman blood, and of sheer, unbridled obstinacy. But in a room crowded with wealthier, more beautiful men, Napier would have turned every female head for he possessed what her old governess had called "a certain *je ne sais quoi.*"

And while he might be hard-hearted, he was at least half a head taller than she, a remarkable accomplishment indeed. It oddly pleased her; they would not look like an awkward couple when she met his family.

By the time he'd finished speaking, Lisette had more or less sketched a family tree, and an old and noble one indeed—though in that moment it had not yet occurred to Lisette that there was still one last and critical detail missing.

"Are you going to remember all that?" he said, cutting into her thoughts.

"I think I already have," she murmured, ticking down the list. "I've a knack for memorizing things once I've read them."

He watched her without commenting. Lisette laid the paper aside. "Well, that's that," she said. "Your grandfather. Your great-aunt. Her companion. Your uncle Saint-Bryce's daughters: one spinster, one married, and one in the schoolroom. And perhaps, if we're lucky, this dashing and disreputable Tony chap will turn up to entertain us. Is there anything else I should know?"

"No." He paused for a long, pensive moment, looking suddenly awkward. "Well. Perhaps. You see, Cordelia—my great-aunt, Lady Hepplewood . . ."

"Yes?"

"She has some unfortunate . . . notions."

When Lisette merely looked at him pointedly, Napier rolled his eyes, and went on. "Sir George says that Lady Hepplewood has taken it into her head that I'm to marry the companion."

"*Marry* Miss Jeffers?" Lisette drew back an inch, a hand set dramatically over her heart. "So *that's* why you need me so desperately. But if I'm to have competition for your favors, I shan't take it well, I give fair warning. I'm not just opportunistic, Napier. I am *possessive*."

His smile was muted, his eyes flicking over her face as if somehow taking her measure yet again. "Excellent," he finally said. "Be quick and brutal if you must. I've no wish to disappoint anyone—and in truth, how could the woman want a man she's scarcely met?—but Aunt Hepplewood says that since the poor girl was to marry . . ." Here, his words dwindled and to her shock, Napier's ears began to turn faintly pink.

Diplomatically, Lisette consulted her notes. "I believe the lady was to marry Lord Saint-Bryce."

"Just so," Napier muttered. "And I suppose that they imagine . . . well, that I am now he."

It took a moment for this to sink in, then Lisette's pencil clattered to the floor. "Good heavens," she murmured. "The heir to the Duncaster viscountcy—Baron Saint-Bryce—is toiling away in government service?"

Irritation sketched over his harsh visage. "Nothing about this is settled."

"Well, I am admittedly no expert," said Lisette, "but if you were born on the right side of the Tarleton blanket and all your uncles are dead without sons, then there's no *settling* to it."

Napier cut his gaze away again. "Good God, you sound just like Sir George."

"*Are* all your uncles dead?" she demanded. "Where is the third?"

"The eldest proved a rake and a scoundrel," said Napier emotionlessly. "He preferred the pleasure of other men's wives—until one of his cuckolds shot him dead on Primrose Hill."

"Truly?" Lisette's eyes searched his face. "And . . . you haven't another, barking around somewhere?"

"I think we've established that I have not," he said coolly. "In any case, just make it plain out of the gate that you and I are betrothed and that your family has strong expectations that I will—"

He stopped, and turned to look at her oddly.

"That you will what?" Lisette pressed.

"I'm sorry," he said, his eyes almost softening. "Do you even *have* a family? I didn't think . . . I mean, with the Ashtons dead. They *are* dead, I gather?"

"Yes, both."

"Then there's someone on your mother's side, perhaps?"

But Lisette wanted no one's pity. "Oh, indeed!" she said, drawing herself up haughtily. "You've the pleasure of addressing the only living granddaughter of the ninth Earl Rowend. Would you care to kiss my ring and pledge fealty?"

The softness vanished. "Do be serious."

"I'm quite serious," she said. "And I can act as high in the instep as any Tarleton. Why, until Papa couldn't pay her, we had a French governess—and no one teaches hauteur like a Parisian born and bred."

But Napier's expression had turned inward. "An earldom, eh?"

Lisette arched one eyebrow. "What, the daughter of Sir Arthur Colburne, dashing but faintly scandalous *bon vivant* was not good enough for you?" She gave a regal wave of her hand. "Very well, use the noble Lord Rowend as you will."

"Is your grandfather living?" asked Napier tersely.

"No, but it scarcely matters. The whole family despised Papa, and very nearly disowned me. They rarely know where I am or what I'm doing."

"Good," he said pensively. "That's good. Perhaps we shall survive this preposterous plan after all."

Lisette was unwisely pleased by his use of the word *we*. Then it dawned on her just what he implied. "Oh, no, Napier, wait one moment," she said, stabbing a finger in his direction. "Do you dare suggest someone might make you honor this sham of a betrothal? Or worse, that *I* might?"

Some inscrutable emotion flared behind his eyes. "Theoretically, a gentleman may not break a marriage engagement."

"Oh, how you do flatter yourself!" Lisette scowled across the compartment. "Only in your fantasies, Napier, would I have you. Moreover, the only family contact I have is when they send the family solicitor round twice a year in the faint hope I've died and will no longer inconvenience them. So be damned to you and your presumption."

But Napier seemed to have absorbed little of her invective, and this time his mouth did decidedly quirk. "I likely am," he murmured, relaxing onto the banquette again. "Damned, that is."

The train rumbled on, the compartment silent, with Lisette glaring across the distance at Napier. After a time, however, his unflinching stare wore her down and she broke it off by scrabbling about for her pencil. "Very well, then," she said when she'd found it. "I'll have the family details memorized by Swindon. Now we've our personal history to settle upon."

As if stirred from a trance, he blinked. "Ah, yes. That will be necessary."

"Regrettably." She gave a sour smile. "And since this betrothal has come about on the heels of a scandal we must explain that away, for it's always the little lies that trip one up."

"There's nothing so welcome as the voice of experience," said Napier dryly. "Very well. What do you suggest?"

Lisette didn't bother to rise to the insult. There was, after all, a painful amount of truth in it. "My name was briefly mentioned in the *Times* as a witness," she simply said. "I daresay they do read newspapers, even in a *godforsaken backwater*. How shall we handle that, Mr. Napier?"

"Ah," he said. "How indeed."

"Were we already betrothed?" she prodded, looking him up and down. "The papers made no mention of such a coincidence. So was it a secret betrothal? Are we *in love,* Mr. Napier? Or do we dare not tax our thespian skills so far beyond the credible?"

He shook his head. "It cannot be an arranged marriage; that won't hold."

She sighed. "And I haven't quite enough money to entice a viscount's heir."

Napier studied her with his cool, steady gaze. "The truth will suffice," he finally said. "We'll say we met when you called upon me in my office to complain about Lazonby, and that I was immediately taken by your . . ."

"—spirit?" she supplied helpfully.

"Actually, it was your proclivity for bribery and seduction," he countered, "along with that tiny peek of your left breast. But yes, let us call it *spirit*."

"How gallant," she said. "And perhaps we met again from time to time so that you might update me as to how the case against Lord Lazonby progressed?"

"Doubtless we did, since I was so charmed by your willingness to unbutton your gown in my office." Napier settled back onto his banquette. "Do keep talking, Miss Ashton. We've all of two hours left."

"But of course, my darling," she said.

"Wait." Napier sat bolt upright again, all pretense vanishing. "Why don't we say you're Elizabeth Colburne? Are you attached to the name Ashton?"

Lisette had learned not to get attached to anything. Upon arriving in Boston, she'd begun using the name because she'd been twelve years old and the Ashtons, childless, had insisted. It had scarcely mattered to Lisette; her father and sister were still just as dead. But the trust documents Bodkins had presented upon her return to England—and even as late as last week—still carried the name Elizabeth Colburne, and she'd spared it not a thought.

"My father had his name legally altered," said Napier pensively. "Did you?"

She shook her head. "I suppose that I *am* Elizabeth Colburne," she murmured. "It feels . . . odd, somehow, to realize it."

He sat now on the edge of his seat, occupying the whole of the compartment, it seemed, with his wide-set knees and hands clasped loosely between them. He was thinking. And looking at her in that dark, deeply intense way of his; looking with such cold penetration that for an instant, she shuddered from the chill. How she would hate to be a criminal under his investigation!

But in a way, she was. And perhaps that's all she was to him: a criminal—for he doubtless suspected her of things more heinous than even Lisette was capable of.

Or perhaps he did not. For when he spoke his voice had softened, with no hint of sarcasm. "And will you do it, then?" he asked. "You don't have to; it wasn't part of our bargain. But if I can say that I'm betrothed to the granddaughter of the Earl Rowend—even an estranged granddaughter—Lady Hepplewood will be unable to find fault with that."

"Why wouldn't I do it?" Lisette held his gaze steadily. "My word is my bond, and I've accepted your bargain. I don't admit to anything, mind you. But whatever else I may be, I am not a cold-blooded murderer, a thief, or a liar—well, not unless I have to be. Now all I ask, before I get off this train in Swindon, is *Do you* have the power to protect me from Lazonby if he turns vengeful, whatever his reason?"

He was regarding her with utmost gravity now. "So far as the judicial system goes, yes," he finally said. "I can't control what the man says in the street. But even Lazonby hasn't the power to hang someone. Not against my will."

That Lisette believed sincerely.

"Then let's agree to this properly," she said, peeling off her glove and thrusting her hand across. "I shall faithfully uphold my end of the bargain if you'll uphold yours. I want your word, Napier, as a gentleman."

He looked at her outstretched hand—even pondered it a moment, she thought—then reached across the narrow compartment and shook it, his large, long-fingered hand warm and sure.

"You have my word, Miss Colburne, as a gentleman—*provided* you are not a murderer or a thief or a liar—that I will protect you from Lazonby's retribution to the utmost of my abilities, legally, and in whatever other capacity I may."

Her gaze holding his, Lisette clasped Napier's hand for an instant longer than she ought to have done, then let it go, wondering if she had truly lost her mind. Wondering when pride and the foolish wish to be thought well of had displaced her good sense.

And worrying about those two little words Napier had *not* echoed.

Cold. Blooded.

CHAPTER 6

In Which Mr. Napier Grasps His Grievous Error

Napier would give the devil her due. Elizabeth Colburne was a master.

And he—well, he was a damned fool. Or a genius.

By the time they stepped down onto the platform at Swindon Junction, his self-described blackmail victim was a woman transformed, having spent the last half hour of their journey rummaging about in her overstuffed carpetbag like some Covent Garden magician tugging rabbits from a hat.

"I'm glad I came a little prepared," she had grumbled into the bag as she extracted a satin jewel box, "rather than simply accept your vague instructions. After all, aspiring to become Mrs. Napier is one thing. But if one aspires to become Baroness Saint-Bryce of Burlingame, a little tarting-up is wanted."

Napier had watched in quiet awe as she redressed her hair, exchanged all her jewelry, dashed a little powder on her cheeks, and stuffed away the simple gabardine cloak she'd worn into Paddington Station. When she was done, she looked nothing remotely like a tart.

Indeed, she scarcely looked like the woman with whom he'd left London. And she looked so little like a radical newspaper reporter that Napier ceased to be certain of his entire theory about how Sir Wilfred Leeton ended up dead in his own dairy.

Elizabeth Colburne now wore a jewel-toned paisley shawl swathed like a cashmere cloud about her shoulders and a short strand of perfectly matched pearls about her neck. A square-faceted emerald identical in color to the green of her velvet carriage dress dropped from the pearls, catching the afternoon light.

Tiny, tasteful emeralds studded her ears and dangled with pearl teardrops. And through her hair she had twisted a length of cream-and-emerald satin roping in a neoclassical fashion that turned her hair into a tousled, flaming tumble of curls.

After whisking her around the hideous twenty-foot marble monstrosity adorning Burlingame's carriage drive—Hades abducting Persephone, he thought—Napier had handed her down from their hired gig and felt for the first time a measure of appreciation for the massive family pile.

And then he realized in some disconcertion that it was because *she* looked so grand. He wished his home to look equal to her visit. Disconcerted by this bizarre notion, he cut Miss Colburne another sidelong glance and felt his breath catch. She stood at the very foot of the grand stairs, looking rich, beautiful, and with her unusual hair, faintly avant-garde.

But Burlingame was not his home. And Miss Colburne—well, she was just a bought-and-paid-for actress, or something near it. A wise man would take care to remember both those things.

"Well, there it is," he said with a wave of his hand. "Burlingame's grand façade in all her Baroque glory."

But Elizabeth Colburne merely took his proffered arm, and lifted her nose. "Has it only *three* wings, then?" she said a little haughtily. "Rowend Hall—the seat of my dear, belated grandpapa, the Earl Rowend—has at least *six*."

"Has it indeed?" he had murmured, escorting her up one side of the wide staircase. "I should very much like to see how the architect managed *that* feat of engineering. But these are called pavilions, I believe. Ordinary wings would never do for the Tarletons."

But the aspiring baroness did not deign to answer, and instead turned the full force of her newfound hauteur upon the erect, elderly woman who stood just inside the front door.

The Countess of Hepplewood leaned much of her weight upon a solid ebony walking stick and watched their arrival with something less than unbridled enthusiasm. Beneath her elaborately coiffed, graying hair, she wore deep mourning and a piercing, hawkish gaze.

Napier greeted her civilly, but not warmly. He did not dread his aunt; indeed, he scarcely knew Lady Hepplewood, and cared even less for her opinion. Or so he told himself— perhaps in self-disillusionment, for he felt oddly grateful for the small, warm hand upon his arm as they suffered the first formal introductions.

It was a slender reed indeed he clutched, relying upon a disingenuous virago who'd been pressed into his service. But moments later Miss Colburne sat as if holding court in Burlingame's grand salon, her spine stiff as a duchess, a delicate ivory teacup held just so, one pinky tilted elegantly aloft—along with her nose—and Lady Hepplewood watching her with a sort of wary curiosity.

Though decorum precluded mentioning it, Lady Hepplewood had reserved a special sort of attention for her visitor's unusual hair, and Napier realized his demand had been not just selfish, but shortsighted. No lady of his acquaintance wore anything but bland buns looped about with heavy braids. But that fierce red chaos of curls and satin . . . well, it was simply *her*. And he would as soon not think about why that mattered to him.

"I fear, Miss Colburne, I know little of your family," said Lady Hepplewood pointedly, "since Saint-Bryce wrote only that he was bringing his future wife."

"Oh," said Napier blandly, his teacup clicking softly back onto its saucer, "did I not mention a name?"

Lady Hepplewood shot a disapproving glance in Napier's direction. "You did not," she said. "Did I hear my grand-nephew aright that you've a connection to Lord Rowend?"

"Oh, indeed, ma'am, the ninth earl was my grandpapa." Miss Colburne made a nonchalant gesture that set her brilliant curls shimmering in the light slicing through the tall windows. "Though I cannot claim we were close. Mamma was his favorite, but dear Grandpapa disapproved, you know, of her marrying a mere baronet—a tragic lapse in discernment which I, of course, was resolved *never* to repeat—" Here, she paused just long enough to turn a doting sunbeam of a smile on Napier, who had wedged his length into an overstuffed chair at her elbow. "—wasn't I, my darling?"

"Oh, you are nothing, my love, if not resolved," he managed.

"How single-minded of you," said Lady Hepplewood coolly, her teaspoon tinkling around her china cup.

Miss Colburne laughed lightly. "Actually, I fear, Lady Hepplewood, that I am quite *incorrigible*." Again, the doting expression fell upon him—row upon row of brilliant white teeth and eyes that sparkled blue-green fire. "And my dear Mr. Napier makes little answer, for he knows I am teasing him."

"Oh?" Lady Hepplewood barely cracked a smile. "May I know in what way?"

Miss Colburne leaned conspiratorially near the lady. "When we first met," she said in a dramatic whisper, "my dear Mr. Napier did not trouble to tell me of his family connections. Can you imagine?"

"Actually, no." Lady Hepplewood looked down her nose at Napier. "I cannot."

"Indeed not, for he was very cruel," she declared, "and for weeks on end quite happily let me think that I'd fallen in love with a pauper."

"And there was such a string of gallants before me," Napier dryly remarked, "one marvels you spared me a second glance."

"Really, my darling, you mustn't fib to your aunt," she warned, eyes firing with humor. "Despite my fine lineage, my age was against me, as well you know. And the hair—well, not every man will have a redhead, I admit, for we are thought quite—"

"—incorrigible," Napier interjected, "I think you said."

"No, willful and hot-tempered, I meant to say," Miss Colburne supplied. "But there, my dear, I never quarrel with your opinion, do I? I'll take a mere *incorrigible* and be glad of it."

"And what of your family?" said Lady Hepplewood delicately. "Have they no objection to your traveling such a distance unattended?"

Miss Colburne looked only slightly abashed. "Frightfully American of me, isn't it?" she said. "When my aunt died two years ago, I gave propriety less thought, perhaps, than was wise. But I had quite resolved not to marry, so I set up housekeeping with dear Fanny, and my elderly nurse. Until Mr. Napier swept me off my feet, I expected to live out my days a spinster."

Here, she broke off to sip her tea, still held so gracefully. "My heavens, Lady Hepplewood, is this a most unusual brew. Do I detect a hint of . . . yes, jasmine, is it not?"

Lady Hepplewood tilted her head in stiff acknowledgment. "It is scented with jasmine flowers," she said. "An unusual tea which I'm told is quite superior to all others."

"Indeed, you were told rightly," said Miss Colburne with an air of sophistication. She paused to sip again. "*Mo li hua cha*, the Chinese call it. But in a green base here, not some common oolong."

"Er, yes." Lady Hepplewood looked surprised. "I believe it is green."

Miss Colburne sat her cup down and gazed about the opulent chamber with an expression that suggested she'd just made up her mind that Burlingame was not, after all, flea infested.

"Lady Hepplewood, I compliment you on your discerning palate," she finally said. "One never knows what inconveniences one might have to suffer in the country, does one? But the house is quite admirable, I think, and the best hostesses in London would not be bold enough to serve such a tea as this."

"Thank you," said Lady Hepplewood, showing little sign of thawing. But the countess had, at the very least, sheathed her claws.

"Well, whatever it is," said Napier, "it's most welcome after a dusty drive."

The claws came back out with a near-audible *snick!* as she turned her disapproval upon him. "And as I hope I made plain, Saint-Bryce, I do wish you'd sent word from Swindon," she said frostily. "Really, it will not do for Duncaster's heir to be seen haring about the county in *hired* equipage."

"Lady Hepplewood is quite right, my dear." Elizabeth Colburne shot him an affectionately chiding glance. "I said as much at the station, did I not? But as usual, you would not listen."

"Does a gig from Swindon's livery even rise to the level of *equipage*?" said Napier evenly. "But if you please, ma'am, I mean to cling to my surname a while longer."

At that, Lady Hepplewood's spine drew another notch straighter, if such a thing were possible. "What nonsense," she replied. "Indeed, Nicholas had no business working himself into such a puerile snit as to change it in the first place. And a Gretna Green marriage in the bargain! He was just a boy, yes, but what he did to spite Duncaster defies all logic."

Napier was on the verge of snapping back that perhaps his father had changed his name to reflect the family he *did* have rather than the one that had cast him so cavalierly aside. But the truth was, he was no longer sure of his father's choices. And after a chary glance at him, Miss Colburne leapt to Lady Hepplewood's rescue.

"Your great-aunt's point is well made, my darling," she said sweetly. "Do as you please in London, to be sure. But here it may confuse people."

Just then, a tray laden with dainties was brought in and set down beside the tea service.

"I thought at this hour, you might be famished," said Lady Hepplewood stiffly. "Do help yourselves."

"Thank you," said Napier, who was starving.

"Ooh, lemon biscuits!" Miss Colburne exclaimed, plucking one. "Wait—" Her gaze fixed on Napier's plate, then narrowed disapprovingly.

"What?" he said.

She reached across and snatched from his plate the sliver of sandwich he'd just picked up. "*Cucumber!*" she chided. "You know, my darling, that it unsettles your digestion. Take a plain bit of cake, if you please."

Napier shot her a dark glance and watched his sandwich go. She bit into it with her sharp white teeth and then, turning her head ever so slightly, shot him a saucy wink.

And in that split second, it happened. Lust shot through him like a red-hot poker, visceral and fierce—along with the burning desire to snatch Miss Colburne up by her bright red curls and lay the business side of his hand to her bottom.

But the spell was immediately broken.

"Or perhaps the egg mayonnaise with cress?" suggested Lady Hepplewood, turning the plate to offer them. "I always find that soothing. Might I ask how the two of you met?"

Napier put his plate down with an awkward *clack!* and attempted to throttle his emotions. Good God, was he taking leave of his senses?

Elizabeth Colburne carried on without him. "Why, we met at a literary reading," she smoothly lied, brushing a crumb from her green velvet skirt. "An evening of poetry at the home of our mutual friend Lady Anisha Stafford—she's the Marquess of Ruthveyn's sister."

"Poetry?" Lady Hepplewood turned to Napier. "I would not have taken you for the literary type, Saint-Bryce. Who was the poet?"

"I've no idea," said Napier. "I turned up because I owed the lady a favor. The fellow was a dead bore."

Just then, the ormolu mantel clock struck the hour. Lady Hepplewood turned to frown at it. "Gwyneth and Diana should have returned from the vicarage by now," she said irritably. "How that pair does dawdle. Really, I wish I had known to expect you today. Anne and Sir Philip are in London—he sits in the Lower House, you know—and Duncaster is unavailable."

Anne was none of Napier's concern, and his grandfather was likely resting at this hour. "I beg you will not trouble yourself over it, ma'am," he said. "I mean to stay some time, as Duncaster requested."

But just then, a faint sound caught his ear. He glanced up to see a liveried footman sweep open one of the massive doors. A pretty, round-figured female in brown stood in the shadows beyond on the threshold, holding a girl's hand. The footman had bent forward to whisper something in the woman's ear.

Her expression stiffening, the woman swept almost haughtily past. In the light, Napier recognized the girl as

Beatrice, Saint-Bryce's only child by his second wife—and now, sadly, an orphan.

Beatrice, Napier had noticed, seemed a peculiar girl. At the age of perhaps ten or eleven, she seemed by turns alternately childlike and guarded. But Napier thought the artlessness a ruse, for unless he missed his guess, there was a certain perceptiveness hidden in her eyes.

"I beg your pardon, my lady," said the woman in brown, "but you did say we might come down?"

The lady was introduced as Beatrice's governess, Mrs. Jansen. She bobbed a curtsy, a wary eye still upon the footman. But by then Beatrice had already slipped her hand and come fully into the room, her gaze cutting shyly toward Miss Colburne.

"If you please, ma'am," she said to Lady Hepplewood, making a dash of a curtsy that set her blonde ringlets bouncing, "I wish to meet the new lady."

Lady Hepplewood again gave her regal nod, beckoned Mrs. Jansen to sit, and sent the footman scurrying for more china.

"A pleasure, Mrs. Jansen." Miss Colburne shone her brilliant smile upon Beatrice. "How do you do, Miss Tarleton? May I call you Beatrice? Or even Bea, perhaps?"

"Oh, Bea is fine," she said, scooting closer to the tea table. "Your hair is awfully red. Why is it so short?"

"Beatrice!" Mrs. Jansen colored furiously.

"That will do, Beatrice." Lady Hepplewood punctuated the command with a hard thump of her stick.

But Miss Colburne merely widened her eyes ingenuously. "Why, we were just talking about my hair," she said, passing a plate to the girl. "Are you by chance clairvoyant?"

"I don't think so." Beatrice paused for a minute, nibbled on a lemon biscuit, then looked up again. "But I was wondering—are you going to marry Saint-Bryce instead of Diana?"

Miss Colburne brightened her smile, if such a thing were possible. "Well, Diana has not asked me to marry her," she teased. "But Saint-Bryce has. Shall I have him, do you suppose?"

Beatrice gazed at Miss Colburne very solemnly. "I daresay you ought," said the girl. "Gwyneth says he's a good catch now, and that Diana is a moon-eyed idiot."

Napier heard Lady Hepplewood's sharp intake of breath. "Beatrice, perhaps you and I might discuss this later?" he gently suggested, leaning forward in his chair. "Perhaps I might visit you in the schoolroom someday?"

"Really, Saint-Bryce, you mustn't encourage impertinence," chided Lady Hepplewood. "Beatrice must remember her place."

Napier bit back his frustration. "Her *place* is in this house," he said tightly. "Beatrice may lack tact but Burlingame is her home, and her father is but recently departed."

Lady Hepplewood shot him a look that made plain she did not welcome correction. "And what, pray, has that to do with anything?"

"Children require certainty," he replied, forcing a calm voice. "They have a right to understand what is happening around them, and *to* them. Their sense of well-being depends upon it."

"How very insightful, my dear," said Miss Colburne, who immediately struck up another superficial conversation, this time directed at Mrs. Jansen—something to do with her French governess.

Napier did not attend. Instead he let his gaze drift about the ostentation of the room and thought about Beatrice. Until recently, her father had been heir to all this, and her place in this house secure. Now, with both parents dead, her half sisters a dozen years older, and Lady Hepplewood thumping that damned black stick at every misstep, Beatrice probably felt uncertain of her position here. God knew he did.

Was it really possible all this would be his to steward into the next generation? And where was that next generation to come from?

Oh, he knew the answer to that one, and it gave him great pause. His eyes settling on the collection of gilt-framed landscapes that flanked the soaring marble chimneypiece, he decided no one could be more ill suited to the task.

On his initial visit to Burlingame a few months ago he had been immediately awestruck by its magnificence. And for the first time, it had sunk into him just what his father had given up, and how greatly his circumstances had been altered by the sacrifice.

The Honorable Mr. Nicholas Tarleton had been a child of great wealth and privilege. Had he imagined, in some fit of childish pique, that altering his name might embarrass this family? So far as Napier could see, the effect had been that of a mosquito bite—a minor annoyance to be complained of only in passing.

No, he sensed no humility here; the sheer hauteur and sense of privilege remained intact, unblemished by doubt. Already he'd seen it in his grandfather. But he had felt almost at once that a sort of darkness hung here, too. And yet he had found nothing—nothing save an old man already lost in a murky world of incoherence.

But Hepplewood had been in his sixties, arthritic and gouty. Saint-Bryce, on the other hand, had been perfectly well. Bea's father had not been young, perhaps, but the coincidence still struck Napier as odd, and the strange sense of gloom he'd felt upon first entering this house still lingered, casting a pall that even he could feel.

Or perhaps that *only* he could feel?

Perhaps this was merely what it felt like to be an outsider?

Lady Hepplewood had made it plain at his very first visit that Napier was scarcely welcome. Even the fact that he had come, not to presume a family connection, but at her dying husband's behest had not swayed the lady to warmth. In fact, it had seemed to irritate her.

But then Napier had been a nobody, for his uncle Saint-Bryce and his bride-to-be had been fully expected to do their duty. It had fallen to Diana Jeffers to place as many potential heirs between Napier and Burlingame Court as were physically possible to conceive.

But two women were already dead from trying to bear a son, and the third had not got her opportunity after all. He wondered if Miss Jeffers was angry, or just relieved.

He returned to the present when Beatrice set down her plate, and Lady Hepplewood rose from her chair. It seemed he had dropped a pall over the conversation that even the glib and glorious-haired Miss Colburne could not throw off. With a sense of relief that tea was over, Napier jerked to his feet and offered Lady Hepplewood his arm.

Grudgingly, she took it. "You will doubtless wish to rest before dinner," she said as they strolled sedately along the wide swath of carpet that led to the massive, gilt-trimmed doors. "I've instructed Gwyneth to put you in the east pavilion, so that—"

But her intent was not revealed. Instead, in that instant, the salon doors were flung wide again and this time Miss Gwyneth Tarleton herself strode past the footman, with Diana Jeffers a dozen steps behind her.

Gwyneth was a tall, horsey female with few graces and a somewhat brusque manner. The lady flicked an assessing glance down his length as she drew up before him.

"Heavens, Saint-Bryce," she barked. "We did not know to expect you today."

"Yes, that point has been driven home to me," he said dryly. "Perhaps my letter could have been more specific. How do you do, Miss Tarleton? Miss Jeffers?"

Miss Tarleton gave a tight smile. "You must call me

Cousin Gwyneth now, I daresay," she replied, looking as if it pained her.

It pained *him* not to point out that they had been cousins since her birth, and that she had heretofore suffered no impulse to call him anything save, he suspected, *that odious Mr. Napier.* But he resisted the petty impulse. He knew nothing of Gwyneth Tarleton, or what her life was like.

Moreover, he was not here to assuage his pride, or even to coddle hers. Instead, he simply introduced Miss Colburne.

Diana Jeffers was delicate and pretty, and if she found any discomfort in greeting to the woman who was ostensibly to replace her as Lady Saint-Bryce, one could not discern it. "Welcome to Burlingame," she said, her voice warm, if a little vague.

"Shall I take Beatrice back up?" asked Mrs. Jansen, as if uncertain whose permission to ask.

"Yes," said Gwyneth and Lady Hepplewood at once.

Lady Hepplewood's glower darkened. "Gwyneth will take you to the east pavilion," she continued to Napier. "Diana, you will return with me."

"Shouldn't I help Gwyneth settle them in?" suggested Miss Jeffers.

But Lady Hepplewood had already started in the opposite direction, her ebony stick clacking hollowly across the white marble of the vaulted entrance hall. "Gwyneth has no need of help," she said, crooking her head to look back with obvious exasperation. "Now do come along, Diana. I cannot find my needlework. I'm quite sure you've mislaid it."

Frustration sketched across Miss Jeffers's face, but swiftly vanished. "Of course, Cousin Cordelia." She turned to shoot Napier and Miss Colburne one last glance. "We keep apartments in the west end of the house. Do visit us there if we may be of some service."

Napier thanked her, then turned to follow Gwyneth in the opposite direction.

"You must forgive Aunt Hepplewood's presumption," said Gwyneth as they walked.

"Must I?" said Napier.

"I suppose Uncle Hep's death and Tony's turning black sheep have left her a tad distraught," said Gwyneth without a modicum of warmth.

Tony, Napier knew, was Hepplewood's heir, and their only child. And if half what he'd heard in London was true, Lady Hepplewood had just cause for her concern. But Napier said nothing, for Tony's moral failings were none of his business.

The trek from the formal salons of the main house was a long one, taking them through one ostentatious room into another until at last they reached one of the long passageways that connected Burlingame's main house to the pavilions.

Here the soaring baroque arches appeared to once have been open but now were fitted with glazed windows that rose some twenty feet high. The passageway floor was laid with alternating tiles of sparkling black and white marble and the ceiling was vaulted on pairs of grand columns that he supposed were marble, too.

Miss Colburne, however, after commenting admiringly on the whole, called the columns *scagliola* and the passageway a *grand colonnade*. Napier made a mental note to ask her what the differences were. She seemed a walking miscellany of obscure facts.

Gwyneth Tarleton nodded her approval, and kept moving. But having apparently decided that Miss Colburne just might *possibly* be worthy of her attention, the lady slowed her pace from time to time in order to point out further architectural details.

Once again Napier found himself grateful for Miss Colburne's presence for she seemed to know just the right things to say and to ask. Oh, his gratitude would likely pass when next she tried his patience—something he expected was inevitable. And that sudden shaft of lust—not to mention the ripe swell of her breast beneath his hand—had been disconcerting.

But thus far, she was upholding her end of their bargain, and admirably so. It felt as if something had shifted between them in the train, and her eyes no longer held as much uneasy suspicion. Nor did his, perhaps. They were, by hook or crook, in this together, it seemed.

At the end of the colonnade, they entered what appeared to be an entirely different house, and one Napier had not previously visited. This, he understood, was where Lord Duncaster resided, and it looked far more like a gentleman's well-worn country manor and less like an overwrought imitation of Versailles. Napier felt oddly better of his grandfather for preferring it.

After mounting a wide, circular staircase, he was shown into an airy bedchamber with a pair of massive windows overlooking a parterre garden rolling out into some sixteen symmetrical squares, and beyond that, a crescent-shaped ornamental lake set with a cupolated gazebo at the end of a little pier. The whole of it, he imagined, must have required a battalion of gardeners.

After confirming his satisfaction with the room, the efficient Gwyneth swept Miss Colburne further down the passageway, and Napier found himself alone. Jolley, it appeared, had been safety delivered from the station with their bags. Napier noted his dressing case already lay open upon an ancient barley-twist vanity, and his dressing gown hung on a hook by the door.

As to the valet himself, he was likely belowstairs sidling up to the cook. Jolley always kept an eye to the main chance. Left to his own devices, Napier headed toward the dressing room. There was no hope, he supposed, of a water tap in this ancient pile, but he glanced inside all the same.

Nothing. He turned around, intending to yank the bell-pull so that he might wash the day's dust away. But as he passed into his bedchamber, the door flew open and Miss Colburne darted in, slamming it shut behind, her odd green-blue eyes alight with what could only be described as burning curiosity.

"Well," she said, leaning back to set her palms flat against the wood, "*who* do you think did it?"

Napier shot her a warning glance, and hoped she took it as such. "I've no idea who's done what to whom," he said, "but account yourself lucky I hadn't stripped down to my drawers to contemplate it."

"Napier, do be serious. You hadn't time." She paused to turn the lock with an efficient *snap!* and then followed him to the windows. "So far, I place my hope in Gwyneth Tarleton. I find her to be frightfully efficient—and the efficient are sometimes ruthless."

For a long moment, Napier said nothing. Though his gaze was fixed upon the lake and the row of topiaried yews that lined its path, he could feel her warmth—her sheer vitality—hovering at his elbow. Her presence soothed him even as it oddly frustrated him. He did not wish to feel either—not where she was concerned.

But the undeniable truth was, from the moment he'd laid eyes on the woman those many months ago, there had been a physical attraction. A dangerous attraction. And though she seemed almost unaware of it, she had only grown more tempting with time.

"I don't suppose there's any point in telling you that you've no business in a gentleman's bedchamber?" he finally said.

She gave a sound of exasperation. "Well, I've no business traveling with a man I scarcely know and certainly don't mean to marry," she said, "but that hasn't stopped either of us, has it? Besides, we must have a place to speak privately if we're to work together."

"That is my very point." Napier turned on his heel to look at her, and wished at once he had not. "We aren't *working together*. You are merely to occupy yourself in distracting that maddening pack of females."

He could hear her toe begin to tap beneath the elegant sweep of her velvet skirts; could see impatience sketch across her face. "Then you quite waste my investigative skills," she blurted.

"Oh?" he said, daring her to confess the truth. "And what sort of *investigative skills,* pray tell, would a grammar teacher from Hackney possess?"

Her face colored furiously. "You know I'm not a fool, Napier," she said. "Very well, *yes*, I worked a little in Boston, helping Uncle Ashton with his newspaper. And I might do a dozen things more here at Burlingame, were you simply to tell me—"

"Miss Colburne," he interjected.

"*Elizabeth*." Her voice broke a little oddly. She let her arms drop and laid her hand on his arm. "Or Lisette if you like. That's what my family always called me. But you can't go on calling me Miss Colburne—not when you're addressing me. It sounds . . . distant."

But it was precisely distance that he needed; distance from her, and from that warm, verdant scent she favored. It mingled now with the dust and heat of the day to form a heady, feminine fragrance that tempted him to do just as she suggested. To confide in her—or worse.

She stepped nearer. "So it's Lisette, then?"

Napier shut his eyes for a moment and tried to remember just who she was—and why she was here. "And you . . ." he managed, his voice entirely too low, "what will you call me?"

A teasing grin curved her mouth. "Saint-Bryce, it would appear," she said, "if your family has any say."

He turned back to the window, and set his hands wide on the sill, almost leaning out of it. A light breeze brushed his cheek, bringing with it the scent of fresh-turned earth and late-blooming apple trees and the soft *hoo-hoo-hoo* of doves awaiting dusk.

Saint-Bryce.

Was *that* who he was?

It did not help his state of mind when Elizabeth edged nearer, braced her smaller, paler hands beside his and leaned out with him.

"What a damnable coil," he muttered, scarcely knowing which coil he meant.

"You aren't contemplating a plunge to your death, are you?" she asked. "Because at this height, you'll only break a leg and be trapped here, bedridden."

He cut her a rueful smile. "Those bay towers out front?" he suggested. "Would that get the job done, do you reckon?"

She pretended to consider it. "I fear the pea-gravel would merely mar that striking face of yours," she said lightly. "But you could climb that monstrous folly we drove past—and if you keep on with your high-handed attitude, I might be persuaded to give you a shove."

Her tone was teasing but something in his heart twisted all the same. "Damn it, Elizabeth, don't—" He stopped, and shook his head.

"Don't . . . what?" Her brows in a knot, she touched his arm again.

He wished to the devil she would not. But he forced himself to look at her, at the translucent perfection of her skin, and what looked like earnest concern in her eyes. He burned for her—*ached* with it—even as he knew the danger.

"Don't even say such things," he managed. "Don't even joke about them."

Don't make me think of what you might be. Don't make me doubt you.

That was what he meant.

Already he was falling under her siren's spell—falling, he

supposed, for nothing save superficial charm and that wild, flaming hair. But beneath that beautiful façade lay a cold, calculating relentlessness. He knew, for he'd seen it firsthand when she'd alternately accused him of incompetence, accused him of taking bribes—offered, even, her own bribe—then offered him *herself.*

And all he'd been able to think about on that long, damnable train journey was that he wished to God he'd taken her up on the offer all those months ago. Even now his cock began to harden at the thought of her lush bottom as she'd squirmed off his lap on the train.

Somehow, he pushed away from the sill and away from her to stand up straight. "Perhaps you'd best go back to your room, Elizabeth," he said evenly. "I'll see you downstairs for dinner."

But Elizabeth, wincing, had begun to unwind the elaborate satin cords from her tousled curls, still oblivious to his lust. "For my part," she added, "I think Lady Hepplewood is an angry and bitter woman. Ah, yes, that's more comfortable."

"Lady Hepplewood is just overbred and overweening," said Napier.

"No, it's more than that." Elizabeth was shaking loose her hair in a way that made him swallow hard. "Did you see her fist on that walking stick? If the human grip could shatter brass, she'd have the shards to show for it. And that poor Miss Jeffers—what is she, the lackey?"

"I gather, yes."

"Poor girl," said Elizabeth. "Having long played the grateful drudge myself, I cannot recommend it."

Napier wanted to ask what she meant, but dared not deepen the air of intimacy. He needed to know nothing more of her; what he already suspected had left him feeling compromised enough.

Instead, he cocked one hip on the sill and crossed his

arms, studying her. "Elizabeth," he said quietly, "why are you not leaving?"

Her satin cords, or whatever they were, having been tossed aside, Elizabeth threw up both hands and looked at him incredulously. "Because we've work to do?" she suggested. "Because the sooner we've done whatever it is you've come to do, the sooner we'll be away from here?"

Away from here.

Away from *her*.

God, he prayed for both—but for far different reasons, he was beginning to think.

Suddenly her eyes widened. She cut a glance at the door, then hastened to it, the green velvet of her carriage dress slithering enticingly over her hips. Then, to his extreme discomfort, she bent over a little and set an ear to a flat spot in the carved wood, providing a delectable view.

It seemed an eternity before she straightened and shook her head. "My imagination," she muttered. "I'm sorry, what were you saying?"

Napier sighed, and altered his strategy. "Make your point, but be quick about it," he said. "In what way might you be of help?"

Again, the ingenuous expression. "Why, it's hard to know," she said, "when I've been told nothing of what brought you here. Nonetheless, I will have time alone with all your *maddening females*—and ladies do gossip. Moreover, they will take no notice whatever of another lady asking a great many questions. Indeed, given my odd predicament, they will wonder if I do not."

"There is some truth to that," he admitted.

"And then, of course, there's Fanny."

"Who, pray, is Fanny?"

"My *maid*," she said impatiently. "Servants' hall tittle-tattle is the purest form of gossip."

"True, my man Jolley is invaluable in that regard."

"Furthermore, Fanny and I are apt to be in parts of the house you will not," she said. "While you're closeted with Duncaster in some stuffy estate office, the ladies will likely take tea in the drawing room, or sew in the parlor, or read in the library. Are you looking, perhaps, for a weapon? Or purloined goods?"

He considered it for a moment, and wondered why he should not take her up on it. Elizabeth Colburne was a clever piece of work, and the fact that she made his cock throb every time she drew near was merely a testament to his stupidity.

"All right," he said, setting one hand high on the bedpost. "I need every bit of gossip either you or Fanny come across, so long as you take no risk to get it. And I need paper."

"Paper?"

"Letter paper," he amended. "From every room in the house, ideally, though that won't be possible. Give it to Jolley, or have Fanny do so."

He could see her brain clocking along like a well-greased gearbox. "Someone has written you anonymously," she said. "Or written something suspicious to someone, at any rate. And you wish to discover if the letter came from this house."

"Never mind what I wish," he snapped. "I just want samples of letter paper. Don't do anything foolish. If you're seen going through a bureau or a desk, just say you needed to jot down a thought or write a letter home."

"Yes, to my dear uncle Rowend, no doubt," she said dryly, "who will need time to plan the wedding."

Napier barked with laughter. "Oh, doubtless."

It was then that he made the grave misjudgment of looking at her—*really* looking at her. A grin had curved one corner of that lush mouth and those eyes were again glittering green with mischief.

Napier dragged a hand down his face.

"What?" she demanded.

But the gravity of his situation had returned tenfold. "I made a mistake," he finally said.

"Oh?" She tilted her head as if to better see him. "Of what sort?"

"Of every sort," he managed. "Bringing you here. The lies. The clothes. That damned wig. I don't know, really, what I was thinking. All of it was . . . unwise."

Her incredulous expression returned. "Well, this is a fine time to decide," she grumbled. "I could have been halfway to the Côte d'Azur by now."

He grunted. "What, I thought you were bound for Scotland, that last, lawless refuge of scoundrels?"

Her gaze swept over him, dark as the velvet of her gown. "Well, I was bound for somewhere far from you and Lazonby, that much is certain."

"And would to God I'd let you go," he muttered.

"Why?" she demanded. "You think me a criminal and—yes, you just said it—a *scoundrel*. Why would you let me go?"

Her head was still set to one side, her eyes drifting over his face, her full lips slightly parted, and that keen intelligence burning fierce and angry in her eyes.

Well, she wasn't intelligent enough, apparently.

With one hand, Napier reached out and dragged her hard against him.

"*This* is why," he said—just before he kissed her.

She scarcely had time to gasp before he'd captured that lush, taunting mouth in a kiss of long-thwarted lust. Her free hand came up to shove him away, too late. Acting on pure instinct, Napier forced her back against the massive oak bedpost.

She gave a soft moan; a sound of surrender, he thought, and on a surge of desire, he pinned her with the weight of his body, his mouth raking hers. Though she kept the hand set stubbornly against his collarbone, Elizabeth did not resist.

Not even when he half hoped she would.

Instead, when he drew his tongue over the delicate seam of her lips, she opened on a soft, welcoming sound and allowed him free rein, her reactions almost artless. Napier seized the advantage, slanting his mouth over hers, thrusting again and again, plundering the depths of her mouth.

Dimly, he wondered at her experience, but the thought washed away on another powerful surge—red-hot desire that shot through his belly and drew his loins taut.

Somehow, they slid away from the bedpost and Napier pressed her back into the softness of the mattress. Dragging himself over her, he deepened the kiss, tangling his tongue sinuously with hers, his unslaked need rushing nearly unchecked.

Her hands flowed over him, tentative and almost shy. Then one warm palm slid down his spine, searing him all the way to the small of his back. Silently he begged her to slide it lower, to draw his body hard against hers in that most wicked and suggestive of ways.

He swam now in sheer, sensual hunger and like a man drowning, felt himself floating toward that dark precipice. Beyond it lay a roaring waterfall of need from which there would be no turning back. Because she was dangerous, and would drag him deep. He'd known that.

He knew it now, but the feminine curves of Elizabeth's long, lithe body molded too perfectly to his, and the warmth of her breasts and her belly pressing against him urged Napier to madness.

They had tumbled sideways across his bed, the down bedding billowing softly about them, and Elizabeth's skirts slithered halfway up her leg. Driven by one thing now, Napier thrust again, rhythmically sliding his tongue along hers in blatant invitation. And when she drew up her knee on a soft sound of pleasure, it was as if the heat of her thigh left him shivering.

Napier was so lost, he scarcely realized his hands now

cradled her face, or that his mouth had slid over her cheek
and along her temple. That he was whispering things: mad
words of worship and desire.

One hand went to the swell of her breast, inching the
fabric down until the hard, sweet bud of her nipple grazed
his palm, sending heat shafting into his groin again.

"*Ah, Elizabeth,*" he whispered, his tongue tracing the shell
of her ear. "*Let me—*"

"N-No." Gasping, she at last put her hand to good use,
shoving it against his shoulder. "Napier, st-stop. I—*we*—we
don't want this."

By God, he wanted it.

But her words were like a dash of cold water. Napier
stopped, his nostrils flared wide, his breath already coming
hard.

Beneath his weight, Elizabeth looked wanton and needy,
her tumble of curls bright against the billowing whiteness
of the counterpane. She desired him; in that his instincts
did not fail. Her lips were wet and slightly parted now, her
eyes somnolent and glassy green. He could feel her body
trembling—but not, he thought, from fear.

"Elizabeth, you want this," he whispered, half hoping she
would deny it. "You want me inside you."

Her eyes flicked to his, her tongue darting out to lick her
lips. "Yes," she rasped. "I won't lie. But . . . we *can't.*"

He kissed her again, more tenderly now, foolishly unwilling to surrender his half-won prize; the thing for which he'd
burned for days on end—if not longer.

But she urged him gently away. "Please don't," she whispered, her long lashes fanning shut like lace above her
cheeks. "We'll regret it. *You'll* regret it."

He let his face fall forward to touch hers, and forced
his breathing to calm. "Yes," he said on a harsh laugh. "I
would."

"And I deserve something better," she said softly, "than a man who will regret me. I am, alas, a hopeless romantic."

He had nothing to say to that. And when her eyes went soft with tenderness, something in Napier's throat constricted.

Good God. She was a romantic?

Napier brushed his lips over her perfectly arched eyebrow and rolled away. For a long moment he lay beside her on the soft mattress, staring up at the plaster roundel in the middle of his ceiling and waiting for his rock-hard erection to subside past the point of pain.

Elizabeth Colburne *deserved better*.

But most women were romantics. Why had he believed her something less?

"You are too quiet," she said, her voice tremulous. "Am I . . ."

"Are you what?" His bollocks tight and aching, the words came out more harshly than he'd meant.

"Have I made you angry?" she said. "Was this . . . part of that price you expected me to pay?"

He cursed beneath his breath.

"Oh, I know you think me some sort of Jezebel." Her voice was strengthening. "Perhaps not without reason. But understand I would have done anything, Napier, to avenge my father's death. I would have paid any price. But this price—merely to save myself?—oh, you need to know here and now that I will not pay it."

"You think that's what this is?" he asked grimly. "A *price* to be paid? Part of that deal with the devil you think you've made?"

"Is it?"

"Christ Jesus, Elizabeth." The knot in his throat tightened again. "What have I ever done to make you imagine me that sort of man?"

"N-nothing," she whispered.

"Damn it, do you see what I mean?" he said. "*This* is what a mistake feels like."

The plaster roundel blurred before his vision—Phaethon felled by a lightning bolt, somewhat aptly. She said no more, and after a time, he somehow found it in him to collect his wits and help her off the bed. But as she turned her back to restore her clothing to order, he saw they had crushed the satin cords she'd unfurled from her hair.

On a pathetic impulse, he picked them up and coiled them tight about his hand—coiled them so tight his blood ceased to flow—then relented and shoved them ruthlessly into his pocket.

She turned around with a wobbly smile, her bodice restored. "You were right," she said. "I oughtn't have barged in. I take full responsibility."

Napier shrugged, and forced a smile that probably looked like a sneer. "A lady may always refuse a gentleman's advances," he said, gripping the bedpost rather too tightly. "My apologies, Elizabeth. There is a train back to London tomorrow at eight. I can see that you are on it."

For a moment, her expression turned inward. "And go back to what?" she said hollowly. "I have no life in London now. I cannot even go back to my charity work at Lady Leeton's school."

She was right, and Napier knew it. Worse, he did not want her to go. "Very well," he said. "Then you may trust this will not happen again."

Her smile had steadied. "So we have reached an understanding," she said. "After all, I'm here. I may as well help you."

He dropped his hand from the bedpost. "Yes, so that I'll keep you safe from Lazonby," he remarked a little harshly, striding to the door.

She did not reply. His hand on the knob, he turned to see she'd lifted her chin.

"Yes, why else would I do it?" she finally said.

Why indeed?

He snapped back the lock, and peered out into the corridor. "All clear," he said, motioning her out.

Without another word, Elizabeth went, brushing past in a cloud of lilies and womanly warmth. He did not watch her go but instead stood just inside, one shoulder set to the door frame, and listened as her footfalls faded down the corridor.

In a moment the creak of hinges echoed hollowly down the passageway. Napier bestirred himself from the wood, and pushed his door shut behind him.

And this time, he locked it.

CHAPTER 7

In Which Beatrice Explains Everything

*L*isette reeked of smoke. Her hair. Her clothes. It singed her nostrils, choking her.

The lamp sputtered. Panicked, she flicked a glance at it. Emptying. She worked furiously. Struck a paragraph. Scribbled in the margin. Wracked her brain for just the right word.

Burned *not* burnt. The brig in Boston Harbor had burned. Ashton hated burnt.

She glanced at the clock. Five minutes. Five minutes until Lem came in to set type. Biting her lip, she looked back down. Her breath seized. The words were vanishing—melting into the paper like hot butter. Behind her, the door swung open.

"Well, girl?" The demand came on a cloud of brandy. "Who's dead?"

"Mrs. Stanton, most likely," she said, furiously scribbling. "She's in a bad way."

Worse than bad. Lisette had learnt the look of death. The frail form had been laid out like an angel on the dock, her green dress and cloak sodden with water, too weak and tremulous even to retch, though she was wracked with the need.

"Enough." Ashton lurched nearer. "Let's 'ave it."

Her stomach twisted. "Almost done, sir."

"Almosh—?" Ashton roared. "I've a paper to sell, you little cow—an' dawdling won't put a roof o'er your head. Not my roof, at any count."

"I just got back," she snapped.

The clock struck the hour. "It's time," he growled, reaching for the paper.

"But it isn't finished."

"Aye, too good to earn your keep, eh?" Reeling, Ashton seized her shoulder and drew back his opposite hand, his face twisting with disgust.

But the blow did not land. It never did.

Because he knew better.

"Miss?" Someone jostled her, the voice coming as if from a tunnel. "Miss, 'tis just Fanny. Now wake up, do."

Confused, Lisette forced her eyes to flutter open. Fanny's face hovered above, her dark brows in a knot.

"*What*—?" she managed.

Fanny released her shoulder, her lips curving into a soft smile. "Miss, it's half seven," she said. "Who were you talking to, anyway?"

Lisette levered herself up on one elbow, dragging a shock of curls from her face as she tried to remember. "Heavens, Fanny," she said, shuddering. "It was Ashton after me again."

"What, that mouthy sot? Ha! You always gave back good as you got. Besides, he'll not catch us now." Fanny had gone to the hearth and was studying it with displeasure. "And whoever laid up this sorry excuse of a fire last night must a' been sotted, too. The smoke could choke a body to death."

Lisette sat fully upright and espied her morning chocolate. Fanny had gone to the window. She threw open the drapes and hurled up the sash, the pulleys shrieking in protest. Cold, clean air flooded the room.

Lisette drew it deep into her lungs, dispelling the last of her fog. "I was dreaming, Fanny, about the *Golden Eagle*," she murmured, her hands curling around the warm mug. "That brig that caught fire leaving Boston Harbor? When all those people had to be dragged from the water?"

"Oh, years ago, that was, and terrible, too." Fanny was flapping her apron at the window as if to chase out the stench. "But t'was the making of our Jack, weren't it? Now Ashton's pickled in his grave, and the poor missus gone, too. As to that black hole of a newspaper—well, that's somebody else's problem, in'it?"

It was indeed. Because Lisette had sold it—dumped it for a pittance as soon as her aunt died, since her uncle's radical politics and penchant for drink had driven the old rag near bankruptcy. For two years after Ashton's death, she and her aunt had somehow kept it afloat but nothing now remained of Lisette's old life save for their old house off Federal Street, now sitting empty.

Lisette almost never thought of those years anymore. Not unless something else disturbed her sleep.

Last night, something had.

Something tall, dark, and deeply irritating.

Hurling back the covers, she hastened to the washstand and sloshed cold water into the basin so that she might wash away what was left of any tears. With light now spilling in, Fanny would miss nothing, and Lisette couldn't bear to be quizzed. She wasn't even sure what her explanation would have been—which made it all the worse.

Patting away the damp, she lifted her gaze to the gilt mirror above the basin. A pale, perfectly oval face stared back at her through a pair of oddly colored eyes. It was her ordinary self. Not the wanton who had writhed and ached beneath Royden Napier's powerful—and rather insistent—body yesterday. So insistent that, for a moment, Lisette feared she'd run the wrong risk with Napier—that this man mightn't take no for an answer.

Instead, he had offered her the chance to go. And in that fleeting instant, she'd held him at a slight—a very slight—advantage. He'd been remorseful, perhaps a trifle embarrassed. But rather than pack her bags, she'd refused his offer.

She'd refused to run when she'd had the chance. *Again.*

Dropping her gaze from the mirror, Lisette gave a pathetic laugh, and considered her own naïveté. Good God, did she really imagine this trip into the wilds of Wiltshire was some quixotic quest for salvation? Did she really believe she might help Napier in some mad pursuit of justice, and thereby find a little redemption for her own sins?

In the bright light of day, she found it easier to admit what was hidden in the back of her mind. For the truth was, had she really wished to escape Royden Napier, she could have fled Hackney days ago. And she might have got away with it.

Instead, she'd foolishly chosen to come here. Because it was a challenge. Because it would distract her from what she had become. And because she'd chosen that elusive path toward redemption.

But there was no redemption for what she had done.

A man lay dead—an evil man, yes—but another man's good name lay in tatters, and that was in part her fault. Her reckless, near-vicious pursuit of Lord Lazonby had brought it ever more clear to Lisette that vengeance really was the Lord's.

Tossing aside the linen towel, she turned to watch Fanny lay out her clothing, wondering how she'd muddled through dinner last night. Napier had been seated at the opposite end of the table, and had scarcely held her gaze. But Lord Duncaster had not come down, so there had been no reprieve by port; everyone had gone straight to coffee in the small drawing room. Unable to bear it, Lisette had scurried back to her bedchamber, claiming travel fatigue.

What she should have claimed was utter stupidity.

Napier was every inch a man, with a man's desires. But she was still his prisoner, or something near it, and Lisette knew she would be wise not to test his restraint too far.

And perhaps wiser still not to test hers.

After dressing and retracing her long hike through Burlingame, she found the room Gwyneth Tarleton had identified as the small dining room and went in to discover that Napier had already eaten and gone back out again. All of the ladies, however, still lingered over coffee. Lady Hepplewood had a newspaper laid to one side of her plate, and Gwyneth Tarleton was inspecting some scraps of watered silk laid across one edge of the table.

Upon seeing her, the three greeted her warmly enough. Diana Jeffers leapt at once from her chair, and followed Lisette to the sideboard. "Shall I ring for warm toast, Miss Colburne?"

"Thank you, no," she answered, picking up her plate. "And please call me Elizabeth—or Lisette, if you prefer."

"Very well." Miss Jeffers's smile was vague. "You must call me Diana."

"And I'm Gwyneth, of course," said Miss Tarleton from the table. "I trust you slept well?"

"Wonderfully," she lied. "Thank you."

Diana showed Lisette what each dish contained, then left her to her own devices.

Lady Hepplewood cleared her throat. "I was wondering, Miss Colburne, if you and Saint-Bryce had set a firm date?"

Lisette turned. "Oh, in the spring," she said vaguely.

"But nothing has been fixed?" Lady Hepplewood pressed hopefully. "Your family has no specific expectation?"

This time, Lisette's smile tightened. "About the only

thing my family ever expects is that I shall_make up my own mind," she said. "But I will certainly let everyone know once the date is chosen."

Her efforts thwarted, Lady Hepplewood returned to her coffee and Lisette to the sideboard. Behind her, she could hear Gwyneth shuffling the fabrics.

"Honestly, Diana, I'm no judge of colors," she said when Diana sat back down. "Though why you're turning out a room done just last year I cannot think."

Diana looked hurt. "Hepplewood told me when we settled here I might furnish all our rooms as I pleased."

"Yes, you always were his pet," Gwyneth murmured. "But he's dead now. He isn't using that room."

Lisette turned from the sideboard to see Lady Hepplewood staring down her nose. "It's a sentimental matter, Gwyneth, something you mightn't understand," she coolly remarked. "Diana chose the green just for Hepplewood. It was always his favorite color."

"Indeed, and I'm still passing fond of it," said a drowsy, masculine voice from the door.

Diana's eyes widened and she leapt from the table, almost oversetting her coffee cup. "Tony!" she cried, rushing toward the door.

Lisette turned around to see a strikingly handsome man in a burgundy silk banyan lingering on the threshold, one shoulder set lazily to the door frame, his blond locks tousled and eyes hooded as if with sleep. He wore a proper shirt and a loose cravat beneath his gown, all to no avail. He still looked like the sort of fellow who should have *sybarite* tattooed on his forehead.

Diana Jeffers had embraced him warmly. Lady Hepplewood observed, her expression bland. "Well, my boy," she said dryly, "can the pleasures of London truly spare you?"

Diana had led the young man into the room. "Tony, when did you come?" she chided. "Why did you not write us?"

"Good morning, Hepplewood." Gwyneth handed the fabrics back to Diana.

"Hullo, Gwen. And Mamma, you're in good looks." The young man drifted languidly past Lady Hepplewood, who turned up a pale, powdered cheek for his kiss. "And I did write, Di. To Mamma."

"With no mention of a visit," said Lady Hepplewood, who did not look all that pleased to see him.

"Well, I finally have some news for you," he said a little warily. But just then, the young man noticed Lisette, still standing by the sideboard, carefully observing the little vignette.

"Gad!" he said, his eyes drifting slowly over her. "Who is this tall, titan goddess hiding in our breakfast room? And here am I, still in my gown like the veriest sloth."

He did not, Lisette noticed, actually apologize for his dishabille.

"You have quite missed the excitement, Hepplewood," said his mother, snapping open a copy of the *Times*. "This is Miss Colburne, Saint-Bryce's intended."

At that, the man's eyes widened, and he shot an almost pained look at Diana. "Saint-Bryce?" he echoed.

"Do call me Elizabeth," she said, putting down her plate and offering her hand. "And yes, I'm Saint-Bryce's fiancée. He will be sorry to have missed you."

"Oh, that." Lord Hepplewood gave a vague smile and began to heap a plate with food. "The Napier fellow— Royden, isn't it?"

"You know perfectly well what his name is." Lady Hepplewood's newspaper rattled as she turned a page. "When did you arrive, my dear? I did not hear you come in."

"Caught the last train from Paddington yesterday evening," said Lord Hepplewood, loudly scraping up the last of the eggs. "Marsh let me in, and I just fell into bed."

Along with about half a bottle of brandy, Lisette silently added. It was doubtless a habit, for she could smell it literally oozing from his pores.

Diana set down her fork with a clatter. "Which bed?" she said pointedly.

Hepplewood slid into the chair by his mother. "*My bed*," he said, as if Diana had challenged him. "The big one in the green room. Papa's old room."

"But I am refitting that room," said Diana insistently. "Didn't you see the draperies were down? Really, Tony, you must take the yellow bedchamber. Gwyneth is helping pick fabrics this minute."

Tony shrugged. "Why is it Gwyneth's choice?" he said. "If it's anyone's choice save mine where I sleep or how it's fitted out, then—well, it's Miss Colburne's, isn't it? This will be her house soon enough. Besides, I like the green."

"Absolutely not." Diana rose and snatched up her teacup.

Lisette brightened her smile. "Diana doubtless knows what's best," she said soothingly. "And I'm sure *I* have no opinion on the subject."

"Indeed you do not." Lady Hepplewood laid aside her newspaper with a *thwack!* "Moreover it amuses Diana to have something to do, so that is the end of it. Now, Hepplewood, what is this important news that could not wait?"

At last a hint of unease passed over the man's handsome face. "Well," he said, taking his seat, "you must congratulate me, Mamma. I am to be married."

"My word!" Gwyneth's cup clattered onto her saucer.

At the sideboard pouring coffee, Diana turned with a gasp.

Lady Hepplewood had fixed her son with a fierce glare. "I beg your pardon?" she said sharply. "Am I to have no say in your choice?"

"Actually, no." Hepplewood hardened his gaze. "And I've chosen Miss Felicity Willet of Lincolnshire."

"Willet? Lincolnshire? I never heard of—" Lady Hepplewood lost what was left of her color. "My God, Hepplewood! What have you done?"

"Oh, *Tony* . . ." Diana was staring at him as if he were a ghost.

Only Gwyneth Tarleton appeared less than apoplectic, but not by much. Lisette looked around for a circumspect way to escape.

The gentleman merely snapped out his napkin and forked up his eggs. "I am marrying Miss Willet," he said. "You said it yourself: Loughford needs a mistress, and I need a wife. She'll do admirably. And Mamma, before you start, no, you do not know her family. They are Midlands industrial folk, and Mr. Willet is worth at least half a million p—"

"*Industrial* folk—?" Lady Hepplewood shoved back her chair and stood. "As in . . . what? Cotton mills? *Coal* mines?" She hurled her napkin down with what looked like suppressed rage. "Not another word, Anthony. You will get up, and escort me to my private sitting room. *Now.*"

Hepplewood's lips thinned. Then, with a silent oath, he tossed his napkin down, and followed his mother from the room.

Diana Jeffers had collapsed back into her chair, trembling. But Gwyneth merely watched her aunt and cousin go, her gaze still emotionless. "Well," she said blandly, "it's a grievous day indeed when a fellow must turn from London's moneylenders to the Midlands' millers in order to keep his creditors at bay."

"*Gwyneth!*" Diana sobbed. "How vile!"

Gwyneth just shrugged. "All I'm saying is Tony must be in deep this time to surrender his precious bachelorhood. And now Aunt Hepplewood is going to flay the hide off his back for his choice."

At that, Diana Jeffers burst into tears, threw back her chair so hard it tumbled over, then bolted from the room with one hand clapped over her mouth. Lisette could only stare at the door through which everyone had fled.

Gwyneth simply sighed, and continued calmly stirring sugar into her tea. "Rather like an overwrought *opéra comique*, isn't it?"

Lisette drew a deep breath. "Would it be frightfully inappropriate of me to ask what just happened?"

Humor sketched across Gwyneth's face. "I wondered how long your circumspection would hold out." Then she heaved a sigh, and laid down her teaspoon. "No, it's not inappropriate, precisely. Tony's right; you'll eventually be mistress of this whole mess."

"Oh, no." Lisette threw up a hand. "I aspire to be mistress over no one, Gwyneth. I just . . . I just feel sorry for them. For Miss Jeffers, especially."

"Oh, never mind Diana," said Gwyneth cavalierly. "She can never bear to see Tony hurt, that's all."

"They are close?"

"As a child she was his little shadow," said Gwyneth with a shrug, "and Anne was worse. But they cannot see that the sweet boy they grew up with has turned rakish and dissolute. Just like Uncle Hep, Anne and Diana imagine Tony can do no wrong. And Aunt Hepplewood is left to clean up the mess."

"How tragic," said Lisette.

"Tragic?" Again, Gwyneth shrugged. "Mostly for poor Mr. Willet. Tony has either already compromised his daughter, or he desperately needs his money—both, most likely."

"*Both?*"

Gwyneth flashed a sardonic smile. "London bred as you are, Miss Colburne, you must surely grasp the term *fortune hunter?* If a man is handsome enough, it takes little effort to entice a girl just up from the country into a dark corner and blacken her reputation—and all the quicker if her father is rich."

Lisette was painfully aware. Lord Rowend had always claimed it was why her parents had wed. Were it true, her grandfather would have been left with little alternative save to accept Sir Arthur Colburne's marriage proposal.

It was the first time, Lisette realized, she'd even considered it from Rowend's vantage point.

"I daresay such marriages do happen," she murmured, wondering how far to press her luck with Gwyneth. "Have the Hepplewoods no fortune, then?"

Gwyneth laughed. "Well, they've a huge house and a fine, old name," she said. "But Loughford is such a money pit one wonders if the rents can keep the place roofed."

Lisette poked at her food, pondering it. "Is that why Lady Hepplewood stays here? Their house is falling to pieces?"

At last Gwyneth looked uncertain. "It hasn't come to that yet, I don't think," she said. "But it's a drafty old place. Still, Diana says Loughford is lovely."

"Then I wonder why Lady Hepplewood doesn't drag Tony back home," said Lisette, emboldened by Gwyneth's candor. "He looks thoroughly under her thumb."

"I think Aunt Hepplewood means to marry Diana off first," said Gwyneth. "Like me, she's been on the shelf too long, and I gather there's no one in Northumberland who'll do."

Lisette had been puzzling over something. "But who will be Lady Hepplewood's companion?"

"Not I," Gwyneth declared. "But Diana is actually a cousin, not a companion. We grew up together, Anne, Diana, Tony, and I."

"Diana's parents are gone?"

"No, her father is Hepplewood's steward. They have a fine house on the estate. But Diana's mother died when she was five."

"We share that, don't we?" Absently, Lisette toyed with a bit of bacon. "Losing our mothers too soon."

"I suppose we do." Gwyneth's expression softened. "And

now Aunt says it's her duty to find Diana a husband—and if ever a woman was meant to be married, it's Diana."

"Well, she did find Diana a husband," Lisette remarked. "She found your father, Lord Saint-Bryce."

"And wasn't that convenient?" Another smile twisted Gwyneth's mouth. "But as soon as Papa put off his blacks, Diana had to put hers on. And then Papa died. And now Mr. Napier is to marry you. And then *he'll* likely toss the lot of us out and wash his hands of the misery."

"Oh, no!" said Lisette. "I am quite sure he wouldn't want—"

She halted abruptly, realizing she wasn't at all sure what Napier would want. *Would* he toss them all out? Or would he even bother to turn up at Burlingame again?

It was as if Gwyneth read her mind. "No, you aren't sure, are you?" she murmured over her teacup. "It's perfectly all right. We likely deserve it, inbred snobs that we are."

Lisette wondered if Gwyneth was relieved Diana would not become her stepmother. And if Gwyneth had hated the notion, what about her sister, Anne?

But Anne was married, and her father's third wife would not have much affected her.

"I wonder if Beatrice knew she was to have a stepmother?" Lisette mused aloud.

"Bea is more shrewd than you might think," said Gwyneth. "And like a vulture, Aunt Hepplewood moved in when Bea's mother was on her deathbed, which made her plan rather obvious. But once Papa passed, that was that, and Aunt Hepplewood turned her arrow to—"

Her words jerked to a halt, and at last Gwyneth had the grace to blush.

Lisette smiled and gave a dismissive toss of her hand. "Yes, I know it was hoped Diana might marry Mr. Napier."

"In Aunt Hepplewood's defense," said Gwyneth, "she thought Mr. Napier entirely unattached."

"And she has been gracious to me," said Lisette swiftly. "So Beatrice's mother had no other children. How sad."

"Poor Julia was like Mamma," said Gwyneth almost wistfully. "They were not good breeders—and in the end, it killed them."

"How very tragic," said Lisette. "Did Julia die in childbed?"

"No, but it left her an invalid," said Gwyneth. "Bea was a miracle. Julia lost six children before she was born. But Papa and Grandpapa, they were desperate for . . . oh, Lord! How awkward I am today."

"Desperate for another heir," Lisette finished. "I know. And I think Mr. Napier would not have minded had they found one, to be honest."

At that, Gwyneth's gaze narrowed. "Perhaps, but what of yourself?"

Lisette widened her eyes ingenuously. "Why, I had accepted Mr. Napier's offer completely unaware," she said honestly. "Indeed, when he made his proposal to me, I understood him to be the Assistant Police Commissioner, and nothing more."

Gwyneth cut her a disbelieving gaze. "Well, Nicholas Napier was a wealthy man," she suggested. "Though how he made his money is anyone's guess."

Given Sir Wilfred's dying words, Lisette was beginning to believe she didn't have to guess, but held her tongue. "Well, I did not claim to think Mr. Napier poverty stricken," she said, forcing a light laugh. "I have seen his carriage, his clothes, and that fine house in Eaton Square."

At that, Gwyneth relented, and relaxed a little into her chair. "Still, you were marrying down," she said. "Quite far, in fact."

Lisette simply shrugged, and told the truth. "My father lived a scandalous life and came to a tragic end," she said. "It alters one's ideas of propriety, even as it tarnishes one's prospects. I respected Mr. Napier, and thought him quite good-looking. And so I accepted his proposal."

"A decision, my dear, which I believe you are now called upon to explain," said a deep voice from the doorway.

The sound of *my dear* spoken in that familiar, almost sensuous timbre sent a dangerous warmth down Lisette's spine—a sensation as unwise as it was unwelcome.

Forcing a bright smile, she turned around in her chair to see Royden Napier blocking the width of the doorway with those impossibly broad shoulders. He wore black again—and a grim expression.

"Good morning, my darling," she said, rising.

"Have you finished your breakfast?"

"Yes, I hadn't much appetite."

Napier held out his hand to her. "Then if you would kindly join me," he said in his low, rumbling voice, "Lord Duncaster requests the pleasure of our company."

"Together?" she said uneasily. "The two of us?"

"Forever and ever," said Napier dryly, "until death do us part."

It felt like an endless trek back to the east pavilion. Lisette walked alongside Napier through the ostentatious state apartments, neither speaking until they reached the marble colonnade. Today the massive casements had been flung up, opening the long passageway to the rapidly warming day, and the sun slanted in upon the alternating squares of marble giving one the impression it had been dusted with diamonds.

In the middle of the colonnade, Napier stopped abruptly, glancing up and down as if to confirm it was empty. The sardonic humor she'd glimpsed in the dining room had vanished from his eyes—eyes that were a dark, storm-cloud blue today.

"Elizabeth," he said quietly, "I wish to—"

"Napier, *don't*." Wincing, she threw up a hand.

"Don't what?" He stood rigidly beside her.

"Apologize," she said, and resumed walking. "Actually, you don't have to do any of this."

But he caught her arm in a firm grip, and gently drew her around. "Elizabeth, wait." His eyes searched her face as one might examine a porcelain teacup, checking for chips and cracks. "What is it you think I'm doing?"

"Being—I don't know—*kind* to me?" Lisette sighed. "You aren't kind. And I'm not fragile. In fact, when you dragged me into this mess, Napier, you implied you thought me ruthless."

"We are all of us fragile," he said quietly, "in our own way."

Oddly irritated by his gentleness, Lisette lifted one shoulder. "My own solicitor recently remarked I'd become hardened and cynical," she said. "And he did not mean it as a compliment. And you—well, *you* think worse of me than that, remember?"

He was still watching her warily. "I hardly know what I think," he admitted. "Understanding you, I begin to believe, is like grasping quicksilver."

She shrugged again. "Just understand, Napier, that I've never lived a sheltered life—not even *before* Papa died, and certainly not after."

"What do you mean?"

She shook her head. She really had no wish to begin this conversation. "My father was a charming scoundrel," she said. "Do you imagine I don't know that? Or that I did not have some sense of the life he lived? As to my life afterward, the Ashtons were in the newspaper business, and in that, no one stays naïve for long. I understand how the world operates, Napier. I understand how men are."

His grip on her arm hardened. "If you think that," he replied, "then you don't understand me at all."

"At last, we are agreed on something," she said setting off again. "Come, let's not keep Duncaster waiting. He might die of old age before we get there. Then where would we be?"

After an instant's hesitation, Napier fell into step beside her, his boot heels ringing even harder on the glossy marble. Lisette tried not to grit her teeth. The infernal man could not bear to be crossed—not even when he was being an idiot.

The fleeting softness having left his eyes, Napier again looked remote and intractable today—for a good reason, she feared. Perhaps no one at Burlingame wished him ill, but neither did they welcome him, that much had been made plain to Lisette. Perhaps Duncaster felt the same.

But it likely did not matter to Napier. He doubtless went where and when he pleased, undeterred by opinion.

Lisette cut another surreptitious glance at his tall, rangy form. The man moved with a powerful, loose-limbed grace and looked, more than anyone she'd ever met, utterly at ease with himself. She sensed in him the confidence of a man who knew precisely what he was, and had made of his life precisely what he wished.

For most people this unexpected inheritance would have been an opportune twist of fate. But to Napier, it was just an unwelcome distraction. That much Lisette truly believed, no matter how many incredulous glances people like Gwyneth Tarleton might cast in his direction.

She glanced at him again, and considered what Lord Duncaster might make of his reluctant heir. Lisette saw nothing of which the viscount might disapprove; in fact, quite the opposite.

She had not lied to Gwyneth when she'd called Napier handsome, though he was not conventionally so. He was dressed today as if for riding in a coat she now realized was actually dark charcoal, paired with a plain black stock and tall black boots with breeches. There was nothing of the dandy in him, thank God. Instead he looked every inch a man's man, with all the virility and lean strength such a phrase suggested.

On an inward sigh, she thought again of the weight and hardness of his body pressing her down into the softness of his bed; of the almost overwhelming power of him. Her face flooding with heat, Lisette decided some idle chatter was in order.

"Did you hear the prodigal son turned up at breakfast?" she said, dropping her voice companionably. "Apparently he, too, has contrived an engagement without his mother's blessing."

"I didn't require her blasted blessing."

"Alas for Tony, it seems he did," she said. "Lady Hepplewood snatched up that wicked black stick of hers and dragged him off for a flogging. So account yourself fortunate. Tea yesterday could have been worse."

"Why, I found tea nearly painless," said Napier dryly, "entertained as I was by your remarkable theatrics."

Lisette felt oddly pleased. "What do you think Lord Duncaster wants?" she continued. "Merely to meet me? Or do you expect questions?"

"I couldn't say," Napier answered as they entered the east pavilion. "I scarcely know the man. The butler brought the summons—a thick, white note card on a salver instructing us to wait upon him in the gun room."

"The gun room, is it?" said Lisette. "Does he mean to shoot us?"

Napier smiled grimly and directed her down the wide, spiraling stairs instead of up. They descended together into the lower level of the pavilion, cool air rising up to meet them. Here the steps were uncarpeted, the walls far older and adorned, not with watered silk or gilt wainscoting, but with faded Flemish tapestries and crackled portraits of dark-eyed, hatchet-nosed ancestors hung against plain white plaster.

Lisette eyed one of them warily as she descended; a particularly imperious-looking fellow in a powdered wig who looked so much like Napier it was haunting.

After leading her down a long passageway, Napier gestured toward a thick plank of a door flanked by medieval suits of armor—décor that might, Lisette mused, be original to this part of the house.

He pushed the door wide on deeply groaning hinges and they stepped into a vaulted, almost castle-like chamber the walls of which were lined with a diverse assortment of guns, swords, battle axes, and even a couple of wicked pikes crossed almost decoratively above an immense stone fireplace.

Two oak worktables nearly black with age ran the length of the room, and at the far end, two men stood conferring upon a pair of firearms laid out upon a heavy blanket. The younger of the two, a slender, fresh-faced man in a rough surtout, nodded and picked up the leftmost weapon, a double-barreled fowling gun.

"Aye, m'lord, that'll do nicely," the young man said, balancing it in his hand.

Napier cleared his throat. "I beg your pardon, sir," he said from the doorway. "You wished to see us?"

The elder man turned, and fixed them with a pair of keen eyes. "Ah, Saint-Bryce," he said, motioning them in. "I think you've not met Hoxton, my new gamekeeper. There's a hawk nesting in the folly, and getting at my quail. Hoxton, my grandson."

Hoxton gave a respectful tug at his forelock, then broke the breech and draped the gun across the crook of his arm. Lisette managed to make a passable curtsy to the viscount.

Her jest about Duncaster dying hadn't been entirely facetious for Lisette had expected a frail, doddering gentleman in a Bath chair. But the man who stood before her looked if not affirmatively vigorous, then certainly well amongst the living. And like Napier, he was dressed for riding.

Though still a man of some height, Lord Duncaster was slightly stooped with age, but his jowls scarcely sagged and his hard, dark eyes were sharp as a crow's, putting Lisette in mind of his much younger half sister, Lady Hepplewood. Here, she estimated, was a man one crossed at one's peril.

Duncaster finished his business with Hoxton and dismissed him. After re-racking the second gun, the gamekeeper gave a departing nod, then strolled out through a set of French windows that opened onto a sunken terrace.

"And don't go onto that devilish parapet," bellowed Duncaster after him. "Shoot from the wood, boy, do you hear?"

"Yes, m'lord." Looking faintly embarrassed, the young man went up a flight of mossy stone steps, and vanished into the greenery of the rear gardens.

Duncaster turned his attention to Lisette, one eye narrowed appraisingly. "Well, so this is the pretty little clew knotting up Cordelia's grand scheme."

"This is my fiancée, Elizabeth," Napier coolly interjected. "As to your sister's schemes, I'm sure neither Elizabeth nor I can speak to them."

"Very wise! Very wise!" said Duncaster, lifting a pair of bushy gray eyebrows almost mockingly. "I avoid them myself when possible. In any case, Miss Colburne, I regret having been unable to greet you upon your arrival."

"Not in the least, my lord," she said. "We'd no wish to disturb your rest."

It was not, perhaps, the wisest thing to have said. "Rest?" said the viscount incredulously. "I was at Birmingham with Craddock buying a new threshing machine."

Lisette and Napier exchanged glances as Duncaster moved with a faint limp toward the fireplace, which looked large enough to roast half an ox. "Well, come along. Sit, the both of you."

Gingerly, he lowered himself into an ancient black chair

carved with dragons for arms. When they were all situated, Duncaster opened his hands expansively, his elbows propped upon the chair's odd arms.

"Well, my boy, here we are," he said, fixing Napier with his glare. "All this is going to be yours now, isn't it?"

Napier's face was perfectly expressionless. "I take no joy in it, sir," he said, "if that's any consolation."

"Well, it isn't," snapped his grandfather. "Burlingame is one of the finest estates in England. It should go to someone who appreciates it and has been trained to take up the mantle of its stewardship."

"I don't know what to say, sir." Napier lifted one hand almost casually. "Saint-Bryce's passing has left no one happy, I do assure you."

Duncaster's mouth lifted in a sort of sneer. "I wouldn't be too certain of that."

Napier leaned a little forward in his chair. "Was there only Saint-Bryce, sir, or have you an estate agent whom you trust, and who could competently run Burlingame should you die unexpectedly?"

"Unexpectedly?" Here the old man chuckled until he wheezed. "It's been expected I should die this last decade or better. Do I look near death to you?"

Lisette intervened. "Indeed not, my lord," she said smoothly. "Royden is much reassured, I know, to find you so vigorous. But travel is exhausting for anyone."

"Well, I'd not ordinarily trouble myself over a threshing machine. But what choice have I with my son dead?" Here, Duncaster's voice hitched as if with grief, but after a moment he regained himself and pressed on. "But yes, Craddock is still steward and a quite competent fellow."

"Perhaps you could hire additional staff?" Lisette suggested. "I believe my late grandfather retained a land agent and a pair of stewards for his various estates."

Duncaster turned the full force of his squinty glare upon

her. "*Hmph*," he said. "Cordelia said you were old Rowend's chit."

"His granddaughter, yes."

"*Hmph*," he said again. "Always was free with his blunt, Rowend. But Burlingame was not built, my dear, on spend-thrift ways." Here, he paused to nod his head in Napier's direction. "As to managing things, that's what *he's* for, wouldn't you say?"

"I beg your pardon?" Napier stiffened in his chair.

Duncaster turned in his seat to better look at him. "It's time to step up, my boy, to your duties," he said firmly. "And we've a vast deal of work ahead of us, so—"

"Thank you, sir," Napier cut him off, "but this is a conversation better had in private."

"Nonsense!" boomed the old man, stabbing a finger at Lisette. "Best the chit here knows what's what. And best you get on with the business of seeing to what's been given you."

"No one has given me anything, sir, that I didn't earn." Napier's voice had gone dangerously cold. "I haven't been sitting idle and coddled in some great mansion waiting for my kin to die off. I have been in service to our government— and working hard at it."

"Oh, come now, my boy!" Duncaster gentled his tone, but not by much. "We're speaking of what must be done *now*. This is no longer about what pleases me, or even about your father's misplaced pride. And this lovely bride of yours, why, she will have no interest, I can assure you, in living in a pokey little house in Town, tatting cushions for some glorified government clerk."

"Well, how charming this is!" interjected Lisette, rather too cheerfully. "I can see, my lord, that you and your heir share at least one distinguishing characteristic."

The old man's head swiveled around, the narrow eye closing to a slit. "Eh? And just what might that be?"

"The maddening habit of assuming what I do or don't want," she briskly replied. "Mr. Napier here believes—"

"Napier, my eye!" The old man's face pulled in mulishly. "His name is *Tarleton*. He must change it back at once."

Napier brooked no opposition. "I understand that's what you want, sir, but I've been a Napier all my life and don't mean to change."

"But your children, Royden!" Duncaster bellowed, his face purpling. "They should have—no, they *deserve*—to carry the Tarleton name."

"It remains to be seen if there will be children," said Napier. "But should I have any, on their majority, they may choose the name they wish to bear. If they prefer Tarleton, so be it."

"Well, they will," declared the old man, "if they've a shred of sense."

"You're likely right." Napier was, as always, utterly calm—and almost ruthlessly cool.

Lisette forced the conversation back to her point. "The thing is, my lord, when Mr. Napier made me his proposal, I believed him the assistant police commissioner, and happily so. I can assure you I will be entirely content to tat cushions and manage his house in Eaton Square. And by the way, sir, have you troubled yourself to see it? *Pokey* is hardly the word."

"*Seen* it?" said the old man. "I bought the dashed thing."

"How kind of you," said Lisette speciously. "Nevertheless, it—"

"Stop." Napier's voice echoed in the gun room. "Stop right there. What do you mean, *you* bought it?"

Duncaster's hands were braced on the dragon's heads, his thumb worrying at one of them almost anxiously. "I *bought* it," he said peevishly. "I bought it and deeded it freehold to Agnes Napier as a—a sort of belated wedding gift. When you were aged eight or nine."

"You bought a house," Napier echoed flatly, "and *gave it to my mother*—? Was that your way of apologizing to her?"

Duncaster twisted in his chair almost guiltily. "I gave it to her because I knew your father wouldn't take it," he snapped. "Knew, you see, Agnes would want what was best for her child—always a woman's weakness, you know, the children."

Napier merely arched one eyebrow. "Why would you even bother?"

"Oh, for pity's sake, boy! Do you think I couldn't see it might come to Nicholas?" Duncaster grumbled. "What with James out carousing and fighting duels right and left. And Harold with two chits and a wife too frail to share his bed."

"Sir, please. There is a lady present."

"Oh, I *please*," the old man grumbled. "I *please* to tell you what your father would not. My God, Royden, do you think a government flunky can afford to live in Belgravia? Nicholas and his overweening pride had the three of you crammed inside a squalid little masionette over some linen draper's shop! And your mother doing her own washing! How is that fit for my grandson? *How*—?"

"Heavens," murmured Lisette, burning with curiosity. "Did your son know you'd done this?"

"He had to have done." Duncaster cast her an incredulous look, then fixed a kindling eye upon his grandson. "So, yes, I bought the house and I made sure Agnes had the money put back to get you properly educated. And then she died, and that was that." Here, he paused to give a disdainful sniff. "I don't know how Nicholas got on after that. But he was always plump in the pocket, or so everyone claimed."

At that Napier's countenance darkened, and Lisette thought again of Sir Wilfred's ugly allegation. "Well, whatever you did for my mother, I thank you, for she was a fine woman and I adored her," he said. "But we seem to have deviated rather far from our original conversation."

"Then let's return in all haste," said Duncaster almost bitterly. "Your parents are far from my favorite topic."

"And the two of you will kindly leave my wishes out of this discussion," said Lisette, "for neither of you know what they are. This is for the two of you to settle."

"Agreed," snapped Napier.

At that, Duncaster seemed to wither in his chair. "All I am saying, my boy, is that you need to learn how to go on here," he said almost whiningly. "Any hope of Harold and Diana supplanting you with an heir is gone, and we must all of us deal with it."

"Sir, with all respect, I'm not sure I must," said Napier.

"Then why the devil have you come?" Duncaster demanded, tossing a disdainful hand at Napier. "Why, here you are, coming down in your riding boots! I thought we were to get on with it. Ride about the estate and spend the next few days with Craddock."

Irritation was writ plain upon the viscount's wrinkled face. The possibility that anything besides money and a title might have brought his grandson to Burlingame had never crossed his mind. Moreover, Duncaster was a man who enjoyed—and expected—the upper hand.

Lisette was beginning to grasp just what had driven Napier's father from the fold.

The room had fallen silent. Duncaster was still worrying at the chair arm—a habit of long standing, Lisette concluded, for he'd worn the finish to the wood, and the dragon's left ear was but a nub.

When at last Napier spoke, his tone was less confrontational. "I've come, sir, for the same reason I first visited Burlingame. Because Sir George asked me to, and because I'm uneasy. And I'm in my boots because I mean to ride over to Marlborough and call on Dr. Underwood."

"Call on *Underwood*?" said Duncaster incredulously. "What in God's name has he to do with any of this?"

"He's the family physician, isn't he?" Napier shot a quick glance at Lisette. "I know Hepplewood wasn't young, but I cannot see how a man of Saint-Bryce's years could die so suddenly—and mere months after Hepplewood's troubling letter to Sir George."

Duncaster drew back. "What, that rambling nonsense about Hep thinking himself poisoned?"

"Poisoned?" Napier echoed. "He said that to you?"

"Oh, Good Lord! He said it to anyone who would listen," declared the viscount. "Claimed Cordelia was trying to kill him! Some days it was smothering, some days poisoning. He had gone round the bend, I tell you."

"But Lady Hepplewood?" Napier's tone was surprisingly matter-of-fact. "Why would your sister wish to kill her husband?"

Lisette noticed that Duncaster was no longer looking directly at either of them. He seemed suddenly smaller, and more drawn, as if he were shrinking in the massive black chair.

"She wouldn't," the viscount finally responded. "Cordelia can be a sharp-tongued shrew, I'll grant you. And God knows they had their troubles. But she always worshiped Hep."

"What sort of troubles?"

Duncaster glared at him. "The kind married folk have," he said evasively. "But if my sister wanted to kill her husband, she wouldn't have dragged him down here to do it."

Lisette found it interesting that Duncaster had not declared Lady Hepplewood incapable of murder, but merely that the facts did not add up.

"Aunt Hepplewood told me he suffered from senility of the mind," said Napier. "Did he seem vague to you when he first moved to Burlingame?"

Duncaster seemed honestly to ponder it. "No, sharp as a tack for a good while. Had to be, to survive those government vultures he worked with." The mulish look returned. "But Hep and I were best friends, so if you think I'd let anyone treat him ill under my roof—even that high-handed sister of mine—you may think again."

Napier shook his head. "No, sir, I don't think that," he said. "But what I cannot understand is how he deteriorated so rapidly as to be incoherent within a matter of . . . what, weeks?" Here, he looked to his grandfather for confirmation.

Duncaster nodded reluctantly. "Well, months," he said, "but not a great many."

"And how could such an intelligent man take it into his head he was being poisoned, or whatever it was he imagined?" Napier pressed.

The old man gave a gargoyle smile. "Old men tend to flights of fancy," he said. "I, for example, imagined my grandson was coming home to do his duty."

Irritation sketched over Napier's face. "Sir, has it ever occurred to you that this *is* my duty?" he said. "It is my duty to the Crown. And if something were amiss, wouldn't you want to know?"

"I . . ." Duncaster lifted both shoulders. "Well, yes, of course."

Lisette watched, mesmerized, as Napier leaned forward in his chair, his elbows propped now on his knees, his hands loosely clasped between them. His eyes had gone dark again, his expression intent and utterly focused, like a hawk scanning a field for prey—but this particular hawk, Lisette was sure, had no interest in something so insignificant as quail.

"It is his words to Sir George that I find most telling," said Napier. "He wrote that Burlingame was choking the life from him. That the walls were closing in and he could not breathe. What did he mean by such a metaphor? I intended to ask him, but by the time I arrived . . ."

"He said a lot of things." Duncaster had clearly tired of

the subject. "Well, go on to Underwood's, then, if it pleases you," he said, flinging a dismissive hand in the direction of the open French windows. "Someone down at the stables will saddle you a mount."

Napier hesitated a moment, as if wondering whether to press further, then apparently thought better of it. "Thank you, sir," he said, rising from his chair. "I don't mean to tire you, or press you to the point of aggravation."

Duncaster did not look happy. "But you have done both," he grumbled. "And in recompense, I shall require four hours of your time tomorrow. If you mean to accept my hospitality, then you will turn at least one eye to this estate. Tomorrow, specifically, you'll begin riding around the tenanted farms with Craddock and me."

Lisette could see Napier was torn; torn between his duty to the Home Office, and the duties that were, inevitably, to fall upon his shoulders.

As to Lord Duncaster, he was putting on a resolute face, but the toll, both emotional and physical, was plain to anyone who truly looked. Lisette did look, and she saw a tyrant who had become petty and childish in his twilight, but in part, perhaps, from grief. It was worth remembering he had buried a wife, all his children, and his best friend.

She rose, and looked at Napier. "Might I walk with you as far as the stables?"

"But of course, my dear."

A few minutes later, they were going up the mossy terrace stairs, following the gamekeeper's path. The stables lay beyond the west pavilion, some distance from their end of the house, and were reached through an apple orchard. Together Lisette and Napier made their way through the expansive rear gardens, which were lush and exceedingly formal.

"Your grandfather is vigorous," she remarked, "for his age."

"Yes." Napier's tone was wry. "But at his age, most men have been dead for a decade."

"Ah," she said quietly. "We do not need to have this conversation, do we? You see what is inevitable. And it's hardly my place to warn you."

Napier shrugged. "As to your place—"

"Yes?" she said.

He seemed to hesitate. "Never mind," he answered as they passed a tall, travertine statue—a Greek goddess pouring water from a ewer into a twelve-foot marble pool shimmering with flashes of gold. They were fish, she realized.

"It's beautiful here, isn't it?" he remarked. "The wealth and the opulence shine upon us even outdoors, like the very sun itself."

Lisette murmured her assent for the remark seemed rhetorical. But the sun was indeed warm on her shoulders, the air rich with roses and new-mown grass. As her shoes crunched softly on the pea-gravel path, she felt increasingly aware of Napier's warmth and powerful male presence by her side. She glanced again at his arresting profile.

He seemed deep in thought, his mood inscrutable.

"I begin to understand what brought you here," she said quietly. "I wish for your sake that Duncaster understood it, too."

Napier gave a dismissive grunt. "He understands only that his iron will is being thwarted," he replied, "which to him is as unforgivable as murder."

"So you do fear there's been a crime?" she pressed. "That someone wanted Hepplewood dead? And perhaps Saint-Bryce?"

"I hardly know what I fear," he replied, "other than having this pile and all its duties dumped on me."

After a time, they entered a long, vine-covered pergola that seemed to lead from the formal gardens into something more wild and natural. At the center was a wrought-iron bench, angled away from the house and stables so as to take in the view of the ornamental lake to the east. On the hill above it, one could see the towering stone folly rising from the trees.

"Napier," said Lisette, "there's something I wish to say to you."

He stopped on the path and paused. She sensed something was troubling him—something besides his quarrel with his grandfather—and she suspected what it might be.

"Duncaster after all?" he asked. "Or something more dire?"

"Something more dire." With a withering smile, she motioned to the bench. "Will you sit with me a moment?"

Though she could see he fairly chomped at the bit with impatience, he nodded. After settling onto the bench, Lisette looked down the rolling expanse of green, all the way down to the lake, so crystalline and smooth it threw up the cloudless blue sky like a mirror. What a pity all of one's choices and decisions weren't as clear.

As if urging her from her reverie, Napier touched her arm and she flinched. He drew back his hand at once.

Lisette turned to face him. "I'm sorry." Oddly, she found herself reaching for his hand, and took it between her own. "It isn't you. I was lost in thought."

He dipped his head as if to better see her, his hand warm and heavy in hers. Lisette knew what she owed this man. The truth. And she knew, too, the questions it would lead to. Questions she really did not wish to answer. So an apology must suffice.

"Elizabeth," he said softly, "what is it?"

She released his hand, and forced herself to press on. "I begin to see how seriously you take your duties with the police," she said. "That, I'm sure, is part of why Sir George turned to you when he was worried about matters here."

"I can't speak to Sir George's views. But in mine, there is

no higher calling than police work. At least not for me." He gave a harsh laugh. "I've no talent for medicine, and I think we can agree I'd be ill suited as a priest. But Elizabeth, did you really pull me onto this bench to discuss my career?"

She cut him a rueful glance. "No, I did it so I might apologize."

"Apologize?" At last she had surprised him.

Lisette drew a steadying breath. She wanted to have done with it. "Almost two years ago," she began, "I . . . I barged into Whitehall and accused you of being incompetent. I believe I may even have called you venal, and suggested you could be bought. I think none of that was true. I think you care deeply."

"Do I?" Almost pensively, Napier forked a hand through his heavy, dark hair. "After a dozen years in this business, I hardly know."

"Those who work hard at things which truly matter are often worn down by them," she said evenly. "And I think you must be very good at what you do. There's a distance in you, yes, but I wonder if one could otherwise survive in your world. It was wrong of me to malign you. I misjudged your character . . . and even *that* was not my worst mistake. I was wrong about the whole business. About everything. *Everyone.*"

To her shame, her words ended a little tremulously.

"Elizabeth," he said chidingly.

She made a sound—a cross between a sob and a laugh— and threw up one hand. "Now be sure, Napier, that I am not putting you on," she said. "I am, or so you imagine, quite an infamously good actress."

"Well," he said quietly, "you do owe me an apology. But you'd do better to worry about Lazonby. He's powerful and probably vindictive, and I am n—"

"What, you are *not*?" Lisette's smile was wry.

His expression darkened. "I've exacted my pound of flesh

by dragging you here," he replied. "I said I'd protect you from Lazonby should it become necessary, and I will."

"I . . . I think you will."

"I *will*," he said gruffly. "But there is something else, Elizabeth, that I need you to do for me."

She lifted her gaze to his, troubled by the sudden edge to his words. "Yes?"

He watched her warily for a moment, his eyes gone dark as a thunderhead. They had looked the very same just before he'd kissed her, and for an instant, Elizabeth's breath caught.

But kissing her seemed the farthest thing from his mind.

"I need you to tell me," he finally said, "*exactly* what you heard Sir Wilfred say in the dairy the day he died. I'm not asking you to tell me more or concede anything. I just want to know, beyond a shred of doubt, what was said."

Lisette knew what he was asking. "About your father."

His jaw flinched. "Yes. About my father."

Inwardly, she sighed. Yet another discussion she did not wish to have—she now counted about four since breakfast. And to do what he asked required her to step carefully indeed.

Lisette licked her lips. "You know I attended the garden party," she began uneasily. "All the volunteers from Hannah's—Lady Leeton's—charity school did. It was Prize Day for the girls. I . . . I gave the Grammar Prize."

"Yes," he said patiently. "I believe Lazonby said as much. But now you bring it up, Elizabeth, I confess I've never understood just how you ended up volunteering there. Especially when you claim you knew nothing of Sir Wilfred's involvement in your father's death."

Lisette had often wondered the same. "I think . . . I think I just wanted to see Hannah again," she finally answered. "I wanted to think of what might have been had Papa's life not gone so wrong. To me, Hannah was always so beautiful, like a fairy queen. And I had always hoped someday she would come to . . . well, to *like* me."

"Hannah—?" he said. "Lady Leeton?"

Lisette shrugged lamely. "I was a little afraid she might recognize me," she confessed. "So I went to the school on a sort of pretense—the wig helped, of course—and then I just got . . . got caught up in my own lies, I guess."

She glanced up to see a puzzled expression on Napier's face. "But Lisette, why *would* she know you? Why might she recognize you?"

Lisette looked at him blankly. "Because of Papa," she said. "Because they were lovers—serious lovers—long before she married Sir Wilfred. Did you not know? That the three of them were all bosom beaus?"

Napier shook his head. "There was nothing in the old murder file about Hannah Leeton," he said, "though Lazonby did suggest there was some competition for the lady's favors."

"It went beyond that. Hannah adored Papa and wanted to marry him." Lisette's voice dropped to a raw whisper. "But now I know the truth. That Sir Wilfred wanted Hannah— and her money—for himself."

Napier's brow was furrowed. "I didn't grasp that," he said. "I thought Sir Wilfred was just a hired killer for some gaming syndicate. Or so Lazonby said."

"Oh, he was," said Lisette, "and well paid for it. The syndicate wanted rid of Lazonby; he was too good a card player. So they paid Sir Wilfred to get rid of him—and they didn't care how."

"And Sir Wilfred confessed to all this?" Napier still looked dubious. "In the dairy?"

"Y-yes," said Lisette. "As I said that day, he bragged about it. He claimed he chose Elinor's rich fiancé as his victim, not just to set Lazonby up, but so that Papa might be driven to panic when the marriage settlements fell through. He wanted Papa to flee his creditors and head for the Continent. To abandon Hannah so that he—Sir Wilfred—might console her."

"Dear God," said Napier under his breath.

Lisette steeled herself against the unexpected press of tears. "How could anyone be so vile? So utterly scheming?" she said, this time aloud. "Sir Wilfred said . . . he said that he saw a way *to kill two birds with one stone.* To take the syndicate's money and rid them of Lazonby, then have Hannah in the bargain."

"And this Lord Percy, your sister's intended—he had a long-standing quarrel with Lazonby," Napier mused. "So of course, to the police it looked like a plausible crime."

Lisette felt the old, familiar nausea well up in her again. "And we all of us believed he'd done it, didn't we? You did. I did. I went . . . good God, I went to Newgate. To the hanging." She set a palm hard against her forehead as if it might block the memory, but it never did. "I was twelve. I remember how the rope snapped taut. Lazonby just dangled there, dead—or so we believed. Then Ellie fainted in the mud. Somehow, I got her up. And the next day, Lord Rowend's solicitor took us to Bristol and put us on a ship to Aunt Ashton's."

Wordlessly, Napier set an arm around her shoulders, and this time she did not flinch. There was no reaction left in her.

"Ellie was dead a fortnight later," she whispered. "A fever, they called it. But I think her heart was just broken. And now . . . dear God, now I look back on all that has happened—all that I believed—and it's like a horrific nightmare."

"I know the feeling," muttered Napier grimly. "Whatever our disagreements, Elizabeth, I'm sorry you had to live through that. But if Hannah was a rich, willing widow, why didn't Sir Arthur marry her?"

Lisette felt her face flush with heat. "Because of Elinor," she finally answered. "Elinor told Papa she would never forgive him if he sullied our family's name in such a way."

"In what way, exactly?"

Lisette lifted one shoulder lamely. "Elinor had just come out that Season," she said. "Papa borrowed horribly to launch her, and many gentlemen were captivated. But she'd set her sights on Lord Percy Peveril, for he was a duke's son. The duke was a frightful snob, and Ellie knew it. She told Papa that Hannah was a pariah who would ruin her chances. That Hannah was a jumped-up shop girl who'd got rich on Jewish money, then used it to run with a fast crowd . . ."

"And?" Napier gently prodded.

Here, Lisette's voice hitched humiliatingly. "—and yes, Napier, the irony does not escape me," she continued, "that the *fast crowd* Elinor disdained was Papa's crowd. And Sir Wilfred's crowd. But men can be forgiven such indiscretions. Women, apparently, cannot."

Napier was very quiet. "I recall vaguely that Hannah's first husband was a wealthy trader in the City."

Lisette sighed. "She was not herself Jewish, I don't think—not that I cared," she said. "And it's true Hannah's father was just an apothecary. But she made Papa laugh, and I do sometimes wonder . . ." Her words broke away, and she shook her head.

Napier squeezed her hand. "What do you wonder?"

I wonder if my sister wasn't a selfish bitch.

But Lisette snatched back the thought as soon as it entered her head.

Ellie had been special: beautiful and charming. People had loved her for that, just as they had loved Papa. And Elinor had been proud of her connection to Lord Rowend—proud of her blue English blood. Was that so very wrong? Was not aristocratic pride the very thing that sustained the English upper class and provided a backbone for the nation?

And yet Lisette knew that in America blood accounted for almost nothing, and the nation little suffered for it. Indeed, some would argue the country was stronger and more equal without it. Mr. Ashton *had* argued it—blatantly, belliger-ently, and on a weekly basis—in his radical newspaper. And for the most part, Lisette had agreed with his politics, if not his execution.

Yet another irony that made her head hurt. Oh, why could the world not be black and white? Sometimes, yes, she did find herself angry with Elinor and with Papa—more and more of late, and it shamed her. She told herself she was just looking for someone to blame for her family's misfortunes now that Lazonby had been vindicated.

She gave a soft, sardonic laugh. "Do you know, Napier, what Hannah used to call me?"

"No," he said tentatively.

"Elizabeth the Unfortunate," she said. "I once heard her tell Papa that Ellie was a diamond, but that I was going to prove 'difficult.' I was too gangly, too pale, my hair too red."

"What utter balderdash," said Napier. "I hope you didn't heed it."

Lisette forced a shrug, a little embarrassed by her childish confession. Indeed, she had indulged her maudlin notions for far too long—and this time, far too openly. She did not want anyone's sympathy, nor had anyone ever given her much.

It was just as well, she imagined. Papa's life had proven one rarely knew who to trust. Napier, moreover, was simply watching her; weighing her, she thought. Wondering, per-haps, if this was all just a cheap theatrical, and if she meant ever to actually answer the one question he *had* asked.

"So there, I've apologized to you," she managed, drawing in a steadying breath. "Beyond that, my personal tragedies are utterly a waste of your time. The business of Papa's death is done, and Ellie's, too. But you . . . you wished to know exactly what Sir Wilfred said about your father."

"Yes," he said tightly.

Lisette realized that his arm was no longer around her shoulders. She half turned on the bench, and forced him to hold her gaze. "Exactly?" she pressed. "I have, regrettably, the gift of near-total recall."

"Exactly," he demanded.

Lisette closed her eyes, and felt the cool, thick air of the dairy furl about her like a musty blanket. She could still hear Lady Anisha, half conscious and sobbing; could still smell the sharp tang of soured milk. No matter how many nights she'd spent trying to get that scent out of her nostrils—no matter how many times she'd shut away the thought of Sir Wilfred's blood trickling over the flagstone into his own spring box—the memory clung like a dampness, a nightmare to be lived over and over again.

"Elizabeth?" said Napier.

"Wait, I'm remembering." Her eyes snapped open. "All right. Sir Wilfred said, and I quote: *'I didn't touch Arthur. I just stabbed Percy. And, yes, I bribed Hanging Nick Napier and that porter chap. And fixed the blame, I suppose, on Lazonby. But that's it. I liked Arthur. I did. And after I persuaded Hannah to marry me, I meant to visit him. In France. Or wherever he ended up.'* "

"Christ," muttered Napier.

"I think that's exact," she said.

And oddly, having to say it aloud had somehow stiffened her resolve. It was over—or would be, she prayed, once this business of Napier's was done. As the rage inside her had slowly settled these past few days, it was coming increasingly clear to Lisette that somehow she must put this long and awful madness behind her.

Somehow she had to find a way to salvage from the wreckage something like an ordinary life. She had to, for there was no one left to blame. No place else to seek revenge. Her family was dead and she couldn't bring them back. And now she had to forgive herself, somehow, for the horrific injustice she'd done Lord Lazonby—even if the man himself never forgave it.

But the one thing she must not do was lean too hard upon Royden Napier. She no longer disliked him, but Lisette knew that he was the sort of man who would place his pursuit of justice above all else, even his own interests. Hadn't he just proven that with his grandfather?

She straightened on the bench, and set her shoulders resolutely back. "I take no joy in repeating that, Napier," she said quietly. "And just because Sir Wilfred said it, doesn't mean it was the whole truth."

"Aye, but was it a part of the truth?" he muttered, his gaze fixed almost blindly on the distant lake. "I have the sickening suspicion it was."

"Have you ever looked at your father's accounts?" asked Lisette pointedly. "At the time of his death, you must have done."

Napier nodded, swallowing hard. "I did. Once or twice."

"Money like that would be hard to hide."

"There were . . . occasional infusions of cash into the household accounts." Napier's voice sounded strained, almost disembodied. "Yes, more money than his salary could account for. I told myself it was horse racing. Something like that."

"Perhaps it was." Lisette shrugged. "And after all that trickery, Leeton's plan didn't even work. There was no flight to France; Papa took one of his morose spells, tamped it down with a bottle of brandy, then shot himself. A niggling detail, of course, to Sir Wilfred. He still got Hannah's money—and for a time, he was rid of Lazonby, too."

"A tragedy all the way round." Napier fell silent for a moment. "Elizabeth, may I ask one other question?"

She hesitated. "I suppose."

But the question, and the sad look in Napier's eyes when he asked it, threw Lisette off her guard. "When Sir Wilfred said what he said about my father," he pressed, "was Lady Anisha there? Did she overhear?"

Lisette could see that, for whatever reason, Lady Anisha's opinion greatly mattered to Napier. But she also remembered Lazonby's warning. "I think you would have to ask Lady Anisha," she hedged, "if Lord Lazonby will permit it."

Sudden anger exploded across his face. "I'll be damned," Napier growled. "I shall ask the lady what and when I bloody well—"

"*Shh!*" said Lisette abruptly. "Hush!"

Napier halted. "I beg your pardon. My language—"

"No, *over my shoulder,*" she hissed, turning on the bench so that she might lean in and set her cheek next to his. "Lord Hepplewood is watching us through the shrubbery—and he appears, miraculously, both sober and unscathed."

"And we should care?" Napier grunted.

"Yes."

Acting on impulse, Elizabeth lightly brushed her lips over his hard cheekbone. "*There,*" she whispered against his ear. "Now we look like lovers caught out."

She pulled away to smile up at him, but Napier's eyes had gone dark as onyx—and about as penetrable. Worse, the tantalizing scent of his shaving soap had come away on her lips.

"*Elizabeth,*" he whispered, "we can't keep—"

The soft crunch of gravel cut him short. "Ho, what's this!" cried a cheerful voice, severing the moment. "A romantic tryst?"

Lisette looked up to see Hepplewood sauntering around the greenery toward the arbor's entrance. Napier cursed beneath his breath.

"Well met, cousin!" said the earl when he finally drew up before them. "And Miss Colburne. I beg your pardon for interrupting."

His golden locks, Lisette noticed, were still tousled, his eyes still drooping heavily.

Napier stood, and shook his hand. "How do you do, Hepplewood," he said a little churlishly. "May we be of help?"

"Indeed, no, it is I who may be of help to you." With a little flourish, Hepplewood produced a letter, the flap of which was already open. "But first, an apology."

"An apology?" Napier took the letter.

Embarrassment that was obviously feigned sketched over the earl's face. "A letter came for Lord Saint-Bryce," he said, "and Marsh gave it to Gwyneth—just as he's been instructed. I fear none of us considered the possibility that it was *not* for her late father."

"Heavens, no, why would you?" murmured Lisette.

"*Ooh,* was that a leveling blow, Miss Colburne?" Hepplewood winced theatrically. "But you may be unaware that, in his youth, Gwen's father was quite the world traveler and forever receiving letters from points afar and people unknown to us. Since his death, Gwen opens them and sends the sad tidings in turn."

Lisette cast a sarcastic glance at the London postmark. "And this one was from . . . ah, yes. East Kalimantan, Borneo."

Hepplewood laughed. "No, Upper Grosvenor Street," he said. "Miss Colburne, you are quite the pip! And the letter is from Ruthveyn House—Lady Anisha Stafford, to be precise." Here, he turned to Napier. "I had heard, cuz, that you were cutting a swath round Town with a beautiful widow on your arm. How convenient she knew to write you here."

"The lady is a dear friend. I like her to know how to reach me." Napier shoved the letter inside his coat, unread. "Thank you, Hepplewood, but you needn't have troubled yourself."

"Not at all! Not at all!"

Napier turned and bowed to them at once. "My dear, I'm off to Marlborough," he said. "I shall see you at dinner. Hepplewood, your servant."

With that, Napier put his hat back on his head, and set off toward the far end of the arbor.

"Be careful, my dear!" cried Lisette after him. "I shall be here, counting the hours 'til your return."

Napier merely threw up a hand, and kept going.

On impulse, she rushed after him, and brushed his cheek with another kiss. "Will you tell me what you learn in Marlborough?" she whispered, looking brightly up at him. "Tonight?"

Napier cut a glance back at Hepplewood. "If I can."

"You must," she pressed. "And I need to tell you about my conversation with Gwyneth."

"We'll see," he murmured.

Frustrated, Lisette let him go and walked back up the path. Her mind had turned to Napier's letter, and to his reaction upon hearing Lady Anisha's name. They had once been a little more than friends, unless she missed her guess. The notion piqued her curiosity even as it left her oddly unsettled.

But Hepplewood was watching Lisette's approach, a curious little smile on his face. When she reached him, he cut an exaggerated bow and presented his arm.

"May I see you inside, Miss Colburne?" he said blithely. "I should find it the highlight of my day."

"Nothing could give me more pleasure," she said with a tight smile. "I would not miss a moment of your charming company."

"Nor I yours," he said, urging her back up the path. "After all, one ought never cower from the competition. Now which of us, do you reckon, is the better actor?"

She looked at him askance. "My dear Lord Hepplewood," she said, "you'd get my vote. I came up in a hard school, and know a scoundrel when I meet one."

"Do you, by Jove?" he chortled. "And I think *I* know what a woman in love looks like."

"Indeed?" said Lisette, cutting another glance up at him. "I shouldn't have thought you the type to much dwell upon such a prospect."

But the warmth had faded from Hepplewood's smile. "Ah, now there," he said pensively, "you might be wrong, Miss Colburne. But I doubt it much matters."

"It might matter to the lady in question."

"Perhaps—if there still were one," he said on a laugh, his light mood returning. "Miss Willet is sensible of the honor I do her, but she does not love me."

"I shall hope, Lord Hepplewood, that you are the one who's wrong—for both your sakes."

"Oh, Lord." He cast his gaze heavenward, clapping a hand over his heart. "Not another romantic."

"Yes," she said quietly. "Perhaps, in the end, I am."

"Ah, well," he said evenly, letting the hand fall. "You'll get over it like the rest of us—and if you mean to marry *that* hard-hearted misanthrope, you'd better. But enough of that for now. At present, I'm ordered to deliver you to the ladies' salon."

"Are you indeed?"

"Yes." His smile looked more benevolent. "Diana and Gwyneth are preparing for their afternoon walk. I collect they mean to invite you."

*T*witchy as a stallion at Newmarket, Napier strode down the hill and out of sight of the gardens. When the stables came fully in view, he slowed his gait and stopped beneath the canopy of the gnarled apple trees that lined the path.

"Damned arrogant coxcomb," he said, casting a glance back up at the arbor.

But it was not, in truth, the coxcomb who troubled him. Nor was it Anisha.

It was Elizabeth Colburne, whose scent still surrounded him and whose aquamarine, all-seeing gaze seemed eternally to haunt him. Her proximity—her vibrant energy, that innate, unaffected sensuality—Christ, this hell of his own making was going to singe him badly before they were through.

But Elizabeth wasn't young—near twenty-seven if he reckoned it right. And with that air of worldly ennui, she certainly left one the impression she was a woman of experience. Yet despite all this, she seemed innocently unaware of her effect on him.

Could she be that naïve?

Perhaps she was just deliberately tormenting him. Perhaps fools simply got what they deserved. He gave an exasperated sigh; then, setting his back to one of the tree trunks, extracted Anisha's letter and shook it open.

He needn't have bothered.

"Damn it all to hell," he said, his eyes sweeping down the page.

She was married.

Married to Lazonby, who did not deserve her and would never be worthy of her kindness. Or perhaps he was. Napier was no longer sure he was qualified to judge anyone's character—Lazonby's, perhaps, least of all. It was worth remembering that Anisha's husband was the man his father had unfairly persecuted and imprisoned.

God, how it stuck in his craw to admit that, even to himself. To know that Lazonby had been innocent—innocent of murder, at any rate. As to the other—the womanizing and cardsharping—perhaps the man was no longer the scoundrel he'd been. Or perhaps he'd never been a scoundrel at all?

What if none of the accusations hurled at Lazonby had been true?

Dear God, it felt as if his entire life—all that he'd clung to, all that he'd believed in—was slowly turning upside down. He did not tolerate ambiguity with grace. Especially the kind Lazonby—and by extension, Elizabeth—had put into his head. The uncertainty about his father's role in this awful tragedy.

And now he'd learned that a part of his family's fine standard of living had come, not from hard work, nor even from old-fashioned bribery, but from *Duncaster*?

From the time he'd been old enough to understand what a viscount was—what *wealth* and *power* meant—Napier had resented these people—hated them, nearly, for how they'd cast off his father. And now he was left to wonder if Duncaster had paid for the very roof over his head. If Nicholas Napier had been duplicitous and venal.

And if Elizabeth Colburne was, in reality, a murderess.

He had no answers. He knew only that pride usually went before a fall, as his father had perhaps learned. Was it possible that, having grown accustomed to the luxuries Duncaster had so subtly provided his wife, Nicholas Napier had been unable to retrench after her death?

Napier's shoulders slumped against the rough bark. God knew it was expensive to keep up a house in Eaton Square, and almost as expensive to dress and educate a son in the manner of a gentleman.

He did not know the truth. He would, in all likelihood, never know.

But he did know that the man he had so deeply disliked had just married a woman he greatly esteemed. However irrational, it was far easier to turn his wrath in that direction. So he did, shoving the letter back inside his coat—this time with a curse that was vile indeed.

"Gentlemen aren't supposed to use that word," piped a voice from high above.

Still leaning against the tree, Napier tilted his head back and looked up at the pink-cheeked face of Beatrice Tarleton. The height at which she sat left him a little cold with fear.

"I beg your pardon, Bea," said Napier, clamping a hand to his hat to steady it. "I did not know a lady was present.

Could you come down a little closer? Looking up makes me dizzy."

Nimbly, Bea swung one branch lower, sending down a shower of dying blossoms. She was still far beyond his reach. "Mrs. Jansen says calling someone arrogant is naughty, too."

"Mrs. Jansen is right," he agreed. "But a lady generally makes her presence known to a gentleman so that he will know not to use such words in her hearing. Can you make your way all the way down, do you think?"

Bea seemed to consider it. "Why should I?" she finally asked.

"Because I'm going to the stables to choose a mount. I could use the opinion of someone who knows a little about the horses here."

"I'm not allowed in the stables," she said evenly.

She stood on tiptoe now, her armpits hitched casually over a branch no thicker than Napier's wrist, her hands dangling loosely. Napier came away from the trunk and turned around, wishing he knew more about children—and wishing he could remember what it had felt like to climb a tree. To his grown-up eyes, Bea's position looked precarious.

"How about this, Bea," he said honestly. "You're frightening me. I'm afraid you might fall. Or that you cannot get down at all. And I'm thinking I ought to run down the hill to the stables for a ladder. Or a wagonload of hay. Just in case."

"Oh, poo." Beatrice giggled. "I climb up here all the time. And no one ever notices."

Napier was very much afraid that was the case: that while the child was by no means neglected, she was no one's priority now—and in his view, a paid governess did not count.

He managed to smile up at her. "Then kindly indulge my weak nerves by coming down," he said. "I am, after all, a guest—and guests are to be indulged."

Bea blinked down at him. "Gwyneth says you aren't a guest anymore," she countered, dropping down another branch, and sending crumbles of bark raining down. "She says you are Grandpapa's heir now. And that Burlingame will be yours. Is that why Aunt Hepplewood told us we must call you Saint-Bryce?"

She spoke offhandedly, but Napier could hear the worry that lurked behind the words. "Gwyneth is wrong," he said. "Burlingame will never be mine. It belongs to the whole Tarleton family, and always will."

Her face peeked from the canopy of curling apple leaves. "But Burlingame was going to be Papa's," she replied, "until he died."

Napier held up one hand. "Come down, Bea, and let's talk about that," he offered. "I am just your cousin. Not your enemy."

The girl eyed him warily. "When you came before, Papa said you were the police," she said, "and that the police catch bad people. Do you?"

"I do have policemen and detectives who work under me," he agreed, "though I've never been an actual policeman. But yes, I've helped imprison some bad people. That's my job."

She said nothing, but he could see her mind mulling it over. "Do all bad people go to prison?" she finally asked.

"If they break the law, yes, it is to be hoped so." He extended the hand further, and softened his voice. "Bea, I am sorry your father is dead. More sorry than you can know. Will you come down and talk to me? Please?"

Her lip sticking out a fraction, the girl finally clambered down, clever as a little monkey, the branches trembling under her slight weight. When she reached the last, she swung off it handily, sailing to the ground in a billowing *whuff!* of petticoats and muslin.

"Thank you," said Napier sincerely.

Beatrice looked up at him, her eyes blinking against the sun. "You're very tall," she said.

"I am, aren't I?" he said. "My valet despairs of me."

Beatrice flopped down in the tall grass, snapped off a piece, and stuck it in her mouth.

Left with little alternative, Napier joined her. "You must miss your papa terribly," he said. "I did not know him well, but he seemed a cheerful sort of man."

Beatrice heaved a great sigh. "He was," she declared. "We did everything together. Papa said I kept him young."

Napier regarded her gravely. "What sorts of things?"

She lifted both shoulders in an exaggerated motion. "Things," she said. "We collected leaves. And birds' nests. We went to the kennels to see the hounds sometimes, and he taught me to ride a pony. Sometimes, in his study, we would read or play dolls."

Napier lifted both eyebrows. "Dolls?" he said. "I confess, your papa didn't strike me as the type."

"Well, I played with dolls," she conceded, "while he wrote letters. He wrote a lot of letters, so that's where the dolls lived. In his pantry. But I'm too old for them now, I guess."

Napier considered it. "It sounds quite nice," he replied. "I confess, my father and I spent little time together. He was rarely at home, and I was always at school."

At that, Bea's face brightened. "That's why I have Mrs. Jansen."

"She seems an admirable governess," said Napier. "How did you meet her?"

"She was Gwyneth's friend," said the girl, "from school, I think. After Mamma died, Aunt Hepplewood told Papa to send me away for finishing, whatever that is. But Papa would not. So Gwyneth wrote to Mrs. Jansen. And I was *so* glad. I don't *ever* want to leave Burlingame."

"And you shall never need to," said Napier swiftly. "Has that been weighing on you, Bea?"

Again, the exaggerated shrug. "What does that mean," she asked, "*weighing*?"

Napier reached out and plucked a leaf from her long,

blonde ringlets. "I mean, have you been worrying that you might be sent away?" he clarified. "Because you won't be sent away, Bea. Burlingame will always be your home, for as long as you wish it to be."

"Until I'm a hundred?"

"Until you're a hundred and two," said Napier, "at least."

Bea giggled, sounding younger than her years. Then just as quickly, her face fell and her gaze narrowed in a very grown-up way. "Are you *sure* you aren't going to marry Diana?" she asked, lifting her chin. "Mrs. Jansen says Miss Colburne is your fiancée and that you'll marry her instead. And then you will come to live with us."

Napier opened his mouth, then hesitated. It was one thing to lie to his meddling Aunt Hepplewood, but quite another to lie to a child who needed certainty; a child who would someday be dependant upon him for the roof over her head, and perhaps even her financial well-being. He had no idea precisely how her parents had left things, estatewise, or what provisions Duncaster might have made for the child.

A part of him wished he'd never laid eyes on Elizabeth Colburne and her wild red curls. With her cap of demure brown hair and her gentle manners, Diana Jeffers was going to make some man a lovely bride, even if she was a few years past the ideal age for marriage.

But then, Napier preferred mature females. And perhaps, had his judgment not been clouded by the taste of Elizabeth's mouth. The feel of her long, lithe body beneath him . . .

Dear God.

Diana Jeffers really was out of the question.

He sighed aloud. "I think Miss Colburne is very beautiful," he said, "and that we might suit, but nothing is certain until the vows are said. What do you think? Do you wish that I would marry Miss Jeffers instead?"

Bea tossed away her stem of grass, and stared at her lap.

"No, I *don't* wish it!" she said fervently. "Only Aunt Hepplewood wishes it!"

Napier regarded her steadily for a moment. "You sound awfully certain about that," he finally said. "Miss Jeffers was meant to be your new mamma, I know, and perhaps—"

"*I* didn't want her!" the girl interjected. "I never did! And Papa didn't, either. I *know* he didn't—no matter what he said. They were all trying to *make* him do it!"

Her words were so vehement, Napier didn't know how to respond. He had little experience with children, and certainly no experience with a child like Bea. He thought again of her gaze, sometimes so solemn and so steady one might imagine her a decade older. But her laugh still held the innocence of youth.

He was glad of that. Deeply glad.

A little awkwardly, he took Beatrice's hand in his. "Well, Bea, no matter who I marry," he said, patting it, "nothing else need change for you. You will not have a stepmamma. Mrs. Jansen seems happy here. So don't worry your head about the future."

"All right." Bea didn't hold his gaze, but instead drew her hand from his grasp to pluck another stem of grass.

"Well," he said quietly, setting his hands on his thighs. "Someone must be expecting you?"

"Only Mrs. Buttons," she said. "She makes crumpets on Wednesdays, and we eat them with Mrs. Marsh in her sitting room. Sometimes Marsh comes, too."

Napier had no idea why Bea would be permitted to dine belowstairs with the cook and the housekeeper. Nonetheless, such traditions likely provided the child a sense of continuity, and that could only be a good thing.

"I wish," he said honestly, "that I could eat crumpets with you. But for now, Bea, I'd best be off."

"Off to where?" she asked.

"To Marlborough, actually."

Her head swiveled toward him. "What's in Marlborough?" she said. "Why can't you stay here? You're supposed to, if you're the heir."

Napier weighed what to tell her, but he wanted to gauge her reaction, too. "I'm going to call upon Dr. Underwood," he said. "I want to ask him some questions."

Her eyes, hard and suspicious, drilled into him. "What kind of questions?"

Napier felt an odd chill go down his spine. "I want to know what made your father ill," he replied. "I want to know the cause of his death, exactly."

Bea tossed away her grass, and leapt to her feet, anger sketching across her face again. "I already know," she said.

"Beatrice?" said Napier softly. "What, exactly, do you mean?"

"*They* killed him," said the girl, her narrow gaze shooting toward the house. "They did it. They plagued him to death— *deliberately*, too—just like he always said they would."

"Now, Bea—" Napier reached for her hand again.

But Beatrice Tarleton jerked from his grasp, then turned and ran back up the hill.

Napier watched the child go, wondering at her words.

CHAPTER 8

The Wisdom of the Samudrika

In the end, Napier did not return in time for dinner. Out of either vanity or lunacy, Lisette put on her best blue dinner gown and tamed her red curls with blue velvet ribbons, all to no avail. The only person even vaguely impressed was Lord Duncaster, who sat, regal and imperious, at the head of his table, while Gwyneth Tarleton made snide remarks about Lord Hepplewood's pending marriage.

It was enough to cast a pall over the entire room, which was rather a feat since the ceilings soared twenty feet high. By the end of the meal, Diana Jeffers was staring at her plate, her face bloodless. Lady Hepplewood was staring mostly at Gwyneth—or rather, shooting daggers at her—and her visage held plenty of color.

Lisette did not lay eyes upon Napier again until dinner the following day. Afterward, they played a rubber of whist with Gwyneth and Hepplewood, then Napier excused himself, saying he had paperwork due back to Whitehall. Duncaster scowled mightily, but said nothing.

The next evening followed much the same, except that

Diana sang while Mrs. Jansen played the pianoforte. Lisette thought their existence dull, and it made her reconsider the life she'd led in Boston. Harsh and hard it might have been; boring, never.

At breakfast—assuming they crossed paths—Napier took it upon himself to make the most mundane conversation imaginable. Their moments of familiarity seemed at an end. If she invited him to walk with her, he politely put her off with obfuscation and excuses.

Though it stung rather more than it should have done, Lisette saw no alternative but to accept it. None, that was to say, save to trot down the corridor and knock on his bedroom door again—a disconcertingly tempting notion. It was as if Napier's touch had woken something long dormant inside her, and the aching loneliness that so often plagued Lisette now felt more acute than ever.

The truth was, she was almost twenty-eight years old, and save for her earliest childhood years, she had known no intimacy. Since her father's death, she could not recall her heart soaring with elation, or warming with contentment. Perhaps her heart had begun to quiet even before then. And now she could not stop herself from wondering what Napier would say if she offered to share his bed.

It was, of course, a mad, foolish notion. The warmth of a man's body—even his passion—could never assuage true loneliness.

But mightn't it hold it at bay for a time?

Oh, she'd meant what she'd said to Lady Hepplewood about not having expected to marry. But now that her life's objective was over—or, more correctly, had shattered like glass—it was if the black void that constituted the rest of her life might swallow her up whole. And in her heart, Lisette feared that a man—not even one so strong and ruthlessly disciplined as Royden Napier—was apt to drag her from that awful precipice.

And so they muddled on until, by week's end, it appeared her betrothed was avoiding her. Even Lady Hepplewood began to remark upon it, however subtly, and to cast hopeful glances in Diana's direction. Lisette laughingly brushed it off, and declared herself a work widow.

Instead, she tried not to indulge her feminine fantasies, and to honorably uphold her end of their bargain. She distracted Lady Hepplewood at every turn, keeping her away from Napier when they were in company. She snatched every straw of scandal that could be gleaned from Gwyneth or Diana, and from her maid's efforts belowstairs, which reaped a bounteous harvest.

Fanny was reliably informed that Walton, the first footman, having been repeatedly spurned by Mrs. Jansen, was now bedding the village postmistress. The postmistress was married to a large and irascible innkeeper. A bad end was predicted.

It was widely believed Lady Hepplewood had come to hate her late husband—quarrels had been overheard—but no one openly accused her of doing the poor fellow in.

Gwyneth was thought to have Sapphic leanings—and leaned, it was speculated, toward Mrs. Jansen—an eternally popular choice, apparently.

One person who seemed disinterested in Mrs. Jansen, however, was the young Lord Hepplewood, who never spared her a glance. He, it was said, had long been meant for his cousin Anne. But at the end of her come-out Season, Anne had insisted upon the bland, modestly affluent Sir Philip Keaton, more fool she. Hepplewood had gone blithely about his business.

As to matters at Burlingame, the staff accounted Diana Jeffers too timid and inconsequential to be its mistress. The jury was still out on Lisette. And lastly, Napier's man Jolley was thought "a trifle slippery"—an assessment with which Lisette cheerfully agreed.

She kept a mental list of this tittle-tattle, on the off chance Napier would ever trouble himself to ask for it. She also collected the promised letter paper, deftly taking two pieces when one would do, writing on the first while tucking the second away.

She wrote to Mr. Bodkins. She wrote to her old nanny and to Mrs. Fenwick. She even wrote to friends and neighbors in Boston: twice to the Reverend Mr. Bowen, her parish priest, who had been a source of some comfort in her youth. The extra paper she slipped into the competent hands of Jolley, who would rub it almost lovingly between his thumb and forefinger before nodding his thanks like a little bird, then trotting off again.

On the following Monday, the weather turned unaccountably hot and by some odd happenstance everyone came down to breakfast at once. Tempers were not much improved when Lord Hepplewood announced over his kippers that Miss Willet was shortly to visit.

Gwyneth snickered aloud. Diana and Lady Hepplewood glared at her.

Duncaster seemed to hold no opinion on Hepplewood's marital fate. When his plate was finished, he cleared his throat portentously. "Have you given any thought, Saint-Bryce, to Squire Tafton's request?"

Napier looked up, setting his knife down with an awkward clatter. "No, sir," he said. "I had meant to ride to Marlborough again tomorrow."

"Whatever can that boring little man want?" asked Lady Hepplewood irritably. "Surely he's not complaining about drainage again?"

"No, no, nothing to do with land." Duncaster stabbed his fork in Lisette's direction. "Seems Mrs. Tafton is perishing of curiosity about the next Lady Saint-Bryce. She wants them to tea at the Grange."

"Oh, *that*." Lady Hepplewood gave a disdainful sniff. "Any little thing to get a step up on the villagers, I daresay, and show off that child of hers."

Napier caught Lisette's gaze across the table.

"Send your acceptance, my boy," Duncaster ordered, stabbing his fork again. "That's my advice. I could drop off this mortal coil tomorrow. Tafton may be a bag of wind, but Burlingame shares a border with the fellow."

Casting her another glance, Napier lifted one eyebrow. Lisette heard the unasked question. "How kind of the squire," she said brightly. "I should love to meet Mrs. Tafton."

"*Hmph*," said Lady Hepplewood.

Not long after, Diana excused herself. "My leather and silk samples came from Manchester this morning," she said, pushing back her chair. "I shall be in the green bedchamber if anyone needs me."

A look of boredom passed over Lady Hepplewood's face. "Then I shall read on my divan," she said, "but first, Diana, you must fetch my book."

"Of course, Cousin Cordelia."

Gwyneth drained her coffee. "Fine, then I'm spending the morning on the west balcony," she said. "I keep a telescope there, Elizabeth. Mrs. Jansen has quite an expertise in astronomy, if you'd care to have a look some evening? Perhaps we might find your birth constellation."

"Yes, perhaps," said Lisette vaguely, "some night."

But she had no intention of climbing up into the high, open balcony with Gwyneth. With an inward shudder, she remembered the last time anyone had talked to her of stars.

It had happened that terrible day of the Leetons' garden party. Lady Anisha Stafford had manned a gaudy fortune-teller's tent, one of the school's fund-raising endeavors. *The Mysterious Karishma,* the sign had read, *direct from Calcutta.*

Lisette had tried, of course, to avoid her. She had long suspected the lady was Lazonby's lover. But eventually her fellow teachers had dragged her inside, laughing.

Lady Anisha had never seen Lisette in her gray dress and brown wig. But it had struck Lisette at once that there was something entirely unsettling about Anisha, who—despite her outlandish costume—had not looked remotely as if she were playing a parlor game. Instead, she had flicked a glance over Lisette's palm, and declared at once that Lisette was Gemini born, and dangerously ambidextrous.

It had gone downhill after that.

Frighteningly so.

"Like many of your kind, you are of two natures," Lady Anisha had said in a dark, distant voice. *"You are torn in half, your better self being dominated by your lesser self. You will be driven to destruction if you do not have a care. You have let your anger and your determination and your denial of joy push you past rational thought."*

It had been, strangely, the words *denial of joy* that had most infuriated Lisette. She had not wanted to face the ugly reality of what she had done to her life. But when she shoved back her chair and suggested Anisha go to hell and take her nonsense with her, the lady had leaned halfway across the table, refusing to release her hand.

Instead, she had warned her.

"If you continue on, you could lose your moral compass entirely," she had whispered, her fingers caught hard around Lisette's wrist. *"Is that what you wish? You must choose a hand. Right? Or left? You must choose a side. Darkness? Or light?"*

It was a warning that, a mere half hour later, Lisette had wished desperately she had heeded.

She wished she had chosen light.

Instead she'd pursued darkness. The darkness of revenge. And Lord Lazonby and Sir Wilfred had paid a terrible price for it. She had pushed herself to the verge of madness, and in the end, perhaps gone a little over the edge.

Even now the self-loathing roiled inside her, sickening her. Even now she wanted . . . *what*? Absolution? Certainly she wanted Royden Napier never to know the truth about what she'd done. Who she really was in the black pit of her soul.

Yes, that was what she wanted. But it was not apt to happen. He was too good at what he did. Already he knew how she'd persecuted Lazonby. But he wanted her to admit it. And to admit how Sir Wilfred had died. He wanted her to say the words aloud. And *that* she would never do.

Yet she felt drawn to Napier in a way that was deeply troubling. It was almost as if, down in that dark corner of her soul, she *wished* to be caught.

Lisette looked down, and realized her hands were shaking. *Good God.*

Was that what this was? A delicate dance of self-destruction? Only the truly mad did such things. But was she tempting fate by challenging Napier? Or had she begun to desire him to an irrational degree? Was she searching for her own small measure of joy and intimacy—but in the most dangerous place imaginable?

"My dear?" The voice came from far away.

Lisette looked around the breakfast parlor to see that everyone had vanished save Napier and his grandfather.

She shoved back her chair a little too harshly. "I'm going to find Diana," she blurted. "Perhaps . . . perhaps I can learn something about décor."

Napier sat at one end of the table, already looking like lord and master and staring at her through those dark, hard eyes as if he could read her very thoughts. Disconcerted, Lisette hastened from the room.

Almost at once, however, Lisette heard someone push away from the table. Soon ominous footsteps were following her. *Napier.* Even now she knew the sound of that long, purposeful stride. She hastened around the corner but he caught up with her just beyond the library doors.

"Elizabeth, wait," he ordered.

She stopped, but did not turn around.

"Elizabeth, what is it?" he said, stepping around to block her path.

"What?" she managed. "Nothing. Why?"

Impatience sketched across his face. "You looked as if you'd seen a ghost."

She flashed a weak smile. "We all of us have a few, I daresay."

At that, his eyes unexpectedly softened. *"Elizabeth,"* he said chidingly, taking her hand.

Napier drew her from the passageway through the open door of the library, which smelled of old books and warm sunlight. She went reluctantly, and when she looked up, his eyes were searching her face again. It was as she'd feared: the man missed nothing.

"It is hard for me to fathom," he said quietly, "that you, of all people, might be afraid of me."

"Afraid of you?" she lightly echoed. "What a fanciful notion."

His gaze was wary. "I thought perhaps you'd rather not go to Tafton's," he said. "Alone. With me. Besides, you never agreed to be trotted across Wiltshire like some broodmare on display."

Lisette shrugged. "It's nothing to me. I shan't have to live cheek by jowl with these people."

"Then what?" he pressed. "Just now—in the breakfast room—your hands were shaking. You looked a little haunted."

She gave a faint laugh. "In my experience," she said, "whenever a person is haunted by something, it's usually just the specter of their own past."

"And is that it?" he asked, his hand still holding her wrist—much as Lady Anisha had done, as if they were both determined to make her face what she was. "I wouldn't know, you see," he went on, gentling his tone. "You've shared nothing about yourself with me."

Her smile faltered. "Nor do I mean to," she said, shaking off his grip.

The concern in his eyes faded a bit. "You really do not trust me, do you?"

"Not in that way," she whispered, stepping back a pace. "How can I? And you don't trust me. We both of us know what the other is, Napier."

He dragged a hand through his hair, looking suddenly bedeviled. "Yes, I suppose," he said. "I mean . . . damn, I don't know what I mean. I'm just trying to work my mind around what's between us. I mean, we understand one another—what's going on here—don't we?"

Lisette hardly knew what he was asking, let alone how to answer. Her life now seemed a pointless shambles, and he was, perhaps, her greatest threat. But she could not deny the inexplicable wish to lean upon that broad shoulder—to spill out the whole, sordid truth.

But what a mistake that would be.

She chose a more ambiguous route. "We have an understanding, yes," she acknowledged. "But we should neither of us forget that I'm here under duress, and that you're still the assistant police commissioner."

His jaw hardened stubbornly. "That's not what I meant," he said. "I'm speaking of that . . . that dangerous physical attraction that keeps flaring between us. And no, I don't flatter myself. I know the look of desire when it kindles in a woman's eyes."

"Desire?" Lisette forced herself to hold his gaze. "No, Napier, I won't deny it. In fact, I rather doubt women deny you much of anything."

His lips twitched. "You'd be surprised," he said.

Lisette lifted one shoulder. "In any case, I thought you were avoiding me rather pointedly."

"Has it ever occurred to you, Elizabeth, that I might be doing so for your own good?"

She managed a light laugh. "How patronizing that sounds," she said. "I think you may depend upon me to take care of my own best interests. Didn't you once say as much?"

"Then perhaps my restraint is for *my* own good," he gritted. "And I'd as soon not make a habit, my dear, of pressing my attentions where they aren't wanted."

It was her chance, she realized. Moreover, she wanted suddenly to sever that ruthless self-control. "Then *perhaps*," she said, dropping her voice, "you should rethink your strategy?"

It was madness, of course, to step closer. Later, she was unable to understand why, but in that moment she yearned to torment him. To set her hand to the wide expanse of his chest and lean into the strength and certainty that seemed to flow from him. To make him acknowledge with his body the words that had just passed his lips.

It was the faintest thing, a mere grazing of skin that was hardly a kiss at all, yet the heat of his mouth seared her. Lisette drew away, her lashes falling half shut, and waited.

But not long.

On a soft oath, Napier yanked her hard against him, one arm catching around her waist. He lowered his face to hers, and she slanted her head. And for an instant, time hung suspended, that wide, sensual mouth lingering over hers a mere two inches away.

"*Yes?*" he rasped, his breath warm on her cheek.

"*Yes*," she said.

Napier obliged her. And this time, when he opened his mouth over hers, it was a slow and deliberate plundering. Willingly she surrendered, opening beneath him and allowing his tongue to curl sinuously around hers.

His mouth was surprisingly soft, his grip enticingly hard. His free hand cupped her cheek, stilling her face—unnecessarily, for her every muscle had melted—as his powerful arm bound her to him. Heat rose between them, redolent with the scent of his shaving soap. Again and again he thrust deeply, taking his time. Tasting her thoroughly.

Rising onto her toes, Lisette invited him to deepen the kiss. The sensation sent something warm and needy curling through her; it twirled around her heart, then spiraled into her belly, drawing her taut with that rushing tide of sensation she was beginning to crave.

It was irrational. So unwise. And yet something inside her pulled her into his fire—as if she might be purified by the heat of him, and unfurled anew like a flower from the ashes.

On a soft moan, Lisette let her hands roam over the hard muscles of his waist, and skate up his back. He shivered at the touch and let his lips slide over one corner of her mouth. They brushed lightly over her cheek, then over her ear, his parted lips warm against her skin.

"*Elizabeth,*" he whispered, "*I want—*"

Just then, the sharp *clack! clack!* of Lady Hepplewood's cane cut into Lisette's consciousness. They sprang apart just as the old woman turned into the room.

"Well," she declared, one eye narrowed assessingly. "I'd begun to wonder if the two of you were suffering buyer's remorse."

Napier had gone dark as a thunderhead. "You may set your mind at ease on that score, ma'am," he said gruffly, "but I'd prefer—"

Lady Hepplewood threw up a staying hand, ivory lace falling elegantly around her wrist. "Never mind, Saint-Bryce; you are dismissed," she said crisply. "My dear Miss Colburne, you are about to part ways with that lovely cashmere shawl. One side is trailing the carpet."

His jaw twitching a little ominously, Napier cut Lisette

one last, lingering look, then bowed stiffly to Lady Hepplewood, his gaze still hot with either passion or temper. With Napier, it was hard to say. But the look warned unequivocally that they were not done.

Lady Hepplewood, apparently, disagreed—at least for the moment.

"Now, Miss Colburne," she said airily, tossing a thin, finely boned hand at the shelves. "Diana foolishly reshelved the book I wished to read. Be so good as to go up those little steps and fetch me down a copy of Mr. Sterne's *Sentimental Journey.* I fear I'm not as nimble as I once was."

"Of course, ma'am."

Her knees still molten jelly, Lisette managed to roll the ladder into place before Napier's footsteps had faded down the passageway. She went up and, trailing her finger along the leather spines, saw that Burlingame's great library held three copies of Sterne's classic travelogue—an unnecessary extravagance, in her view. But she tugged one out, relieved to see her hand did not shake.

After going back down again, she placed it in the old lady's hands. "I think this is what you want, ma'am."

Lady Hepplewood scarcely regarded it. "Miss Colburne," she said coolly, "might I presume upon our impending kinship?"

Lisette was instantly on guard. "Presume in what way, ma'am?"

"To give advice," said the old woman. "I was wondering, you see, if you fancy yourself in love with Saint-Bryce."

Lisette weighed her answer. "I hold him in great esteem," she hedged. "I think him honest and capable—and handsome in his own way. And I believe we shall be compatible."

"An excellent response." A smile seemed to play at Lady Hepplewood's lips. "In our world, Miss Colburne, it does not do for a wife to become overly attached to her husband."

"I confess, I never thought of it."

"Then I beg you will consider it now." Lady Hepplewood arched one imperious eyebrow. "Indeed, I beg you will not succumb to bourgeois notions and imagine Saint-Bryce must be the great love of your life. If you do, you'll find it a source of never-ending disappointment. But I daresay you already knew that."

It was a veiled reference, perhaps, to her parents' marriage. Or perhaps Lady Hepplewood knew something about Napier's past that Lisette did not?

On the other hand, perhaps the old woman was just trying to spook her away. If so, then Lisette's bland answer had probably dashed that hope altogether. But it scarcely mattered; she was not going to be Napier's wife.

After giving Lady Hepplewood a faint curtsy, Lisette thanked her, then left the old woman perched like a black-bird on a stiff-backed chair by the windows. In the passageway, she exhaled in relief as she turned in the opposite direction from the one Napier had taken. But her mind had turned back to that kiss.

Really, had she quite parted ways with good sense? Once this sham of a betrothal was at an end, she would have to live with the scandal and the memories. The scandal she could run from—and likely would. But another kiss like that, and she feared the memories might follow her to the ends of the earth.

She regained herself somewhat on the long hike through the house, eventually making her way into Lady Hepplewood's apartments. This required, however, a great many twists and turns along with the aid of a footman—not the philandering Walton, but the more genial fellow whose name at that moment escaped her.

Upon passing through the double reception room, Lisette was thankful the dashing, disreputable Lord Hepplewood was nowhere to be seen. As she followed the servant deeper into the apartment, Lisette realized Duncaster's sister had been given the use of an entire floor in the west pavilion, a space larger than the whole of Lisette's cottage and encompassing a private dining room, the withdrawing room, a parlor, a gentleman's study, and, she later realized, at least six bedchambers.

For a girl born in a narrow, rented town house, the wealth required to maintain such a place was impossible to fathom. Moreover, all the rooms seemed washed with light, and decorated in elegant but neutral shades complemented by furniture that appeared quite new.

The footman stopped and bowed with a flourish of his hand. "The bedchambers lie along this corridor, miss."

"Thank you, er . . . Prater, is it not?"

Prater smiled. "Indeed. Shall I show you which door?"

She smiled gratefully. "Yes, please."

After following him around another corner, Lisette turned into the last bedchamber. Inside, Diana stood over a heap of billowing green; a waist-high heap of drapery fabric and watered silk wall covering.

In fact, the entire room was in disarray, the windows and all the walls save one were stripped down to wood and plaster, and a ladder sat against one wall as if painting were about to begin. A grand suite of walnut furniture had been shoved against the wall that had not yet been stripped, along with a divan lushly upholstered in green brocade that perfectly matched the elaborate velvet bed hangings. The odor of vinegar was strong in the air.

At the sound of door hinges, Diana spun around. "Oh, Elizabeth," she said a little breathlessly. "What a surprise."

"I hope I'm not interrupting?"

"Not at all." But upon seeing the footman, Diana's brow furrowed. "Oh, and Prater—"

"Yes, miss?" said the servant, already half out the door.

"Was I not clear that this was all to be hauled away and

burnt?" she said, gesturing at the heap of green. "And last week, if memory serves."

"We've been short, miss," said the servant apologetically, "what with Walton ill."

"Walton was not so ill he couldn't go haring off to the village Sunday." Diana spoke in a peevish, somewhat girlish tone. "Was he not assigned to help me here? Honestly, I might as well be a lamp table in this house, for all the heed I'm paid."

"Beg pardon, miss," said Prater as he drew the door shut. "I'll ask leave to help you."

Lisette was surveying the disarray. "Oh, dear, I *am* interrupting," she said, just inside the threshold. "I'm sorry."

The furrow fell from Diana's brow. "Oh, not at all." Her voice was at times so soft as to be nearly inaudible. "Are you hiding from Gwyneth and her frightful telescope?"

Lisette managed to grin. "I'm hiding from any number of people," she acknowledged. "I think we might make a list."

"Well, you may take safe harbor here," said Diana, motioning toward a worktable in the middle of the room. "Come see my samples. And do forgive my speaking so sharply to Prater. It's really not his job to help me here. It's Walton's. He began tearing all this down, then left it in a heap with one wall not finished."

Lisette laughed. "From what my maid reports, Walton suffers frightfully from lovesickness," she said, "but if it helps, he actually has been very ill with a dyspeptic stomach."

Diana's mouth quirked. "Yes, and won't Mrs. Boothe be disappointed to hear it."

Mrs. Boothe, Lisette had learned, was the postmistress. Diana had laid out, Lisette noticed, a row of leather samples alongside the fabric from the previous week, obviously attempting to pair something up.

For a time, Lisette merely watched Diana work. Her hands were quick and clever—and she was not, after all, a nail biter. Instead she had a short third finger, and for a moment Lisette feared an accident. But the nail was intact; it was merely an anomaly.

She must have noticed Lisette staring. "Curious, isn't it?"

"I'm sorry." Lisette felt her face heat. "I didn't mean to stare."

Diana laughed. "Gwyneth has a short, flat thumb," she said, "and Tony's middle toe is curiously long. We used to call ourselves the Odd Fingers. We even had a club—and we wouldn't let Anne join. Cruel, weren't we?"

Lisette smiled. She wondered what the absent Anne was like. "Which of you is eldest?" she asked.

"Gwyneth, then Tony, then me, then Anne," she said, her brow furrowed. "Yes, that's right. Anne is younger than me, but not by much."

But a fabric had caught Lisette's eye. "Ooh, I like this silk." She reached across the table to point at a piece of champagne-colored fabric.

"Yes, I thought perhaps that for the draperies," said Diana, who was pinning a slightly darker piece to a large square of muslin. "Gwyneth liked it. But it isn't silk."

Lisette picked up the loose sample. "But it has a sort of sheen to it," she murmured, fingering it. "What is it?"

"It's a fine cotton," said Diana around a pin now stuck in her mouth. "The manufacturing process is new. The fibers are treated with chemicals that make it shiny."

"Truly?" Lisette was amazed.

Diana blushed. "My mother was from a Lancashire milling family."

Lisette tried not to look astonished, but she thought again of Lady Hepplewood's disdain toward her son's fiancée. Miss Willet was from an industrial family, too.

"Well, many a man has made a success of himself in that line of work," said Lisette evenly.

Diana took out the pin, deftly stabbing it into her fabric sample. "I'm not sure Grandpapa did," she said, "though mother was brought up to be a lady. My uncle is still trying to drag that old mill back from the brink. He sent me all these fabrics."

She sounded suddenly sad, and a little wistful.

"Tell me about your mother," Lisette suggested. "What was she like?"

Diana's gaze instantly softened. "Mamma was very beautiful," she said, going to the nearest window and holding her creation to the light. "And exceptionally well educated. I think that's what drew Lady Hepplewood to her in the first place."

"Lady Hepplewood?"

"Oh, yes." Diana glanced back from the window. "Did you not know? Mamma was Tony's first governess. She met Papa her very first day at Loughford. Do you think this filters the light sufficiently?"

Lisette set her head to one side. "We're facing a little north, so it should do," she said. "I'd forgotten your father was Hepplewood's estate agent, as well as his cousin."

"But Papa was only visiting then," said Diana, coming back to the table. "He was just up from university, trying to settle on a career. He wanted Hepplewood's advice."

Lisette smiled. "Was it love at first sight?"

Diana laughed again. "Mamma said that, for her, it was," she said. "I think Papa did not fall completely prostrate at her feet until he returned to take up his post. How did your parents meet?"

At Lisette's wince, Diana stuck out her lip. "Oh, come, I adore romantic stories!"

"I sometimes wonder how romantic it was," said Lisette on a laugh. "My mother was a seventeen-year-old debutante and Papa was society's greatest scoundrel. He said he fell in love with her the moment their eyes met. His flirtation caused a frightful scandal. In the end, though, they did marry."

Diana's eyes were shining. "And did they live happily ever after?"

"Oh, I don't know." Lisette shrugged. "Does anyone, really?"

"Yes." Diana circled around the table to her. "Oh, yes, Elizabeth, they do! Don't you plan to live happily ever after with Lord Saint-Bryce?"

Coming on the heels of Lady Hepplewood's philosophy of love, Diana's optimism was refreshing. "Well, one always hopes for happiness," she said vaguely. "But sometimes fate intervenes in ways one cannot expect."

"But you *do* love him, do you not?" Diana surprised Lisette by seizing both her hands. "Oh, my dear, if you do not, you must on no account marry him. Please, promise me you will not. Nothing should stand in the way of true love—and if you marry now, you'll never find it."

Lisette was confused. "But . . . you were going to marry the previous baron," she said.

Diana hesitated for a heartbeat. "Well, my situation was different," she said, squeezing Lisette's hands hard. "But I was so very fond of Saint-Bryce. I had known him since childhood. He was a fine man. A good man."

"And Lady Hepplewood insisted," Lisette added, "didn't she?"

Diana cut her gaze away.

"Diana, did you have to marry him?" she asked, dropping her voice. "I mean, you can marry elsewhere, can you not? You . . . you have been provided for?"

Diana turned back, her eyes softening almost tenderly. "Oh, yes!" she said. "Well provided for. Lord Hepplewood set aside twenty thousand pounds as my marriage settlement in gratitude to Papa. As to Papa, he has done very well for himself. He invests in railroads. I'm his only child."

"Then you have only to meet your knight in shining

armor," said Lisette brightly. "But Diana, you aren't apt to meet him here. You . . . why, you should go to London. You should have a Season."

Diana shrugged. "I did; I came out with Anne," she said, returning to her drapery samples. "Cousin Cordelia sponsored us the same year. But I'm beyond such nonsense now. Honestly, I should rather we all just went home."

"Home, to your father?"

"Home to Northumberland." Diana did not quite meet her gaze. "Yes, to Papa. To . . . all of it, really."

At last Lisette saw the truth. "Oh, Diana," she murmured, "do you dislike it here so very much?"

For a time, Diana just fiddled with her fabrics. "We don't belong here," she finally said, crushing a wad of cream-colored linen onto the table. "It's Gwyneth's house to run now—well, until Duncaster dies—and she doesn't want anyone's help. She certainly didn't want me to marry her father. Anne affirmatively hates me. Cousin Cordelia is miserable and if Tony stays in Town, he's apt to get . . . well, all I'm saying is I don't know why we must stay on."

"Oh, Diana . . ."

Diana gave a sharp sigh. "Lord, I must sound so ungrateful!" she said. "Yes, Cousin Cordelia says we will probably take a little house in Town eventually. And she says Gwyneth must go as well, and stop keeping Mrs. Jansen from her duties."

But she did not look especially happy about any of it. Lisette was beginning to think Diana and Lady Hepplewood were like millstones around each other's necks. As to Gwyneth and Lady Hepplewood—or Gwyneth and Mrs. Jansen—Lisette dared not speculate.

"Then next year, perhaps Town will have more appeal," she said neutrally.

"Well, we might have gone this year." Diana had opened

a small pasteboard box filled with tassels and was poking through it. "But everyone's in mourning."

Lisette propped one hip on the edge of the table and watched her work for a moment. "Diana," she said curiously, "how did Lord Saint-Bryce die? I never heard."

Diana looked up from the box. "Apoplexy, Dr. Underwood said, though for a time we thought he might recover."

"So it was not . . . sudden?"

"No, he survived for a time," she said. "But he could not speak, and his right arm and leg would not work. Walton and Prater had to carry him to his bed."

"Well, thank goodness they found him," said Lisette.

"But they didn't," she said, blinking rapidly. "*I* did."

"You did?" Lisette echoed. "Oh, Diana, how terrible!"

She looked suddenly grief stricken. "I was passing by his study on my way to the schoolroom," she said. "I heard this frightful thud and just knew something bad had happened. When I went in, he could not speak. Fortunately, Walton and Prater were just around the corner."

"Well," said Lisette pensively. "How life does change, and in the twinkling of an eye. Speaking of which—will Lady Hepplewood reconcile herself, do you think, to Miss Willet?"

Diana laughed. "Oh, that betrothal will never last," she said, holding the tassels straight out in both hands. "Which do you think? The blue? Or the gold?"

"Well, there isn't much color in the main reception rooms," remarked Lisette, who had begun to drift about the bedchamber. "They are neutral, but pleasingly so."

"I know," said Diana. "I chose all the furnishings. I love ivories and golds. And Cousin Cordelia really does not care, so long as everything is of the finest quality imaginable."

"Is that what Loughford looks like?" Lisette stopped by the hearth, and turned. "Everything of the finest quality?"

"Oh, yes, but everything there is old," said Diana, warming to the topic. "Classically so. Loughford is—oh, it is, I think, the most beautiful house on earth."

"And yet it is in disrepair," said Lisette.

Diana's head jerked up from her work. "Who told you that?"

Lisette felt her eyes widen. "I—why, it was Gwyneth, I think."

"Gwyneth is full of nonsense." Diana sounded exasperated. "The house is well kept."

"Perhaps Lady Hepplewood merely suggested otherwise to her brother?" Lisette lightly suggested. "Perhaps she wished an excuse to stay here instead?"

Diana opened her mouth, then shut it again, apparently pondering. "That may be so," she finally admitted. "But the pair of them—Duncaster and his sister—are thick as thieves."

"Ah."

Lisette continued to drift for a time, admiring the elegant chimneypiece and a landscape hanging upon it. Diana pinned the samples and took them to the window in turn, occasionally asking her opinion. When she'd settled on the champagne with gold tassels with a white muslin backing, Diana turned to the pieces of leather—Lady Hepplewood wished to have a pair of sofas to flank the hearth, she said.

It seemed a frightful extravagance for a room to be used only on occasion, and Lisette could only conclude Lady Hepplewood suffered no shortage of funds. Or perhaps Duncaster gave her an allowance for the furnishings? Or paid the bills outright?

Musing on it, Lisette bent down and picked up an oddly pierced kettle that hung from a long hook in the firebox. "This is lovely," she remarked.

"Isn't it?" said Diana, sorting out her scraps. "Saint-Bryce—Gwyneth's father, I mean—brought it home from his travels in the Orient—or was it was Africa? He was a great traveler in his youth. I don't know what the thing's purpose was—some heathen ceremony, no doubt—but we found it useful for steaming herbs."

The thing was remarkably ornate and heavy, with a chamber for water, and a pierced platform above. "What sort of herbs?" she asked.

Diana took a pin from her mouth. "Like lavender and rosemary for restlessness," she said, "or eucalyptus for congestion. Lord Hepplewood rested far better when it was steaming."

"How soothing," she said, putting it back on it's hook. "Well, have you decided?"

"No, come look," asked Diana a little fretfully. "Do you think this will alter in the afternoon light?"

Lisette put the contraption back and returned to the table. As they began another round of pinning and choosing, she began gently to pry. "Lord Hepplewood's last days must have been difficult for Lady Hepplewood," she said absently. "I understand he had become senile?"

Diana flicked her gaze up. "At first he was just weak and a little confused," she said. "Toward the end, though, yes, he began to ramble incoherently."

Lisette leaned over the table. "Is that why they argued so often?" she asked, dropping her voice conspiratorially. "Had he gone out of his head? Become hard to manage?"

Lips pursed, Diana set her pincushion aside. "Lord Hepplewood wanted us all to go home," she said. "Perhaps they quarreled about that once or twice. I believe that . . . well, perhaps he feared he was dying? And one always wishes, I think, to die at home in one's own bed."

"But Lady Hepplewood did not wish to return?"

Diana shook her head.

"Why?"

Diana lifted her slender, birdlike shoulders. "Cousin

Cordelia says Northumberland is too cold," she said. "And that it's time Tony got out on his own, and experienced a taste of life in London."

"Apparently he got more than a taste," said Lisette dryly. "Besides, he must be nearly my age. Had he never ventured from home?"

"He spent, I think, two years at Oxford," said Diana, "but it did not suit him. And he whiled away a Season or two in London, but nothing came of it."

Lisette was confused. "When the late earl was working in London, did Tony and Lady Hepplewood not accompany him?"

"Sometimes." Diana picked a bit of lint from her fabric. "Generally, though, he took the train down alone, and stayed in Clarges Street," she said. "Tony never seemed to have much interest in politics—and until recently, no interest in society."

It was odd, thought Lisette. The new Earl of Hepplewood did not sound quite as bad as the prodigal Napier had described. Perhaps it was true that Diana had blinders on where Tony was concerned.

Lisette pondered how to ask her next question, and came up with nothing tactful. "Duncaster told us Hepplewood accused Lady Hepplewood of trying to kill him," she said quietly. "He didn't credit it, of course. And then there were some strange letters Hepplewood wrote to Whitehall . . ."

"Letters?" Diana looked stricken, her head jerking up like a startled deer. "Is that why Napier—Lord Saint-Bryce—started coming here?"

"I'm not perfectly sure." Lisette shrugged. "We don't often discuss his work. Did you help care for Lord Hepplewood?"

Diana swallowed hard, and nodded. "We all did. I sat with him almost every day. Gwyneth, too. When he was ill, we soothed his brow with cool compresses and cajoled him into taking his beef tea. We took turns reading the Bible, and even the newspapers."

"You must have loved him very much," said Lisette softly.

"I did!" She looked suddenly as if she might burst into tears. "He was—why, he was like a grandfather to me. I owed him *everything*. I was devastated when he died. We all were."

"Even Lady Hepplewood?"

"Yes." Diana nodded vigorously. "Oh, yes, even given their age difference, theirs was a love match. In later years, yes, they may have had quarrels. What couple does not?"

It was precisely what Duncaster had said—and it left Lisette deeply puzzled. In her admittedly limited experience, quarrels came early in a relationship, not after long years of marriage.

She opened her mouth to press the issue but was interrupted when the door swung open again. It was Prater, who had cast off his livery in favor of a long canvas apron.

"Marsh has given me leave to help you, Miss Jeffers," he said. "Just tell me what I'm to do."

With a murmured apology to Lisette, Diana excused herself and went to the pile of discarded green fabrics. Lisette watched for a moment, her mind turning over all that she had learned. But Diana was obviously well occupied now.

After a murmured good-bye and an absent wave, Lisette began the long trek back to her bedchamber, feeling oddly uneasy—and more uncertain—than ever.

CHAPTER 9

Every True and Perfect Thing

"All the world's a stage," Shakespeare once wrote, "and all the men and women merely players." And in Royden Napier's estimation, no one embraced that concept more thoroughly than his temporary fiancée. Even he, long hardened by skepticism, could at times believe the infernal woman half in love with him.

The resulting emotions left him feeling perplexed and oddly thwarted.

Over tea at Squire Tafton's tidy manor on a graying afternoon, Elizabeth played the doting wife-to-be to perfection, tucking close against him on Mrs. Tafton's snug camel-backed settee, and gazing adoringly up at him at every opportunity.

With her warm scent wafting up to tease at his nostrils, Elizabeth regaled their hosts with hilarious anecdotes from his childhood—made entirely of whole cloth, but gleaned, she glibly lied, from his dear old nanny. Then she explained in dramatic detail how her eyes had first met Napier's across a crowded drawing room. She had known at once, Elizabeth declared on a breathless sigh, that he was *The One*.

The squire smiled, and declared Napier the most fortunate of men.

Napier thought he was instead the most stupid—and perhaps the most besotted—for listening to Elizabeth's tales even a tiny bit wistfully. She was patently dangerous. And he—well, when in God's name had *he* turned starry-eyed?

He was the last man on earth who should have done so. As a child, he'd never even read fairy tales, let alone believed them. In his work at Number Four, he dealt on a daily basis with the darkest deeds a man's soul could conceal. Oh, he had known women—delightful, deeply desirable women, some of them—and had the honor of bedding a few. But not a one had made him feel a hearts-and-flowers sort of longing.

And he didn't feel it now, damn it.

What he felt was lust, he assured himself. A burning, seething lust for a woman who was a near stranger to veracity—a lust he'd half a notion to put to an end in that most expedient and effective of ways: by taking the red-haired vixen up on the suggestion that sometimes lingered in her eyes.

Suddenly, Napier realized that, for decency's sake, he needed to shift a little bit away from said vixen.

He forced his focus mind back to his hosts and imagined *them* naked in bed. It was an effective countermeasure, his burgeoning erection shriveling at once. Missing several teeth, Tafton was a lanky, sprawling, good-natured fellow who took his tea with more enthusiasm than grace.

His wife was round and plump, and almost shyly bedazzled by her guests. Unaccustomed as he was to blinding anyone with his charm, Napier tried not to snort out loud.

As to Elizabeth, she quickly set Mrs. Tafton at ease. Too

much at ease, perhaps, for Napier's comfort, because as soon as the tea tray was removed, Mrs. Tafton asked a little wistfully if Miss Colburne would care to see the newest little Tafton?

For the first time, Napier saw a look of grave uncertainty dash across Elizabeth's face. But it was quickly veiled.

"Oh, yes, if you please, ma'am," she said breathlessly. "It would be my greatest pleasure."

"We have our two girls, both half grown," said Tafton once his wife disappeared up the staircase, "and the apples of my eyes they are. But a son—well, I don't mind telling you, my lord—we'd pretty nearly given up hope."

Napier understood that, to a country squire, a son was of the utmost importance. Daughters, it was to be hoped, would marry well and go on to live their own lives with whatever family they married into. But a son was expected to stay behind, to help his father run the farm, and in time, run it himself.

In a trice, Mrs. Tafton was back down the stairs with a bundle in her arms, a young housemaid trailing dutifully behind. "And here is our Andrew, Miss Colburne," she declared, bending over to present him for Elizabeth's inspection. "Just up from his nap, he is, so in a fine temper, too."

Napier leaned over and dutifully declared the infant the handsomest of children—which, in his limited experience, was perfectly true. Andrew Tafton had the roundest blue eyes he'd ever seen, and a pair of fat, cherubic cheeks to go with them. And when the child encircled Elizabeth's index finger in one of his tiny fists, kicking his feet with such joy and vigor, Napier felt something almost painful tug inside his heart.

But Elizabeth merely sat speechless, her face gone a little pale.

Mrs. Tafton seemed not to notice, and thrust the child at her. "Would you care to hold him in your lap, Miss Colburne?"

Elizabeth seemed to return to herself with a little jerk. "Oh, *yes*," she whispered, extending her arms.

Mrs. Tafton placed the bundle gently in her arms, and for an instant, Elizabeth sat rigidly forward on the sofa, the child borne awkwardly across her elbows.

"Oh, you may tuck him close, my dear," said the squire's wife dotingly. "Andrew shan't shatter, I promise."

At that, Elizabeth cast a shining, almost hopeful gaze up at Mrs. Tafton, then drew the child to her breast. Fisting both hands, the babe yawned hugely, then relaxed into a drowse again, his pale, feathery lashes sweeping half shut.

For a time the room was held captive, as Elizabeth rocked the child and cooed the silliest things while the squire and his wife looked on with delight. But it was not the happiness upon his hosts' face that tore at Napier's heart.

It was the look upon Elizabeth's.

As she gazed down at the child held so gingerly to her heart, her soft expression held both joy and sorrow, and told him more than a thousand words might have done.

He wondered, fleetingly, if she were unable to bear children. She was some years past the age when a woman would be expected to marry, and God knew she was beautiful in an unusual way. But many men, he knew, simply would not consider taking a barren wife—though the very word grated on Napier. It was cold term, and full of ugly implications.

And in her case, it seemed especially cruel, for a woman of Elizabeth's intelligence and determination would have so much more to give a man than a mere child.

Yet it was her intelligence and determination that had brought her life perilously near ruin, Napier suspected. Perhaps that accounted for her unwed, childless state? Perhaps Elizabeth's priorities had required her to coldly pare away certain choices from her life.

What a shame—and what a loss—were that true.

Soon enough, however, Elizabeth passed the child back to Mrs. Tafton, her face fixed into that smooth, smiling countenance again, her every true emotion carefully masked. There was no point, he realized, in mentioning the fleeting pain he'd seen on her face. It couldn't be his concern. And he knew Elizabeth would have denied the emotion.

When at last they had taken their leave of the squire and his lady, Napier handed Elizabeth back up into their borrowed curricle, and tried to forget how she'd looked with the child tucked to her breast.

"Well, how did that go?" she murmured when he leapt up beside her.

He cut her a dark, sidelong glance. "Those poor people are destined be twice disillusioned," he muttered, snatching up the reins. "Once when the wedding falls through, and again when it dawns on them what a sorry specimen of landed gentry they're getting for a neighbor."

Elizabeth gave an unladylike guffaw, sounding entirely recovered. "At least you've begun to accept your fate."

"Which fate would that be?" he said quietly, giving the reins a snap. "The fact that you wouldn't have me? Or my pending lord-of-the-manor incompetence?"

At that, the laughter left Elizabeth's eyes, and she looked at him very oddly.

Damned bloody idiot, he thought.

Where had those words come from? But her mouth slowly twisted into a wry smile. "Oh, I think we're both too jaded to believe our own lies," she said. "But as to you, Napier, I think you give yourself too little credit."

"Oh?" he managed, cutting her another sidling glance. "How's that?"

She waved a dismissive hand. "Why, managing an estate like Burlingame Court cannot be any more difficult than managing the Metropolitan Police—vastly easier, I daresay."

"I can't think how," he said, "when I scarcely know corn from hay."

"Do you know every street corner and watch-box in greater London? Every magistrate in Westminster? All the laws of the land?"

"No, but—"

"No, but you administer justice all the same," she interjected. "You'll find administering an estate no different. I expect it's more about having a knack for management, and a grasp of human nature. It is not about one's book knowledge, for that can be had from . . . well, *books*."

Oddly, her opinion reassured Napier, though she could not have known much more on the subject than he did. "Speaking of a knack for management," he said dryly, "you managed our hosts rather handily."

She looked at him archly. "Is that not what I was employed to do?"

"You do it rather too well," he complained. "You're charming and witty and beautiful—and I'll be thought an idiot and a cad when you throw me off."

"Oh, Napier, such lofty compliments! Careful your tongue doesn't turn black." She lifted her chin, eyes sparkling green with mischief in the afternoon light. "Besides, perhaps you will throw me off instead?"

"And be thought an outright scoundrel?" he said, frowning. "Come, Elizabeth. We had this discussion somewhere between Twyford and Reading. I cannot do it."

Elizabeth sat uneasily at his elbow as they spun between Squire Tafton's gateposts and onto the village road. Suddenly, she glanced back over her shoulder with a wistful expression. "I liked them, but they will forget about us soon enough," she said in a voice that held more hope than certainty. "Won't they? Everyone, I mean. We will go back to London, and if God is kind, your grandfather will live a while yet. We will go back to our ordinary lives."

He made a dismissive sound. "You wouldn't know an ordinary life if it jumped up and bit you," he said, casting his gaze heavenward. "Nor, perhaps, would I. And now look. It's going to rain."

"Blame the unseasonable heat, not me." Elizabeth was neatening the pleats of her carriage dress. "Just hurry your horses a little."

He did, but the drive back to Burlingame's gate was six miles by village road, and another four along the winding drive that led to the house. Soon the rain began to patter a little, the temperature dropping precipitously. In the trees that lined the road, leaves began to ruffle in great waves, and then to flick upside down.

Napier pushed on, but as they passed through the village, an ominous crack of thunder rattled the windows in the Duck and Dragon. He started to pull in—and should have done—but in the graveled yard a snorting, white-eyed bay was wheeling his hindquarters wildly, kicking up gravel and grit as an ostler fought to hold its head, while a black-and-red mail coach was drawing up from the opposite direction, three thoroughly drenched fellows swaying upon the top bench.

Thinking the poor ostler had his hands full, Napier drove on. It was to be the least of his mistakes that afternoon. Half a mile later, Elizabeth was pulling her shawl tighter, and casting up anxious glances.

"Perhaps we might wait it out?" she finally suggested. "The folly tower, perhaps?"

"Too far," he said, "and Craddock has it locked so they can rig up scaffolding. The parapet's giving way."

"Yes, Gwyneth borrowed the key from Marsh last week," she replied. "I nearly died of exhaustion climbing up, but if you make it to the very top and lean far, far over the edge, you can see for fifty miles."

He shot her a dark look.

"What?" Lisette threw back her head and laughed. "I'm teasing. We were careful. And it's only thirty miles."

Napier just shook his head. "We had better go in by the back drive," he said. "I know a place we can stop."

By the time they did so, however, the rain had commenced in earnest with a promise of a true torrent rolling over the horizon, the source of the mail coach's drenching, no doubt. After a quarter mile, Napier gave up and turned his team down a side lane. In a matter of minutes, they reached the little spinney he remembered that stretched beyond either side of the road.

Leaping from the seat, he went around to hand Elizabeth down. "The gamekeeper's cottage is through those trees," he shouted over the rain. "Better a cup of tea with Mrs. Hoxton than your taking a chill from the damp."

"I assure you, I'm not that frail," said Elizabeth.

Napier turned to secure the horses. "And I hear we've a footman half dead already," he said. "So have a care."

"It's dyspepsia, not a chill."

"Then it's a dashed bad case," Napier answered, grabbing her hand and starting into the wood. "Duncaster said they'd sent to Marlborough for the doctor. Poor devil turned convulsive in the night."

"Dear God." Elizabeth looked suddenly solemn. "I hadn't heard."

Taking her hand, Napier led her along the footpath through the trees. Here the rain was a bit less fierce as the silence of the wood settled around them. But his boots were beginning to sop and he could only imagine the state of Elizabeth's dainty slippers.

A few yards along, they reached the house he'd espied on one of his rides with Craddock; the old gamekeeper's cottage, the estate agent had called it. But Napier should have taken better heed, he belatedly realized, of that word *old*, for after dashing up the steps he realized there was a decided air of abandonment about the place.

Abandonment, perhaps, was not the word. The house was well kept like all of Burlingame, but the curtains were drawn, the stoop scattered with leaves, and no sign of life within. Hammering upon the door with one hand, he drew Elizabeth into his lee with the other.

"No one lives here," she said, beginning to shiver. "J-Just lift the latch."

After a moment, he did so, pushing open the door to a cool, shadowy parlor and a hearth that likely hadn't seen a fire in months. The sharp tang of lime dust hung in the air, but the room was partially furnished with an oak settle, a table with chairs, and a thick, well-worn red carpet beneath the whole. More importantly, a coal scuttle sat near the grate.

Lisette sniffed. "Someone's plastering."

"We'll wait it out here," he ordered. "Put your shawl and shoes by the hearth. I'll build up a fire."

An old match tin hung from a nail near the mantelpiece, and after laying up a bit of kindling, it did not take Napier long to set the room aglow. He could hear Elizabeth in the back of the cottage rummaging about.

She returned to the front parlor, sliding her hands up and down her upper arms. "*Is* there a Mrs. Hoxton?" she asked, casting her gaze about the place. "Someone's been repairing plaster and paint, but there are no personal effects whatever."

Still kneeling by the hearth, Napier pondered it. "There's a Hoxton Farm on the east edge of the estate," he said. "Could the fellow still live with his parents?"

"He did look young." Elizabeth shrugged, and sat down on the wooden settle near the fire.

Napier added the last bit of coal and rose, his leather boots squeaking.

"You need to take those off," Elizabeth advised.

There being an old iron bootjack hammered into the floor by the hearth, Napier took her advice. That done, he padded across to the mullioned window set deep into the thick stone wall, and threw back the curtains. Fat raindrops were racing one another down the leaded panes, and catching in the Vs of the solder.

"This won't last," he said over one shoulder, praying he was right.

But the words were barely spoken when a fearsome crack of lightning lit the cottage and thunder rumbled like a giant beer keg across the cottage roof. At once the rain began to hammer down.

She smiled up at him. "Do you know, I don't mind it here," she said, scooting her stocking feet back and forth on the blood-red carpet. "It's cozy. Burlingame is oppressive, and everyone seems on edge."

He turned, speaking a little gruffly. "I'm sorry you don't like it."

She scowled back at him. "Lord, Napier, don't glower at me," she said. "You don't like it, either. *Do* you?"

He returned to the hearth, stripped off his frock coat, and tossed it over an old ladder-back chair, uncomfortable with his sudden pique. Why should her opinion matter?

"It's too grand, yes," he said, propping one shoulder against the mantel. "But I've little choice in the matter. Nonetheless, I don't wish you unhappy."

She gave a short laugh, and took off her hat. "Recall, if you will, that you didn't give a jot for my happiness when we started all this," she said, her voice falling. "And, to be fair, it doesn't really matter."

"What do you mean?"

She lifted both shoulders, her smile crooked. "Do you know, I honestly can't remember the last time I was truly happy."

"Try," he said, surprising himself. "I would like to know."

Elizabeth had bent over to shake out her short, fiery curls, raking her fingers through the dampness. "Oh, perhaps my twenty-first birthday?" she suggested, swiveling her head to look up from the floor. "Aunt Ashton dug out Mother's gold locket. It had been stored away in Ellie's trunk."

"And that made you happy?" he murmured, watching her across the small room.

"For the hour that I wore it, yes." She sat back up and shook her curls into place in that way that always made his breath catch. "Then Uncle came home half-sprung and insisted it should be his in recompense for putting up with me."

"Good Lord."

She smiled thinly. "A great row ensued," she went on. "Ashton jerked one of the bowls from Aunt's silver epergne and hurled it. It shattered against the chimneypiece. She burst into tears. And then—"

He waited, but she said no more.

"And then what?" he pressed.

Lisette flicked him a weary gaze, her jaw hardening. "And then, when her tears dried, she blamed me. That's how things went in Boston. Nothing could ever be Uncle Ashton's fault, and peace was to be kept at all cost."

"Ah," he said quietly. "One of those marriages."

She looked at him curiously. "What do you mean?"

He stirred from the mantel, dragging a hand down his face as he wondered how to answer. "I see them, sometimes, in my line of work," he finally said. "But we cannot stop them. The law permits a husband great latitude. It is a sort of mental cruelty—and, I daresay, he beat her physically, too?"

Elizabeth swallowed hard. "Yes. Sometimes."

Napier felt his blood boil. "And you?"

"*Never.*" The word was fierce and hard. Like her.

"I'm glad of that, at least."

"Because I'd have run away," she added, "or cut his throat

in his sleep, if I had to. And he knew it. He browbeat and he threatened, yes. But somehow . . . somehow, in the end, he always walked a wide circle round me."

That, Napier did not doubt. Bullies always sensed how far they could push. And he—well, he was fast realizing one ought never push Elizabeth.

"Do you have the locket still?"

She lifted her chin, and drew a finger beneath her neckline. "Ashton was so drunk he didn't recall it the next morning," she said, drawing it out. "Otherwise it might have been sold."

The delicate locket nestled between her breasts, brilliant gold against the fabric of her gown. "And is that all you have to remember your mother by?" he asked, forcing his eyes up.

"I have better things," said Elizabeth. "The necklace and earrings I wore to Burlingame, and other pieces she brought to the marriage. After her death, Mr. Bodkins put them in his safe. But some of the stones had already been pried out and replaced with paste to settle Papa's debts."

Her voice, he noted, was dispassionate but she sat a little slumped on the settle, tilting toward the fire that was beginning to chase the damp from the room. She had suffered tragedy upon tragedy, he realized, and enough indignity to last a lifetime. And it had made her what she was. Bloody, perhaps, but ever unbowed, Elizabeth Colburne was a fighter.

And clever. Oh, he did not for one moment discount that. It was how she'd managed to survive in an unwelcoming world. Her father had been nothing but a slick, spineless roué who'd simply shot himself when life threw up a hard hurdle. Lord Rowend had failed her utterly. And the drunken, bourgeois Mr. Ashton sounded worst of all.

It left him wondering if there had been one person in her life who had loved Elizabeth unselfishly. One responsible adult she could look up to or count on. It seemed not—and it made Hanging Nick Napier look almost doting by comparison.

But when had he come to care so much?

He was, as she'd once pointed out, accounted a heartless bastard. He'd earned an ugly nickname honestly, because there was damned little he wouldn't do to see a criminal convicted, or to simply mete out justice—justice as *he* defined it. But this visit to Burlingame—or her—*something* was throwing him off. He felt . . . odd, as if he were being altered by it somehow.

Restlessly, he rolled his shoulders beneath the tight constraints of his waistcoat.

"I know what you're thinking." She turned around on the settle to pin him accusingly with that cool green gaze. "You're thinking my father was a cad. That he did not love us. But it isn't true. It *isn't*. He was improvident, I know, but he was the most convivial of men, and we had . . . oh, we had the best times, the three of us. And he adored us, Ellie and me."

Convivial Sir Arthur might have been, but Napier still burned to reach into the grave and strangle the bastard's cold corpse. A blithe disposition and a pack of cards wouldn't feed a man's children or put a roof over their heads. And in her heart, she had to know it.

Elizabeth was just clinging to what might have been, reaching up from a deep well of sorrow to grab on to the memory of some knight in shining armor; seizing onto a dream in the faint hope it could keep her from drowning in her own sense of loss. And she had, indeed, lost everything. But he kept these thoughts to himself.

"You don't remember your mother?" he said instead.

Elizabeth shook her head. "Not well. I remember she was warm and very beautiful—and that she always smelled of *Esprit de Fleurs*. Papa would buy it for her in the rue de la Paix whenever he went to Paris."

And bought it out of guilt, Napier suspected, though he did not say as much. The gaming hells of Paris were legend.

Suddenly something occurred to him. "*Esprit de Fleurs*—is that by chance the scent you wear?"

"Lately, yes," she said, smiling up at him. "It's . . . warm. Like lilies and jasmine. I'm surprised you noticed."

And again he felt that shaft of lust drive deep into his belly—that intense, frightful thing that came out of nowhere, swamping him. That same thing he'd felt at tea in the withdrawing room. In his bedchamber. In the library.

And he realized suddenly that it might have been easier for both of them to have driven on in the rain and risked dying of a chill.

The journey to Tafton's had been made under a placid sky, the conversation entirely matter-of-fact, as if they both hoped to edge back from the thing that had flared between them yesterday. Nothing had been said of that wild, heated kiss, nor had he apologized for it—and truth to tell, he couldn't make himself regret it.

Elizabeth had spoken only of the gossip she'd picked up, and relayed bits and pieces of her conversations with his family. He, in turn, had spoken of his afternoons spent with Duncaster, and of his frustration at having been unable to run the elusive Dr. Underwood to ground. Mundane things, for the most part.

But now it was as if the benign sky had conspired against them, for nothing about the quiet intimacy of this dark cottage felt mundane, and already he could feel that inner storm roiling. He returned almost hopefully to the window, half wondering if he'd already fallen in love with her.

But how could that be when, as she'd pointed out, he knew precisely what she was?

Knew better, really, than to trust her.

And it made no difference.

Napier burned for a woman he was well nigh certain was a murderess. Empires had fallen for less. Certainly his career would collapse; the Home Office would be scandalized. And yet, something about Elizabeth Colburne—her unconventional charm or her pale, ethereal beauty—*something* left him willing to throw his morals and his life to the wind.

But his life was already on the cusp of an awful change that was not within his power to stop. Duncaster might be tough as old shoe leather, but his days were numbered just like everyone's. And soon, like it or not, Napier's allegiance would lie beyond the Home Office.

He set a hand to the glass and soaked up the cold against his skin as if it might jolt him to sense. Beyond the glass, black skies pressed down and the world seemed on the edge of twilight. He, too, felt on the edge of something portentous. He had begun to want Elizabeth with a near bone-deep ache, and it was no use to pretend otherwise.

It was as if she read his mind. "Napier, do you ever wonder," she said softly from the settle, "if perhaps you overthink things?"

He fisted his hands at his sides, so hard he felt his nails digging into his palms. "Lisette—" he said, the words hoarse as he stared through the rain. "Lisette, what are we to do about all this?"

She did not even pretend to misunderstand. "I don't know," she whispered from her settle. "But at least you've stopped calling me *Elizabeth*."

He turned from the window, crossing the room in three strides. Wordlessly, he stopped before the old settle, extending down his hand.

She looked up, her dark lashes falling shut, feathering across her cheeks almost shyly. Then she placed her hand in his, her fingers cool as they curved around his, and opened her eyes again.

"Is there nothing of the romantic in you, Napier?" she asked, the intensity of her gaze piercing him. "Nothing at all?"

"No," he answered.

"Good," she said, standing. "Pretty words come cheap to most men."

It was, he realized, one of the truest things she'd ever said.

His hand was still cold as he cupped her chin, lifting her face to his. He kissed her tenderly and slowly this time, saying with his mouth and his hands what he could not speak. Eloquence was not his strong suit; he was a gruff, plain man. And those pretty words she spoke of likely couldn't have been beaten out of him with one of his constable's truncheons.

But he wanted her above all things.

And in this moment, at least, he wanted her to know it.

When he lifted his head, she was watching him. "Lisette," he whispered, cupping her face in his hands. "I'm not pushing you onto a bed again. I'm not doing anything remotely against your will."

"Nor would I let you."

He let his hands slide up her arms, his nostrils flaring wide, and he dragged the scent of lilies and woman deep into his lungs. "Then tell me you know what this is," he whispered. "Tell me you want it."

She pushed him a little away then. "I want *you*," she said simply. "And I think you want me. But I really doubt, Napier, that either of us has a clue what this is."

He greatly feared she was right.

And he feared, too, the bond that kept drawing him to her—not the sweet bond of lips or even loins, but the intense bond of eyes. Of *honesty*. Though how it could have been that the most disingenuous woman he knew could look so deeply and so penetratingly—so straight into his soul, it felt—utterly escaped him.

"*Do* you desire me, Napier?" she whispered.

He felt his entire body shudder with long-suppressed lust. A knowing smile lifted one corner of her mouth. He kissed her there, slanting his face to take her lips as his fingers slid around her cheek, then into her hair at the nape of her neck.

But again and again, Napier felt the pull of those eyes drawing him, forcing on him a truth he would as soon have evaded. Those odd, startling eyes that, first seen, had blazed turquoise hellfire upon him. The eyes that had followed him like some pale Mona Lisa's gaze, as he'd moved across that Greenwich garden.

Napier had more knowledge of women, perhaps, than an unmarried man had a right to. And in his experience, women shied from eye contact when making love, preferring to kiss, or to simply put out the lamps when possible. But as he slowly undressed Lisette, he held her gaze as she held his. Even as he pushed the dark blue silk off her shoulder, and fumbled awkwardly to unfasten her clothing.

Because the eyes were the window to the soul, and he wondered if he might see hers.

"Napier."

With lips like warm satin, Lisette kissed him. His mouth. His faintly bristled cheek. Even the turn of his neck. She stood on tiptoes in nothing but her shift and whatever lay beneath, tempting him, entwining her tongue with his until their breath began to come fast and his cock began to thicken and throb impatiently.

Eyes a little feverish, she rolled back down on her heels, her pale, slender fingers furious at the buttons of his silk waistcoat. "There is a bed," she said hastily. "In the back room. But myself—I favor this red carpet by the fire."

"And I," he said, dipping his head to nuzzle her throat, "have always favored red *anything*."

Her fingers caught a moment in his buttons, then awkwardly finished. On a soft sound of impatience, she pushed the waistcoat off his shoulders, and looked up, eyes glowing.

He finished the job, ripping loose his stock, then yanking out his shirttails. That done, he dragged the shirt over his head and flung it aside.

Lisette's small, clever hands were already tugging at his trouser buttons. First the top, then the next, fell open. Blood surged southward, hot and pulsating, until he was blatantly swollen and hard for her.

Suddenly her fingers stilled, and his heart stopped with them.

Hesitation hung in the air, heavy as coal smoke.

Please, please, please, he prayed.

"Napier," she said hoarsely. Her eyes—and her fingers—were still fixed near the bulge beneath his fly.

After exhaling with slow deliberation, he tipped up her head and dredged up his willpower. "I understand, Lisette," he said. "The rain will let up. We can go soon—now, if you wish."

"No," she said, lifting her gaze to his a little warily. "It's not that."

"Then . . . what?"

"It's just that you're awfully . . . or that I should probably say . . ."

Her cheeks had turned a pretty shade of pink. It lit her opalescent skin, warming her entire face. And suddenly, he knew. Should have known, he realized, all along.

He let his hands fall, disappointment crushing him. "You're a virgin?"

She nodded, the merest jerk of her head.

Dear God.

But what had he imagined? She'd already told him she was an incurable romantic. That she deserved something better than regret. She was bold, yes, and mendacious when it suited her purpose, but save for the rash, desperate offer she'd made him all those months ago, nothing about Elizabeth suggested she was fast.

On an audible sigh, he lifted her hands from his trouser buttons, and carried them to his lips in turn.

The gesture didn't appease her. "And that's it?" she said accusingly. "You mean to turn honorable and patronizing on me now? And I'm to have no say?"

"Lisette." He drew her hard against him, sliding one hand into her hair as he held her. "Oh, Lisette. Think what you're doing."

"I'm doing, I think, what I've wanted to do for some days now." Her voice was muffled against his chest. "And you are not romantic, remember?"

"No, but you are," he said. "And I hope I know the value of a woman's virtue."

"It's of no value whatever to me," she replied a little tartly. "I find the very word demeaning. I'm twenty-seven years old, Napier. Even if I meant to marry, a man who valued virtue over what is in my heart would not be worth my time."

She had a point, he realized.

But more cogently, she had a hand on his cock.

She eased her fingers firmly down the front of his fly and Napier's breath seized. Before he could think better of it, he'd shucked the last of his garments, easing off stockings, drawers and trousers as one, and letting them fall in an awkward heap.

Eyes widening, Lisette stepped back, her hands tugging up the hems of her shift. He caught it, and she shimmied out of it to unveil a pair of small, perfect breasts, and hard nipples the color of ripe peaches.

Later, he had only the vaguest of memories as to how the rest of her clothing fell away, or how they ended up on the carpet with Lisette beneath him. Driven by desire, he knew only that time was of the essence; that if he delayed, good sense would overcome him.

His mouth sought hers, and he kissed her exultantly. All his good intentions had flown, taking his doubts and his hesitance with it. She was Elizabeth, and his desire for her had simmered, he realized, for months.

He would as soon not think of the folly of *that*.

But he was going to have her. He was going to give her the pleasure she'd begged for with those expressive, all-seeing eyes. He pinned her to the carpet with the weight of his body as the firelight danced over her creamy skin. Lisette was perfection: long and lithe, with a dancer's body. And, he sometimes thought, a warrior's heart.

She opened to his kisses, granting him every liberty, and tasting him thoroughly in return and her hands roamed restlessly, and a little artlessly, over him. When at last he pulled away, he let his gaze drift over the fine oval of her face. Over that slender nose and high, aristocratic forehead. Over her eyes, widely set and faintly almond shaped, and a chin that should have been too sharp and yet was perfectly her.

"God, Lisette. I think I've wanted you since the moment you strode into my office."

"I gained a stone," she whispered, "and hacked off my hair."

He dipped his head, and flicked his tongue over the hard bud of her nipple, causing her to gasp. "That stone went to the right places," he said. "And that hair—God, you must know what it does to me."

"No," she whispered, "not really."

But he made no answer and instead let his lips slide down the swanlike turn of her throat, breathing in her scent. Lisette smelled . . . right. Soft and welcoming. Sensual and comforting. Like every true and perfect thing a man might yearn for in the long blackness of a winter's night.

And if she wasn't entirely true—if she was not what he believed and hoped—then that was trouble for another day. This stormy afternoon was for loving; even, perhaps, for pretending. That this was something more. Or that they were different people, meeting under different circumstances.

His mouth found her breast and captured it, suckling hotly. Lisette cried out, arching up against him. In response, Napier circled the tip with his tongue and felt it harden to a nub. Then ever so gently, he eased a hand down between them. Shifted his weight, he stroked one finger through her soft thatch of cinnamon curls.

She shuddered in his embrace and Napier lifted his head, still rubbing her gently. In the hearth some feet way, a bit of coal sheared, sending up a shower of hot sparks that cast her in a glow. But the heat that burned in her eyes had nothing to do with the fire.

Later he might wonder if it was all just another charade, but in that moment her need felt more real than his own flesh and blood. The soft warmth in her eyes, he decided, said she knew what she was doing. What she was surrendering.

Gazing down, he cupped one hand around her cheek, and drew his finger deeper between her legs, teasing at, but not quite touching, that sweet center. Her hips rolling restlessly, Lisette drew in her breath on a sort of sigh, then turned her face into his hand, her mouth a little open. Lightly, he ran his thumb over the full swell of her lush bottom lip and to his shock, the pink tip of her tongue flicked out, stroking wet heat across the ball.

His every nerve ending jolted.

It was just a thumb, for God's sake.

But when a soft moan escaped him, Lisette caught his thumb between her lips, sucking hard. Hot need drew through him like a rope pulled taut, making his cock throb. She let it pop from the wet warmth of her mouth, and swiveled her head back to look at him, mischief glittering in her hot green eyes.

"*Wicked girl,*" he whispered, and stroked his finger deeper, rubbing hard over her clitoris, savoring her thready cry.

Lisette felt her whole body tremble at Napier's touch. Need surged and her hips bucked. Again and again he stroked, sliding deeper into the damp folds between her legs. She was not a complete fool; she had lived a worldly life. She knew what men did to women.

Sort of.

And having it done to her—by him—*dear God.*

"Napier," she whispered urgently. "Can we—"

"No," he said sternly. "Not yet."

Then he dropped his head, his straight, heavy hair falling forward like a curtain of black silk, his mouth capturing her breast again. Hotly he suckled her, his tongue mimicking the stroke of his finger. And then two fingers.

When he slipped one fully inside her, Lisette gave a soft, startled cry.

"Shush, love," he cooed, making her stomach bottom out.

And then ever so gently, he bit down on her breast, and the ache shot through her—all the way from her breast to her belly and then to the wet place he was touching. Lisette felt a strong throb beneath his finger.

It was too intense to be borne. "*Stop,*" she cried. "Oh, God. Napier, stop and—and do . . . *something.*"

Though her eyes were closed now, she felt him shift his weight, and felt the stubble of his lean, hard cheek brush over hers. "Lisette, if I do . . ."

"There is no if!" Her eyes flew open. "*Oh.* I can't bear it."

"You need to let me worry about the when," he said firmly, brushing his lips over the end of her eyebrow. "It's going to hurt."

"It hurts *now.* I ache for you from the inside out." In the gloom, she could hear her own breath coming fast. "Please."

He let his full weight come over her then, bearing her down into the softness of the rug. He kissed her deep and hard, then pulled away. "You, my dear minx," he murmured, "are too much accustomed to having your way."

"Napier—" she gritted.

"*No.*" He kissed her hard, capturing her hands in his. But

when she sobbed again, he took mercy and wedged one thickly muscled thigh between her legs to gently nudge them apart. She felt the weight of his erection rest heavily between her legs. She wanted to touch it, yet felt so uncertain.

Napier eased his fingers inside her again, then his thumb found that aching spot between her legs and began to stroke small circles. "*Ah,*" she whispered.

And then it was as if something inside her gave way, as if some dam inside her burst, breaking into shards of light. His touch became fleetingly a part of her as something powerful washed through her, wave after wave of a pleasure indescribable.

He was going to break her heart.

That was her next clear thought. And on its heels was the knowledge that this—yes, *this feeling*—would be worth the pain.

When the flood abated and she came back to the world, it was to see Napier kneeling between her legs, looking dangerous and deeply pleased with himself. He was, she thought, the handsomest man she'd ever seen. Not beautiful, no, but thoroughly male, with wide shoulders, his arms layered with muscle and corded with tendons.

And as with everything he did in life, Napier looked deadly serious. A shock of heavy, dark hair had fallen over one eye, and his manhood rose up between them, unmistakable and a little daunting. Tentatively, she captured it in her hand, amazed at the silken weight of it.

He bared his teeth an instant, his breath seizing. Lightly she circled her thumb over the swollen head, mimicking the gesture he'd employed to such delightful effect, and a tiny bead of moisture welled up.

"*Umm,*" he moaned.

Then he pulled her up a little from the rug, dragging her into his embrace, the weight of his manhood pressing hard against her belly. His fingers sliding into her hair at her nape, he stilled her head to a kiss that was beyond sensual and into something she had no words for. It was a thorough possession, leaving her his to command. Lisette's body began to thrum again, and she felt the throb between her legs commence anew.

Beyond the little cottage, the rain hammered down now. A crack of thunder rent the sky, and the room lit up. She could feel Napier's heart beating against her chest as they kissed—and hers, too, faster and faster. As his skin heated up, Lisette's senses were flooded with the scent of lime shaving soap and thoroughly aroused male.

Acting on pure feminine instinct, Lisette thrust her tongue along his, parrying his deep thrusts. Napier shuddered against her, and jerked his mouth away.

"Now," he said, urging her down onto the rug. In one smooth motion, he crawled over her, the muscles in his arms rippling almost predatorily. The weight of his erection settled between her legs, and Napier guided it deeper with his hand.

Instinctively, she drew up her feet and widened her legs. A hot hardness pressed into her, then slid inside an inch, invading her. She jerked a little, then forced herself to still, and then to relax. Napier bore his weight on one arm, hard tendons cording the length of it, his eyes squeezed shut. Experimentally, Lisette rocked her hips.

"*Wait*," he growled. "Christ Jesus."

She could hear her own breath in the gloom. "You're very dictatorial when you make love," she managed. "But then, I wonder I'm surprised."

He laughed, and let his forehead tip forward to rest on hers. "Lord, Lisette, you're too tight," he said. "I'm going to hurt you. I can't bear it."

"I can." Lisette exhaled slowly, and tilted her hips upward to take him. On a harsh grunt, Napier slipped deep and the pain was like the sharp stab of a knife. She must have cried out. His eyes flew open, hot and a little angry—angry, she realized, with himself.

A questioning gaze swept over her. Lisette caught her lip in her teeth and rocked again.

"*Aah—*" he whispered.

Drawing up her knees another inch, Lisette let her hands skate around to the sculpted muscles of his hips and urged him fully between her legs. Napier pulled back a little, and pushed inside again, this time deeper.

His gaze caught hers and searched her face, questioning the pain.

Questioning, perhaps, everything.

"*Yes,*" she said.

He thrust home on a groan of male triumph, claiming her, a sound so pure her heart ached. Oh, she longed for this. Not a longing for sex—though God knew she felt that, too—but for the intimacy of two people thoroughly drowning in each other.

Longing, really, for *him*.

She let herself drink him in, tucking the memory away in the hidden corners of her heart for another time—and another place—when all this would be over.

Napier let his head fall, bearing his weight forward on powerful arms as he set a steady pace, sliding deep, brushing the sweet spot between her legs. Lisette felt her passage slicken as his flesh pulled at hers. His thrusts sped up, his tendons cording with the strain.

She felt herself open like a flower welcoming the sun's heat, her need matching his, stroke for stroke. Soon that glorious sensation edged near again. The fleeting moment of pain was forgotten and only that white-hot pleasure remained, tantalizingly beyond her reach. She felt herself rising up to meet him as she shuddered, their bodies coming together as one. And then the light shattered again, and this time it was as if something inside Lisette broke away and flew to him—taking her heart with it.

She cried out softly beneath him, then felt her every muscle flood with pleasure. Napier thrust again, his head going back. Every sinew in his neck strained with his efforts as a molten warmth surged inside her, sweet as the pleasure itself. Twice more he drove inside her, then his head tipped forward, his intense dark eyes burning into hers.

Then he cursed softly beneath his breath, and collapsed.

They must have dozed for a while, for when she stirred it was to find one of Napier's heavy legs thrown over hers, and his head nestled upon her breast.

It was, she could not but notice, a long, well-muscled leg, sprinkled with dark hair that curved into a beautifully shaped buttock so fine it might have been carved by Bernini. That perfect, semicircular globe was going to warrant a good deal of further attention once she knew more what she was about with this lovemaking business.

But that assumed a future they likely didn't have, and Lisette had learned long ago to steel herself to disappointment. Nothing had changed between them. Even if Napier found a way to forgive who she was, he was not apt to forget what she'd done.

On an inward sigh, she turned her face toward the window. Though the sun wasn't out, rain no longer hammered at the glass, so perhaps the worst was over. Lisette stretched experimentally to find certain parts a little sore, but in a deliciously wonderful way.

At the faint movement, Napier opened his eyes, watched her intently for a moment, then lifted his head to kiss her with exquisite gentleness.

"Dear God in heaven," he groaned, falling back onto the rug, and taking her with him. "I knew you were trouble the instant I laid eyes on you."

"And you said you weren't romantic," she purred, sprawled over his chest.

His laugh rumbled deep. "Ah, there's my ineloquence again."

But almost at once, a pensive look passed over his harsh countenance, and he lifted a hand to tuck a wayward strand of hair behind her ear. "But Lisette, for you . . . for this glorious feeling . . . perhaps even an old dog could learn a new trick?"

She forced a light laugh. "Oh, that feeling is just fleeting male gratitude," she murmured, "and if those were your old tricks, you may rest comfortably upon your laurels. Besides, Napier, I ask nothing of you."

He relaxed against the rug, pulling her hard against his chest. "Let's hope you never have to," he said quietly.

But when she asked him what he meant, Napier's gaze turned inward and he made no reply. Lisette did not press the point. Instead, they lingered a little longer in each other's arms, her cheek pressed to the wide plane of his chest as she listened to his strong, steady heartbeat.

Soon, however, the rain had stopped altogether and dawdling further was out of the question. Concern—perhaps even alarm—might be raised at Burlingame if they did not soon turn up.

But there was one last thing she wished—no, *needed*—to say.

She lifted her head and smiled down at him. "You wanted to know, Napier, the last time I was happy," she said, stroking a finger through the dark hair that dusted his chest. "And I think I lied to you."

He crooked one eyebrow, his expression a little wary. "Did you now?"

"Yes," she said pensively, "because strangely, I've found a sort of happiness in all this—in coming here to Burlingame with you, I mean—and in having a sense of purpose again, for however long it lasts. And I am happy now—in this moment, I mean—*sublimely* happy. And I thank you."

"I hope," he said quietly, "that you will always thank me. That you will never have cause to regret, Lisette, what we did here together."

"Will you regret it?" she asked, holding his gaze.

He shook his head, his dark hair scrubbing a little on the old rug. "No," he said solemnly. "I very much fear I *won't* regret it—however it all turns out."

Then, after a few last lingering kisses, Napier drew on his shirt and drawers and went out the back, the cottage door slamming after him. He returned with a bucket of cold water for washing—but it might have been better used, Lisette inwardly considered, to dash her silly daydreams, for she was suddenly and foolishly caught up in them.

They drove back to Burlingame in near silence, Napier taking more care, perhaps, than was strictly necessary in cutting his team around the wide puddles. Lisette sat quietly on the seat beside him, the enormity—and the risk—of what she'd just done slowly sinking in on her.

She did not regret it, no. She had done it with her eyes wide open. But she understood, she thought, the reason for Napier's quiet curse. Were they to go in this fashion, she would have to learn to look at her calendar, Lisette realized, and for that she would require Fanny's advice.

It was a lowering thought. And beneath it lay a frightening uncertainty.

For her, their afternoon interlude had not been simply a matter of physical pleasure and Lisette was not fool enough to think otherwise. She had begun to lean on Napier—to take from him a sort of strength and emotional sustenance she had not known in a very long while.

A frightening uncertainty indeed.

CHAPTER 10

In Which Dr. Underwood Makes a House Call

Royden Napier spent the next three miles of his life in a pair of sopping wet boots and a state of inner frustration. Of the two, he far preferred the boots. A resulting bout of pneumonia, he inwardly considered, might have laid him up long enough to regain his senses.

He was to be temporarily distracted from this mental flagellation, however, for when they arrived at the house it was to find a black cabriolet sitting at the foot of the steps, the calash thrown up against the weather and a pretty gray waiting in its traces. Just as he spun the curricle around the monstrous statue of Hades, a thin gentleman carrying a black bag came out the front door, then stopped and turned around as if to address someone within.

A waiting groom took Napier's horses and by the time he'd lifted Elizabeth down, holding her as near as he dared, the gentleman was coming swiftly down the steps with a fretful expression and a dark look in his eyes.

"Good afternoon," he said, approaching with one hand extended. "I think you must be Assistant Commissioner Napier?"

Napier was taken aback to be addressed professionally, but threw out his hand. "Indeed, yes."

The gentleman swept off his hat. "I'm Dr. Underwood," he said, then bowed when Napier introduced Lisette. "Mr. Napier, I hate you waited in vain for me last week. I was detained with a patient far more ill than I anticipated."

"The perils of a doctor's life, I'm sure," said Napier, taking in the man's obvious disquiet. "Tell us, how did you find Duncaster's footman?"

"Very ill, sir. Very ill indeed." Dr. Underwood's gaze shifted uneasily to Elizabeth. "Might we speak in private?"

"If you prefer," said Napier, "but you may certainly speak plainly in front of Miss Colburne."

"Very well." Dr. Underwood still looked unhappy. "But we had better go inside."

Napier knew with a policeman's instincts that something was wrong. They hastened up the steps and Napier turned into the first private room to be found, the narrow butler's office off the grand entrance hall. It was unoccupied.

"Your being from home, I was just on my way to see Squire Tafton," said the doctor when Napier had closed the door. "He's the nearest justice of the peace since your Uncle Harold's death."

Surprise sketched over Napier's face. "I didn't know Saint-Bryce had been a justice," he said. "But why do you need one? What has happened?"

The doctor glanced back at the door. "I cannot like Walton's symptoms," he said, dropping his voice to a whisper. "I am most uneasy. I greatly fear, sir, that he . . . well, that perhaps he has been *poisoned*."

This Napier had not expected. "Good God," he murmured. "By whom? Or was it accidental?"

"It mightn't be either," said the doctor. "But he has become very ill, and I'm given to understand that . . ."

"Well, go on," said Napier impatiently.

The doctor set his bag down with a thud atop the butler's chest, which was folded open to reveal the green leather writing surface. "Oh, dear, this is most awkward."

With a solicitous smile, Elizabeth leaned in and patted him lightly on the hand. "I was just telling Mr. Napier earlier that Walton had been less than circumspect in matters of the heart," she murmured. "One must consider the postmistress's husband, mustn't one?"

The doctor's eyes widened, his pallor whitening even further. "*I* mustn't," he said. "That is for the justice to decide—or for you, Mr. Napier."

"I fear I've limited authority in Wiltshire," said Napier, not entirely sure that was true. He had come at the behest of Sir George Grey, who had tremendous authority. "What are Walton's symptoms?"

"On its face, it looks a bit like *cholera morbus*," said the doctor, again glancing uneasily at Elizabeth. "But . . . it just isn't. I know it isn't."

"He suffers from purging? Vomiting?" said Napier flatly. "Acute gastric pain? Rapid heart rate?"

Underwood looked relieved. "You've seen it, then?"

"More times than I care to count," said Napier, cutting a speaking glance at Elizabeth. "Arsenic, most likely. My men in Scotland Yard call it inheritance powder. But if he is no longer convulsing, and if he ingests no further poison, he might recover."

"My assessment precisely," said Underwood, "*if* it's poison at all."

"How does one make sure?" asked Lisette.

Again, Underwood's gaze shifted back and forth. "Without a suspicious compound to test—and I found nothing at hand—one can be certain only by postmortem. But my apologies, Miss Colburne. I'm sure your delicate sensibilities preclude such a discussion."

"Oh, not in the least," said Lisette with a breezy wave. "You'll notice Napier here doesn't hesitate to throw out purging and vomiting."

"Don't forget the acute gastric pain," added Napier dryly. "Underwood, I fear my future bride comes from a newspaper family and—so far as I've seen—possesses no delicate sensibilities."

"Oh." Underwood gave a withering smile. "That's . . . convenient, I daresay, given your line of work."

"Well, there is that," Napier acknowledged. "So, have you performed such a postmortem?"

"No, no, merely read about them," the doctor confessed. "But I'm given to understand the damage will be primarily gastrointestinal, presenting with a reddening of the lining of the esophagus."

"And it will be streaked with bloody mucus, most likely," Elizabeth interjected. "One might even see the appearance of coffee grounds in the stomach—the bits of digested blood, you see."

Napier turned to stare. "Really, my dear?"

"In cases of direct ingestion, yes." Lisette shot him a bland smile. "In fact, I once wrote—I mean *read*—about a case in which grains of arsenious acid had adhered to the victim's stomach lining. That was a dead giveaway—no pun intended."

"Hmm," said Napier darkly.

Underwood had gone a little pale, and was staring at her.

Then Napier's expression relented. "But let's not jump to conclusions," he said, raising his hand. "We're supposing a malicious and deliberate poisoning. Arsenic poisoning is more apt to be slow, and by exposure or some sort of accidental absorption."

"In which case," said the doctor glumly, "a postmortem will be of far less use."

Lisette felt a heavy uncertainty settle over the small room. Dr. Underwood was looking less happy by the minute. Napier had paced to the narrow window designed to give the servants a discreet vantage point from which to observe approaching carriages.

One hand was set on his hip, pushing back the dark fabric of his frock coat to reveal the athletic turn of his waist. He was scrubbing the other hand around the faint shadow of his beard in a pensive gesture and staring out at Hades and Persephone with a distant look in his eyes.

Their passionate interlude, it seemed, was forgotten.

Lisette tried to take no offense; she'd known from the first Napier was driven by his work. And just now the whole of his focus had returned to the strange goings-on at Burlingame.

When he turned from the window, his expression was sober. "We can certainly search the house top to bottom," he said, "and throw the entire household into disarray in doing so. Then we can go into the village and do the same at the Duck and Dragon, even inside the post office itself. But we will almost certainly find some sort of arsenic compound in both places. Nearly every large establishment keeps it. And what will that have gained us? We will merely be fueling—or worse, giving rise to—dangerous speculation."

"My thoughts exactly," said Underwood grimly. "Mr. Boothe—the innkeeper—is a nasty piece of work. I'd fear for his wife if we raised suspicions. That's why I thought of Tafton. But what he would be able to do differently is . . . well, nothing, I suppose. Not unless Walton dies."

Napier just shook his head. "A grim business," he said, shoving his hands in his pockets. "And it brings us, I suppose, to my reason for calling on you last week."

"I thought perhaps it might," said Underwood a little glumly. "You look in the pink of health."

"Quite, thank you," said Napier. "I came in more of a professional capacity. I've seen the coroner's reports, of course, but I wanted your more specific opinion—or even your honest guess—as to what killed my uncle, and Lord Hepplewood before him."

Underwood looked horrified. "As the records state, Hepplewood suffered a bilious derangement," he said. "At least, that was my assessment at the time. It came on slowly, a sort of chronic condition, before suddenly and acutely worsening. Have you reason to suspect something else?"

"Did you ever see Lord Hepplewood alone?" Napier barked.

The doctor shook his head. "Not that I recall," he said. "His wife was always present."

"Hepplewood wrote to his friend Sir George Grey expressing fear for his life," said Napier, "though not very coherently or specifically. That, you understand, was what first brought me to Burlingame. I was *sent*. By the Home Secretary. As I am now."

Implicit in his words was the fact that Napier had not come to dance attendance on his cantankerous grandfather, or to hang about awaiting some sort of family largesse. And for the first time, Lisette wondered what that had cost him; to swallow his pride and come all those months ago to this place where he had not been not wanted. To this house and this family—this life of aristocratic splendor—from which his father had been so coldly banished.

But he had come, because it was his duty. Napier was the sort of man who would always do his duty, putting it before his personal wishes—and perhaps even before his heart.

To Lisette, that knowledge was a harsh reminder of her reality—a fact as admirable as it was chilling.

But Underwood was slowly shaking his head. "I knew Hepplewood was fearful at the end," he said. "But dying men often become fanciful, particularly the elderly. He did sometimes babble things that made no sense."

"So was it bilious disease?" Napier demanded. "Or just the senility that comes with old age?"

Underwood flashed half a wince. "Lady Hepplewood believed the latter," he said, "but in my experience, senility tends to make the elderly childlike. They recall the past better than the present, as Hepplewood seemed to do. Toward the end, you see, he . . . well, he kept calling out a name."

"A name?" said Napier. "What name?"

Here, the doctor blushed faintly. "Jane," he said, dropping his voice to a near whisper. " 'Jane, Jane, Jane,' he would say, 'I think they are trying to kill me.' And it was said most pitifully."

"*Jane?*" said Napier. "Who the devil is Jane?"

Underwood lifted both shoulders. "That's the thing," he answered. "According to Lady Hepplewood, her husband had an aunt Jane to whom he was deeply attached. But she's been dead thirty years."

"Are there no other Janes? It's a common-enough name."

"Burlingame has a housemaid named Jane who sat with him occasionally when Miss Jeffers and Miss Gwyneth were unavailable. But by then Hepplewood was near insensible. And he was so . . . fretful. Almost *fearful.*"

"Could he have been poisoned?"

His expression faltering, Underwood opened both hands almost plaintively. "Possibly, but as I said, he died slowly, and at the end, in a vast deal of distress."

"Physical distress?"

"Yes, mostly," said Underwood. "But there must have been something going round at the time. For a few days, Miss Gwyneth Tarleton felt unwell, too, with similar but far milder symptoms. She recovered quickly, but Hepplewood, given his already frail condition, seemed unable to shake it off."

"What about Saint-Bryce's death?" Napier pressed. "Hemorrhagic apoplexy, the coroner's report said."

"Now that one, I stand by that," said Underwood firmly. "All the symptoms were present, and I have no doubt a postmortem would have revealed excessive blood in the brain."

Lisette had been wondering about something. "Doctor, can hemorrhagic apoplexy be caused by poison?"

The doctor shook his head. "There are theories, unproven," he said. "Most commonly the cause is a head trauma or Bright's disease. Or, if one suffers from brittle arteries, an extreme exertion or an emotional outburst might precipitate such a hemorrhage."

Napier's brow was deeply furrowed. "Did Saint-Bryce quarrel with any—"

Just then they were interrupted by a sharp knock on the door.

"Marsh isn't here," Napier called, his voice sharp.

But the knock came again. "I beg your pardon, sir," said an irritable voice, "but this *is* Marsh."

Napier strode to the door and yanked it open.

The butler stood straight as a soldier on the threshold, his face bloodless, his eyes going straight to Underwood's. "I very much fear, Doctor, that you are needed back upstairs," he said.

"Oh, God," Lisette whispered. "Is Walton—?"

Marsh gave a tight shake of the head. "Not Walton," he said. "Prater."

$\mathcal{L}$ife at Burlingame took on a more subdued rhythm over the next few days. Mercifully, perhaps, circumstances prevented Napier from wallowing mawkishly in the memories of his interlude with Elizabeth. Walton lingered at death's door, often rambling incoherently and lashing out at those who nursed him.

Prater was less affected but still violently ill, his symptoms identical, the doctor said, to those Gwyneth had suffered before Hepplewood's death.

Underwood came each day, always pausing to exchange words with Napier. But in reality there was little to talk about. To Napier's frustration, the doctor immediately retreated from his diagnosis of poisoning in favor some sort of contagion since the two footmen shared a bedchamber. Napier was not so sure.

But the strapping young footmen were far more resilient than the aged earl had been, and all scenarios of gloom and doom were to go unrealized. After a good deal of nursing and a near constant infusion of fluids, Prater was hitching on his livery by week's end, somewhat worse for wear, and soon Walton was alleviating his boredom by pinching the bottom of one of the less charitable housemaids while she was bent over by his bed.

It was a grave misjudgment. The maid popped back up, backhanding the fellow with his own chamber pot, fracturing his nose.

Mrs. Jansen could barely contain a smile over dinner upon hearing of this contretemps, and the following morning, to no one's surprise, Underwood pronounced Walton fully recovered—save for his nose, which was accounted likely never to be straight again.

Gwyneth laughed out loud at the news. "One can only hope," she crowed, "that a lumpy black-and-yellow nose will not put Mrs. Boothe off *too* badly."

And so, with the house slowly returning to normal and the fear subsiding, Napier tried to force his attention back to the one thing that, from the very first, had sat uneasily with him—the business of Lord Hepplewood's death, and by extension his uncle's—for if he did not dwell on that, he knew he'd find himself contemplating something a good deal more troubling.

But Hepplewood's fate could no longer distract him from the temptation that was Lisette Colburne.

Napier felt restless and bewitched, caught in the throws of a nameless longing that felt by turns like both agony and temptation. Temptation when Lisette caught his gaze over the dining table, something enigmatic simmering in her green-blue gaze, and agony—well, the agony came at night, particularly when he counted off the steps that separated their bedchambers. Which totaled precisely twenty-three.

With both footmen returned to service, dinner on Monday evening resumed its usual form with all the formality of a great English house, and more courses than Napier cared to count—or eat. One chair, however, sat empty, for Mrs. Jansen claimed another headache and did not come down and soon Diana, too, left the table early to entertain Beatrice in her stead.

By the time coffee was finished in the drawing room, Duncaster had fallen asleep, slumped in a chair with his fingers laced over his waistcoat, and Gwyneth and Lord Hepplewood were squabbling over a hand of piquet, the former having declared *carte blanche*.

"I know perfectly well," said Hepplewood, his words a little slurred, "that you've a knave hidden behind that eight of hearts."

"Tony, how utterly vile!" Gwyneth retorted. "No, I won't show them again. Do you imagine me an idiot?"

"You're a cheat, Gwen," her cousin retorted. "You do it all the time."

"All the time?" Gwyneth had turned beet red. "Really, Tony? That's your excuse? I did it once. When I was *twelve*. And you've already got a sheet in the wind. Perhaps you might put down that glass of sherry, and simply play your hand?"

"And perhaps you might put down that overbearing attitude?" Hepplewood suggested, tossing his cards onto the table. "Or just go back upstairs. Doubtless Mrs. Jansen can be persuaded to give you a game you like better."

Lady Hepplewood snatched up her ebony stick. "The two of you," she said coldly, "are to set an example for the lower orders, not act like them."

"Mamma, I—"

"Spare me your excuses," Lady Hepplewood snapped, planting the stick firmly on the carpet. "If you wish to display vulgarity, Tony, kindly go down to the village tav—"

Duncaster punctuated this discussion with a loud *snk-snk-snoork!* then let his chin fall back into the folds of his cravat.

Napier jerked from his chair and proposed a walk in the gardens, looking rather pointedly at Lisette. "Perhaps," he added, "we might go so far as the lake? The moon is nearly full."

The plan, however, backfired. Her posture still rigid, Gwyneth rose and, with a flick of her wrist, sent her cards skimming across the table into Hepplewood's lap. "A capital notion," she said. "I, for one, find this house oppressive."

"I should adore a walk." Lisette picked up her cashmere shawl that lay across the arm of her chair. "It looks to be a cloudless night."

Hepplewood might have been in his cups, but not so impaired he couldn't grasp he was about to be abandoned to the tender mercies of his mother. "Love to go," he declared, coming a little unsteadily to his feet. "Unless the betrothed wish a moment alone?"

"Oh, no, we should love company," said Lisette so brightly Napier could have strangled her.

And yet she was doing, Napier suspected, precisely what he'd been doing for several days now. Evading. Avoiding. Pretending. And trying, perhaps, to convince herself that they had not crossed all boundaries. That he had not taken from her something that was not his by rights.

And that she had not willingly given it.

Yes, perhaps Lisette was suffering regret. But he would never know, he realized, if he did not speak to her of it; might never understand what was truly in her heart if he could not bear to ask.

But it was not so much her feelings for him that he questioned; he did not overly flatter himself in that regard. Instead he found himself increasingly desperate to know *her*. Her nature. Her character.

At first glance, it had been so easy for him to assume Elizabeth Colburne was ice-hearted— even a little unstable. Or a murderer. Yet with each passing day, it grew harder to appraise her at a distance—not even when she kept such a distance between them. He simply desired her, and feared he was fast falling in love with her. And more disconcertingly, what he might learn beyond that simple fact was rapidly ceasing to matter.

No, at this point, it was more a matter of simply figuring out how deeply he was in—then living with himself ever after.

Blithely unaware of his unsettled emotions, the three of them followed Napier out by the back terrace and through the gardens. It was just as well. He had more chance of resolving the deaths at Burlingame than the one left hanging over him in Greenwich—which wasn't saying much.

He walked on, scarcely absorbing the moonlit beauty of the gardens. On the outs with Gwyneth, Hepplewood soon hitched his arm through Lisette's and began to regale her with hilarious escapades from his boyhood summers spent gallivanting about the estate.

Left to walk in near silence with his cousin, Napier offered her his arm. Gwyneth Tarleton had a businesslike stride to match his own, and soon they were some distance ahead.

Beyond the shadows of the house, a stillness reigned over the gardens, settling around them like cotton wool to muffle the world beyond. The only sounds were the melancholy hoot of an owl in the wood beyond the lake and an occasional trill of laughter behind them. Napier drew the cool, clean air deep into his lungs and realized that though he might miss the bustle of London, a life of peace and quiet had much to recommend it.

Soon they turned from the formal gardens onto the long, yew-lined path that led down to the lake. Behind them, Hepplewood had begun to flirt with Lisette.

Gwyneth cast a dark look over her shoulder. "You mustn't mind Tony," she muttered. "He's harmless, I assure you."

"Oh, I don't mind him in the least," said Napier honestly.

"Well, most men do," said Gwyneth. "Shockingly good-looking, the devil. But all charm and no gravitas. An intelligent woman would never fall for it."

"No," said Napier dryly, "but many a stupid one likely has."

Gwyneth laughed, but when he said no more, she spoke again. "You're very quiet tonight, cousin."

"Am I?" he said. "You'd better rattle on about something, then. I'm an inadequate conversationalist at best."

"Oh, I've no talent for social banter," said Gwyneth, "according to Aunt Hepplewood. So, deficient as we are, how shall we begin? Here, I'll attempt it. Burlingame's gardens are beautiful at night, don't you think? I love how the moon reflects on the water."

"Everything about Burlingame is beautiful," Napier quietly acknowledged. "Breathtakingly so. One cannot begin to comprehend it in one visit, or even two."

Gwyneth seemed daunted by this open admiration and lapsed into silence again.

Napier cleared his throat a little gruffly. "Miss Tarleton," he said, "I hope you understand I mean you no—"

"Gwyneth," she said hastily. "You really must call me Gwyneth now. And you are Nicholas Royden, after your father, are you not? I can call you Royden, if you'd like, rather than Saint-Bryce."

"I wish you would," he said.

"Royden was our great-great-grandmother's surname," Gwyneth continued in a conversational tone. "And by tradition, someone in the family always bears it in her honor."

"Then it seems odd that I, of all people, should have it."

Gwyneth shrugged. "Your father was Nicholas Royden Tarleton before he changed the surname," she said. "I daresay he simply wished to name his son after himself. As to Grandmamma Royden, it was her massive dowry that made Burlingame the grand house it is today, and built the folly tower. That's what it is properly called—the Royden Tower—but I daresay you knew that?"

"Actually," he admitted, "I did not."

And for an instant, Napier felt an almost childish stab of resentment that she should have the privilege of knowing such family intimacies when he knew almost nothing at all. But that had been his father's choice, not Gwyneth's. And when had he begun to have a sense of longing about this place?

"The tower," he said evenly, "must be a hundred feet tall."

"Well, not quite," she replied. "It's said Grandmamma Royden built it so that she could gaze upon her father's house in Berkshire when homesick." Gwyneth smiled up at him in the gloom. "Until she married in, Burlingame was just a ramshackle little manor."

"One can scarcely fathom it," he murmured as laughter punctuated the air somewhere behind them.

Gwyneth ignored the sound. "Well, old history little matters in these modern times, however families might cling to it," she said with an ease he would not have credited. "Besides, I have heard that round Scotland Yard, they rarely call you either Napier or Royden."

He chuckled. "No, oftentimes not."

"Is it true, then?" said his cousin, her face breaking into a smile in the moonlight. "Do they really call you Roughshod Roy?"

"Yes, and honestly earned," Lisette called after them. "I expect it comes from his . . . well, let us politely call it his lack of diplomacy."

"A failing I shall strive mightily to overcome, my dear," he returned over his shoulder.

"Yes, well, I shan't hold my breath," said Lisette before returning to her chatter with Tony.

"In all seriousness, Gwyneth," said Napier, returning to his earlier point, "Burlingame is magnificent, but I am ill suited to lead it. I marvel I should even be meant to do so. I should rather ten times over that my uncle Harold—your father—had lived to take it on, as he was brought up to do. I hope you can believe me."

She turned to look at him as she walked, but they were in deep shadow now and he could only sense the faint smile on her face. "It is all rather ironic, is it not?" she said.

"What?"

"No one had more to gain by my father's death than you," said Gwyneth. "And yet you seem the only one concerned about it."

"I hope that is not the case."

She shrugged. "Oh, Bea is utterly crushed and Grandpapa is badly cast down, but I suppose he simply accepts that we can none of us bring Papa back, however much we might wish to. But you . . . well, you are prodding a little, are you not?"

"And when you say *prodding*," Napier murmured, "what, precisely, do you suggest?"

"Oh, come now," said Gwyneth in a knowing undertone. "Do you think I cannot see what you're doing? Talking to Grandpapa and Dr. Underwood and even Beatrice. And Miss Colburne's subtle questions, however delicately placed, scarcely deceive me. Now she might—*might*—be merely curious, as females often are. But you have been here three times now asking questions about Hepplewood. And now Papa, too."

"I trust I've not troubled anyone too greatly," said Napier, realizing Gwyneth was far more perceptive than he'd given her credit for.

"Oh, only Aunt Hepplewood." Gwyneth gave a sharp laugh. "It is a good thing you brought Miss Colburne along, else you'd have suffered the constant onslaught Papa did. Indeed, I'm not sure Aunt has entirely given up her schemes."

Napier did not pretend to misunderstand. "You are speaking of Miss Jeffers's future, I collect," he said. "But I am quite sure she can do better than me."

"And I am quite sure," said Gwyneth, "that she hopes so."

Napier was unsure who the *she* in that comment was meant to be. Miss Jeffers? Lady Hepplewood?

"Might I ask a little about you, Gwyneth?" he said smoothly. "What are your hopes? Your dreams? Aunt Hepplewood tells me you don't mean to marry."

"I'm thirty years old," she said, her voice suddenly sharp. "Does it look like I mean to marry?"

"Well, I merely meant—"

"You meant, I daresay, that you'll want rid of me, too, as soon as Grandfather's in the grave," she said through nearly clenched teeth. "Indeed, to a man, there can be nothing so burdensome as an unwed female relation left hanging off the family tree, cluttering up his house."

"Gwyneth," he said gently, "I suggested nothing of the sort. And if the world were fair—"

"But it is not fair, is it?" she interposed. "If it were, women would be allowed to inherit. And Burlingame would be *mine*. Not yours."

Napier drew back an inch. But Gwyneth had spoken with

less bitterness than frustration. Perhaps he was not the only one to feel slighted by fate.

"You are quite right," he admitted. "It is not fair. Can it be altered? I think it cannot. The laws of entail are entrenched."

"Deeply entrenched," she agreed, her ire receding. "And no, I don't want a husband. I just want what I've always wanted, and the one thing Papa would never—"

Her words fell away, and despite the shadows, he could see the chagrin sketch over her face. They had reached the planked pier that led from the glorious green lawn out into the lake, ending at a nearly water-bound structure that was more a gazebo than a boathouse. The water gently undulated all around it, throwing up the moonlight like slivers of glass.

Lisette and her new admirer had fallen a few yards behind. Napier paused at the end of the pier, hoping Gwyneth would continue speaking.

"What did you want, Gwyneth, that your father refused?" he finally said. "I should like to know."

She hesitated a heartbeat. "I wanted the dower house," she finally said. "Rather, the loan of it, for my lifetime."

"I didn't know we had a dower house," he replied, noting with some disquiet his use of *we.*

"It's a fine old house with a pretty garden on the other side of the village," said Gwyneth, her voice trembling with emotion. "I wished to remove there, and to take—or rather, to employ, Mrs. Jansen. As a lady's companion. Papa and I quarreled horribly about it. But how could he expect me—" Gwyneth stopped, and shook her head.

"What?" he pressed.

Her lips were drawn in a thin line. "How could he expect me to live *here*," she whispered, "with Diana as mistress of my home? Is it not bad enough Aunt Hepplewood dismisses my opinion at every turn? At least that is temporary. But Papa wished me to hand everything to Diana? As my step-mother?"

"If you want the dower house, Gwyneth," he said, "then I'm happy for you to have it. Shall I speak to Duncaster?"

Again, she shook her head. "He won't agree," she said. "When the tenant left, I begged—"

Just then, raucous laughter erupted as Lisette and Hepplewood drew up behind them. Gwyneth turned around, and Napier with her. Even by moonlight, one could see Hepplewood was laughing so hard his eyes were tearing.

"God save us from fools," Gwyneth muttered.

"No, Gwen, *listen*," said Hepplewood, motioning her nearer. "I was just telling Miss Colburne—Lord, it's just *too funny*—d'you remember that time we all jumped off the roof of the boathouse? Into the lake? And Anne tore that great, gaping hole in her shift?"

Gwyneth's smile was muted. "Indeed, Tony, who could forget?" she answered. "Anne caught her seam on a nail and you got *quite* an eyeful."

"I should say!" Hepplewood clapped a dramatic hand over his eyes. "To you and Diana, perhaps, it didn't matter. But my boyhood innocence ended in that moment—and just look what *that* has led to."

"Indeed, I joked years later that that was why you wouldn't marry her," said Gwyneth mordantly. "That a man didn't have to buy a pig in a poke when he'd already seen the pig in its altogether. As I recall, she tossed a glass of madeira on me."

"*Gwen!*" Hepplewood dropped the hand, his expression horrified. "Gwen, for God's sake, surely you never did anything so cruel? Besides, I never said I wouldn't marry her. I *never* said that."

Gwyneth drew back, stiffening at the neck. "But you didn't ask her," she retorted. "You let her entire Season go by without so much as a word."

Hepplewood, however, looked flummoxed. "Because, dash it, I *couldn't*," he said. "Not even with Grandpapa and

Duncaster hanging over me like vultures waiting to pick a carcass. I just . . . Gwen, don't you see? I *couldn't*."

"No, you simply *wouldn't*." Gwyneth had both hands on her hips now. "She was crushed, Tony. She'd been meant for you from the cradle and everyone knew it. *You* humiliated her, my boy. Not I."

"The devil!" Hepplewood sputtered. "What did I ever do to Anne?"

"Nothing," snapped Gwyneth. "That's the very point. My sister whiled away her entire Season scarcely daring to dance with another gentleman because she was waiting for you. And when you didn't come up to scratch, all society knew she'd been spurned. She had to accept that milquetoast Sir Philip Keaton at the last minute. To suggest *my* joke was her undying humiliation, oh, that's rich, Tony. Truly."

But Hepplewood had turned and was marching back up the hill. "The *devil*!" he said over his shoulder—apparently possessed of a limited vocabulary. "The devil take you, Gwen!"

Gwyneth, however, was more fluent, and began casting a variety of multisyllabic aspersions at Tony as she set off on his heels. Tony turned and began to walk backward, quibbling back in a dark undertone.

"So much for peace," said Napier under his breath, "—and cotton wool."

Lisette turned from gazing up the path. "I beg your pardon?"

"Never mind," he muttered. "Would you like to stroll out to the boathouse?"

"Well, I would like *not* to have to go back up the hill with Gwyneth and Tony," said Lisette. "Yes. The boathouse sounds lovely. Thank you."

Napier offered her his arm, very certain that matters would not end with the boathouse.

Even on the water, however, one could still hear his cousins arguing in the distance. And it suddenly seemed to him that they were bent, the whole damned family, on sullying Burlingame with their petty quarrels and undercurrents of animosity.

It was a beautiful place, yes. But like a glistening apple with a rotten core, it felt suddenly distasteful to him.

The boathouse was an open octagon railed all around in an oriental style, save for two sides left open to land boats. In the low, open rafters someone had stored a single scull and a small skiff, but they looked little used. Napier led Lisette just inside, then spun her around, urging her back against one of the columns.

Her breath caught teasingly when he wedged one leg, pinning her. "Oh, my," she murmured breathlessly. "What *can* you be thinking, Mr. Napier?"

"I'm thinking I should like to kiss you," he said, lowering his mouth, "and you well know it."

Humor lit her eyes. "Ah," she said softly. "And I thought you'd decided me dull."

"Oh, you're a lot of things, my dear," he rasped, "but dull will never be one of them."

Then he kissed her thoroughly and she permitted it, opening willingly beneath him, both her hands flattening against his back then sliding inexorably lower. When she entwined her tongue with his, Napier felt that familiar surge—that inexplicable rush of desire and yearning and, yes, a little fear—just as he'd known he would.

But this time there was no desperation in it. The longing felt as enduring as it did unassuasive. There was no need to rush. Not when a man was already lost.

When at last he pulled away, her humor had turned to something else. Lisette's lips were swollen with desire, her eyes wide and limpid in the moonlight. On a long exhalation, he set his forehead against hers.

"Lord, I needed that," he said, "to get the vile taste of Gwen and Tony out of my mouth."

She gave a thready laugh, and set a hand to his cheek. "You've been avoiding me again."

He still stood with one hand braced on the column, his head bowed. "I have tried, Lisette, to show restraint," he said quietly.

Her hand fell. "And you have," she answered, "until now. Just be aware all that restraint gives Lady Hepplewood hope."

"Hope? Of what sort?" But he shouldn't have been surprised; Gwyneth had suggested the same.

"Hope that you've tired of me," Lisette clarified. "Hope that she might still make a match between you and Diana."

"Did someone tell you that?"

Lisette caught her lip between her teeth. "Diana did," she finally said. "Yesterday."

Napier gave a bark of laughter. "Still afraid of being saddled with me, is she?"

"Yes," said Lisette, "and she is an utter fool."

Napier looked down at her, searching her face, but Lisette had gone perfectly still.

Suddenly, she drew a quick breath and went on. "In any case," she said, the words rushing forth, "I begin to think your great-aunt would marry that poor girl off to the village blacksmith given half a chance."

"So I've risen in Lady Hepplewood's esteem, then?" said Napier sardonically. "Until now I imagined myself ranked somewhere behind the boot boy."

Lisette laughed, but almost at once the heavy silence fell again. On an inward sigh, Napier kissed her—on the forehead this time—then gave her his arm and led her in a sedate stroll around the pavilion as she looked out across the glistening water. But his mind was in turmoil, searching for something he really should not wish to find. Hoping, perhaps, for something that simply did not exist.

Lisette was an actress nonpareil, he reminded himself. She had to be. She could never have survived otherwise, masquerading for all those months as a hard-bitten newspaper reporter with a taste for vengeance—something he was pretty near certain she'd done.

Moreover, he greatly feared she'd lived—probably been *forced* to live—a similar ruse in Boston. Perhaps her latest role as doting fiancée was simply bleeding over the edges of her script. And driving him mad in the process.

"Well," she said when his smile had entirely faded, "have you found your mysterious letter paper yet?"

He shook his head. "Thank you, though, for your efforts. Jolley has been mightily impressed."

"Alas, I've run out of places to steal it," said Lisette, "unless I start to pilfer unoccupied bedchambers. Well, everyplace save the late Lord Saint-Bryce's study."

"Indeed?"

"You must admit it's tucked rather out of the way," said Lisette defensively. "One would think a gentleman's study would be in a grander location."

"Marsh told Jolley that Saint-Bryce had his study moved upstairs when Bea was born," said Napier. "His wife was not well, and he wished to be near the child."

"I think I would have liked your uncle," said Lisette a little wistfully. "But for whatever reason, his study is always locked when I pass by."

"Locked?" said Napier. "That's a little odd."

She cut him a sidling glance. "I might take a hairpin," she suggested. "I have, admittedly, never actually *picked* a lock, but I'm not above trying. It's the most ordinary looking mechanism imaginable."

"*No hairpins*," he said darkly.

"Oh, good heavens," she said. "What can they do, have me drawn and quartered? In any case, Napier, trust me. I'm too quick to be easily caught."

"That," said Napier grimly, "has certainly been my experience."

She stopped, turning to face him. Even in the gloom, her face seemed to pale. "What, pray, is that supposed to mean?"

Napier was weary of the charade. "Damn it, Lisette, you know what it means."

She arched one brow. "It sounds as if you hope to catch me at something," she suggested. "But I thought we had a bargain?"

"Don't twist my words." He set his hands on her slender shoulders and gripped her hard. "And no, I don't deny you're good at what you do. Perhaps life has left you little choice. But are you ever going to trust me, Lisette? With anything other than your body?"

She shook her head; one swift, short jerk. "No," she whispered. "And you don't want me to. If you can't think of me, Napier, think of your career. Your honor."

He tightened his hold on her shoulders. "As if I haven't already compromised both of those?" She tried to turn away, but he forced her back. "Lisette, I'm long past worrying about deniability. My God, I've climbed in bed with the Earl of Lazonby—the most devilish, duplicitous fellow imaginable—to protect you."

At that, she went rigid. "No," she corrected, "you climbed in bed with him to protect *your father.* And if you've begun feel guilty for that—if you can't live with yourself—don't blame me for the choice you made."

She was right.

Damnation! When had his determination cleaved so cleanly he'd lost sight of his intent? When had her desperation become his?

"But perhaps you no longer need Lazonby's good will." Her voice was cold. "Perhaps you can prove your father's fine standard of living was all because of Duncaster."

He dropped his hands and pinched hard at the bridge of his nose. "This is not the conversation I wished to have right now, Lisette."

"Nor I," she said. "Nonetheless, it seems to be the one we're having."

"Then, no, it wasn't just Duncaster's money," Napier snapped. "I'm not an idiot, Lisette. I told you I looked at those accounts. Besides, we both know Sir Wilfred told the truth about my father; a man doesn't lie when he's got a gun to his head and about to meet his Maker."

It was no more than a turn of phrase, but it seemed to push her over some sort of edge. She made a pitiful sound; the faintest thing. Then she turned and sank onto one of the benches by the railing, her eyes wide.

He had hit upon the truth, he realized, or a part of it.

Certainly someone had got a confession out of Sir Wilfred—and the tool used to do it was more apt to have been the gun that shot him than any sort of gentle persuasion.

"Perhaps I can guess what happened, Lisette." He stood rigid before her. "Because I know you. Because I know what you're capable of. Especially when you're angry and in pain."

"Do you, then?" She licked her lips uncertainly, refusing to hold his gaze. "Well. My congratulations to you, Napier. Because I have no idea what I'm capable of. And I'm not sure I can even feel pain anymore."

"Lisette." Napier knelt before her, gripping her shoulders again. "Lisette, just *tell* me you didn't—"

But she leapt off the bench and strode away, planting her hands upon a span of railing on the opposite side—away from him. She looked as if she were shaking. He had no wish to frighten her, but damn it, he had to *know*.

Was there even a shred of truth to Lazonby's mad story? Or had Lisette simply shot a man in cold blood? And if she had, did it even matter to him anymore? He had the most dreadful feeling that it didn't. That he'd do anything—lie, cheat, forsake his duty—*anything* to protect her.

He wanted suddenly to take the first train back to London, and shake the truth from Anisha. But that assumed Anisha knew the truth. That she'd been conscious, or even present. And it assumed he could get past her new husband—past Lazonby, who had every reason to want Sir Wilfred dead and every reason to lie—at least for as long as it suited him.

And then, yes, Lazonby might well turn on Lisette and blame her with the murder, for theirs was an unholy alliance. Jack Coldwater and the *Chronicle* had had ruined him in the court of public opinion, methodically and viciously, and Lisette had been behind it all.

And now Napier was left to pray that Lazonby was a better man than he'd believed. He had to take comfort in Anisha's judgment in marrying the fellow, and perhaps in her capacity for mercy. Were Lazonby fool enough to go back on his statement—not something a man would do lightly—then surely Anisha would stop him?

He drew a deep breath, and let it out slowly, resisting the urge to tell Lisette that whatever she was, whatever she had done, it simply did not matter. Yet he remained frozen in place. Not because it wasn't true, but because Lisette would never have believed him.

There was nothing but the sound of water sloshing around the pillars below now. Gwyneth and Tony had long ago gone inside. Even the owl had stilled. At last Lisette turned around. Behind her, the lake glittered like a backdrop of diamonds, but her face lay in shadows.

"You brought me here, Napier, because you thought I was a good actress," she said, her voice surprisingly resolute. "And because I can be determined and yes, perhaps even a little ruthless. So let me do what I came here to do. Let me, for once, do the right thing."

"And just what would that be, Lisette?" he asked quietly.

"Well, I know what it is *not*," she said, her voice grim. "It is not right for either of us to continue to blame Lazonby for our troubles. You called him devilish and duplicitous. I . . . I once thought the same. But whatever he is, I had no right to ruin his life. I had *no right*. And I am so deeply ashamed. I will live with that all of my days."

It was as close to an admission as Napier was apt to get. "Lisette," he said, stepping toward her.

She threw up a hand, palm out, to stop him. "I cannot undo the pain I've caused Lazonby or anyone else," she said. "For my sort of sins, perhaps there is no redemption. But perhaps I can right someone else's wrong. I can get inside Saint-Bryce's office. If I'm caught, I'll bat my eyes and play dumb. I'll tell them I meant to visit Bea and got turned round. That the door was unlocked. Let them sort it out."

Lisette drew in a ragged breath, and waited for Napier to speak. She did not think she was on thin ice here; no, not yet. But she was sick in the pit of her stomach, and very uncertain. Moreover, a part of her was tired of worrying. Perhaps she should confess everything to Napier, pen a note of abject apology to Lazonby, and let them throw her in prison for killing Sir Wilfred. Doubtless it was what many people would think she deserved.

Napier stood now by the bench, his long, harsh jaw set like stone, his dark hair tossing lightly in the breeze coming off the water. When he turned to face her, Lisette knew that he was wrestling with some sort of demon. A choice he did not wish to make.

She only prayed it had nothing to do with her crimes.

That telling hand went to his waist again, and he began to pace. Slowly. Like the predator he was, perhaps. Yet despite the danger and the thwarted emotion he radiated, Napier looked every inch the wealthy aristocrat in his dark frock coat and elegant breeches.

Duncaster insisted upon old-fashioned formality at dinner, attire that became Napier's finely muscled legs. Even now she could see in her mind's eye the hard bulges of his bare calf and thigh; could almost feel the weight of his leg thrown over hers, and the soft brush of hair that dusted—

Dear heaven!

How could she think of such a thing just now? She must have made a sound—a laugh, no doubt, at her own stupidity, for Napier was staring at her. Then the scant clouds shifted, casting him in shadows.

"Lisette—" he said, his voice raw.

She threw out a staying hand, and shook her head. "I know you are apt to be my undoing, Napier," she said, the words a little unsteady. "I've known it since the moment you came walking up Sir Wilfred's lawn. I could see it in that awful, purposeful stride of yours. I feared I'd eventually be done for, and that even Lazonby—with all his tricks and machinations—would not be able to save me from myself."

"Lisette," he said. "Lisette, I am *not* your enemy."

She kept the hand up, for what little it was worth. "I don't know anymore," she said. "I didn't count on you . . . on this . . . this *thing* I feel. I can't bear it. Please don't let me make a fool of myself, Napier. Not over you."

He crossed the boathouse toward her, his tread heavy and ominous. "How am I to know what *this* is?" he whispered. "How am I to know how you feel? Or know anything about you?"

"I *feel* like a fool," she said harshly. "That's how I feel. As to the rest, you know what you need to know. May we let it go, Napier? *Please*. I'm doing what I promised. I'm keeping my end of the bargain, and you know it."

Anger sketched across his face. "So you just want me to let everything go," he said. "You don't want to trust me with the truth. You don't want anything more than this hellish bargain between us. You don't want us to . . . to be honest. To be intimate in any meaningful way."

Lisette closed her eyes and slowly shook her head. "Oh, Royden, you know I desire you." His name slipped so easily from her lips. "One more of those knee-melting kisses, and probably I'd lie with you right here and now."

"But it would be just sex," he gritted, stepping toward her. "And you would have no finer feelings for me."

For a long moment, she hesitated. "No," she whispered. "It's lust, Napier. And if we're wise, that's what we'll both call it."

He walked away then, all the way to the edge of the dock. There he hesitated, silhouetted in the moonlight, his hands clasped behind his back so tightly it looked painful.

"Then you leave me in an untenable position," he finally said, his tone harsh. "If I argue, you'll call me a cad. If I tell you I don't care what you are, you'll call me a liar. You'll sleep with me if I press the matter. So long as we don't talk. About anything personal. Does that about sum it up?"

"I—yes, I daresay it does." She hung her head.

"Then we do indeed find ourselves at an impasse," he said. "Shall I leave you now, Lisette? Is that what you wish?"

She threw up her hand impotently. Oh, she knew what she wished—and what she deserved. She felt the hot press of tears behind her eyes.

Napier radiated anger now. "Just tell me, Lisette, to go," he said, "and I will. Tell me never to kiss you again. Never to touch you. To surrender all hope of having anything more of you. And trust me when I say that, in this moment, all those words would feel like a mercy."

She swallowed hard, and finally found her voice. "You don't want me, Napier," she said, lifting her hand again. "Don't imagine yourself in love with me, for God knows I don't want to fall in love with you."

Napier felt something deep in his chest twist like a knife. Before he knew what he was about, he'd closed the distance between them and dragged Lisette hard against him. "Fine, then, lie with me here and now," he rasped. "As you say, it's just lust. It won't matter."

"Napier, I never meant—"

But his mouth seized hers, shutting off the words with a kiss more domineering than tender. It was pure male possession. Something frighteningly akin to rage roiled inside him as Napier thrust deep into that warm sweetness that was almost painfully familiar to him now.

She trembled, but didn't pull away. Entwining his tongue with hers, Napier pressed his hips into Lisette's with unmistakable intent. In response, she made a soft, feminine sound of uncertainty. Hot need—that raw male wish to have her— shot through his body like a lightning bolt.

But the heels of her hands were still wedged hard against his shoulders. Lisette shoved, but the desire and the rage and that aching sense of loss had churned up anew and Napier could not relent. He burned for her. And she burned for him. Let her walk away if she could summon the will; he would damned well not make it easy. He needed to have his way in this one, simple thing, needed to force her actions to belie her cold words—or force her to backhand him royally.

It seemed he hardly cared which, for when her hands relaxed, Napier deepened the kiss, urging her back against the wooden column of the boathouse, plunging his fingers into her mass of curls to still her face to his kisses. He could hear his own pulse pounding in his ears. Could feel his cock surge hard as a tipstaff against the soft swell of her belly.

He wanted to kiss her until her breath came in gasps and her eyes were hooded and heavy with need. Wanted to thrust and caress and suckle until her cold, pale beauty was in utter dishabille. Wanted to force Lisette to . . .

To what?

To love him?

It was logic bordering on insanity.

And if he wanted a fight, he was not to have that, either.

Instead, Lisette had begun to kiss him back. Deeply. Hungrily.

He set a hand to her cheek, and on a soft groan, her hands slid around his waist, then under his coat, leaving him shivering with lust. He wished suddenly for the moonlight's return—ached to see her eyes and the finely carved bones of her face. To see her desire for him—or at least the desire for what he could give her—writ plain upon her face.

On a rough exhalation, Napier shifted his hands to cup the full swells of her breasts. Lisette sighed into his mouth. He snared his thumbs in her décolletage, and tugged both dress and chemise down until the pale mounds surged over her corset and into his hands.

At last he lifted his mouth from hers, and let it slide lingeringly down her throat to catch a sweet, hard nub between his teeth. Gently he bit, teasing at the very tip with his tongue.

"Oh. Napier."

The words were mere exhalations. Utter surrender. Lisette let her head fall back against the column, thrusting her bare breasts higher. Offering herself up for his pleasure. He accepted, suckling her hard—nipping first tenderly, and then not.

She cried out, trembling against him. When he turned his attention to the other breast, her hands slid lower, all the way down to the hard muscles of his hips to pull him toward her in that most carnal of ways. Napier continued his torment, drawing the swollen bud more fully into the heat of his mouth, sucking until her breath began to come in soft, quick gasps. In the heat of their passion her seductive scent rose, maddening him.

At last her fingers plunged into his hair on a cry.

Napier was vaguely aware of the risks he ran. The risk of the moon's return. The risk of discovery.

The risk of losing his heart forever.

He forced it all from his mind and instead fisted up her skirts in a rustle of silk, winding them higher and higher in his hand. Slipping the other hand between them, he urged her legs apart with his knee and found his fingers wet with her silk. She gave a little cry of pleasure at the touch, and Napier pressed his mouth to her ear as he slipped one finger inside her slick sheath.

"Is this . . . *just lust*?" he whispered.

She swallowed hard, her head still tipped back against the column, her knees sagging weakly. "Damn you, Napier," she finally said. "I always knew you were the devil."

On a soft sound, he drew his fingers through her wetness again, this time grazing her sweet, quivering nub. She did not struggle when he shoved her skirts to her waist, nor when he pulled loose the tie of drawers.

He watched in satisfaction as the silk sailed down her legs to puddle on the planks. Lisette had slender, beautiful legs that begged to be hitched about his hips, giving him free range to thrust and plunder. But first, he was determined to enslave her as he was enslaved, if only fleetingly.

She stiffened with shock when he went down on one knee, and cried out threadily when he plunged his tongue into her heat.

"*Napier . . . ?*"

It was madness, perhaps. Especially for a man as calculated as himself. But he made love to her with his mouth all the same, easing two fingers into the wet tangle of curls, then into her silken passage. For long moments he thrust his fingers gently, tormenting her with his tongue, listening in satisfaction to her breathy sobs.

She clutched the railing behind with one hand, the nails of the other digging into his shoulders. "Oh, God," she cried.

As her climax drew near, Lisette began to shake as if frightened, her hands moving as if to stop him. But he did not stop, and her fingers plunged into his hair again. Then she gave a soft, keening wail, shuddered, and then came apart beneath the gentle onslaught, her long, lithe body wracked with waves of release.

She was so beautiful, caught in the throes of her passion, and that beauty only ratcheted his own need higher. He stood and held her as she rocked with the last waves of release, then swiftly opened his trousers, yanking hard at the buttons. Shoving the fabric down in a wad, he lifted her and pushed himself inside her awkwardly. He lifted her another fraction, and felt the hot length of his cock slide deep into her pulling wetness.

Instinctively Lisette lifted one leg, hitching it over his hip. On a groan, Napier pinned her to the column with the strength of his body, lifted her in his arms, then took his own pleasure in thrusts so deep and so fast they would have shamed the greenest of schoolboys. There was no grace in his actions; it was a vulgar, desperate act, and Lisette was no woman of experience.

Yet the shame did not slow him. His breath heaving from his chest, Napier thrust and thrust again, lifting her with each stroke until his pleasure came, blinding white and pure in his head. And as the last surge of his seed pumped into her, and the deep, shuddering weakness took him, Napier knew without question he was lost.

CHAPTER 11

Fanny to the Rescue

$\mathcal{L}$isette and Napier returned to the house together, picking their way back up the path with rather more care than had been required to come down. The clouds had thickened now, and the moon showed little inclination to reappear. It was as well, Lisette decided, for the darkness helped to dispel the lingering awkwardness that now hung unspoken between them.

But perhaps words had become superfluous? As with all things, it seemed that Napier could look straight through to the truth inside her. He sensed her most intimate desires, could edge near her most closely held secrets, and knew, perhaps, her darkest fears.

Not for the first time, Lisette wished desperately she were more like her sister or her father. Easily self-deluded. Able to cling to hope when hope was but a pipe dream, ever certain that a life of happiness was not just around the corner, but that it was deserved.

Instead Lisette felt the curse of Cassandra upon her shoulders. This would not end well for her; she was in deep, her heart already half broken, and she knew it.

Nor, in the end, was she to have a reprieve from the awkwardness. Napier jerked to a halt halfway up the hill, and turned to face her in the gloom.

"Lisette, I'm sorry," he said. "What we did just now . . . nightingales in Covent Garden, I daresay, are treated with more grace."

She stood rigidly on the path. "Did I ask you for grace?" she said quietly. "You are an exquisite lover, Napier—a fact you doubtless use to your advantage. But if I told you I didn't enjoy what we did just now, then we'd both know me for a liar."

"A lady deserves something a little more elegant than to have her skirts thrown up," he said, his voice rueful in the dark. "A lady deserves . . . romance, Lisette. To be properly courted. Flirted with."

"But you are not a romantic, remember?" She forced a smile, though he could not see it. "And in truth, Napier, I cannot imagine a man less flirtatious."

"Christ, Lisette. That's harsh."

"I don't mean it so," she replied. "It is who you are, and you've always been honest about it. And for a man who's not a romantic, not flirtatious, and who possesses little in the way of charm, I'd say you're doing pretty well for yourself. I haven't yet found the will to refuse you. And I . . . well, I fear I never will."

She could feel him watching her in the dark.

"Let it go, Napier," she whispered. "Yes, we desire one another. And that might be unwise, but it's neither vulgar, nor a crime. Let's get back to worrying about what brought us here, and how we may resolve it."

For a moment, she thought he didn't mean to answer. Then, after a long pause, Napier set off up the path again.

"You're right," he said. "The sooner we're finished here the better."

"Thank you." She ignored the slight sting in his words. "Just tell me what to do."

"Very well." He spoke in hard, clipped tones: the impersonal giving of orders that she remembered from Hackney. "Tomorrow morning after breakfast, go into the library. Alone, if at all possible."

"Certainly," she replied. "And once there—?"

"Act as if you are looking for a book," he said coolly, "and keep one eye on the door. Eventually, Jolley will walk past. Follow him at a distance into the great hall. He will go up the main staircase to the south side of the second floor."

"South?" she said. "Toward the schoolroom and study?"

"Yes," said Napier tightly. "Jolley carries in his pocket a lock pick—"

"Ah," she murmured. "Why am I not surprised?"

"Just follow him," Napier ordered. "If no one is about, he'll have Saint-Bryce's study open in a trice. I'd have him search it—he's capable enough—but there's no excuse for his being there should someone see him. And if you are seen—"

"If I'm seen, I'll deal with it," she interjected.

His lips thinned. "Very well," he finally said. "Make a mental list of what's in the room using your—what did you call it? Near total recall? God knows neither Jolley nor I have it. So survey the room and go through the desk. Take samples of any letter paper you find."

"Yes, of course," she said. "Where will you be?"

"Unless it rains, I'm headed to Berkshire with Craddock to inspect one of Duncaster's lesser estates," he said. "We might be away the night. But Jolley can fetch me if need be."

"There will be no need," she promised. "You may count on me."

"Thank you," he said a little stiffly. "But after this, Lisette, I think we must make some hard decisions."

"What do you mean?" The words came out more sharply than she'd intended.

He hesitated. "I should rather cross that bridge another day," he finally said. "But I see little more to be done here."

He then offered her his arm—a sort of truce, perhaps—and they continued in silence for a time, soon reaching the edge of Burlingame's formal gardens. Lisette curled her hand into the softness of his coat sleeve, all too aware of the strength that lay beneath.

"Have you been in the schoolroom yet?" he eventually asked.

"Yes, but I've been unable to have a good look at it." Idle gossip seemed safer than dwelling on what had just happened in the boathouse. "Someone is always there. Do you suspect Mrs. Jansen of something? She seems the most benign of creatures."

Napier shook his head, but she felt some of the tension leave his arm. "I don't know whom I suspect—nor even what I suspect them of," he said. "Two deaths and two more perilously near it—and all in a few months' time? Perhaps Underwood is sure Saint-Bryce died of apoplexy, but . . ."

There was something he wasn't telling her, thought Lisette. Something besides a rambling letter from an old man on his deathbed, and a pair of sick footmen. But at least they were back on their old footing.

"And poor Prater," she murmured. "Who could wish him ill? I cannot say as I care for Walton—he eyes women far too lasciviously to suit me. He's begun to sneer at Mrs. Jansen. The poor creature is frightened of him, I believe."

"Walton had better be frightened of Gwyneth," said Napier grimly. "She's definitely capable of poisoning someone."

"Oh, it's not just Gwyneth. There's enough suppressed rage in that house to blow the roof off should someone strike a match wrong." Lisette pulled her shawl tighter. "And then there's that awkward business with Mrs. Jansen."

He flicked another glance in her direction. "What do you mean?"

"Well, perhaps that's why Walton sneers at her now?" Lisette felt her face heat. "Because his cause is so obviously lost, and his good looks are useless? I mean, really, don't all you Englishmen have one of those odd, old-maid aunties tucked in a cupboard somewhere?"

"You seem to become conveniently American when it suits you," Napier remarked, "and I believe Mrs. Jansen is a widow. But do continue. I find your assessment fascinating."

"For all that they're often together, I think Gwyneth and Diana hate one another," she mused. "Though hate may be too strong a word. And Lady Hepplewood runs over Gwyneth, overruling her household decisions, and seems to quite disdain Diana. In fact, Lady Hepplewood gives the impression of being—well, just grief stricken. Weighed down with it. All the time. I think it's made her bitter in her old age."

"Grief stricken? That's not the term I'd have chosen."

Lisette shrugged. "But that's what it is," she said quietly. "I know grief when I see it. And I comprehend bitterness."

Napier fell silent a moment. "And Mrs. Jansen?" he finally said. "What do you make of her?"

"She's very quiet," said Lisette, "but I like her well enough."

"I like her, too," he said. "Does she fancy herself . . . er, emotionally attached to Gwyneth?"

"I think it quite likely," Lisette acknowledged. "They are in one another's company whenever Mrs. Jansen's duties permit. But what can that have to do with Lord Hepplewood's death?"

"In my experience, passion can be the source of much trouble," said Napier.

With a wry smile, Lisette considered how very true that was. "For my part, I worry more about Lady Hepplewood," she said. "Why is she even living in Wiltshire? First we hear the house in Northumberland is drafty and run down. Then Diana—who would surely know—says that's not the case."

"Perhaps there's just no pleasing Lady Hepplewood," Napier muttered.

"It's more than that," Lisette countered. "And now we hear that Gwyneth is angry because Tony spurned her sister Anne—by the way, Anne is coming up from London tomorrow, had you heard? And bringing Miss Felicity Willet with her?"

"I'd heard rumblings, yes."

"It's all very odd," Lisette went on. "Tony's known in Town as a skirt-chasing wastrel, while Diana paints him a regular homebody who just wants to put his boots up by the fire. I rather like the fellow—one cannot help it—but I think he's much deeper, and far more shrewd, than he lets on."

"Or perhaps Diana is naïve?" Napier suggested.

Lisette twitched her shawl tighter again. The clouds scuttled past the moon, once more washing the gardens in light. Something was stuck in the back of her mind. Something that had flitted through her brain in the green bedchamber some days ago, and again just now. But she could not get it to alight long enough to be grasped.

"Oh, well," she said. "Diana may be a romantic ninny-hammer, but in other matters, she's no fool."

"And being romantic generally makes one a fool?" he asked.

She cut him a sharp glance. "Usually, yes."

"Ah, I begin to grasp your logic." Napier fell silent for a time. "But have you never had romantic leanings, Lisette? You are, after all, a self-confessed romantic."

"Yes, but I could ill afford such fantasies," Lisette retorted. "I was never the perfect princess, Napier, like Lady Anisha Stafford. My life was never a fairy tale. I will always be flawed. Always be different."

"But surely in Boston there was someone courting you?"

Lisette disliked the direction they were taking. "A few young men, yes," she said, "especially when Uncle Ashton's health began to fail and it was clear I'd inherit the paper."

"Ah, yes, the opportunists," he said softly.

"Gluttons for punishment, more like," she said as they turned into the carefully hedged parterres. "The paper lost money more years than not."

"And so you turned them away, brokenhearted?" His voice was faintly sardonic.

"I saved them from their own folly," she snapped. "And I had other plans."

"Yes," he said grimly. "I think you were too busy pursuing your mad notions of justice and revenge to think of your own future, Lisette. To think of what you might be giving up. I saw you with that child in your arms at Tafton's. I saw the want and the ache in your eyes. So don't even bother pretending what you've lost doesn't matter. It bloody well does matter."

She jerked to a halt on the graveled path. "How dare you talk to me of pursuing mad notions!" she said, her frustration rekindled. "You've come all the way to Wiltshire for reasons you cannot even articulate. And whatever I've given up, at least the choice was *mine*."

For a moment he stood stock-still, blocking the path before her. Then, "*Touché*," he said softly.

Lisette felt herself trembling inside. "You offered earlier tonight to leave me to myself," she replied. "May I now accept that offer? I should like to sit in the gardens for a while and enjoy the calm."

He bowed once, very stiffly, at the neck. "But of course."

Suddenly, and entirely on impulse, Lisette reached out for him, catching his hand. "Napier, I'm sorry," she said. "I wish—oh, God, how I wish that life were different. That we'd met in a different time and place, and that we'd neither of us have any regret when all this was over."

His mouth turned up in a sardonic smile. "Damn me for a fool, Elizabeth, but I don't regret anything we've done," he said. "All I regret is the distance and the deceit." Then, to her shock, Napier leaned into her and set his lips lightly to her forehead.

And on her next breath, he was gone, turning and striding through the last of the gardens and up the veranda steps. Fleetingly, his broad shoulders and impressive height were silhouetted in the lamplight that spilled from the house. Then Walton pushed the door wider, and without so much as glancing back, Napier vanished.

Drawing her shawl tighter still, Lisette stood in the suddenly cold air watching the house. After a few moments had passed, she saw his shadowy form go striding through the long colonnade. On a sigh, she sat down on the first bench she could find.

Only then did she realize her hands were shaking quite visibly.

He was not going to be satisfied, she realized, with her help here in Wiltshire. And he was not going to be satisfied with the pleasures of her body.

No, Napier wanted her to cut open a vein and bleed the truth. About *everything*. About things she dared not even face herself.

Well, she could not do it. She had stayed the course in the face of far more brutal storms than Napier was capable of stirring.

She only hoped she could stay the course in the face of her own passion.

She wanted to kick herself for her own stupidity. Like the stray cat she was, Lisette lived on her instincts. As Jack Coldwater, the androgynous, red-haired reporter, she had consorted with criminals and thugs—and more dangerous still, politicians—all in order to muckrake for the *Chronicle*. She had followed Lazonby into hells and dark alleys and once even the rookeries of Whitechapel in pursuit of something that might put him back on the gallows.

Her instincts had carried her safely through it all.

But now, because of a desirable man, they might fail her? Oh, *surely* she was smarter than that. *Tougher* than that.

Or at least, she had been.

Before Royden Napier and his all-seeing eyes.

Lisette had no idea how long she sat alone in the gardens contemplating her own mortal weaknesses, but when at last she rose, it was to find that though the urge to cry had left her and a little of her resolve had returned, her teeth had begun to chatter.

After hastening up the rear steps, she followed Napier's path through the house. By the flickering sconces in the grand entrance hall, she could see the gilt tallcase clock showed a few minutes past midnight. She passed through the colonnade and started up the east pavilion's winding staircase.

Just then, her ears caught a sound high above her head, and the mere impression of motion. She froze like a rabbit, gingerly looking upward.

A dark shadow pulled away from the balustrade, and she heard Napier's familiar footsteps heading down the passage-way in the direction of his bedchamber. He had been waiting for her, she realized.

But when she rushed up the stairs to . . . well, to do some-thing both rash and unwise, Lisette was saved from her folly by an empty corridor. Napier's door was shut tight and only the faint scent of his shaving soap remained.

Like the gentleman he was, Napier had merely waited to be sure she returned safely from the gardens. It was a com-forting if disappointing realization. For a long moment, she simply stood there, hand lifted as if to knock on his door.

But to say . . . *what?*

On a sigh, Lisette passed the door by, and went down to

her room to find Fanny stitching up a torn hem by the light of her bed lamp.

Her gaze flicked up from her work, swift and knowing. "Evening, Miss Lisette," she said, tucking the fabric away. "You look a tad disheveled."

"Fanny, why aren't you abed?" Lisette sagged into a chair before the dressing table and began to tug out her hairpins. "But since you're not, will you help me get these ribbons out of my hair? Blast, will the stuff ever grow out?"

Fanny sighed, rose, and set to work on her hair. "It *is* growing," she said. "Besides, some ladies do still wear their hair short."

"Oh, yes." Lisette scowled at the mirror. "Consumption victims."

"Some ladies, somewhere, do, I'm sure," Fanny chided. "French ones, probably. No, put down your hands. You're just getting in my way."

Suitably chastised, Lisette put her hands in her lap. "What was the gossip today, Fanny?" she asked lightly. "I heard Miss Tarleton's sister is to arrive tomorrow."

"Oh, yes, and a proper favorite she is belowstairs." Fanny was tugging at a tangle with the comb. "Mrs. Marsh had a letter from her. Seems Miss Anne—or Lady Keaton, she is now—met this Miss Felicity Willet at church and struck up a friendship."

"So that's how Hepplewood met Miss Willet," Lisette mused.

"Aye, and Lady Keaton is over the moon about the betrothal," said Fanny, "or so she wrote."

So perhaps Gwyneth was wrong. Perhaps Hepplewood had not compromised Miss Willet at all. They did not love each other, no, for he'd admitted as much to Lisette in the garden. But perhaps they were genuinely fond of each other?

The hope lightened Lisette's heart a little. Dear heaven,

was she becoming as romantic and as dreamy-eyed as poor Diana Jeffers?

"What do the servants say about Sir Philip Keaton?" she pressed, turning the topic.

"Oh, they like him very well indeed." Fanny put down the comb. "A proper gentleman, Marsh called him."

"Gwyneth called him a milquetoast."

Fanny snorted. "Aye, well, anyone would be, compared to her," she said. "Oh, and I gave your last piece of paper to that Mr. Jolley—and ain't he a downy one, by the way?"

"What, that cloud of white hair?" Lisette laughed.

"No, downy as in . . . quick-witted." Fanny was tossing pins into a porcelain dish on the dressing table. "Resourceful, you'd call it."

"Oh, I fear we don't know the half," said Lisette.

"Aye, and don't want to know, like as not."

Lisette lifted her gaze to the mirror and watched the maid's clever fingers work. "You're always so shrewd, Fanny," she said after a moment had passed.

Fanny looked over Lisette's head, and caught her eyes in the mirror. "*Hmm*," she said. "What's the trouble, miss?"

Lisette looked down at her lap. She'd begun to pick at one of her cuticles, always a bad sign—a sign that she was about to do something foolhardy. But she could no more stay away from Royden Napier's bed, she feared, than fly to the moon.

"Fanny, I was wondering," she said, "how hard—or, rather, how easy is it to . . . to *not* get . . ."

"To not get what?" Fanny's voice had an uneasy edge.

"—with child," Lisette managed.

"Oh, Lord." Fanny dropped a fistful of hairpins in the dish. "Come to that, has it?"

"Well, I'm not perfectly sure," Lisette fibbed, "yet."

Fanny's lips thinned disapprovingly. "Aye, well, that Mr. Napier's a big, strapping buck of a man, to be sure," she said, "but awfully grim if you ask me—and vicious, too, that Mr. Jolley says, when he's crossed."

Lisette shot her a dark look in the mirror. "How to you know it is Napier?"

Fanny snorted. "Who, then?" she said. "That handsome Lord Hepplewood with all his silky words and fine ways? No, miss, you're too downy yourself to fall for that. But Napier"—here, she gave a little shudder—"that one's a tad too far the other direction. I'd think twice, miss, about warming that black-eyed devil's bed."

"Actually," said Lisette, "his eyes are blue. When you get very close."

Fanny sighed. "Well, then, if you're getting *that* close," she said, dropping the lid on the dish with a clatter, "then I may as well quit flapping. And you'd best get your calendar and come over here by the lamp."

CHAPTER 12

In Which Jolley Plays the Screwsman

"*L*ooks like rain to me, sir," Jolley grumbled the next morning, holding open his master's riding coat. "Pity I fagged me elbow glossing up them tall boots."

Jolley helped Napier slide the garment up his arms, careful not to bunch his shirtsleeves. Then, taking up a little brush, he carefully swept the shoulders and lapels, tidying the fabric's nap.

It was something Napier had never quite grown used to, this custom of being helped with one's dressing. In the past, he had believed it an affectation of the rich, who hadn't nearly enough to do. But Duncaster had sharply corrected him.

A wealthy man's estate, his grandfather explained, provided employment for a vast array of people—from the lowliest stable hand to the talented Craddock himself—and allowed them in turn to feed their families. There was great pride, the old man said, in serving a noble house like Burlingame.

Napier had never looked at it quite that way.

Nor had Jolley, apparently. He let his hands fall, giving the brush a cavalier toss. "Right, then," he said, patting his pocket. "If that's enough of a morning mollycoddle for you, yer lordship, I'd best be off with Betty here, hadn't I?"

Napier cut him a warning glance. "Just be sure you and Betty don't get caught," he said. "And that you keep Miss Colburne out of trouble."

One hand already on the doorknob, Jolley grimaced. "I might be a first-class screever, sir, and a dab hand with me pick, but there's not a fellow born can manage a redhead— and that one doubly so, if you ask me."

"I didn't." Napier cut him a dark look. "Just tell me where the damned boots are."

"Dressing room, sir, just to the left," said Jolley evenly, "and so shiny you'll be able to see that great nose of yours in the polish."

With that, the door slammed, leaving Napier, sullen and sleepless, to tug on the tall boots himself. He did not blame Jolley nearly as much as he wished to. The poor devil certainly hadn't volunteered for this duty, and it wasn't his fault Napier's eyes had scarcely closed last night. Nor was it Lisette's.

No, as usual, he'd brought the trouble on himself.

The tall boots wrestled on, Napier went to the window by his bed and simply stood looking down at the lake, wondering if Jolley were right in his assessment of redheads.

There was a mist on this morning, a gray and feeble thing that crept over the water and clung to the glass like the uncertainty that had crept into his soul. On impulse, he threw up the window and leaned out into the damp, drawing it deep into his lungs. Embracing, perhaps, the ambiguity.

But he had reached a decision in the wee, restless hours of the morning, he realized.

He was going to take Lisette back to Hackney.

And he would do it by week's end, at the latest. What she did after that—even if she absconded to Scotland, Boston, or the Italian coast—he told himself it would have to be her choice. He couldn't make her love him. He certainly couldn't make himself bring her to justice, whatever that was. And bringing her to Burlingame had been folly of the worst sort. The self-deceptive sort.

He had known, since that first moment in Whitehall, that the woman fascinated him beyond all logic. And last night had brought home to him the realization that he could trust neither his heart nor his actions—not where she was concerned. His longing for her unleashed in him a sort of madness that defied his own will. And he knew that if she were guilty of a crime—even a crime of the worst sort—he could not have prosecuted her.

In fact, he would have rationalized it away. His logical self knew this.

His illogical self simply knew she was innocent.

He had become one of those people to whom, under certain circumstances, the truth simply did not matter. He would believe what he chose to believe.

For a man who'd so long lived by black and white, this blurring felt—on some strange level—a little liberating. For if truth did not matter, perhaps what his father had done was not so egregious? Perhaps walking away from a life of service, a career that both frustrated and fulfilled him, was not a selfish choice?

But neither of those things had anything to do with Lisette, whose happy life had been so unfairly stripped from her by Sir Wilfred Leeton and a warped, imperfect justice system. She had been hurt to the point that she'd claimed she was no longer sure she could even feel pain.

Well, by God, he felt it.

He felt it enough for the both of them.

And the only way through it was forward. He needed to

get Lisette away from here, settle what little he could of this business at Burlingame, then return to London and hand his resignation to Sir George. Because it wasn't just his heart he couldn't trust. He could no longer trust himself to do his job. He had crossed that line between black and white, and he did not mean to return.

With Sir Philip and Lady Keaton soon to arrive, along with their child, there would surely be enough goings-on to keep his Aunt Hepplewood occupied, even with Lisette away. Moreover, his theory about his anonymous letter had not been borne out, and he was fast coming to believe that the mysterious author was more of a troublemaker than a concerned citizen.

But thinking of the letter reminded him of a pressing missive from Sir George, and after glancing at the clock, Napier decided he had just enough time to answer it. He drew up a chair to his writing table, realizing that while he missed his duties at Number Four, he did not miss them nearly as much as he'd feared he might.

He could be content here at Burlingame, he realized. Or as content as he ever was anywhere—particularly so once the house had been emptied of meddling relations.

But he was not at all sure he would ever be happy.

He felt the awful sadness grip his heart again, and cursed his own weakness. It was in moments like this that he longed for the days of black and white. The days when he had been confident in the righteousness of his every decision. When he'd been relentless in his pursuits—be it the pursuit of justice, or the pursuit of a woman.

The days before he'd fallen in love with Elizabeth Colburne, and begun to worry about estates and corn and his orphaned cousins. Next it would be puppies. Or a damned rose garden, perhaps. He had lost his hard edge. Gone soft. Begun to give a damn.

Christ, he hardly recognized himself.

He was a better human being, perhaps. Of course he was. But at what cost? The cost of his heart?

But if he could not have Lisette, weren't there a thousand other things both great and small to which he might turn his energies, if not his heart?

God forbid Duncaster should die anytime soon, but when he did, Napier had resolved to give Gwyneth the dower house and pack his great-aunt back to Northumberland on the first train, sending Miss Jeffers along with her. The young lady could fend for herself, or decorate a damned house for her widowed father. Heaven knew it was what she seemed good at, with her scraps and her sketchbooks always to hand.

In the end, only Beatrice would remain at Burlingame, and only then if neither of her sisters better suited her. Napier had meant what he'd promised the child about this being her home as long as she wished, though he had no idea how he would go on with an eleven-year-old girl in his care.

It felt more daunting, in some respects, than the actual running of the estate. And it was just as important—if not more so. Moreover, a child needed a woman's touch. Someone wise and protective. Someone both fierce and gentle.

Sensing the direction his thoughts were taking, Napier cursed beneath his breath, and dipped his pen into the ink. Ruthlessly shoving Lisette to the back of his mind, he hastened through his letter to Sir George, then went down to breakfast.

The room was empty. Lisette had gone, of course, along with everyone else. He dined alone, then set off in the direction of the estate offices.

His trip was in vain. Craddock sat by the hearth, a fire built up against the damp, a lap desk propped awkwardly on one knee, and his left foot up on a pile of cushions, bare of shoe or stocking.

"I do beg your pardon, sir," he said, trying to set the desk away.

Napier threw up his hand. "Don't get up, Craddock," he ordered. "What's the matter?"

A faint blush rose on the man's cheeks. "I fear, sir, that I'm in the gout," he said. "It's . . . mortifying, really. It is an old man's disease, or so I imagined it."

"It is a bloody painful disease, at any age," said Napier, crossing the room to peer at the swollen red toe. "My good fellow, you cannot possibly put a boot on that foot."

"Nor even a stocking," Craddock admitted. "Riding is out of the question."

"It's just as well," Napier assured him, straightening. "My man Jolley predicts rain, and he's nigh infallible. If you don't believe me, just ask him."

Craddock managed a smile. "Would you like to go over the breeding records for the home farm instead?" he offered.

Napier set a hand on the man's shoulder. "What I'd like is for you to go back to bed with a stout tincture of opium and a peck of sour cherries," he said. "And go at once."

"Mrs. Buttons is fetching them now," Craddock admitted.

"Excellent, then. May I help you back upstairs?"

Craddock looked further embarrassed. "No, thank you, sir," he said. "I trust you can otherwise employ yourself?"

"Oh, yes," said Napier. "I shall doubtless think of something."

*M*r. Jolley, Lisette discovered, was nothing if not dependable. After another miserable, sleepless night, she was perusing Volume IV of the Encyclopedia Britannica at precisely half past eight, one eye upon the door, when the elderly, white-haired man walked past, his gait purposeful and his shoulders stooped.

Lisette shoved the encyclopedia back into its slot, snatched up a volume of fairy tales she'd laid aside, and then counted off ten seconds before breezing out the door and down the hall.

It was no trouble to hang back and out of his sight since she knew where Jolley was headed. But as Lisette passed through the grand entrance hall, she was surprised to see Lord Hepplewood and Diana standing in the depths of the west colonnade in what appeared to be an intense, whispered discussion.

With his tousled curls, dark blue coat and matching striped waistcoat, Lord Hepplewood looked, as always, dangerously handsome. Diana, however, looked distraught. Hepplewood gripped her arm just above her wrist, as if holding her back from something.

Suddenly, on a sharp word, Diana shook her head, yanked from his grasp, then swept past him and into the hall, brushing by Lisette with a curtest of greetings, her heels rapidly clicking across the wide, vaulted chamber. It looked as if she were blinking back tears.

For an instant, Lisette hesitated, feeling she ought to go after her, but Jolley had vanished around the turn of the stairs.

Lord Hepplewood saved her the decision, striding across the hall with a grim look in his eyes. "Let Diana go," he said gently. "It's just Mamma again."

Lisette felt her face color. "They have quarreled?"

"Hardly." Hepplewood's smile was muted. "One does not really *quarrel* with Mamma, does one?"

"Lord Hepplewood," said Lisette abruptly, "why do I somehow get the impression you're a far better man than you make out? In fact, I sometimes wonder you're much of a rake at all."

At that, he grinned, his flawlessly white teeth flashing. "Ah, my dear Miss Colburne!" he said. "Have you finally surrendered to my facile charms? Women generally do, in the end. Even my dear Miss Willet, I think, has succumbed."

Lisette opened her mouth to reply, but it was not necessary. Lord Hepplewood had cut her a deep, elegant bow, then passed her by. For a moment she could only stare after him. Perhaps he *was* a cad. She didn't know, and it wasn't her problem. Shaking off the urge to follow Diana, Lisette hastened up the stairs.

Jolley, apparently, had hesitated long enough to permit her to catch sight of him turning the next corner. Lisette sent up a little prayer of thanks. And by the time she'd trotted up two flights of stairs and wound her way through the rabbits' warren of corridors, Jolley was walking away again, and tucking something back into the pocket of his coat.

Lord Saint-Bryce's office door stood ajar.

Lisette slipped inside, started to close it, and then thought better of the notion. Were she to be discovered, a closed door would be suspicious. Instead, she threw it wide, and began methodically to search, alert to any sound.

The room was not terribly large. Swiftly, she surveyed the fitted bookcases flanking the hearth. No volume leapt out. With an eye to the door, she pulled the two books that had obvious bits of paper tucked inside.

Both were agricultural tomes marked with scraps that held nothing of interest: a boot maker's receipt and a scribbled note from Mr. Crawford about repairing a granary roof. She shoved them back and turned her attention to the stacked drawers that should have held files.

She pulled out each drawer to find all had been emptied. And rather recently, for there was not a speck of dust inside. Disappointed, she looked behind the draperies, then tipped aside the three landscapes that hung about the room, peering behind each for hidden papers or perhaps even a safe.

Nothing.

She tried the desk. It appeared to be locked. Quelling her impatience, Lisette pushed and pulled each drawer in turn, all to no avail. On a muttered curse, she examined the surface. There was a blotter, well used. An inkwell, empty. An antique silver wax-jack, tarnished and absent its snuffer—clearly a sentimental piece.

Lisette put it down and moved on. A stack of books sat neatly piled on one corner; a Bible, a dictionary, a treatise on animal husbandry, and the Book of Common Prayer, all well thumbed. Hastily she flipped through each and found nothing.

Just then, Lisette froze. Footsteps—light and quick—were coming down the passageway. Snatching up the fairy tales, she left the desk and stepped swiftly to the door, then turned her back to it setting one arm akimbo.

"Miss Colburne—?"

"Oh, dear!" Lisette spun around, deeply furrowing her brow. "Oh, Mrs. Jansen, there you are. But . . . where am I?"

Mrs. Jansen looked unhappy. "You are in Lord Saint-Bryce's study," she said with faint disapproval. "Gwyneth—Miss Tarleton—wishes it kept locked until she has finished cleaning it out."

"Really?" Lisette tried to look stupid—which, after last night, didn't feel like much of a stretch. "The door was cracked when I came by, and so I thought—" Here, she looked about the room, then shook her head. "Somehow I thought this was the door to the schoolroom."

"The schoolroom?"

"Yes, but all the doors on this floor look very like, do they not?—at least to one unaccustomed to grandeur." Lisette gave a sheepish smile. "In any case, I found a book of fairy tales in the library and thought I might show it to Beatrice?"

"Then I fear you simply went left when you should have gone right." She turned and, with an efficient snap of her wrist, locked them inside the room. "The rooms are back to back, or nearly so."

"But you—you just locked us in," said Lisette, staring uneasily at the lock plate.

"We'll go another way." But Mrs. Jansen was looking at her oddly. "Miss Colburne, are you perfectly well? Your eyes, they look a little—"

"A little red, I know." Lisette forced a sheepish smile. "The grass this time of year makes me sniffle. I ought not have walked through the gardens last night with Lord Hepplewood."

"Ah," said the governess.

"In any case, the way out is . . . ?"

"Follow me."

Then Mrs. Jansen crossed to a panel of wainscoting topped by the smallest of the landscapes, and cleverly pushed a piece of molding. Lisette felt suddenly foolish. A wall panel she had not noticed swung neatly out, taking both wainscoting and painting with it.

Surprised, Lisette gazed at the narrow, unlit passageway beyond. In the gloom, she could see it was lined with cupboards over counters on one side and open shelves on the other, some of which were stacked with books and toys. One shelf, the lowest, was neatly lined with dolls, carefully seated, while the taller shelves above were set with miniature pieces of furniture.

"How clever," Lisette murmured. "What is this room?"

"An old butler's pantry," she replied, waving at the shelves as she passed through. "I keep some of Beatrice's books in here, but mostly it stores her toys."

Lisette knelt to look at a miniature sofa. "This is precious."

Bea's governess glanced back. "Those shelves, I fear, are—or were—Bea's makeshift dollhouse."

"Indeed, I can see that this shelf is the parlor," said Lisette. "And this one is a child's bedchamber. And here— look, a tiny kitchen!"

A wistful expression sketched over Mrs. Jansen's face. "Beatrice tells me that she is too old for all that now, but I do still find her hiding in here sometimes, rearranging the furniture and giving her dolls instructions." Suddenly, her voice hitched. "That's when I know she's missing her father."

"Did they often play together?" asked Lisette, rising.

"Oh, yes, that's why he moved his study upstairs," said the governess. "Lord Saint-Bryce adored Bea."

Here, however, her face fell as if she feared she'd spoken out of turn. Then Mrs. Jansen set a finger to her lips, and pulled open the door at the other end of the pantry.

"Oh, Beatrice," she sang out, "look who has come to call."

The girl sat at a long worktable, her head bent over a slate, her bouncing blonde ringlets pulled over one shoulder as she worked a row of numbers. On seeing Lisette, her eyes brightened at once, and she tossed her chalk down with a sharp *clack!*

"Miss Colburne," she said excitedly, rising to manage a perfunctory curtsy. "Have you come to visit me? Would you like to see my leaf collection?"

"Actually, I brought you my favorite book of fairy tales." Lisette cut a swift glance at the governess. "But honestly, the leaf collection sounds more interesting. Might she do so, Mrs. Jansen?"

"Oh, by all means. But there are some fifty specimens in it now. To make it educational, shall we see if Beatrice can identify them all?"

"I know I can," bragged the girl, going to a deep shelf and pulling out two massive albums.

"The challenge is on, then," Lisette declared.

The child slipped back into the chair beside Mrs. Jansen, her back to the door. Just then, a shadow fell across the threshold. Lisette looked up to see Napier standing in the doorway, his broad shoulders filling the space, one long-fingered hand set flat to the door's surface, pushing it wide.

The same hand that had touched her so intimately last night. At the sudden memory, something hot and melting rushed through her, leaving Lisette with the urge to flee. Or throw herself shamelessly at the infernal man.

His gaze caught hers, his eyes dark and questioning as he stepped inside. He, too, likely noticed the evidence of her miserable night.

Suddenly Beatrice saw him. "Lord Saint-Bryce!" she said, leaping up.

"Good morning, poppet," said Napier, making her a neat little bow. "Am I interrupting?"

"I was just about to do all my leaves," she said on a breathless rush. "Will you watch me? They think I cannot know them all, but I do. I'm quite sure I do."

"I don't for an instant doubt you, child." Napier dipped his head in Mrs. Jansen's direction. "If I may be permitted, ma'am?"

"But of course," said the governess. "Beatrice looks forward to your daily visits."

Lisette was unaware of Napier making any visits to the schoolroom, but there was no mistaking the comfortable familiarity that existed between the two. It reminded her again how little she knew of him. How little he'd shared of his purpose in coming here; of his hopes or his dreams or even his fears—assuming Napier had any of the latter.

"Is your trip canceled?" asked Bea hopefully. "I thought you were going away with Craddock."

"Mr. Craddock is under the weather," he said, "so we've postponed a day or two."

He was indeed dressed for riding, in a dark coat and a pair of glossy brown riding boots that molded to his calves. But no amount of elegance, Lisette imagined, could have offset the hard angles of his face or the weariness in his eyes.

Mrs. Jansen had leapt up to pull out one of the small chairs. "Do sit down, Mr. Napier."

Lisette watched as Napier attempted to fold himself into it and scoot it beneath Bea's worktable. He may have looked incongruous given his long legs and grim countenance, but Lisette had to commend the effort. Bea's welfare might soon fall to him, and he was wise to cultivate a friendship with the child. Lisette had been precisely Bea's age when she'd lost her own father. She understood with painful clarity what it was like to be an orphan.

"Now, on to the leaves." Napier leaned back and extracted a gold watch from his pocket, thumbing it open with a theatrical gesture. "And let's do the thing properly. Shout out when ready, Bea, and I shall time you."

A grin spread over the child's face. "Then ready, set, *go*!" she cried, flipping the first page.

She did indeed begin as if it were a race, rambling off *alder*, *ash*, *aspen*, and *beech* as she tore through the pages. But by the time they had reached the assorted oaks— *pendunculate*, *holm*, and *sessile*—they had all begun to laugh and clap. Then, finishing tidily with *wych elm* and *yew*, Beatrice slammed the book shut and beamed around the room.

"Ninety-three seconds," declared Napier, snapping the watch cover shut, "assuming one allows for Miss Colburne's bursts of applause."

"That did slow me down," the girl chided.

Just then, Napier shifted, doubtless attempting to stretch his cramped legs. But when his booted calf brushed Lisette's, she jerked. The extraordinary wave of sensual awareness swept her again, warming her cheeks.

Of course the arrogant devil noticed, his gaze catching hers across the table, one eyebrow lightly lifting.

Mischief needled Lisette. With a faint smile, she slipped her foot from her shoe and brushed it quite deliberately up the length of his boot. All the way up, over the deeply turned cuff, until her toes could tease the inside of his knee through the snug breeches, then stroke slowly along his inner thigh with just the right sort of pressure.

And then she stopped short—but ever so slightly. Napier's eyes flashed with warning—but there was an unmistakable heat, too.

"Oh, may I have a look at your collection, Bea?" asked Lisette sweetly, returning her foot to its shoe. "I like to keep my hands busy—and sometimes even my toes."

"The vicar says idle hands are the devil's work," said the girl, turning the heavy book, "but he's never mentioned toes."

Without looking at Napier, Lisette reopened the scrapbook to flip back and forth between the pressed leaves. "Heavens, are all these native to England?"

"Oh, yes," said Beatrice. "But those in the second volume are not. They're the leaves Papa collected during his travels to Asia and Africa before I was born. Even before *Gwyneth* was born."

"My, Asia and Africa!" said Lisette. "How adventurous he sounds."

"Papa was an explorer," Beatrice declared proudly. "Well, until my eldest uncle died. Then Papa had to settle down to do his duty."

She said the words in a parroting fashion, perhaps with little idea what they meant.

"Well, duty is an important thing," Lisette murmured, remembering Napier's story about the rapscallion heir shot dead at Primrose Hill. "For my part, I've never been anywhere, really, unless one counts Boston."

"Of course one must count Boston," said Mrs. Jansen defensively. "I'm told Massachusetts is the most beautiful of all the colonies."

Lisette did not trouble herself to correct the term and instead smiled down at Beatrice. The girl had taken a fresh leaf from a little wicker basket on the table, and was tracing it onto a sheet of thick, cream-colored paper.

The paper, curiously, appeared to have something printed on the reverse side, and Napier, too, was watching Bea, and fixedly. No hint of desire heated his eyes now.

"What of yourself, Mrs. Jansen?" he murmured without glancing up. "Have you lived all your life in England?"

"Why, no, as it happens," she said. "I lived on the Continent for a time."

"Where you met your husband, perhaps?" said Napier offhandedly. "You see, I once knew a family named Janson—with an *o*—from Northampton. But your name is spelled with an *e,* in the Dutch fashion, I'd guess? And sometimes pronounced differently, too, I expect?"

"Just so, Mr. Napier," she said, "though I was born a plain Miss McDonald from Glasgow. My late husband was a spice merchant from Amsterdam."

Napier finally looked up. "You must miss him greatly," he said, holding her gaze in an odd, measured fashion.

Mrs. Jansen blushed, and looked away. "I—yes, I do," she said. "But he was a good deal older than I. And sadly, we were not married long."

"I hope it was not a protracted illness," said Napier solicitously.

"A few months." Her face saddened. "It was a bilious condition, but I never quite understood the particulars."

"Tragic," murmured Napier. "And the business?"

"It fell on hard times," she said, "so I sold it."

"Well, that was likely for the best." But his brow had furrowed absently, and Napier had begun to pat through his coat pockets.

"I'm glad it was sold," said Beatrice, now sketching veins onto her leaf, "because Gwyneth brought her to live with me. And I shan't let her leave Burlingame—never, *ever.*"

Napier had given up on his pockets. "I beg your pardon," he said, cutting a rueful glance at Mrs. Jansen, "but I seem to have come away without my notebook. Might I trouble you for a piece of paper? A minute ago, Craddock told me something I meant to jot—"

"Oh, dear." Mrs. Jansen had flashed a pained expression, and risen to pull out a drawer. "I haven't anything proper," she said, digging through it, "unless I go to my room. But I can give you this, and you might use the back of it?"

"Oh, anything," said Napier with a wave of his hand.

She turned around, smiling, and passed him a piece of cream-colored letterhead.

"Thank you, you have saved me," said Napier, proceeding to jot some numbers on it. "Craddock spews out the most frightful facts and figures, and imagines I'll remember them."

Lisette looked down at the letterhead. *De Groff en Jansen* it said across the top, the type an ornate script with great loops and swashes, and below it three lesser lines in a language she could not make out.

She reached over, and drew her finger along the words. "Mrs. Jansen, what does this say?"

The lady colored again, and bent over the table. "*De Groff and Jansen,*" she said, pronouncing the last more like *Yonsen*. "*Importers of Rare Spices and Fine Teas.* And below that, our old address in Sint Antoniesbreestraat."

At Lisette's surprised look, the governess shrugged almost sheepishly. "I thought it a waste to throw good paper away," she said. "We use it here in the schoolroom. It's perfectly serviceable for that."

"Most economical of you," Lisette declared.

Napier, however, was carefully folding the paper and tucking it away in his pocket, and Lisette thought she knew why. She had not long to consider it, however. In the next moment, there came the sound of footsteps hastening down the passageway and Gwyneth Tarleton almost burst into the room, her face genuinely alight.

"Come, Bea, quick!" she said, extending her hand to the girl. "It's Anne and the baby! The carriage just turned it!"

They were, for the most part, a convivial group in Burlingame's state dining room that evening. Despite the small size of their gathering, Duncaster had ordered the massive chamber thrown open and the thirty-foot dining table appropriately shortened.

Though she had to force herself not to stare at Napier through much of the meal, even Lisette could see that Anne, Lady Keaton, was the darling of the family and Duncaster's favorite grandchild.

The prettiest of the Tarleton sisters, Anne was a petite young lady who possessed Gwyneth's fine eyes and Bea's heavy blonde ringlets. Her personality, however, seemed far more outgoing than either of her sisters. Her visit put Duncaster in a rare good humor, and despite the presence of Lady Hepplewood's nemesis, Miss Willet, the viscount demanded Marsh break out the best wine with every course until Lisette was a little dizzy with it.

As to Miss Willet, she was a handsome if not beautiful girl of perhaps nineteen years old. Thankfully, the chill her presence cast over dinner was not quite severe enough to leave anyone frostbitten, and lasted only through the fish course, for Duncaster seemed disposed to approve of anyone Anne had befriended. Even Lord Hepplewood looked smitten with his betrothed.

This left Lady Hepplewood in the awkward position of staring down her nose at the girl without Duncaster's moral support. Thus Miss Willet was given the general impression of being welcomed into the family, and if the anxious gazes she occasionally cast in Lady Hepplewood's direction suggested the girl knew better, the remaining party was merry enough not to notice.

Lisette had had no opportunity to ask Napier about the paper he'd taken from the schoolroom though she burned to do so. The entire household, it seemed, had rushed down the corridors and out of the house to greet the Keatons and their infant son, the latter being swept up affectionately and taken immediately to the nursery by Beatrice and the Keatons' competent-looking nanny.

Lisette watched Napier now across the dinner table, where he had been situated between Miss Willet and Mrs. Jansen. Though they had not shared so much as an instant alone since bitterly parting in the gardens, she could sense in him tonight some tautly drawn emotion, and could feel his gaze fall frequently upon her from beneath his heavy, hooded lids.

She had accused him last night of having mad notions. Of having come to Wiltshire on a wild goose chase. And though Napier had owned it to be true, in the light of a new day, Lisette had known it for the unfair charge it was.

Napier was not wrong. Something black and ugly hung over this house and over this family. Even now, as wine ran like a Highland stream and toasts were drunk around the dinner table, Lisette could feel the subtle undercurrents as cold as the glass in her hand.

Did Napier suspect Mrs. Jansen of something? It seemed improbable. Nonetheless, Lisette knew the man well enough to comprehend he had not been making idle conversation in the schoolroom. Mrs. Jansen, perhaps, had known it, too.

Lisette remembered with some unease the frisson that had run down her spine upon seeing the governess lock them both into the study. But that had proven to be a silly notion, and one not worth sharing with Napier.

Still, dinner seemed interminable, as she waited, hoping for a moment alone with him. Hoping, foolishly, for a good deal more than that. Though Lisette knew she walked a tightrope where Napier was concerned, her desire for him seemed destined to blind her to all danger. But soon—very soon, if her instincts were right—they would leave Burlingame, and whatever it was that burned between them—call it love or lust or insanity—would be at an end.

For her part, however, Lisette knew what to call it.

And it was not the sweetness and light that the poets praised, but a dark, rich thing that swamped her heart with its weight and curled hot in her belly like a torment. A desire so deep she had begun to feel her need for Napier like an ache in the marrow of her bones.

She knew it was a righteous punishment. To have met such a man at this terrible juncture in her life—well, one could only conclude God's justice was swift.

Beyond this time and this place, Napier would not pursue her—not in the romantic sense, certainly. Far better she should pray he simply forgot about her, or at the very least, that his steely resolve would keep them apart. For she very much feared that, where he was concerned, hers was not to be relied upon.

She was recalled to the present when, farther down the table, Gwyneth asked for the bordelaise. Still heatedly aware of Napier's gaze, Lisette lifted the sauceboat with a slightly unsteady hand, then politely turned her attention to the gentleman at her elbow.

Sir Philip Keaton was a reserved gentleman who wore a pair of gold-rimmed spectacles and sported very little hair. But Lisette warmed to him over the dessert course when the young man shyly confessed that his mother was American, then spoke of his happy memories of having attended university near Boston. He even had a passing familiarity with her family's newspaper.

"I'm surprised you remember it," she confessed.

"Well, I was living in Cambridge, you see, when the

Golden Eagle burnt leaving Boston Harbor," he explained. "It happened quite late at night, and I remember the *Examiner* was the only paper to carry the story the next morning. One couldn't lay hands on a copy for love nor money."

"Yes, I recall it," she said, smiling.

Specifically, she recalled every word, for the story had marked Jack Coldwater's journalistic debut. Ashton having been drunk as a lord that night and incapable of giving instruction, Lisette had shoved her long tresses into an old cap and pulled on a pair of trousers so that she might go unimpeded about the docks herself.

She had counted on the gloom and the confusion to shield her.

She had not needed it. No one had spared her—or her notebook or her pointed questions—a passing glance. And it was then that Lisette realized how very easy it was to deceive people: how very rarely anyone looked beneath the surface of anything. Instead, people went like automatons through their daily lives, seeing only what they expected to see.

"I thought it an unforgettable story," said Sir Philip, carefully buttering a bit of bread. "I mean, what with every soul aboard saved. What were the chances, given that frightful fire? And everyone jumping madly into the pitch-black water?"

Lisette laid her fork down a little awkwardly. "Not everyone was saved," she said quietly. "There was a lady who died the next morning."

"Ah, water in the lungs?" said Sir Philip sadly. "The effect can be more lingering than one suspects."

"Actually, it wasn't that," Lisette corrected. "It was something rather more freakish. Oh, heavens, forgive me; I'm hardly making pleasant dinner conversation."

"I believe I brought it up," said Sir Philip kindly. "By the way, what became of the *Examiner*? Is it still a going concern?"

"I fear it shared the *Golden Eagle*'s fate," she said lightly, "and more or less sank."

"Really, must we speak of *business* over our dinner?" interjected Lady Hepplewood, lifting her wineglass as she cut a glance at Miss Willet. "Sir Philip, pray tell us who is in Town this Season? Has your uncle found a husband for that lovely young cousin of yours?"

Sir Philip laughed. "I fear Lady Emily is too choosy, ma'am," he said. "Uncle declares she's holding out for a duke."

"But mightn't an earl have done at one time?" said Lady Hepplewood with a faint sniff. "I was quite persuaded, you know, that she and Hepplewood were going to make a match of it last year."

"But I was not *Hepplewood* last year, Mamma," Tony teased, though Lisette caught a flash of irritation in his eyes. "I was a mere lordling-in-waiting."

"And now we're all in mourning," said his mother tartly. "I wonder you've met anyone new at all."

"I'm afraid that was my doing," said Anne in a firm voice. "I've been having Tony to dinner regularly, along with a few dear friends. It keeps him out of the gaming salons. And I scarcely think my mourning Papa requires I not eat."

"Quite so, quite so," said Duncaster, motioning for more wine all around. "Perfectly proper, Cordelia, for the boy to dine with his cousin. Besides, neither Hep nor Saint-Bryce would want any of us utterly cast down. Why, I daresay both would be charmed by Miss Willet and happy for Tony."

"No doubt they would," murmured Lady Hepplewood sourly.

"How long can you stay, Sir Philip?" asked Duncaster as the glasses were topped up.

"I must return tomorrow afternoon, I'm sorry to say," the young man said. "We've a critical debate in the Commons. But I shall return to escort the ladies home."

"My dear, you are too indulgent." Anne cast her husband

what looked like a sincerely affectionate glance. "Philip thinks ladies ought never take the train alone."

"And so they should not," agreed Duncaster gruffly. "Particularly not *my* granddaughters."

At this remark, Gwyneth rolled her eyes. Hepplewood shot her a warning glance, and turned the topic back to London. The rest of the meal passed in a discussion of the Season's debutants, and who amongst them had made the best match. Although Anne had not put off her blacks, Sir Philip sat in the Lower House, which kept them well abreast of society's goings-on.

As the names were bandied about, Lisette exchanged an accordant glance with Napier, who gave an almost imperceptible shrug. They neither of them recognized any of the names, nor did they care. It was an oddly heartening moment, yet it made her realize again how much she wished she'd met him under different circumstances.

That she were a different person.

After dinner, a few brief turns were taken at the pianoforte. Even Miss Willet was persuaded to sing a tender aria while Lord Hepplewood accompanied her. The young man possessed more musical ability than Lisette would have credited, and Miss Willet's was the purest, most carrying voice she'd ever heard—not that she had a vast deal of knowledge on the subject.

Still, Lisette began to think that perhaps Hepplewood had done very well for himself. Miss Willet gave every impression of being the perfect, well-bred wife. Hepplewood seemed to agree, for as he played the last chords, he cast an affectionate glance up at the girl, and an almost audible sigh ran through the room.

Seated behind them, Gwyneth leaned between Lisette and Diana, both eyebrows lifted. "Good Lord, she's perfect," she whispered. "Can it be Tony's finally succeeded at something that doesn't involve cards, horses, or whores?"

"Gwyneth, don't be vulgar," said Diana hotly.

"I think he really has fallen in love," said Lisette, leaning into them. "And I fear his mamma will not be well pleased by it."

Certainly none of them dared speak directly of Miss Willet to Lady Hepplewood. Instead, Gwyneth stood, and proposed the group make up two tables for whist, but Mrs. Jansen excused herself to tuck Beatrice in.

Snatching up her black stick, Lady Hepplewood followed her, clacking off toward the great hall, this time without barking at Diana to come along. Nonetheless, after extracting from Miss Willet the promise of a long walk the following afternoon, Diana dutifully trailed after her, murmuring something about some sewing she needed to finish.

By then Duncaster had nodded off into his cravat again. The evening was over—and, as usual, at a very early hour. Fifteen minutes later, Lisette was strolling out on Napier's arm, having made it a point to leave the drawing room as he did.

"What did you find this morning?" she whispered as soon as they entered the long colonnade.

He did not pretend to misunderstand. "Besides your foot stroking up my inner thigh?" he murmured, throwing a glance behind them. "I found what I half expected to find all along, I think. But we aren't going to talk about it here."

"*Napier.*"

"Lisette," he said tightly, "hush. These corridors carry like the Royal Opera House."

Eventually they reached the top of the stairs to a silent, dimly lit passageway, Lisette bristling with impatience. Napier's bedchamber was second on the right. He stopped before it and set one hand on the doorknob, turning as if to bid her good night.

"Napier, wait." Lisette set a hand to the door frame, willing him to invite her in.

He did not, but instead stood silent and implacable by the door. "Very well," he said in his low voice. "I'm waiting."

Lisette knew, of course, that she should go—that she shouldn't press her luck or her heart any further. There was a dark edge to his gaze tonight, his jaw rigidly set. But she was a fool.

"You can be a hard-hearted man, Napier, and stubborn," she finally said, her tone aggrieved. "Will you make me say it, then?"

His mouth turned up sardonically. "I've had little luck making you do a blasted thing," he said, "other than accompany me here—which we're both apt to regret in the end."

"Perhaps we should." Flicking a quick glance up at him, Lisette moved her hand from the door and placed it against his chest. "What worries me is that . . . *I don't.*"

"Ah, come to dance with the devil again, have you?" he said bitterly.

"Against all wisdom, yes." Then, rising onto her toes, Lisette leaned near and brushed her lips over his.

Napier's restraint seemed to snap, his hands catching her shoulders to still her to a kiss that was hard, possessive, and swift. Then just as swiftly, he set her away.

"Damn it, Lisette, we're fools, the both of us," he said. "It would be better if we just didn't—"

"Please, may I come in?" she interjected, glancing at the still closed door. "I'm sorry. I've said some things that weren't—oh, I don't know!—this trip with you has addled my brain. But we can't just stand here nattering at one another. If nothing else, may I hear what you learned today?"

"If you come in, Lisette," he said warningly, "it won't stop at that. *I* won't stop at that."

"And what if I don't want it to stop?" she asked, her lashes falling half shut. "Do you think I care so little for you, Napier, that I won't miss this—miss *you*—when it's all over? That I won't remember your touch, and sometimes ache for it?"

Napier dropped his hands wearily. "I swear to God, I sometimes think you'd turn a screw into a man's heart," he said grimly. "No, I don't know what to think, Lisette. What do you want from me?"

She opened her eyes and looked at him with as much honesty as she dared. "I want, for this one evening, not to be lonely," she said, "or alone. I want to be with you. To just spend an evening with you. An ordinary evening. Does that seem so implausible?"

"Oh, *ordinary*," he murmured. "How could any man resist such flattery?"

"Don't twist my words," she said. "You know . . . you know how you make me feel. I mean ordinary as in . . . the sort of evening partners—*lovers*—might spend. The sort of evening where we stop bickering and just pretend we're normal."

"Nothing about this is normal," he said. "That's the hell of it, Lisette."

She regarded him in silence a moment. "Do you despise yourself that much, Napier, for wanting me?" she finally whispered. "Am I that far beyond redemption?"

"*Lisette*," he said, tipping up her chin with his finger. "Oh, too harsh, my girl. Do I wish you trusted me? Yes. But you never will; you've learnt to trust no one, I think, and it's not my place to judge that choice. But last evening did not end especially well for either of us."

"No, but that middle part"—she managed an unsteady smile—"oh, *that*, I thought, was wickedly wonderful."

The little muscle near his mouth twitched tellingly. "Ah, so under certain circumstances—in exchange, perhaps, for certain pleasures—the lady might tolerate my cold, hard heart?"

"Oh, the pleasures seem *very* certain," she whispered,

leaning near enough to brush her lips over his cheek. "And no, it is not your hard heart that intrigues. It is your . . . well, your very hard, exquisitely firm . . . mind."

"Ah," he said. "My mind, is it?"

Lightly, she shrugged. "Stubbornness, apparently, arouses me," she said. "It's the only explanation I have for this hold you have over me."

His gaze did not much soften, but he pushed the door open on silent hinges. "Well, my dear, on that great tarradiddle, I bow to you," he said. "By all means, come in."

She brushed past him into the room to see the bed had been turned down and a fire burned in the grate, a feeble defense against the day's incessant damp. The air was faintly warm and redolent with his scent, and even in utter darkness Lisette would have known the room was his.

On the table, Napier's dressing case sat open, while at the foot of the bed lay his neatly folded nightshirt. A pair of slippers was tucked beneath his night table, while atop it a book rested, marked with an old envelope. It was a scene so personal, so utterly intimate, that it made something in Lisette's heart well up.

Napier had lifted his chin high and was yanking impatiently at the elaborate knot of his cravat. "There's sherry on the side table," he said, cutting his eyes toward it, "and some brandy. Make yourself at home."

"Here," she said, moving to face him. "Let me. Or will your valet turn up?"

Napier snorted. "Not of his own accord."

Having occasionally worn one herself, Lisette found it a simple matter to untie his cravat. But it was not so simple a matter to stand near him—near enough to inhale his shaving soap, that now familiar scent of lime and bayberry mingled with his own male essence.

"There," she said softly, her hands falling away.

On an efficient jerk, Napier stripped the loosened cloth

from his collar and tossed it on the bed. Lisette went to the table and poured both sherry and brandy, watching from one corner of her eye as Napier shrugged out of his coat.

After hanging it in his dressing room, he joined her on the small sofa by the fire, his shoulders appearing even wider beneath his snug waistcoat and the fine cambric of his shirt. She pressed the brandy into his hand, feeling suddenly anxious.

"So," she asked lightly, "how are we doing so far? At being ordinary?"

Napier hesitated a moment, then looked away. "It feels surprisingly domestic," he said, "and not unpleasant."

"Not . . . *unpleasant*." Lisette let her head fall back against the sofa. "Lord, we are like alley cats, Napier, tiptoeing round one another."

He barked with laughter. "Fine, then, it feels good," he said. "Disarmingly so. There, happy?"

"Oddly, I am happy," Lisette whispered. "Sometimes. With you. But I think I told you that at the cottage. And I . . . I meant it, Royden. When all this is over, I hope you will look back and remember that you brought me both pleasure and happiness."

His gaze fixed somewhere beyond her, Napier said nothing. Still relaxed against the sofa, Lisette tilted her head to the left, her eyes drifting over his profile, taking in those dark, weary eyes and that harshly aquiline nose she loved so well. Past the long turn of his jaw, already shadowed with tomorrow's stubble.

And that mouth; yes, that wide, mobile mouth that could thin to the point of ruthlessness, then in the next moment soften with a tenderness so apparent to Lisette that it belied his outward demeanor.

She had come to love him desperately, she realized—so much so, she'd sooner die than disappoint him. And it was that realization which had been the font of last night's tears.

Royden Napier was a decent man, one of the few she'd ever known.

What a pity she had not chosen that light Lady Anisha had spoken of, instead of a vengeful darkness.

On a sigh, Lisette lifted her hand, and stroked a finger lightly along the firm line of his jaw. "Do you not think," she murmured, "that if we'd met under different circumstances, if we were different people—just a little, mind—that we might have got on like a house afire?"

Instead, he merely snared her hand and carried it to his lips for an instant. "I'm too old for you, Lisette," he said. "At least that's what I've been telling myself."

"Good Lord." She blinked at him. "You cannot be above five-and-thirty."

"Too old in a way that has little to do with years," he said quietly. "And I'm thirty-four, by the way."

"That is no difference at all," she said dismissively, "and when it comes to being old beyond one's years, Napier, I think you forget to whom you're speaking."

"Aye, perhaps."

They fell into a pensive silence for a moment, the quiet pierced only by something that popped in the fireplace, shooting a shower of sparks up the chimney. From without, the day's heavy mist had turned to rain that still spattering lightly at the windowpanes. Napier sat now with his head hung almost broodingly, staring into the golden depths of the brandy he cradled, warming it with his palms.

"Tell me you found something of interest in Saint-Bryce's study," he said after a time.

Lisette straightened, and shook her head. "Nothing," she said. "The file drawers were empty and recently dusted. I saw no safe. No ledgers. No books of interest. The desk, oddly, I found locked—just before Mrs. Jansen found *me*."

Napier cursed beneath his breath.

"It was quite all right." Swiftly, Lisette explained.

"And she suspected you of nothing?"

"Merely of being a goose," said Lisette, "which I often am. Case in point, here I sit with you, giddy at the pleasure of it, ignoring all risk to my heart. In any case, after finding me, she took me through to the schoolroom."

Napier was looking at her oddly now. "I'm sorry," he said after a moment. "She took you through how?"

"There's an old butler's pantry that connects it to the schoolroom." Lisette turned and tucked one leg beneath her, cradling her sherry in her lap. "At one time, the study must have been a breakfast parlor."

"Or a nursery," he said musingly. "These great houses sometimes had a place to prepare trays for the children. Is it possible to hear from one room to the other?"

Lisette shook her head. "I think not, but if one were in the pantry—yes, almost certainly. But it's full of Bea's books and toys. Dolls, mostly. I can't think why anyone else would go in there."

"Dolls, yes," he murmured, shifting his gaze to the fire. "She mentioned it one day in the orchard. That her dolls lived in the pantry. That she played with them while her father wrote letters."

"*Hmm.*" Lisette set away her sherry, her head still a little light from dinner. "Well, in any case, that's what little I learned. Now, what did you discover from that sheet of paper you rooked out of poor Mrs. Jansen?"

Napier sighed, and slid forward on the sofa. A large morocco-bound book entitled *A Geographic Survey of North Africa* lay on the tea table before him. With a flick of his wrist, he opened it and extracted two pieces of thick, creamy vellum, one two inches shorter than the other.

"Have a look," he said. "Though I can already tell you the two are a dead-on match. Jolley's checked the watermarks—they're Dutch, by the way—but the first one, the letter, has been trimmed across the top."

They exchanged knowing glances. "That cannot be co-incidence," she said. "And this was sent to you? Anonymously?"

"Yes, as you guessed days ago," he admitted. "It came to my house in Eaton Square—and, more interestingly, addressed to Baron Saint-Bryce."

But Lisette was reading it now. "Good Lord, *a concerned citizen*?" she muttered. "And *wickedness*?"

"Not exactly damning language, is it?" said Napier dryly.

"Well . . . no," she admitted, "but whoever wrote it wanted you here. And they knew your new title. Your home address."

"And the paper came out of Mrs. Jansen's drawer," he added.

Lisette winced with doubt. "Yes, but anyone could have found that paper."

"But why would anyone *look*?" he said. "It's a schoolroom. There's better paper—paper that doesn't require the letterhead cut off—in nearly every room of the house."

"It sounds as if one of the servants could have written it," mused Lisette. "Which one of them cleans the schoolroom?"

"Jane," said Napier darkly.

"Jane?" said Lisette in surprise. "Isn't she the maid who sometimes sat with Lord Hepplewood when Gwyneth and Diana weren't about?"

"Yes, but Jolley tells me the girl is illiterate," Napier mused. "I think it cannot be her."

"Mightn't she have taken it for someone else?" Lisette suggested.

"I fancy not," said Napier.

"Then . . . Mrs. Jansen?" Lisette found it hard to credit. "Why would she? And if she had, why would she have given you that paper so readily?"

"Indeed, she is more apt to have wanted rid of Saint-Bryce," said Napier, "not bring me running down here to investigate his death."

Lisette stared at him. "Why would she have wanted rid of Saint-Bryce?"

Napier looked reluctant to continue. Then he exhaled sharply. "It seems she and Gwyneth wanted the dower house rather desperately," he confessed, repeating all that Gwyneth had told him. "I gather Gwyneth quarreled with her father over it. On more than one occasion."

"And you fear that they perceived Saint-Bryce was standing in the way of their happiness?" Lisette was walking it through in her mind. "Yet that assumes they imagined they could eventually get round *you* in his stead. And more easily. But they would have to be utter fools to think you softhearted."

"Thank you," he said dryly, "but I'm afraid I already promised it to her."

"To . . . to Mrs. Jansen? You promised her a *house*?"

"No, to Gwyneth," he muttered, looking vaguely embarrassed. "In a moment of weakness the other night, whilst you were giggling like a schoolgirl with Lord Hepplewood."

"Ah, so I was acting like a schoolgirl and you were flinging away bits of property that you do not even possess as yet." Lisette laughed. "Good Lord, Napier, are we both utter frauds?"

"Perhaps we are at that." Then, his mouth turning up in a weary smile, Napier shifted around to better face her. "Ah, Lisette . . ."

"Yes? Go on."

"Here we are again," he said, one shoulder propped against the sofa. "Nothing has changed since that day in the cottage. I still want you so desperately it hurts."

"Well, then." A soft smile curving her mouth, Lisette toed off her satin slippers, and climbed across his lap, setting one knee to either side. "Let me encourage your desperation."

Napier smiled faintly, then, sliding his hands around the turn of her face, kissed her slowly and lingeringly. It was their first shared kiss, she realized, not driven by temper or rash desire. Instead it was a slow exploration of each other's warmth as Napier's fingers slipped deeper into her hair.

When he lifted his mouth away an inch, his eyes had gone soft with desire and with something that looked like frustration. "Lisette," he whispered, "is it just the here and now? Is that all we have?"

"It's all anyone ever has." Lisette held his gaze unwaveringly. "Take me to bed," she whispered, her nails curling into his shoulders. "Please. Make love to me."

"Tread cautiously, love." He kissed her again, the mere brush of his lips over her cheek. "For I'm no gentleman, no matter how many titles they chain to my name. And for you— well, for you there's an awful risk. You understand, yes?"

"A risk of a child," she said, her face searching his, her hands warm and light on his shoulders as she balanced. "But there won't be. I counted. Carefully."

"Ah," he said.

Faintly, she nodded. "I counted *carefully*," she said again. "I'm very . . . predictable, you see. And quite good at arithmetic."

"I wish to God you wouldn't tempt me," he whispered. "This—*us*—it's so unwise."

"Unwise for whom?" Lisette trailed a teasing finger around the turn of his jaw. "You desire me, at least a little. Even that first day in your office. I was half afraid, from the burning wrath in your eyes, that you might take me up on my foolish offer."

"*Witch*," he said hoarsely, cupping her face in his hands. "But I can't believe that's who you are, Lisette. You aren't that woman at all, and—"

"Don't romanticize this," she interjected, pushing away a little to search his face. "Don't you see? Therein lies the risk. If this is just desire—if it's just pleasure—then it's not so dangerous."

"Ah, yes, your theory of non-attachment." His voice had flattened. "I think we had this discussion already."

"Yes," she said swiftly. "But tonight, Napier, I'm tired. Of being alone. Of wanting you."

"Lisette, it will never—"

"Shush." She set her fingertips to his lips. "I don't delude myself. In a few days, we'll go back to London. We'll go back to being what we used to be."

"To one another?" His gaze drifted down her face. "And what was that, Lisette? Mortal enemies?"

On another faint laugh, she shook her head. "Nothing," she said. "We were nothing to one another. We scarcely knew of one another's existence. I won't be staying in London, Napier—perhaps not even in Britain—so I'm not looking to . . . to *ensnare* you in any way."

He caught her wrist, kissing her pulse point. "And what if I wished to ensnare you?" he whispered.

"You would soon rue it," she said honestly. "And you would always wonder—"

He dragged her to him and cut off her words with his kiss.

Napier wasn't even sure when the longing in Lisette's eyes became something he could scarcely bear. She wanted him to pleasure her—and he would agree to it, of course. No sane man would refuse her.

So he kissed her determinedly, as if he mightn't stop, cradling the back of her head in his hand as his other hand worked down the buttons that fastened her blue dinner gown. The silk was cool against his hand, her mouth hot and seeking beneath his.

And as he worked each button free, he closed his eyes tighter, unable to bear the desire that softened her eyes and left her languid in his arms.

Couldn't bear it because it wasn't enough.

Not until she totally surrendered to him.

And Elizabeth Colburne surrendered to no one. She might

surrender to his body—for this, for what he could make her feel. And he *was* making her feel—rather desperately, if her breathy sighs were any measure. She straddled him now, her head thrown back as he worked her bodice down. Her breasts sprang free, full and ripe, begging for his mouth.

Still cradling her head with one hand, Napier suckled Lisette until her fingers tangled in his hair and she began to whimper, and then to murmur what she wished him to do to her.

And he surely meant to oblige her; had meant to since allowing her in the door, if he were honest. Indeed, at this point, he could hardly have stopped himself. Scooping her in his arms, one hand sliding beneath her lush bottom, Napier rose from the sofa and carried her to the bed. Lisette was kissing him now, her lips sliding down his neck with murmured supplications, her long legs wrapped around his waist, her hands twining around his neck, sinuous as a cat.

Perching her on the edge of the high mattress, he undressed her with slow deliberation. When her fingers went impatiently to her hooks and buttons, he pushed her hands gently away, unwilling to surrender the pleasure.

Unwilling to give in to her completely.

"Patience, love," he murmured. "I want to savor this."

She dropped her hands and sat docilely. Lisette desired him for this one thing. And in this one thing, he was determined to have his way. With this one thing, he could enslave her—if only for an hour or two.

Or three, perhaps, if he measured himself out carefully.

Already Lisette's eyes were glassy with need. The silk dress settled around her waist in a pale puddle, luminous against the cream of his counterpane. Her loosened corset followed, and her shift fell after that. Kissing his way down her breastbone, Napier snared the tie to her drawers in his teeth and pulled it free, pausing only to tease at her navel with the tip of his tongue.

She shuddered on a breathy sign. Then Napier lifted Lisette to her feet and let it all fall, leaving her bare save for garters and stockings. After dispensing with those, he swiftly undressed himself and this time she stood watching passively save for the occasional catch in her breath.

When his shirt drifted to the ground, she reached out and set her hand over his heart. He pushed his drawers and trousers down in an untidy heap, and her hand slid lower.

"Slowly, love," he said, urging her back onto the bed.

Napier mounted her, crawling over her and pressing her down into the softness with his weight as his mouth took hers on a deep, plundering kiss. Lisette's head fell back into his pillows. She exhaled on a little shudder, her hands going to the rounded muscles of his shoulders. He thrust his tongue into her mouth again, sliding it sinuously and repeatedly along hers in that age-old mimicry; warning her of his intent.

In response, Lisette sighed and let her eyes fall shut, her thick lashes feathering over her pale skin. Urging her legs wide with his knee, Napier turned his attention to her breasts, his cock lying thick and throbbing against the alabaster flesh of her thigh.

Strangely, she did not reach for him—did not run her fingers over his sensitive head or tease from him his essence as he'd thought she might. Instead Lisette lay quietly but wantonly beneath him, as if she knew what he wished.

What he needed.

To take her. Not against her will, no, but to be in utter control of her body—assuming there was no winning her soul. His hand weighed her swollen breasts in turn, thumbing her nipples into sensitive, dark rose nubs as he sat back on his heels and watched her breath ratchet up. Teasing her until the pleasure of his fingers became too much for her to bear and he was compelled to lean forward and soothe her with the tip of his tongue.

"*Napier . . .*" she whispered urgently.

Her patience—and passivity—was coming to an end, he sensed. As if he'd bidden her touch, Lisette began to move restlessly, the fingers of one hand stroking down the turn of his waist, then lower. His hand caught her fingers, then Napier sat up and drew them together through her nest of curls until her dew glistened both their fingers.

Her eyes widening, Lisette still lay against his pillows, her wild curls shimmering around her head like a halo of rubies, brilliant against the white linen. She looked like an angel—an angel, he feared, sent to show him hell here on this earth.

The hell of what he could not have. Not in any way save the most fleeting.

But fleeting passion, he had decided, was better than none at all.

In his mind, Napier considered all manner of tactics to torment and delay. He wanted to teach Lisette to touch herself as he watched. To tease her sweet nub with his mouth again. Perhaps even to feel the warmth of her mouth on him.

But she was untutored and already arching restlessly beneath him, and he—well, he was fighting down his own impatience. So he situated himself between those impossibly long legs and let his eyes feast, fearing he'd be wise to let Lisette's feminine perfection sear his memory. For it was all, in the end, he might have.

"Lisette," he whispered, "you are beautiful."

And he meant it. Lisette was all leggy, coltish grace with firm, high breasts and a soft, creamy dip of a belly that invited a man to cradle his head upon it.

She gazed up at him through somnolent but knowing eyes. "And you are hard, physical perfection," she whispered. "Come. Come inside me. Let me feel how perfect."

Her throat worked up and down, her eyes pleading with him. But Napier had no intention of being rushed.

"*Now*," she whispered.

In answer, he let his hands skate up the alabaster flesh of her inner thighs—all the way up—until he could run his thumbs along the lush folds of feminine flesh that embraced her delicate treasure.

Ever so gently he parted her and let his gaze take in the glistening, pearl-pink skin and the sweet jewel within. Lisette's breath seized at the intrusion, her hand sliding restlessly down.

"Patience, love," he said, touching her gently.

"*Aah*," she whispered, her hips rolling against his hand. "Please. Inside me. Now."

Again her hand lashed out, this time reaching desperately. And Napier knew if the witch stroked him once, he'd likely be lost. But it was no hard feat to snare her wrist in his and push her hand back up.

"Napier," she begged, restlessly rolling her hips, "just hurry—"

But he was bloody tired of hurrying; he wanted to savor what little he had. To deny for as long as he could that the end neared.

"*Don't make me wait*," she whispered.

And suddenly the devil really was in him.

Later, when good sense returned, Napier blamed despair. But in that instant, he felt only raw, male frustration.

Reaching blindly around with his empty hand, he groped in the gloom until he found the cravat he'd tossed onto the bed. And before he'd had time to think better of it—before she'd even grasped what he was about—Napier had the linen looped around Lisette's wrist and was urging it over her head.

"Napier?" Her eyes flew wide in the firelight. "What are you—?"

"Helping you temper your patience, love," he interjected, looping it around the other hand and drawing the knot fast.

She gave a little jerk, only half testing the knot. "Ah, for my own good, is it?" Something was kindled in her eyes now; something that was not irritation and certainly not fear. "I ordinarily question when a man says that."

"Some women beg for this, you know." Napier wrapped the next turn on a little grunt, and felt raw lust surge through his loins. "Not that I asked."

"My, how arrogant you are," she said evenly. "Have I mentioned that lately?"

"I don't believe so." Napier drew the next knot tight, a little disturbed by how arousing he found it. "But you did touch on *stubborn* and *devilish* and—oh, what was it?—oh, yes. *Hard.*"

"This," she said darkly, casting her eyes up, "had better be good."

"Oh, it certainly will be good for me," he murmured, yanking snug the next knot. The back of Lisette's hands slapped the headboard. "For I mean to have my wicked way with you. Stubbornly and devilishly, of course."

"And hard," she murmured. Her eyes were drifting down his cock, now swollen so thick the veins stood out. "Very . . . *literally.*"

"And for as long"—he drew Lisette's wrists tight together with the last knot—"as is humanly possible."

At that, she shuddered beneath him. "Napier, please." This time she did not sound quite so bold.

Finally Napier sat back with satisfaction at his handiwork: the pale, slender arms fastened loosely but fairly firmly above her head.

Could she wrench herself free?

He decided it was possible—but not easy. Moreover, he was morally confident he could distract her from her efforts.

"You must admit, Lisette," he said, his eyes trailing over her, "that thus far you've been mighty dictatorial in this relationship."

"That I have *what*—?" Her voice was softly incredulous.

"It's a little humbling, my girl, for a man to find himself so utterly willing to answer every crook of a woman's finger," he went on. "I warned you tonight. I suggested very strongly you not come in here."

"And yet . . . *here I am*," she said.

"Yes, and entirely at my mercy," he replied. "And it shames me to admit how erotic it looks—though I know it won't last."

On a laugh, she tilted her head back and gave her hands a hard yank. The knots held, soft but unyielding. Slowly Lisette's face fused with color and with it came reality.

That this was no game. No, not quite.

"Napier," she said hotly, "let me go. This very minute."

"*Five* minutes," he returned. "Just . . . five minutes, Lisette. Is that so much to ask?"

"Five minutes of what?" she asked, her voice breaking.

But Napier had let his hands ease up her warm inner thighs again. "Five minutes of savoring this," he said, holding her gaze. "Oh, Lisette, let me live the fantasy, even fleetingly, that you are in some small way within a man's control. And then, if you ask prettily, yes, I'll let you go."

"Royden," she fumed, "this not funny."

"No, but it's arousing as hell," he said. "And by the way, I notice I'm *Royden* now. How sweet it sounds on your lips, love."

Suddenly, she gasped. And this time she did not yank at the headboard, for he'd drawn his thumbs through her dew again, teasing lightly near her clitoris.

"My God, this is intoxicating," he murmured, grazing the nub lightly on the next stroke.

"*Ohhh*." The word was a soft moan.

He stroked again—the merest nothing—and she began to shake.

"Oh, Lisette," he said warningly, "*I think you like this*."

She closed her eyes, her throat working frantically. "*Touch me again,*" she whispered.

"Oh, yes," he said, "I will, love—until you beg me to stop."

He did better than touch her. He bent forward to nip his way down the soft flesh of her belly, sending another shudder deep through Lisette's body. Then he soothed the trail of bites with the tip of his tongue, retracing until he reached her damp curls.

"*Royden,*" she murmured, her hips rolling restlessly.

Then, probing gently through her damp folds, he found her perfect spot with the tip of his tongue. He stroked once, firmly, and felt a deep shudder go through her. He stroked twice more, lightly teasing. Then Lisette went rigid and came apart, her sweetness warm against his mouth.

Good Lord. Never had he seen a woman so easily—so wildly—aroused.

He watched it in stunned awe. He'd meant, in all honesty, to untie her. Instead, he found himself crawling over her like some feral beast, pushing her wide with one knee as he thrust himself deep.

Lisette arched on a soft, startled cry. Napier felt half mad with need. Grabbing the headboard with both hands, he thrust and thrust again as Lisette's spasms slowly waned, tugging around his cock. Her eyes were wide, rolling back in her head, her hands bearing down on the knot on a shudder.

He rode her then, the soft sounds of their flesh sweet and wet in the dying firelight. Lisette's knees came up, clasping him hard over the hips as her belly drew taut, urging herself against him. Over and over he thrust, his fingers clenching the walnut headboard as he moved on her.

Sweat beaded his brow. Ruthlessly he held himself back, summoning every inch of will. A dozen strokes later, Lisette was again gasping and pleading for release again, whispering his name and even more. Whispering words— promises—she would likely never remember.

Napier drew them in, held them to his heart. Then, lifting himself, he shifted just a fraction higher, renewing his thrusts. It was as if someone tossed a burning lamp onto the bed. Hips bucking against his, Lisette opened her mouth as if to cry out.

Napier took her mouth with his, swallowing her cries. It was his last clear realization. And then he was exploding, his own release like a roar in his head. Heat rushed from his loins and gushed from his heart, pumping and pouring into her. Drawing him deeper. Then the bone-deep shuddering dragged him under, swamping him with a pleasure so profound it weighed down his limbs and dulled all rational thought.

Long moments later, Napier came slowly back to the faint crackle of a dying fire to realize he still lay over Lisette. The rain was over, the room now glowing with a soft, white moonlight that shone through the draperies he had not bothered to close.

Shifting his weight, he rolled away, onto his back so that he might thumb open the drawer of his night table and scrabble in the gloom for the knife that old habit kept close to hand. Beneath him, Lisette gave one last sigh.

"Hold perfectly still," he murmured, slicing up through the fine linen like so much butter.

The fabric fell away, and Lisette's hands collapsed, limp-wristed, onto the pillows. "Good Lord, Napier," she managed to rasp, "you are going to pay for that."

"Am I, love?" he whispered, gently threading his fingers through her hair.

"Eventually . . ." she murmured, " . . . perhaps . . ."

Then she rolled against him, tucked her head into the crook of his arm, and promptly fell into a deep sleep. He merely held her for a time, savoring the warmth of her body and the soft rise and fall of her chest as she breathed.

Dear God, it felt so simple—so very natural and right to lie with her this way, stretched out on his back, utterly re-

laxed, with Lisette's body curled around his. He marveled
how her every curve and valley seemed to fit his own. How
the weight of her head cradled on his shoulder felt perfect.
How, when he dipped his head to kiss the crown of her head,
the scent of her hair smelled like comfort.

Like home, really.

The home that should have been, because it felt as if Lisette had been meant for him. He'd known it for a while
now, and was tired of denying it. At the thought, Napier felt
something pressing a little like tears behind his eyes.

Christ Jesus. What was he going to do about such a damnable quandary?

Marry her.

Take the quandary out of it, and leave the rest for someone
else to deal with.

Yes, he could simply marry Lisette—assuming he could
convince her to have him. But Napier rarely failed once he'd
set his mind to a task. And it seemed suddenly the most rational choice imaginable.

But it was not, quite, was it? His logical self—his *old*
self—understood. Marriage to Lisette would require a great
deal of forethought, and the first and swiftest step must be to
press on with his resignation from government service. For
Lisette—whoever she was or whatever she'd done—simply
mattered more.

Drawing her scent deep, he kissed her brow, then found
himself staring up at the plaster roundel in the middle of
his ceiling again. It seemed destined to be his fate, over and
over again, to lie here with Lisette, falling just a little more
in love every time she drew breath.

That breath had now relaxed into slow, deep exhalations.
He turned to see she lay now in a wash of moonlight that
seemed to cast her with an ethereal glow. Her halo of curls
looked like rich, red mahogany against his skin; her pale,
almost opalescence face was so beautiful in sated repose.

His bride.

Was it possible?

It had to be. Somehow, he would make it so. But he dared not let her sleep too long. Certainly he could not keep her here the night, though he desperately wished to do so.

Gradually, he kissed her awake, tucking his head to press his lips lightly across her temple. In his arms, she stirred and stretched like a cat. "*Umm*," she said, "I'm sore."

"Christ, I ought to be horsewhipped," he choked, snaring her wrist. "Let me see."

"Not *there*," she said on a spurt of laughter. "Somewhere a little lower—and not, I think, in the sort of way one's lover ought to apologize for."

"Ah," he said, relaxing again.

Lisette looked up at him, her blue-green gaze still soft with sleep. "You were a beast," she whispered. "It was . . . wicked and bad and utterly divine."

He kissed her again, tentatively, as if she were made of spun glass. "I wonder, actually, if I've lost my mind," he muttered. "I might have done you a harm."

She rolled toward him then, pushing him onto his back and into the softness of the bed. "Oh, I think your cravat took the worst of that little encounter," she said, sprawling half atop him. "But if it will make you feel suitably chastised, I shall think of a proper penance—not, I imagine, an actual horsewhipping. I couldn't bring myself. Though one does hear of ladies in Covent Garden who can—for a price."

She was toying with a lock of his hair now, and grinning at him a little wickedly, but Napier was still kicking himself. Oh, Lisette wasn't entirely innocent. He knew that. One couldn't troll the sordid side of London in the guise of a young newspaperman—which he was sure Lisette had done—without learning and seeing things a lady oughtn't know.

But merely *knowing* about certain things wasn't the same

as having engaged in them. "You aren't a woman of experience," he said.

"I am now." Then her expression sobered, and Lisette propped her chin on his chest, staring into his eyes. "But perhaps you think me . . . oh, a little green still? Doubtless you are accustomed to lovers who are—"

"Shush." Crooking his head to look down at her, Napier laid a finger to her lips. "If I ever had other lovers—which I doubt—I cannot now recall them."

Lisette snorted with laughter. "You are the most egregious liar."

But Napier was very much afraid he was not; certainly in this moment he could not recall so much as another woman's name, let alone a face. And he was suddenly struck by the conviction that, after her, all others would pale.

Setting a hand at the nape of Lisette's neck, he threaded his fingers through her thick red hair and set his lips to the warmth of her temple. "I've fallen, Lisette," he said quietly. "Utterly fallen for you."

He felt her stiffen in his embrace. "You don't need to say that," she said, lifting her head to look at him. "Napier, you . . . you just don't. I'm not like that."

"Oh?" He crooked one brow. "Like what, pray?"

She answered with a feeble smile. "You know, like one of those women who . . . who always needs to hear—"

"What, the truth?" He gave a dismissive shrug. "That's what it comes down to, Lisette. I've fallen in love with you."

"Oh, Napier, I can't—"

"*Royden*," he said, "remember?"

She cupped her hand around his face, her expression softening almost painfully. "Oh, I remember," she said. "But I shouldn't talk—*we* shouldn't talk—of such things. Please. Just make love to me again. Or toss me out and say good rid—"

"Oh, if you want out of this, my dear," he interjected, "you'll have to walk away."

She rolled onto her back. "I don't want out," she said softly. "That's half the problem."

"Ah," he said softly. "It seems we've reached another impasse. Or a crossroads, at the very least."

She lay perfectly silent for a long while. He could hear the mantel clock ticking off the interminable seconds. "I can't have this discussion, Royden," she finally said. "Please don't make me."

She was blinking back tears, he realized.

Napier felt, suddenly, like the dog he was. He had pursued her to Hackney, forced her here to Wiltshire—forced her to live a lie, merely to suit his purposes—then to thank her, he'd taken her innocence.

Now he'd tied her up in his own bed and ridden her like some half-crazed animal. And that was not even the worst of it. How could she know what to say to him just now? Weighed down by guilt as she so obviously was and dragging a lifetime's worth of grief, could Lisette even know how she felt?

Perhaps not. A cold fear began to slowly settle in his gut: the heavy certainty that if he pushed her too far, she'd simply run. She was still afraid—afraid of Lazonby, afraid of what she'd done. And still afraid of him, too, on a level he couldn't fathom.

And if she ran, God only knew where the girl might go. She was too clever by half to make it easy. Oh, he'd find her. He'd search to the ends of the earth. But how long would that take? And how much damage would he have done?

No, far better to get a chokehold on his impatience. To call upon that cold rationality that had always served him so well.

Suddenly, Lisette spoke again, in a voice so small he scarcely recognized it. "It's unfair of me, I know," she said into the ceiling, "but I cannot keep from wondering . . ."

"Wondering what?"

"Well . . . if you loved her, too."

He turned his head, confused. "Loved who?"

She rolled to face him, her expression softening. "Lady Anisha," she whispered.

"Lord, no. Who sold you that bit of moonshine?"

"No one," she said. "I just thought . . . everyone said . . ."

Suddenly, he understood. "Everyone, I daresay, did not include the lady or me," he said more gently. "Do I like her? Yes, greatly—though I fear the friendship won't survive her marriage."

"Does that make you sad?"

Did it make him sad? Apparently, it did not; he'd scarcely spared her a thought these last many days. "No, life constantly alters," he said. "Anisha knows where to find me should she have need of me. And Lazonby—well, he'll look after her. Of that I'm confident."

Lisette lay curled on her side now, pensively trailing a finger through the hair on his chest. "When you were young, Royden, were you ever in love then?"

He wanted to tell her he knew damned well what love was, if that's what she was after. But he bit back his impatience and rolled onto his back, staring at the damned roundel again. He was grateful Lisette was still talking. That she hadn't bolted.

Perhaps it was better, after all, to keep things light and even for a time.

But had he ever *been* young?

"When I was eighteen," he finally said, "and a tall, strapping lad just down from Oxford, I imagined myself passionately in love with an alderman's widow."

"A widow?" Lisette lifted her head a little. "Truly?"

"Oh, yes," he confessed dryly, "and I worshipped her with the sort of ardent desperation that only virginal young men can suffer."

"Oh, my! *Were* you a virgin at eighteen?"

"It pains me to admit it," he said. "And she was nearly thirty, plump in all the right places, and a frightful flirt. She had this habit of plying her fan rather cleverly whilst eyeing me over it—across the aisle at church, no less. So one Sunday over dinner, I declared my intention of courting her. My father was furious. He utterly forbade it."

"Oh, dear," she murmured. "That was imprudent."

Napier laughed. "Yes, perhaps," he said, "not to mention the pot calling the kettle black, given what he'd done at my age. But I was a young buck, and imagined myself broken-hearted and filled with angst."

"So what did you do?"

"Oh, I did what young men always do when they're feeling randy, fervent, and thwarted," he said. "I vowed my undying love to spite him, and began to court the lady in secret—which pleased her greatly and hurt me not a little. And that, you see, should have been my clue."

"Your clue?" Lisette looked at him blankly. "To what?"

"To the fact that the lady and I had, in actuality, quite different objectives," he said. "Though for a time, we spent a great many nights getting hers met."

"And yours . . . ?"

Napier pulled a glum face. "Alas, as it happened, the lady did not wish to marry me," he said, "nor, truth to tell, to be seen on the arm of a greenling just down from university. Not unless she absolutely had to in order to get what she wanted."

"So . . . what did she want?" Lisette's brow furrowed charmingly. "Your fortune?"

"Come, Lisette, I had no fortune. I was a law student at Lincoln's Inn, and barely that. No, I had only one thing the lady wanted—and for a time, I gave it to her with unflagging enthusiasm."

At last recognition dawned, widening her eyes. "Aah," she said.

"Yes, *aah* indeed," he replied, shoving one arm beneath his head. Lord, he hadn't thought of the bounteous Mrs. Minter in years. "So I lost my virginity and I lost my heart—and in the end, I lost my beloved."

"What happened to her?"

"She married an elderly ironmonger who'd made a right royal fortune selling fire-dogs in the Strand," he said. "But *he*—she later explained—turned out to be so frail he preferred to go to bed with the chickens instead of his wife. And *I* was most welcome to call upon her most any evening—after the chickens had roosted, of course."

"Oh, I see," said Lisette knowingly. "And did you?"

Napier felt his mouth twist a little. "I did not," he said. "Whilst I'd turned to fornication pretty cheerfully, I somehow didn't fancy adding adultery to my long list of sins."

Lisette giggled, and covered her mouth.

He turned his head to look at her, willing his eyes to be gentle. "And I believe," he said quietly, "that I once asked you a similar question about being in love, but you declined to answer it."

After a time, she sighed. "No, I said a few young men tried to court me," she answered, "assuming, I suppose, that I'd inherit whatever was left of Uncle's newspaper."

Napier saw an avenue to a question that had been nagging at him. "Lisette, was it always Mr. Ashton's intention to put you to work? Was that why he wanted you and your sister?"

Lisette's gaze grew distant. "No, he did it because Lord Rowend paid him a stipend to take us. Besides, Ellie would have been of no use in that regard. If brains were feathers she couldn't have flown from one side of the street to the other. But she would certainly have married money—and brought Ashton influence—because she was so pretty."

Napier caught her chin in his hands. "Yes, she was pretty in the way a rose blossom is pretty. But you're beautiful, Lisette, in a bone-deep way that never fades. And you're intelligent. Determined. Only a fool would wish to trade those things for mere prettiness."

She shook her head, and he let her go. "I *don't* wish it," she said. "I never have. And, yes, I had suitors, but nothing ever *took*. Always, in the back of my mind, I was thinking of Lazonby. How he'd escaped death whilst Papa and Percy and Ellie had not. How that, someday, I'd run him down like the dog he was."

This time, Napier was not fool enough to begrudge her anger.

"But we recaptured Lazonby, and put him in prison," he said gently. "Didn't that free you to live your own life?"

She shrugged. "I suppose, but by then Uncle was dead and Aunt Ashton and I were just trying to keep the paper afloat. We were desperate—and everyone knew it."

"I see," he mused. "So that's when you became—" He couldn't think how to word it.

"Became what?" Her brows had knotted so prettily, it distracted him an instant.

"—Jack."

He dropped the name like a mortar shell, right into the middle of the bed.

All the color drained from her face. It was too late to wish back the word.

And really, what was the point?

"Come, Lisette," he said quietly, "this has become a fool's game. You know that I know Jack Coldwater doesn't exist."

"Tell that to Lazonby," she answered curtly.

"Lazonby merely relayed a story that could be neither proven nor disproven," said Napier, "and told it with his tongue tucked so firmly in his cheek it's a wonder he got it out again."

She wasn't looking at him now. "Apparently you must decide for yourself what the truth is."

"I decided that weeks ago," he said gently. "Now, I still

don't know who killed Sir Wilfred or why—most probably it was you, but it could have been Lazonby or even Anisha—hell, perhaps the dastard shot himself or the butler did it. I'm not sure I care anymore."

"And yet we find ourselves still talking about it," she retorted. "Why is that, I wonder?"

"Because, Lisette, I'm merely trying to understand . . . *you*."

"Trying to understand me—?" She turned a little away from him, and sat up on the edge of the bed, one long leg still tucked beneath her. "Tell me, Napier—do you think me mad? Or dangerous?"

"*What?*" Napier swallowed hard.

He had misjudged the intimacy, he realized. He reached for her, hoping to undo the damage. "No, of course not. Lisette, love, come back here."

But her fingers were digging into the edge of his mattress, and she would not turn around. "And have I done, Royden, all that you've asked of me in your investigation?"

He dropped his hand. Her voice had gone utterly cold.

"You've done more than I've asked," he said. "Christ Jesus, Lisette!—I've been half terrified if there actually was some wickedness afoot, you'd put yourself in danger resolving it—but what has that to do with this?"

She stood, her hands shaking but her voice oddly steady. "We had an understanding in Hackney," she said, snatching her shift from his carpet. "You said you meant to keep an eye on me until you were sure I wasn't *mad* or *dangerous*. And then, if I'd done everything you'd asked, you'd drop all this. And you'd keep me safe from Lazonby if he turned vengeful."

"And by God, I will."

But Lisette was already dragging her shift on. "Yet you keep browbeating me," she said, the words coming swiftly—and a little angrily—as she shoved her arms through. "You keep on insisting on having something I don't wish to give, and looking past what I'm offering. My body. My desire for you. I don't wish to shut you out. I care for you, Royden. I do. Far more than I wish to. You are an exquisite lover. And . . . and I don't mind you haven't any charm. Or pr-pretty words."

Something in her throat caught at the very end, her face softening wretchedly.

Napier rolled off the mattress, and came around the bed. "So you care for me and I'm a fine lover," he echoed, watching as she grabbed up her stockings and corset. "And I've declared fervently that I love you. But you have tears welling in your eyes. Forgive me if I cannot grasp the problem."

At last she straightened up, and looked him hard and square in the eye—in a way few women dared to do—and he knew with an awful certainty his life was edging toward ruin.

"The problem," she said, ramming a wad of blue silk under her arm, "is that if we go on in this vein, one day you'll look back and remember this conversation. You'll remember the moment I told you the truth and made it so hideously real for you. You'll remember to the very breath that instant when you made your hard choice to do nothing and just keep fucking me. And eventually, when the heat fades, you'll look back and wonder if you compromised your integrity for lust. If I orchestrated this whole bloody seduction."

Napier fisted both hands to keep from dragging her back to bed and laying a hand to her bottom. "Lisette, I am not *fucking* you," he said tightly. "I am making love to you. *We* are making love with one another. And everything else you just said is utter balderdash."

"But what if it isn't?" She started for the door, one stocking trailing from the bundle. "In the passageway—before passion addled your brain—you didn't even want to let me past the door. You said you thought I'd shove a screw in your heart. But I practically pushed past you, then pushed my way into your bed—and I meant to do both, if I could get away with it."

He was on her heels, angry and a little frightened. "Oh, so you seduced *me* tonight?" he said. "And then you managed to tie yourself to my headboard in the bargain. And forced me to bed you breathless with a cockstand the likes of which I haven't seen since I started shaving. Oh, that *was* a clever trick."

She whirled around, her face bloodless and frozen. "And God knows I'm nothing if not clever," she whispered. "I can raise duplicity to an art form. Those were your words, not mine. Don't forget them now, Napier, merely to have them come back and haunt you later."

He reached around her, and slammed his hand flat against his door. "Oh, I haven't been seduced, my dear, since Mrs. Minter took my virginity," he growled, "so I think I'm old enough to know the difference between love and lust."

"Kindly move your hand."

Instead, he leaned against it with all his weight. "I *know* the difference," he reiterated. "And whatever I do or don't know about you has become almost irrelevant."

Her eyes drilled into his, ageless and hard as she leaned very, very near. "If it were so irrelevant," she said softly, "you wouldn't be haranguing me."

"Oh, *haranguing*!" Still wedged against the door, his arm was as rigid as his erection had been mere minutes ago. "Now you listen, Elizabeth, and listen well. I *will not* be gainsaid in this. And what I feel for you is a simple fact."

The anger drained away, replaced by an age-old weariness as she shook her head. "Oh, Napier, surely you cannot be that naïve," she answered. "Nothing is ever simple. Least of all facts. Much of the time, they're dashed inconvenient. Particularly so when we'd like the world to be as we wish it. When we need desperately to see what we want to see, and to live a life of certitude. But facts are always there, getting in the way—even if we manage to forget them for a time."

He dropped his hand, and she whipped around, yanking the door open.

"Lisette," he demanded, seizing her arm and causing her to drop a stocking. "Lisette, for God's sake. This is madness. You're going out into the passageway in a damned shift."

"You think *that's* madness?" She spun around, her expression incredulous. "You want me to bare my soul and confess to you that I murdered Sir Wilfred Leeton? But you're worried someone might see me in my *underwear*? Have you any idea, Royden, how bollixed up that is?"

He shoved both hands through his hair, fighting the urge to seize her and drag her back inside. Standing there like some bare-arsed fool, and wondering what he might say or do to simply *fix it*.

In response, Lisette's lip just curled, but whether from derision or tears, he could not say. Then she turned on one heel and walked away.

Napier just stood there, staring into the emptiness. The fear and rage still warred inside him. He felt desperate. Blindsided. There was only way he could think of to make matters worse—and that would be to stride after her in a great ruckus, and force her back into his bed to finish this.

He likely would have done it, too, but he was still turning the notion in mind when he heard the slam of her door, and the sound of her lock snapping shut—like the hammer on a dry-fired pistol, a hard, ominous *snap!* in the gloom.

But Napier had already been shot down. He felt as cold and as bloodless as Sir Wilfred, laid out on that flagstone floor, his life leeching away into his own spring box. He felt that awful press of warmth behind his eyes.

He had failed. And Lisette hated him.

How in heaven's name had it happened? Did he really understand women so little? Was her affection for him so nascent, so desperately fragile, his ham-fisted ways had crushed it?

Or was she right? Was his love for her contingent on something he'd as soon not think about?

Damn it to hell, she'd put mad thoughts in his head. She'd done what she'd set out to do: to make him doubt. To make him question his own judgment.

Somehow, he forced himself to breathe—found the presence of mind to pick up the stocking she'd dropped and shut the bloody door. He returned to his night table, half sick at his stomach. His drawer still gaped open, the steel blade of his knife winking up at him. Taunting him in the pure white light by which he'd spun his own gossamer fantasy.

The fantasy of a bride by moonlight.

Slowly, he let the silk slither from his hand to pool atop the satin cord she'd tossed on his bed so many days ago. Years ago, it now seemed. Good Lord, he loved her.

He loved her.

And whatever they had shared, it seemed over. Lisette was not going to listen. There mightn't be another chance. His bullheaded insistence had driven a stake through her trust.

The hell of it was, she was right. He *had* harangued her. He had done—over and over again—the one thing she'd begged him not to do. Something caught in his chest. A sob that wouldn't come. An awful ache simply caught in the void where his heart had been, and was likely never to leave him. He sat down on the bed, grief curling around his heart like tentacles of ice.

His hand shaking, he rummaged in the still-open drawer, and drew out the green cording, wrapping it around his hand so tight the blood could barely flow. Until the pain wasn't pain but just a dead numbness that throbbed with the beat of his heart.

CHAPTER 13

Our Concerned Citizen Confesses All

Lisette stood in the open doorway of the green bedchamber, studying with some dispassion the room's swift transformation. It was beautiful, she supposed—the walls were the color of warm stone, the draperies a complementing shade of champagne. The furnishings, however, were still in disarray, with both the massive dressing chests pushed to the center amidst half a dozen boxes and trunks.

After drawing a steadying breath, she knocked on the door frame. "Might I come in?"

Lady Keaton's head jerked up. "Oh, Miss Colburne!" Seated amidst the jumble, she leapt up from a three-legged work stool. "What a pleasant surprise! Where have you been all morning? We missed you at breakfast."

"Good morning, Lady Keaton." Lisette looked tentatively about, pausing just over the threshold. "How do you do?"

"Why don't we just be Anne and Elizabeth?" Attired today in a simple black dress, the petite blonde picked her way through the open trunks and cartons, pushing a loose curl from her forehead as she came. "And I do very well, thank you. But my dear, I wonder if you do?"

"Do I look a fright?" Twisting a handkerchief in her hands to keep them from shaking, Lisette stepped into the bedchamber. "I confess I did not sleep well, nor have much appetite."

"I'm sorry. Come, sit." Anne caught her hand. "I was just helping Gwyneth and Diana clean out all these drawers."

"I was looking for Gwyneth and Diana, actually," Lisette confessed, tucking the wrenched handkerchief away. "Marsh said I might find them here."

"Oh, dear. You just missed them." Anne had drawn her to a second stool situated by an old traveling trunk, its lid thrown wide. "Diana leapt up in the midst of all this, declaring she'd forgotten a walk she'd promised Miss Willet."

"I somehow thought they meant to go in the afternoon."

Anne shrugged. "In any case, next I knew, Aunt Hepplewood was here to fetch her, expecting she might accompany her to the vicarage. But since Diana had gone, Gwyneth offered to go instead."

"*Gwyneth* offered?" said Lisette, perching herself on the stool. "How very . . ."

"—out of character?" Anne supplied, chagrin sketching over her face. "Yes, I fear it speaks to Gwyneth's desperation."

"Desperation?"

Anne's smile returned. "You've doubtless noticed, Miss Colburne, that my elder sister is less than enamored of household chores," she said. "And Diana, whilst she adores the more artistic aspects, finds routine drudgery far less compelling. I shamed the pair of them in here, and now they've squeaked out again."

"Heavens, and left you sorting all this?" Lisette was glad to feel sorry for someone other than herself. "May I help? I'm sure I shouldn't mind."

"I ought to refuse, since you're a guest." Hands on her hips, Anne surveyed the disorder. "But then, I suppose I am, too. And soon enough all this will be yours to sort anyway."

"I do wish people would quit pointing that out," said Lisette on a faint laugh.

"Well, in any case, I accept your kind offer," she said, returning her concerned gaze to Lisette. "It will give us a chance to chat. My husband tells me you're frightfully well-read. I so look forward to knowing you better."

"You're both very kind," said Lisette—and she meant it.

She had greatly enjoyed Sir Philip's company at dinner, and his wife, too, seemed most amiable. With Anne, there was none of Gwyneth's prickliness, and none of Diana's demure reserve.

But Anne was motioning about the clutter. "So, that contains Uncle Hep's stockings," she said briskly, pointing at a drawer hanging open. We're sorting everything into three cartons: mending, charity, and rubbish. Pull out the dressing slide if you wish, and use your best judgment. Uncle was a frightful packrat."

Grateful for the distraction, Lisette began at once. "Your uncle has been gone some months, hasn't he?" she asked casually.

"Yes, but Aunt Hepplewood couldn't bring herself to do this. And Diana just never got round to it. Now the room must be readied for Tony and Felicity, not left to languish." Anne heaved a slightly put-up sigh. "I shall be so glad, Elizabeth, when you are Lady Saint-Bryce."

"Shall you?" Lisette turned. "Why?"

Anne snapped the wrinkles from a nightshirt. "Oh, this grand old house hasn't had anyone to love it properly in an age," she mused, examining the seams for tears. "Since Mamma died, I daresay. Gwyneth tries, but her heart isn't in it."

"Bea's mother was frail, I collect?"

"Quite, yes, but very kind." Anne folded the shirt and laid it in the carton marked *Charity*. "Now, Elizabeth, allow me to pry. I wish to know what's caused those frightful smudges under your eyes."

"It's this dratted pale skin," said Lisette despairingly. "It shows everything."

"But why did you not sleep, my dear? I cannot imagine my husband's dinner conversation was so stimulating it kept you awake into the night."

Lisette laughed. "I found your husband fascinating, and deeply thoughtful."

"Thank you! I do, too!" Anne's eyes danced for a moment. "Papa always thought Philip dull, but he did not know him as I do. Philip has an incisive mind—and a sharp wit, once he knows you. But there, you didn't answer my question. About your bad night?"

"Oh, I had a letter," Lisette lied, her gaze firmly fixed upon the stockings. "I didn't read it until after dinner. My old nanny is unwell."

"Why, that is terrible!" said Anne, her pretty face falling. "Are you still close? Obviously you are. You look stricken."

Lisette managed a feeble nod. "She lives with me. In Hackney. I think I must go home. That's what I came to tell Gwyneth and Diana, you see. That I'm leaving."

"And I just got here." Anne pulled a sad face. "The loss is mine, Elizabeth. Saint-Bryce must be disappointed, too. Or will he see you home?"

"I . . . no, he won't," said Lisette. "I mean, he doesn't know I'm going. I haven't told him yet."

"Ah," said Anne, cutting her an odd glance. "Well, then. When do you go?"

"In the morning," she said. "I'll be able to get a train, won't I?"

"Heavens, yes. They run all day." Anne snapped out another nightshirt. "Lud, look at this! Mended at least eight times. Uncle's valet was seventy-five—devoted, but nearly blind—and Uncle would not put him off. That's why his things are in such a frightful state."

"Your uncle must have been both frugal and loyal," said Lisette. "And his wife must have loved him very much. I mean, if she could not bear to . . ."

"To sort out his things?" said Anne on a sigh. "Yes, she was utterly devoted, though he was quite some years her senior. Duncaster introduced them. I cannot imagine her grief."

But Lisette's mind had turned back to that long-ago conversation with Lady Hepplewood in the library. "I would have guessed her more of a realist than a romantic," she murmured, pairing up two stockings and tossing them into the appropriate carton.

"Oh, Aunt was not always the dour creature you've probably observed," said Anne gently. "She has changed vastly."

"Since her husband's death, do you mean?"

Anne lowered the shirt she was folding and considered it. "I think it was before then," she finally said. "Around the time I married, I think she . . . *altered*, somehow." Anne shook her head as if to shake off the thought. "And then she and Uncle Hep began staying here all the time. And Tony went off to live in London."

But Lisette wondered what had driven the Hepplewoods apart, for that surely seemed the case. "In any event," she remarked, "no one seems to mind that she and Diana remain here."

"Lord, no," Anne agreed. "Besides, Loughford is Tony's now—and, as Gwyneth and I were remarking earlier, it hasn't a dower property attached."

"Has it not?" Lisette folded another pair of stockings. "Well. I cannot quite see Lady Hepplewood returning to Loughford after the wedding to live under Miss Willet's purview."

"And really, who could blame her?" Anne agreed. "But Burlingame is three times Loughford's size, so we can all rattle round in here like marbles, scarcely striking one another."

"Will Tony and Miss Willet be spending much time here after the wedding?"

"Why, I daresay they shall," said Anne. "This has always been Tony's second home. And Felicity seems to like it very much."

"When do they mean to marry?" asked Lisette.

"Diana was just asking me, which is what prompted the dower discussion," said Anne. "The wedding is set for mid-August."

"Goodness, that's just weeks away." Lisette cut Anne a sidelong glance. "But Diana said that—"

Anne looked at her sharply. "Diana said what?"

Lisette shook her head. "I may have misunderstood."

Anne flashed a mischievous grin. "I doubt it," she teased. "Come, we are practically cousins already! What did Diana say?"

Lisette gave a weak shrug. "She merely suggested the betrothal would not last. I collect she meant that Lady Hepplewood would stop it."

"Well, Aunt mightn't be terribly pleased, but she'll reconcile herself." Anne gave a weary smile. "As to the remark, that was likely Diana being—well, let us charitably call it *protective*. She wasn't any happier when Gwyneth told her Tony and I were promised. She felt like the odd one out."

And yet it had been Diana and Tony—along with Gwyneth—who'd shut Anne from their little clique as children. "But you were very young then, weren't you?" she blurted.

Too late Lisette realized she looked like a gossip.

"Ah, Gwen's been tattling, hasn't she?" said Anne, chuckling. "Yes, there was a mad marriage scheme between

Grandpapa and Uncle Hep, but none of us really heeded it."

"You never cared for Tony in that way?"

Anne lowered her hands, now clutching a striped waist-coat. "Tony and I adore one another and always have," she said, looking a little exasperated. "Yes, I thought I might as well marry him. I daresay we'd have got on. But then I met Philip. And a week later, I realized—"

"Realized what?"

Anne shook her head. "Never mind."

"I should like to know," said Lisette, "if it isn't personal."

Anne bit her lip. "Well, it isn't personal *to me*," she clarified, glancing about the room. "It's just that I never told Gwyneth. I *wanted* to. But just wouldn't have done, you see. Gwen can be so defensive of me—as if I'm incapable of looking after myself."

It was an odd and rather tender view of Gwyneth, and one Lisette had never considered. "Why on earth would she need to defend you?"

Anne sat back down on her stool, crushing the waist-coat in her lap. "It's just that I had come out that year with Diana," she said, her eyes a little guilt wracked. "But half-way through the Season, I met Philip. And oh, Lisette, I liked him so much! We shared so many interests—books, poets, politics! But I felt as if I were meant for Tony—that he needed me, you know?"

"But I can't imagine," said Lisette, "that Tony would have expected such a sacrifice."

"Apparently not." Anne's lips quirked with humor. "Because one evening—some weeks after our come-out ball—I caught him in the library kissing Diana."

"Kissing *Diana*?" Lisette's brow furrowed. "But kissing her . . . how?"

"Good try," said Anne wryly. "But it was not a brotherly peck. He had her bent over his arm and she had a hand on—ah, but never mind that."

"Oh," said Lisette softly. "Well. Were you angry?"

"A little." Anne looked chagrinned again. "But I waited a few more weeks, and when nothing came of any of it—Tony seemed fixed on neither of us, to be honest—I just stopped feeling so frightfully loyal. I told Papa I wished to accept Sir Philip's suit, and that I would not be denied. Aunt Hepplewood was very angry."

"Heavens, what did you do?"

Anne gave a lame shrug. "Eventually, I had to tell her why," she said. "She was outraged at first. Then, on her next breath, she made it out to be a mere dalliance. But then she suggested—in this grim, irritated tone—that Tony would likely get round her objections in the end."

"I gather Tony is rarely refused anything by any female."

"So far as I know, it's never happened," said Anne on a laugh. "But to marry the steward's daughter? That was looking low indeed, to Aunt's way of thinking. Still, she always did give in."

"So what happened?"

Anne lifted both hands, palms up. "Oddly, nothing," she said. "It was very strange. I married Philip the following spring. And eventually, Diana accepted Papa's suit. And now Tony is fixed as well."

"You married the person who was perfect for you," said Lisette reassuringly. "And soon Tony shall. As to Diana, once she's over the grief of your father's death, she'll find someone. She's already said Lady Hepplewood means them to go to London next Season."

"Oh, excellent!" Anne's face brightened hopefully. "I must begin to think of someone perfect for Diana. By then you'll be married, too. We must put our heads together."

Lisette thought Anne one of the most charitably disposed human beings she'd ever met. Her presence—and her sheer normalcy—went a long way toward assuaging Lisette's view of the whole family.

And what a pity that, in the end, it would mean nothing. Lisette would be gone from this place, and soon forgotten.

"Well," she said brightly, pushing in the drawer. "That's emptied, Anne. What shall I do next?"

"The walnut night tables." Anne pointed left and right. "Each has two drawers cramp-full of heaven knows what. I think you'll want to draw up a rubbish bin."

The drawers being small, it seemed easiest to pull them out and carry them into the sorting area. The first was filled with gentlemen's periodicals, all months out of date. Lisette emptied it carefully, returned the drawer, and carried over the second.

This one, rather oddly, was stuffed with a folded length of brilliant green fabric, some of it cut to bits. Lisette lifted out a piece, and let it dangle. "These are just scraps," she said. "But the larger piece might be salvaged."

Anne looked up from a tangle of braces she was pairing. "Lord, don't pitch any of that out," she said, throwing up a hand. "Diana will have our heads."

Lisette dropped it and picked up another piece, almost identical. The fabric was a lush, heavy green velvet—and very familiar-looking velvet, too.

"Anne," she said curiously, "aren't these Lord Hepplewood's old bed-hangings?"

"Yes, and his curtains, too," said Anne, flicking a glance up. "Or, more correctly, that the fabric was *left over* from the sewing of his hangings and draperies. After she fitted out the room all those months ago, Diana stuffed the scraps in a drawer."

"Like *this*—? All hacked up?"

Anne's brow furrowed. "No, in one piece in the bottom of that wardrobe, I think," she said. "But Gwen found it and began cutting it up for compresses when we were nursing Uncle Hep."

"Oh." Lisette looked at her curiously. "Were you here?"

"Oh, yes, when I could be," said Anne, triumphantly freeing one of the braces. "When Uncle was restless, we'd soak compresses in cold vinegar for his forehead and wrists. It was a trick my stepmother often used for fever."

"Nanna did that when my sister and I were small," said Lisette. "It's oddly soothing."

Anne shrugged. "And velvet, we thought, would feel quite nice," she said. "But Diana had a fit. She said she was saving it to make a Parisian green counterpane."

Something inside Lisette went perfectly still.

Parisian.

Paris.

For a long moment, Lisette stood there, scarcely daring to breathe as she scrabbled through her brain, one arm hitched beneath the little drawer.

"Anne," she said a little sharply, "did Diana perhaps say a *Paris Green* counterpane?"

Anne looked up, her expression bland. "She might have done. Uncle adored green. But he was so ill by then, it seemed awfully optimistic. Still, Gwen stuffed what was left of the velvet away to appease Diana."

Inwardly, Lisette ran through her logic again.

Good Lord. Could it be so simple? But what were the chances of such a thing happening? And entirely by accident?

A chill ran through her. Both Gwyneth and Mrs. Jansen understood scientific things; astronomy and mathematics and yes, chemistry. Abruptly, she set the drawer down, stuffed a velvet scrap in her pocket, and then strolled toward the hearth.

The strange kettle still swung from its hook in the firebox.

No. It was not possible.

Still, she spun around, her heart suddenly pounding. "Anne, I beg your pardon," she blurted. "I just remembered—the letter—I should post a letter to Nanna. To tell her I'm coming home."

Anne was standing by one of the tall dressing chests, pushing one of the drawers in. "Yes, of course," she said. "You've been a great help. But Elizabeth, you'll likely arrive home with the letter—or within hours of it."

Lisette nodded, and tried to calm herself. "Perhaps so," she said. "But I mightn't go tomorrow, you know? It might be Friday or Saturday. I should let her know, do you not think? Just so she'll know I'm definitely coming? That I haven't forsaken her?"

"Oh, it will cheer her immeasurably, I am sure," said Anne brightly. "Thank you for your help. Shall I see you at dinner?"

"Oh, yes. I shall look forward to it."

Swiftly, Lisette made her escape.

*Q*uite by happenstance, Napier timed his visit to the schoolroom for half past ten. It was an hour when Mrs. Jansen was most apt to be taking Beatrice out for a morning romp since no trace of rain remained, and the day had dawned brilliantly sunny, with a stiff breeze that had dried the landscape.

His task, it seemed, could no longer be put off.

Napier strode through the house a bit like a man bound for the rope. He'd hoped to delay another day or two, but Lisette's anguish and Craddock's gout left him with no excuse to dawdle. He was going to have the conversation he'd been avoiding since coming to Burlingame—certainly since his last visit to the schoolroom.

Napier met the winsome pair coming down the staircase, Mrs. Jansen with a large bonnet in one hand and what looked like a novel in the other.

"Saint-Bryce!" said the child, her face lighting up.

"Good morning, Bea." He stopped on the landing to make

her a little bow. "Mrs. Jansen, you are in good looks today."

"Oh, how do you do, my lord?" said the governess. "Are you not off to Berkshire?"

"No, Craddock was willing, but his foot still looks a misery," said Napier. "I thought I might walk in the orchard with Bea instead—assuming you've no objection?"

Mrs. Jansen blushed prettily. "No, my lord, not in the least."

Napier turned and offered her his arm. "Perhaps you might like to sit on the bench above, just to keep an eye on us," he suggested. "Bea might decide to climb up a tree again. In which case, you'll have to come down the hill and get her out, since I'm afraid of heights."

At that, both females laughed and Beatrice began to tease him unmercifully. A few minutes later, they had deposited Mrs. Jansen and her book upon the bench and were making their way down the hill toward the stables in a stiff but not unpleasant breeze.

"You *aren't* going to climb up a tree, are you?" he asked warily.

"Not if I have something better to do," said the child, grinning up at him.

"Ah," he said. "What did you have in mind for today?"

The girl shrugged, and flopped down in the grass beneath her favorite tree. "We might go down to the boathouse," she suggested, "and skip stones on the water again?"

"Aye, we might," he said reluctantly.

Later, Napier was to wish that he'd encouraged the child's notion. But in that moment, he simply wanted to avoid the damned boathouse—as he'd been doing for days now. Merely glimpsing it through his window reminded him of his passionate interlude there with Lisette, and of the crashing argument that had followed.

It was the same pattern they'd followed again last night, but with far more harrowing results.

Lisette had not even appeared at breakfast this morning. Napier was sure, for he'd gone down early, having been unable to sleep, and lingered until everyone else had dined. He had lingered so long, in fact, that the servants had begun to mill about, anxious to clear the sideboard.

Finally Napier accepted that Lisette didn't mean to come down at all; that even as he sat hunched over a cold cup of coffee, his stomach in a knot and his heart half broken, she was likely packing her trunks and wishing him to the devil.

But if he was going to dwell upon the chaos that constituted his love life, he might as well go down to the lake and throw himself in. Far better to turn his attention to someone he perhaps could help.

He joined Bea in the grass, with little regard for the grumbling that would ensue when Jolley saw his trousers.

They had met here with some frequency, he and Beatrice, Napier having learned the girl's schedule and gained, in some measure, Mrs. Jansen's trust. He had been relieved to learn the woman always hovered near, well within earshot and usually carrying a book or something pertaining to Bea's lessons. Though there was a fine line between the two, he'd decided the child was not neglected, but was instead given a healthy amount of independence. In that knowledge, at least, he'd found some comfort.

Napier stretched out his legs and crossed them at the ankles. Beatrice followed suit, her tiny brown boots peeping from beneath a froth of lace. Then she fell back into the grass and stared up into the branches now clattering a little in the wind, crossing her hands over her heart.

He glanced down at her. With her blonde ringlets fanning around her head, Bea looked rather like an angel. He had developed a great fondness for the girl, he realized, and no small amount of tenderness. Suddenly, that unfamiliar emotion gripped his heart a little—wounded, wrung-out organ that it had become these last miserable hours.

But it would not do to be maudlin on such a lovely day. Beatrice had enough of that in her quieter moments, he suspected. Instead, he inhaled deeply. "Ah, smell the fresh air, Bea," he said. "I shall miss this when I return to London."

"Is the air in London truly foul?" asked Bea absently. "Mrs. Jansen says it smells worse than the sewage canals in Amsterdam."

He laughed, and fell back into the grass beside her, staring up into the skirling canopy of green. "It often does," he agreed, wedging his hands beneath his head. "Especially when that notorious odor is blended with the acrid stench of coal smoke and the reek of the riverbank, and the whole miasma is pressed down upon the city by a fog. They call it a London Peculiar, and you can scarcely see through it."

"If it stinks so, why would you go back?" The girl sounded wistful.

"Oh, because of my work," he said vaguely.

"But what about Miss Colburne?" said Bea. "Aren't you going to marry her and bring her here to live?"

Napier hesitated, still unwilling to mislead the child. He gave a soft sigh. "I'm afraid we may not marry after all, Bea," he said quietly. "Miss Colburne is having second thoughts."

Bea swiveled her head to look at him, her eyes giving up little. "Diana had second thoughts," she said quietly, "and that didn't end well."

He smiled faintly. "I'm afraid I brought Miss Colburne's second thoughts on myself," he said. "Will you mind so very much?"

The child lifted both shoulders in an exaggerated motion, rustling the grass. "Will you marry Diana, then?" she said a little sullenly.

Napier turned his face back into the branches. "No, Bea," he said softly. "I think I've given my heart to Miss Colburne. It would not be right to marry someone I did not love."

"Aunt Hepplewood told Diana that love was a cartload of nonsense," said Bea evenly. "That it was better to marry with the head than the heart."

"She might be right," Napier admitted, "but it's too late for me. That said, I'm going to ask you to keep my secret about Miss Colburne for now. Just in case I can convince her to change her mind. Can you do that?"

The girl nodded. "Yes," she said solemnly. "I can keep a secret."

Napier hesitated a heartbeat before plunging forward. "Indeed, I think you must be very good at keeping secrets," he said, "which is an admirable quality under most circumstances."

She was still looking at him through the swaying stalks of grass. "But not all circumstances?"

"Not always." He rolled up onto his elbow, and withdrew the letter from his pocket. "For example, I think, Bea, that you secretly wrote me this letter some weeks past."

He held it out between two fingers. The child looked at it unblinkingly, her blue eyes narrowed a little against the sunlight.

He let his hand drop. "Actually," he said, "I know you wrote it. And I should like to know why."

"How do you know?" she asked doubtfully.

"Because it is my job," he said. "My job—sometimes—is to uncover secrets. Oh, it looks, perhaps, as if a servant might have sent it. Cleverly done, I thought."

She was silent for a long while. Napier refolded the letter and tucked it back into his coat. "Bea, you don't have to say why you sent it, if you don't wish to," he said, "but just know that it was perfectly fine for you to write me."

"Was it?" she said in a small voice.

"Certainly," he said. "In fact, whilst I'm still living in London, you may write to me at any time, and about anything. If something troubles you—even the most trifling thing—I should *wish* you to write me, and to do it straight-away. But do sign the letters, Bea. I would be very happy to get them, and to see your signature."

She sat up then, curling one leg beneath her. She looked coltish, and very pretty. Indeed, he thought it quite likely her beauty would surpass even her sister Anne's.

The child was fast approaching a vulnerable time in her life. Soon enough there would be balls and suitors and mar-riage proposals to be weighed. The thought chilled him. And because of it, Napier dared do nothing to jeopardize the child's growing trust.

Bea began to twist a stalk of grass into some sort of loop. "I might write to you again," she said, "someday—if you don't come back to Burlingame."

He reached out and squeezed her hand. "I will come back, Bea," he said quietly, "from time to time. And if anything should happen to your grandfather—to *our* grandfather—if Duncaster's health should fail, I mean—then I would come at once. And I would stay."

"All the time?" she whispered.

"All the time," said Napier.

And he was suddenly struck with the realization that the idea no longer troubled him as much as it once had. Sir George had been right. There was no escaping his fate. Moreover, there was much to learn here, and the fortunes of many depended upon Napier's ability to learn it.

But his days spent traveling the estates and reviewing the accounts with Craddock had reassured Napier that Lisette had been right, too. The running of a great estate required, above all, a keen grasp of human nature and a knack for management.

But Bea was still looking at him a little pensively.

Lightly, he patted the letter in his pocket. "Why do we not play a game?" he suggested. "Why do I not guess at the reason you sent this letter? And if I am right, you may simply say so?"

She looked up from her grass chain, and stared at him for a moment. "All right," she said.

Napier appeared to consider it. "I think you became a bit afraid last year when your Uncle Hepplewood grew ill," he said. "He became a little . . . distraught, didn't he?"

Again, she lifted her slender shoulders. "They would not let me see him," she said quietly. "But I could hear him sometimes. Saying . . . things. He was scared. Then he died."

Napier thought he understood. "That must have been frightening," he said, "to know that your uncle was so ill he could not think clearly."

She gave a little nod.

"And when your papa died a few months later," said Napier, "I'm sure that frightened you even more. But Bea, he died of an apoplexy. It was unforeseeable."

"I suppose." Her chin came up almost defiantly. "But Uncle Hep kept saying that people were trying to kill him. And then P-Papa said . . ."

Her face began to crumple a little.

Napier reached out and laid a hand on her shoulder. "He said that people were trying to plague him to death," he gently suggested. "Is that it? But he did not say it directly to you, I'm guessing?"

She gave a short shake of her head that set her ringlets bouncing.

"Perhaps you heard him saying it to himself?" Napier gently pressed. "Perhaps when you were playing in the pantry, and he did not know you were there? It must have sounded a little like the things Lord Hepplewood said."

"Well, no one believed Uncle Hep, and look what came of it." Bea's lip thrust out a little stubbornly. "And I did not make it up. Mrs. Jansen thinks I did, but I did not. Papa said it all the time. He even said it to Craddock once. You can ask him."

Napier patted her shoulder. "Oh, I believe you," he assured her. "But Bea, it is something grown-ups just *say*. It's just an expression—and our saying it means we're frustrated. It doesn't mean we actually believe people wish us ill."

Her gaze locked with his, hard and fierce. "But Papa *did* die," she said grimly. "He said it would happen—over and over—and then *it did*. They nagged and they shouted and they said vile things until he just *died*."

Her vehemence shocked him. For a long moment, Napier considered it, and when he spoke, he chose his words with great care. "And when you say *they*, Bea, who do you mean, exactly? It will be our secret—and I'm very good at keeping secrets, too."

Beatrice stared into the grass, her blonde eyebrows knotted. "*Gwen and Diana*," she whispered accusingly. "Gwen shouted at him and Diana cried—Diana *always* cries—I *hate* her. And then—and then I *don't know* what happened! Not for sure. But Papa fell down! And then he—he just *died*."

Napier caught her hand in his and gave it a reassuring squeeze—and this time he held it. "Bea, were you in the pantry that day?" he said. "Remember, I'm just guessing. But you wrote to me, Bea, for a reason. Because you were worried. And because I catch bad people, yes? I don't think there are any bad people in this story—merely some unhappy ones—but let's be sure, *hmm*?"

With what looked like grave reluctance, she nodded.

"All right," he said calmly. "Now, was the pantry door open?"

She gave a tight shake of her head.

"But there was some sort of quarrel?" he said. "With Gwyneth and Diana?"

"First Gwen," she said resentfully, "then Diana."

"Bea," he said solemnly, "I think you should tell me, as best you can, exactly what you heard."

When she did not respond, he tipped her chin up with his finger. "Bea, it troubles you," he said. "I know it does. But I cannot understand it—or more importantly, explain it to you—unless you tell me."

She exhaled slowly, then her gaze caught his, regretful and wary. "Gwen came into Papa's study. She started a big fight. It was about Mrs. Jansen and that house again."

"Ah, the dower house, perhaps?"

"Yes, that," said the girl. "She wanted it, and she wanted to take Mrs. Jansen away to live in it."

Napier nodded. "And what did your Papa say?"

"That Gwen needed to hush up and go to London and find a husband," said Bea. "They fought about it all the time. But this time Gwen said that if he would not give her the house, she was going to take Mrs. Jansen and go back to Amsterdam. And Papa said she was not so big he could not put her over his knee. That she was un-*unnatural*—and wanted straightening out. And then they yelled some more, and Papa said she was going to plague him to death."

"Ah," said Napier quietly. "And then what happened?"

Again, the little shrug. "The door slammed, and Papa said some bad words. Then he went to the table and got his brandy. I heard him put it on the desk, and take out the stopper. It makes a *chink!* sound."

"Yes, I know exactly." Napier wished all his witnesses had such a memory. "You're very good, Bea, with your descriptions."

"Then someone knocked on the door, and it was Diana."

"Ah. And did they quarrel, too?"

The girl's fretful look returned. "Not at first," she said. "Diana just cried. And then she said she did not want to marry him."

"I see," said Napier. "Had you overheard such discussions before?"

Bea nodded in an exaggerated fashion. "Yes," she said darkly. "But this time Diana said that she was begging him. That she would do anything, if only he would tell Aunt Hepplewood."

"And what, exactly, did Diana want him to tell her?"

"That he didn't want to marry her," said Bea.

"Ah," said Napier.

It made sense. Diana was cowed by Lady Hepplewood. Her father was dependent upon the Hepplewood estate, not just for his position as steward, but for the very roof over his head.

"And what did your father say to that?" he went on.

"He said she was just having bridal nerves again," said the girl, "and that it would all go away once the vows were said, and that he would be gentle. Then she cried even worse, and said she couldn't bear it. That she did not love him, and could never love him, and did not want him to touch her. That the very notion was ab-abhorrish or something—to her."

"Abhorrent, perhaps?"

"Yes, that."

Napier winced. Strong words indeed—and ugly ones, too. He was glad Bea didn't seem to grasp their full import.

"I see," he said quietly. "Well, Bea, that is unfortunate. I think we are very right to keep it a secret."

"And *then* they had a quarrel," said the girl, more intently. "They started shouting. Diana said she hated him, and she was not a broodmare, whatever that means."

"*Hmm*," said Napier warily.

"And Papa started yelling—he never yelled—but he did, and he said she was mad as a hatter, and that a gentleman mightn't beg off and that she could just damned well do it herself."

Jesus Christ.

For an instant, Napier shut his eyes. "And then what?"

"I heard him cry out," she said. "And then I heard glass break. And Diana ran out screaming that Papa had collapsed. She lied, and said she'd just found him like that. But . . . she plagued him to death. That's what *I* think."

Napier took her hand again. "Bea, I always want to know when something worries you. But Dr. Underwood told me that your papa had an apoplexy. That's something no one can see and no one can predict."

She lifted her slender shoulders again and sighed. "Anyway, he's dead now, isn't he?" she said sadly. "And now I wonder if—"

"Yes? If what, sweet?"

Bea cut him a dark look. "What if someone starts plaguing Grandpapa?" she said quietly. "What if he is . . ." Her little face started to crumple.

"They won't," he said, giving her hand another squeeze. "Bea, I promise."

She lifted her gaze to his, looking somewhat reassured. "Well," she said, "I still think Gwen is just mean. And I still hate Diana."

Napier drew the child close, and set an arm about her shoulders. The responsible adult in him knew he should tell her not to hate anyone. But the policeman in him knew that many people had earned a measure of hatred.

Was Gwen one of them? Or Diana?

No. Gwen might be a bit blunt and mannish, and Diana was trapped in the thankless role of poor female relation. She had no power over her own dominion, and perhaps it had driven her to despair.

"I'll tell you what I think we should do," he said, standing and pulling Beatrice to her feet. "You should let me worry about all this from here out, and trust that I will deal with it. Can you do that?"

The child nodded.

"You may count on me, Bea," he said as reassuringly as he knew how. "And tomorrow, perhaps you and Mrs. Jansen and I might take a walk into the village?"

"To the village?"

"Yes," said Napier. "Perhaps you might like to gather some flowers for your Papa's grave? Then we'll take them, the three of us. I used to do that with my father. Especially when I was uncertain about things—work things, especially—I'd just go and talk out loud to him."

"So he's dead, too?"

Napier nodded. "Yes," he said. "He was your Uncle Nicholas, you know, and I'm sorry he did not live long enough to meet you. But we can still talk to them, Bea. And it will reassure you, I hope, that your father is happy in heaven, and always watching over you."

"All right," she said softly.

He gave her an awkward pat on the head. "And after that's done," he added, "I think we should stop at that bakery. The one with those little cakes you told me about."

"The *sesame* ones?" Her eyes widened.

"Absolutely," he said, taking her hand. "The *sesame* ones."

CHAPTER 14

A Voice from the Grave

$\mathcal{L}$isette arrived, breathless, at the top of the east staircase. The corridor was as quiet as it had been in the wee hours of the morning when she'd rushed back to her room practically naked to collapse into a sobbing heap, intent on ruthlessly forcing herself to face the truth.

Her *affaire de coeur* with Royden Napier was at an end.

She had known, of course, it could not last—that the heated passion would scorch her in the end. Yet she had allowed herself to be lulled into denial by his touch. But Lisette had laid her life's path long ago, and if her older and wiser self now yearned to go back—to alter that awful course she'd taken—it still could not be done.

Nonetheless, she could not make herself regret a moment spent in his arms. She didn't even regret their quarrels. She would have those memories to cling to when Napier was gone from her life.

Hastily, she passed by his door, wondering if she should knock. But she simply could not face him again until she was more settled in her mind. Instead she burst into her own room to see that Fanny was there before her.

The maid was already laying out the clothes that were to be packed. "Oh, hullo, miss," she said. "Just leave the door open, if you please. That Mr. Prater's gone up to the lumber room to fetch down your trunks."

Lisette scarcely heard her. "Fanny," she said breathlessly, "where's my brown morocco folio?"

Fanny's brow furrowed. "Ah!" she said, turning and going into the dressing room. "Never took it from your carpetbag, I daresay."

Lisette followed her in, watching anxiously as Fanny rummaged. On a triumphant sound, the maid drew out the tall, thin book. Lisette seized it from her hands. Going to the window, she flipped it open on the sill and began to page frantically through the news clippings she and Fanny had diligently pasted in it for years on end. Jack Coldwater's journalistic oeuvre, such as it was.

"What are you after?" asked Fanny curiously.

"An old *Examiner* article," she said. "The one about the *Golden Eagle* burning."

Fanny set a hand on her arm. "Settle down, miss. The house ain't afire. Look to the very front."

Lisette started over, finding it at once. "Actually, no, not this one," she said her eyes rapidly scanning it. "The one from the *next* day. Or perhaps the day after that. About Mrs. Stanton."

Calmly, Fanny flipped to the next page. "It's right here, miss," she said. "But awfully old news."

Hastily, Lisette reread it, then gave it a good yank, ripping the entire page—newsprint, paste and paper—from the portfolio. Her mind worked frantically. Mrs. Stanton had died quickly—and for reasons no one could immediately discern. Lord Hepplewood had lingered. And then—suddenly—the end had come.

"Pencil," she ordered, holding out a hand as she read.

"Righty-ho," said Fanny.

Sitting down at the desk, Lisette began circling the pertinent parts of the article, Fanny bent over her shoulder. "I surely don't see, miss, why you're so fixed on poor Mrs. Stanton again."

"It's that dratted dream," Lisette muttered, now scribbling in the margins. "It's haunting me, Fanny."

And the thing was, indeed, more nightmare than dream, variants of which she'd suffered through the years. Usually the dream was of Ashton reeling drunkenly as he tried to snatch the article. Other times the words vanished as fast as she wrote them.

But sometimes—more and more of late—the dream began on the docks with the gruesome sight of Mrs. Stanton convulsing and near death. Since coming to Burlingame, Lisette had dreamt pieces of it over and over. The first might have been happenstance. But beyond that? Well, there was no accounting for inner workings of the human mind.

Her scribbling finished, she folded the article and weighed her options, none especially attractive. Doing nothing was really quite out of the question. There was an inherent risk, perhaps, in passing the actual article along. But if she could not give Napier an answer to the one question he kept asking, could she give him this, at the very least?

For a moment, she drummed her fingers on the desktop. "Have you any idea, Fanny, where Mr. Napier might be?"

Fanny had returned to her pile of clothing on the bed. "Mr. Jolley said he meant to ride to Wiltshire."

"Ah." Something inside her fell a little.

But really, what had she expected? To find the man prostrate with grief on her threshold this morning? She snorted aloud. Royden Napier probably couldn't even spell *prostrate*.

Still, she had promised in good faith to help him. Lisette might be a lot of things, but she did not go back on her word.

Could she resolve this before his return, and prove Hepplewood's death accidental? Diana, hen-witted though she was, might be of help.

But the time had to be now: Lisette was leaving in the morning, and this wouldn't make for pleasant dinner conversation.

Hastily, she stuffed the page into an envelope and jotted Napier's name across it. If her conversation with Diana turned up anything, she could decide then whether to leave it for him.

Leaping up, Lisette snatched her shawl from the open wardrobe. "Fanny, would you lay out the yellow silk for dinner?"

"Righty-ho," said Fanny again. "Where are you off to in such a tizzy?"

Lisette was indeed already flying toward the door. "To find Diana," she said. "I want to ask her about—"

Just then, Prater came through, carrying Lisette's massive traveling trunk balanced neatly on one shoulder.

"Oh, Prater, thank you," said Lisette. "How strong you are."

He set the trunk by her bed with a grunt, then rose, blushing. "Thank you, miss."

Suddenly it struck Lisette she was overlooking a possible font of information. "Prater," she said, turning around again, "you worked in Lord Hepplewood's bedchamber, did you not, taking down the watered silk?"

"Yes, miss." He looked at her oddly.

"I was wondering—how did you do it? I mean, it's pasted, isn't it?"

The young man shrugged his wide shoulders. "I'm sure I don't know, miss," he said. "But we sponged it with warm vinegar. Devilish stuff, it was."

"Walton did most of it, didn't he? And removed the curtains and the bed hangings?"

*N*apier left Beatrice in the schoolroom under the watchful eye of Mrs. Jansen. They were preparing to focus on Euclidean geometry for the afternoon, since Lord Duncaster, thank God, held the unfashionable view that education was not wasted on women.

It was but one more enlightenment he'd had to suffer with regard to his grandfather, he inwardly grumbled, shutting the door behind him. Duncaster was a stubborn old devil, and like most of his class, a bit arrogant. Yet through the whole of his stay at Burlingame, Napier had seen nothing to give him a distrust, or even a dislike, of the man.

It ate at him a bit as he made his way through the vast, vaulted colonnade, his heels ringing hard upon the black and white marble. More and more it felt as if all that he'd believed in—and built his life upon—had been torn asunder by this visit.

He was going to end up with a ward, it seemed—a child he liked vastly. He had discovered a deep appreciation for fresh air. He'd learned that an overabundance of gilt, marble, and gaudy French furniture did not ruin one's life, and that the father he'd idolized from afar and followed so diligently was looking less like a tireless crusader, and more like a flawed character from a Shakespearean tragedy.

And then, to add agony to injury, he'd fallen in love. Desperately, heartbreakingly in love—with a woman who, despite all the gilt and French furniture, would likely never agree to be Baroness Saint-Bryce.

Oh, he had not given up—and he wouldn't. But his heart was heavy with dread, and with the certain knowledge that he had brought this misery on himself; that he'd made the sort of mistake the greenest constable would have known never to make. He had pushed when he should simply have listened.

Years of experience had taught Napier that people rarely

needed urging on. Were a police officer worth his salt, he'd often learn a vast deal more by simply waiting and letting the object of his query speak. Everyone showed his colors sooner or later—and usually it was sooner.

But he already knew Elizabeth Colburne's colors. She was true as Coventry blue.

He was grimly, determinedly certain that she was the woman he'd waited for all of his life. And somehow, he had to find a way to salvage this.

He arrived upstairs to a cool, shadowy corridor. But beyond his bedchamber, some six doors down, Lisette's room stood open, permitting the morning sun to cut across the passageway. Just then, Prater came down the servants' stairs, a pair of portmanteaus in hand.

"Mr. Prater," he said. "Good morning."

"And to you, my lord." The footman carried the bags through Lisette's open door.

Something inside him went cold with dread.

As if drawn by a magnet, Napier strode past his own room, apprehension weighing heavier with each step. In Prater's wake, dust motes settled back into the blade of light, dancing on the air. He turned into it, following the footman, not even thinking to knock.

Inside, the sun-warmed air was redolent with Lisette's scent. A yawning trunk sat open in the floor. Prater set the portmanteaus at the foot of the bed. Atop the mattress, Fanny was folding clothing into the truck's tray—and one scarcely needed a team of crack detectives at one's disposal to grasp what was *unfolding*.

"When is she leaving?" The words came as if from a deep well, Napier barely realizing he'd spoken.

Fanny looked up in some surprise. "In the morning, sir," said the maid, lifting her chin. "First train, she said."

"I see." Napier tried to think. "Yes. Well. Where is she now?"

Fanny hesitated, but Prater was less discreet. "Gone looking for Miss Jeffers," he said. "Toward the ornamental lake."

But Napier did not shift his gaze from the maid. "She can't go, Fanny," he said hollowly. "I can't let her go. Not without me. Do you understand?"

The maid shrugged. "It scarcely matters, my lord, what *I* understand."

But what sort of answer had he expected? She was Lisette's servant—and confidante, no doubt.

Napier turned about on his heel, something akin to rage unfolding inside him like a slow burn. Not rage toward Lisette, but toward circumstance. Toward his own unbridled stupidity. Good Lord, was he to have no opportunity to make this right? Did she mean to give him no chance at all?

It did not bear thinking about. It would not happen. And to hell with his notion of chasing her to the ends of the earth.

After retracing his steps back to the entrance hall, he went out and down the terrace, scarcely noticing the wind had picked up to whip at his cravat. At the edge of the parterre, one of the gardeners was shoveling pea-gravel from a wheelbarrow, his blade grating rhythmically into the stone.

"Have Miss Colburne or Miss Jeffers come this way?" asked Napier bluntly.

The gardener tugged at his cap. "Miss Colburne, m'lord," he said, gesturing downhill. "Saw her just as I come out."

"Thank you," said Napier, hastening on. Along the path, wind thrashed the topiaried yews. Below, he could see no one, but as he scanned the lake's shore, he caught a flash of movement in the tree line beyond. Someone was going up the wooded path to the folly.

It wouldn't be Lisette, he thought. She wasn't foolish enough; not in this stiffening wind.

But she was looking for Diana.

Quickening his pace, Napier set off down the hill.

*L*isette had climbed the dratted tower for nothing. No voice answered her call up the steps save the whistle of the wind. But after heaving one last breath, she pulled herself onto the parapet with the iron handrail and stepped up into a bold, blue sky that seemed for an instant to wheel about her head.

Later, looking back on it, she wondered if she'd known even then something was terribly wrong. Something—an awful sound—caused her to turn abruptly. In that instant, her hair whipped back to reveal the terrified face of Felicity Willet. Blood trickled from her temple as she crouched, whimpering against the crumbling wall.

For an instant, Lisette couldn't grasp the horror. Then her brain jerked into motion.

"*Diana, no!*" she screamed, leaping forward.

Diana's head whipped around but an instant, her eyes alight with an unholy glow, a twelve-inch kitchen knife glittering in her hand. Lisette stopped herself, almost too late.

"You mustn't come any closer, Lisette," Diana suggested in her sweet, breathless voice. "There's about to be a tragic accident."

"Diana." Lisette kept her hand out. "Diana, for God's sake, think what you do!"

"I've been trying," she said, sounding mystified. "I *am* trying. But why did he bring her here? *Why*—? He lied to me, Lisette."

"Diana, let her up!" said Lisette in a low voice. "That parapet—it's crumbling."

"I know," said Diana gently. "But if she would just jump—why, it wouldn't hurt. It would break her neck. And she wouldn't even feel the rocks. Oh, Felicity, I'm so sorry."

Miss Willet whimpered again.

"Diana!" Lisette choked back panic.

"*P-Please* just let me up. Let me go." Miss Willet's hand

curled in to the rubble, sending down a hail of pebbles and mortar.

"Miss Willet, do hold still." Inching forward, Lisette forced herself to be calm. "This is a misunderstanding. Diana, give me the knife."

"No," said Diana, her voice suddenly cold. "I want her to *jump!*"

Lisette's eyes swept over the scene. A six-foot stretch of the waist-high wall had crumbled into a swag. Even the flagstone's mortar beneath the girl's feet had riven. She'd crouched so far back into the rubble, attempting to avoid the knife, a mere flinch might send her over in an avalanche.

She began to sob in earnest. "Oh, *please.* I—I don't want him." Her eyes shot wild toward Lisette. "Please, I *swear* it."

Diana went rigid. "I don't believe you!" she cried, jabbing the knife until Miss Willet jerked. Behind her shoulder, a large stone rumbled ominously then tumbled over the edge.

"Oh, God!" Terror sketched over the girl's face. "I don't want to die! Take him!"

"Diana," Lisette repeated, "*give me the knife.*"

Diana seemed not to hear. "But he's too honorable, Felicity," she said as if addressing a child. "Don't you see? A gentleman can't break an engagement. So I must help him. Because he loves me. He always has."

"Yes, h-he adores you!" Frantically, Miss Willet nodded. "He told me. And I j-just want to go *home.* To London. *Please.*"

But Diana was leaning inexorably forward, watching the trickle of blood as if mesmerized. Lisette crept an inch nearer, leaning hard into the wind.

"Diana," she said, reaching out her hand. "Tony will never forgive you. He does not want this."

Diana jerked as if she might turn around, then thought better of it. "*Tony doesn't know what he wants,*" she screamed, "*until his bitch of a mother tells him!*"

"So you mean to kill Felicity?" asked Lisette softly. "You want revenge. I sympathize. But then what? Will you try to kill me, too?"

The reality was sinking in on Diana, but she tried to hold fast. "If I must," she snarled, "then, yes."

"That's regrettable," said Lisette, inching forward, "because you'll find, Diana, that I don't cower."

"You'll see!" Diana's knife trembled like a snake anxious to strike. "When I've my knife in your face, you'll see!"

Balanced on the edge of the cracking flagstone, Lisette kept her hand out. "Diana, I don't wish you ill," she said coolly. "But trust me, you haven't a chance. If you hurt her, only one of us will walk away. And it won't be you."

"Just hush!" Diana barked, her eyes cutting back wildly. "It's not your concern! I *won't listen!*"

Lisette was fast; she knew she could lunge for the knife. Possibly send Diana over if she had to. But would Miss Willet hold? Would she panic? Or would the flagstone give beneath all of them, and go sliding over the edge?

She softened her tone, and said the only thing she could think of. The only thing that might get through.

"Diana," she said quietly, "have you ever watched someone die?"

"Hush *up!*" she screeched.

"I have," said Lisette, her own voice trembling. "I killed a man once. Because I was angry. Because I wanted revenge for what he'd taken from me. So I held a gun to his head. I made him get on his knees—yes, just like Felicity—and I told him to pray. I told him I meant to kill him. And I did, at first. I wanted, with my whole heart, to watch him die."

"If he took something you loved," Diana snapped over her shoulder, "then he deserved it."

"He took *everything* I loved." Lisette tried to steady her voice. "He took my whole life. And revenge seems such a comfort—such a *necessity*—until one has it. Then it becomes like a cancer, Diana. And it eats straight into the heart of you. It destroys you utterly."

"I don't believe you."

"Believe what you will," Lisette answered, "but not a day goes by I don't regret yanking that pistol from my reticule. And if you kill her, Diana, you will lose *everything*. You will lose things you never dreamt of wanting. But by then, it's too late. And assuredly you will lose Tony."

"*You* didn't lose anything!" Diana screeched. "*You* still have Napier!"

"Only because he doesn't know," said Lisette. "Not with certainty. Are you prepared to lose what you love?"

"No." A tear traced down Diana's cheek. "No, and I won't," she whispered. "I can't. He's the only person who ever wanted me."

"Tony will never want you again," said Lisette gently. "No man will. To have a murderess in his bed? In his heart? Just think about that, Diana. Think how this will ruin everything."

"But I can't let *her* have him!" Diana was sobbing now. "He's mine! He's told me over and over. That we'd marry. That no one would ever stop us. And then he brings *her* here? I won't have it! I won't!"

"But Felicity understands now," said Diana. "She *wants* to go home. Let her. Then talk to Tony. You can fix this."

Diana still wouldn't look at her. "I can't!" she sobbed. "His mother—she—she turned him against me! Good God, can't you see? I've waited and waited. I've been *so good*. I've licked her boots and kissed her arse 'til I'm choking on it."

"No, it's all right," said Lisette fervently. "Anne said so. Just this morning. Why, she told me Cordelia knew you'd marry Tony. That she'd accepted it."

Diana lowered the knife an inch and licked her lips uncertainly. "She—she did say it, yes. But she changed her mind.

Long ago. She talked to Lord Hepplewood. Then he spoke to Tony. It was poison! All of it! *Everything* changed."

"But Lord Hepplewood is dead now," said Lisette, the wind still in her face.

At that, Diana sobbed and grasped her abdomen. "*I know, I know, I know!*" she wailed, bending over as if she'd been kicked, one hand still fisted about the knife. "I didn't mean it! I *loved* him. I . . . I just wanted him to need me! And I wanted us to go *home*! If he were ill, she'd have to let us go. *Wouldn't she—?* But Gwen—stupid, stupid cow!—she killed him!"

Dear heaven. Diana had known?

All along, she had known? The pierced kettle, the poisoned footmen, could it all be of a piece . . . ?

But Diana was sobbing hysterically now, and inching up on Felicity with the knife pointed at her throat. Just then, Lisette caught a flash of motion. Flicked a glance over her shoulder.

Napier. He stood on the top step, his eyes hard, his face gone white. Relief rushed through Lisette—and on its heels, alarm. She gave a tight, swift shake of her head. Another inch right, and Diana would see him. She might panic.

The wind had risen to a howl now, and clouds were rolling in. "Talk to me, Diana," Lisette begged, throwing up a hand to stay Napier. "I'm your friend. I can help you."

"It's too late," Diana sobbed. "Gwen already killed half the people I love."

"But it was an accident," said Lisette. "She didn't understand. You need to go back, Diana. To tell Gwen what she did was dangerous. To make things right with Tony."

The knife lowered an inch. "I can't," she whispered, hunching further. "I can't. Something's gone all wrong. And they . . . they won't tell me *what* . . ."

She gave a mechanical jerk—a sort of start toward the col-

lapsing corner of the tower. Suddenly, Lisette saw her intent.
She meant to jump.

Everything happened at once then. Napier lunged, seizing Diana about the waist. She let out an agonizing scream.
Hacked downward with the knife—short, brutal stabs.

Napier barked a curse. Lisette glanced back but an instant.
Diana was clawing wildly. He was dragging her to the stairwell.

Lisette turned. She thrust a hand at Miss Willet. "Give me
your hand," she shouted.

Behind her, Lisette heard the knife clatter onto the flagstone.

"Lisette, watch your step!" Napier barked.

It was precarious. She edged onto the cracking flagstone.
Miss Willet was sobbing, frozen, her arms wrapped around
her head as if to shield it.

"Give me your hand!" Lisette ordered.

At last she did so, unfurling one arm to reach out. Lisette
yanked her from the wall and flung her away.

Suddenly, there came an awful, cracking sound. The sagging wall crumbled in a roar. Flagstone splintered. Began
sliding beneath her feet. Lisette scrabbled for purchase. She
landed on her knees. Felt herself going over the edge. Something caught her wrist, yanking her arm from its socket and
snapping her neck.

When the roar receded, she was looking up through a
cloud of gray ash.

Napier had his hand locked around her wrist. "Hold still,"
he said through clenched teeth.

Lisette blinked away the ash. She lay at a precarious
angle, lower legs dangling. The back of her hand felt warm.
Wet. She struggled to make sense of it. Blood was gushing
down Napier's arm.

"You're hurt," she shouted.

On a fierce grunt, Napier hauled on her arm. But Diana's knife had sliced down Napier's right forearm, ripping both flesh and sleeve. *Dear God, he was going to go over with her.* Lisette dug her hand into the rubble.

"Push," he gritted, hauling harder.

Napier did not relent. Lisette fought down panic. The stone was going to give. But she'd begun to inch up. Acting on instinct, she dug her knees and then her soft slippers into the scree. Clawed into it with her other hand.

Inch by ruthless inch, Napier hauled her back up, Lisette digging at the stone. It had sheered, thank God, at an angle, giving opportunity for purchase. But it was Napier's unbridled strength that hauled her up until finally, with one last heave, he dragged her over the edge.

Lisette found solid flagstone, crawled forward, then Napier's strength dragged her to her feet. He caught her tight against him but an instant. Then he seized her around the waist, hauling her bodily into the stairwell. And then the tower wall gave way again, another two feet vanishing in a roar and clatter of rock.

Lisette blinked, and the very floor on which they'd stood was gone.

CHAPTER 15

In Which Jane Is Revealed

$\mathcal{M}$rs. Boothe, it was widely allowed, could not have chosen a more convenient morning to conk her innkeeper husband soundly across the sconce, nor a more efficient weapon with which to do the job.

"Postal scales," Dr. Underwood grunted, throwing open his black bag. "Solid brass, drilled into a slab of oak. Took eight stitches to the back of the head. But the accident put me near to hand, eh? Even my catgut's strung."

Napier sat stoically in his grandfather's black, dragon-armed chair by the hearth, never flinching as Underwood sliced away his coat sleeve and Lisette watched, her heart still in her throat.

A quarter hour earlier, she had practically forced Napier in through the gun room, the first door she saw open, to find young Hoxton cleaning an old pepperbox pistol, its parts laid neatly out upon a blanket.

The gamekeeper had gone at a run to set the footmen off after Diana Jeffers, fortuitously flying past the doctor in the entrance hall where he was trading gossip with Duncaster.

"A nasty bit of work," grunted Underwood, tossing the fabric aside and setting Napier's elbow into a basin of hot water. "I'm going to irrigate it, my lord. Unnecessary, perhaps, but it's becoming the done thing nowadays."

Napier set his jaw hard as the painful process was begun. Lisette had drawn a small chair to his side. She was still shaking with relief.

"Dreadful!" Duncaster himself was pacing back and forth by the row of French windows. "Dreadful business, Royden! Good God, you might have been killed! Then where would we be?"

"You'd do better to concern yourself with Lisette, sir," said Napier, his eyes cutting a glance at her. "She very nearly *was* killed. And for that, I would never have forgiven myself."

"Indeed, the two of you must set up your nursery at once!" Visibly shaken, the old man was talking almost to himself. "No time to waste. None whatever."

"No, not if the family means to go round stabbing one another," said Napier coolly.

Duncaster turned about at once. "That infernal woman is not our blood," he replied. "She is nothing but Hep's distant cousin."

"Oh, I wouldn't count on that," said Napier—just before he hissed through his teeth.

Diana's knife had gone deep into the muscle of Napier's forearm, then drawn two long but blessedly shallow slices down its length. Never squeamish, Lisette nonetheless felt herself begin to swoon as Underwood's needle pierced the first flap of flesh.

Indeed, it might as well have *been* her flesh, so much did the man seem a part of her. As if, in some deep, unfathomable way, they had become one, joined together by a thousand bits of bone and sinew.

And if she had lost him? Dear God . . .

Her vision began to darken a trifle at the edges.

"Duncaster—?" Underwood jerked his head in Lisette's direction.

The old man leapt with surprising vigor. "My dear girl," he said, kneeling by her chair, "do bend forward. Here, rest your forehead in my hand. Yes, all the way down."

"But I never faint!" Lisette whispered into her skirt, which was now bloodied and shredded.

Duncaster's hand was blessedly cool. "I blame myself for this," he muttered.

"If anyone"—Napier paused to grunt as the next stitch was pulled—"is to be blamed for dragging her into this, it's me."

Her head still set against Duncaster's hand, Lisette drew a deep breath. It brought with it the scent of dried blood and mortar dust, reminding her of what they had survived. And if she could survive that, surely she could watch Napier's arm stitched up. Bracing her hands on the chair's arms, she pushed herself up again.

"I'm all right now, sir," she managed. "Truly."

Duncaster rose reluctantly, and Napier's good hand crept over Lisette's, giving it a hard, reassuring squeeze. Heedless of the doctor, she lifted it to her lips, and pressed a fervent kiss to the back of his knuckles.

Just then, the massive oaken door flew open, and Tony rushed into the room. "Good God!" he cried. "Where is she?"

"Gone upstairs," said Lisette. "She's frightened, but fine. I've sent Fanny to tend her."

"No—the devil!—not *Felicity*." Tony strode fully into the room. "*Diana*. They—dear heaven!—they won't hurt her, will they?"

"I beg your pardon," said Lisette hotly, "but it's Napier here who's cut well near to ribbons."

Tony jerked to a halt. "Gad!" He looked at the partially stitched wound, stricken. "Napier, my good fellow. That's frightful. But Diana—good Lord—she didn't mean it! Wouldn't hurt a fly, the poor girl."

"I begin to wonder how well you knew her," Lisette muttered grimly.

"Oh, this is all my fault!" choked Tony, dragging both hands through his hair. "I should have seen—might have guessed—oh, bugger all! I must go after her."

"Language, my boy!" boomed Duncaster.

Underwood looked around in irritation. "I could do with some silence, if you please."

"Sit down, Tony, and hush," Duncaster commanded. "The servants will find Diana."

The viscount had gone to a table by the windows, and was filling a tray of brandy glasses. It was very odd to see the grand old man himself carry the tray about, pressing one into Napier's good hand, and then into Lisette's and even Tony's.

The handsome young man had fallen into a chair opposite Lisette, his face bloodless, his full, faintly petulant mouth drawn into an uncharacteristically thin line. At his grandfather's appearance, he flicked a quick glance up, took the brandy with a nod of thanks, and downed it in one swallow.

They sat thus, the three of them, watching as Underwood worked his way down the arm, Napier wincing but otherwise stoic. By the time the doctor's work was nearing an end, Lady Hepplewood had clacked into the room on her black stick, followed five minutes later by Gwyneth. At Duncaster's warning glare, they sat silently together on the sofa opposite the hearth.

"Well, that's that," Underwood finally said, giving his surgical scissors a little tap on the basin, dislodging the last bit of bloody thread. "Twelve stitches to close the worst of it. But clean cuts, my lord, and only the one gone deep into the muscle. Still, I'm going to wrap it and put it in a sling."

"No sling," said Napier grimly. "Just bandage it, thank you. We've important business to settle—and settle it we surely will, before someone else gets hurt. Someone besides that poor Willet girl, who's likely traumatized for life."

Only then did Lady Hepplewood burst into tears, her shoulders hunching forward on an awful cry, her head falling into her hands. Surprisingly, no one moved. Not even Tony, whom Lisette would have expected to go to his mother's side. For once, Lisette hadn't the strength.

Instead, it was Gwyneth who consoled her aunt, patting her lightly on the back as she sobbed. "There, there now!" she gently chided. "It's not as bad as all that."

"Oh, isn't it?" said Tony, his voice deep with anguish.

Gwyneth flicked a glance around the room. "By the way, they caught Diana," she said in satisfaction. "Marsh told me as I was coming down. Hoxton found her huddled in one of the box stalls."

"In the *stables*?" said Tony, his expression horrified. "Where is she now? What will they do to her?"

"Probably not what she deserves," said Gwyneth mordantly. "Now, can someone kindly tell us what's happened? There are all manner of wild rumors upstairs."

Napier exchanged knowing glances with Lisette.

"I'm not perfectly sure," she said. "Nor am I sure we ought to discuss it here."

"Discuss it!" Tony leapt to his feet. "Damn and blast, I'm tired of keeping secrets."

"*Tony—!*" said his mother on a sharp, pitiful cry.

"No!" He spun on his heel to face her, his face ashen. "No, Mamma, with all respect, you caused this! It's you and your damned secrets—your overweening pride—that's driven the poor girl half mad."

"More than half," said Gwyneth evenly. "After all, she tried to kill poor Felicity."

"At the end, I think not." Napier's authoritative voice silenced the room. "I suspect she meant to throw herself over the parapet. That, at least, was my assessment." He turned a steady gaze upon Lisette. "My dear? You were nearer than I."

"Yes, without a doubt," said Lisette decisively. "You're right, I think, Lord Hepplewood. Diana hadn't the will to kill Felicity. But had Diana jumped, she'd surely have taken part of that collapsing wall with her. And that would have sealed Felicity's fate."

"And yours," Napier grimly reminded her. "It is easy, perhaps, for me to be magnanimous, Hepplewood. My bride has been spared. But you—I greatly fear you've lost yours. Miss Willet means to leave. This afternoon, she says. And I do not think you will be seeing her again."

Tony lifted one shoulder. "Felicity must do what she thinks best."

"Anne is already packing their things," said Gwyneth a little ghoulishly. "Unless, that is, Felicity is needed as a witness?"

Napier appeared to consider it but an instant. "I fear we've a hard decision to make, sir," he said glancing up at his grandfather, who now stood behind Lady Hepplewood. "The gossip cannot be entirely stopped. Rumor of Miss Willet's canceled wedding will have gone round Mayfair before tomorrow's out."

"Yes," said Duncaster solemnly. "I daresay you're right. But what else is there to decide?"

Napier cast a glance around the room. "A few family matters," he said darkly. "Specifically, how did Diana Jeffers come to imagine herself secretly betrothed to Hepplewood? And what must we now do with her?"

"Send her to jail, won't we?" said Gwyneth.

Napier tilted his head almost warningly. "I should be very slow in deciding that," he said, "though I've little doubt I can get her convicted, if that's what you wish."

"Well, why shouldn't we?" Duncaster blustered. "She's no kin of ours. Not really."

Lisette watched Napier's gaze turned wary. "I believe, sir, you'd best ask your sister about that. Or better still, ask your nephew the question I just put to him. How did that poor, mad creature come to think herself engaged to marry him?"

"Because he's been tossing up her skirts for years, I don't doubt." Gwyneth thrust a finger at her cousin. "Go on, Tony! Tell them! It's why you wouldn't do what Grandpapa told you to do—to marry Anne, as you were intended, isn't it?"

"Good God, Gwen, you disgust me!" cried Tony, leaping to his feet. "Does no one care about poor Diana? Yes, I once said I'd marry her! She seemed to want it so desperately, and—why, she was *dear* to me. And she's fragile, always has been. Can none of you understand that? Or are you so unfeeling you cannot care?"

"I care," said Lisette softly. "But you have been Lord Hepplewood some months now. If you wished to marry Diana, why didn't you simply do it?"

At that, Lady Hepplewood rose from the sofa, and hobbled to the French windows. Setting one hand on the door frame, she stood on the threshold as if she wished to flee. Then quietly she bent her head and began to sob in earnest.

"*Mamma—!*" Tony warned. "Don't start. It won't work again. I'm sorry; I've no wish to see you humiliated. But Diana cannot bear the brunt of this! She's not strong; you know that. She's not like you."

At that, Lady Hepplewood spun about, her face a mask of rage beneath the tracks of her tears. "No, she's not like me!" she retorted. "She's fanciful—and *spineless*. But go ahead; if you're willing to throw your poor mother to the gossip hounds to be slavered over and ripped to bits, I cannot stop you."

"Perhaps I should go," murmured Underwood, half rising.

Napier caught his arm. "No," he said warningly. "You'll be needed."

But Tony was still staring at his mother. "This is *our*

family, Mamma," he said quietly. "Underwood is our *physician*. Duncaster is *your brother*."

"It sounds as if something's gone on too long," said the viscount a little grimly. "And secrets kept, Cordelia, simply fester. What have you done to Diana?"

Lady Hepplewood drew herself up stiffly. "How can you, of all people, suggest I meant that girl ill?" she said sharply. "I brought her up cheek by jowl with my own son after her mother died. And to thank me, she decided to fancy herself in love with him! Of course, I'd feared it for years; she idolized the boy."

"Yes, yes," said Duncaster impatiently. "That's why Hep wanted a match between Tony and Anne. To discourage the chit. And I supported it."

"And it's why he sent Tony off to school," said Lady Hepplewood, "and then off to London. But you, Tony—you just kept giving in to her wheedling, didn't you, and coming back home again? You could never refuse her manipulations. But I did as well by Diana as I could. I will not be blamed for thinking her not good enough for you, for she wasn't. Still, I did my duty. I brought her up, and brought her out, too—and in a high style."

At that, Lisette's memory stirred. "You did better than bring her out," she said. "Your husband settled twenty thousand pounds on her."

"A decision I opposed," said Lady Hepplewood bitterly. "But my husband scraped it up—and it should have made marrying her off a simple task. Yet Diana cast aside every suitor until . . ." She stopped, and shook her head.

"Until one day, Anne explained what she'd seen?" Lisette pressed. "That's right, isn't it? Anne told you she'd caught Diana kissing Tony."

"Kissing him?" Lady Hepplewood tossed a derisive glance at her son. "If that's what Anne called it, then she's a lady indeed."

"Mamma, don't listen to Gwen's vile mouth," said Tony darkly. "I never did anything more than kiss her."

"But she kept throwing herself at you in secret," his mother snapped. "She kept playing upon your guilt until, in the end, you told me *it was Diana, or it was no one.*"

Tony turned his palms up, and gave the faintest of shrugs.

"So I did what you asked, didn't I?" his mother continued. "I went to your father. I told him the business with Anne—with anyone else—was at an end. That only Diana would do, and I meant to announce your betrothal at once. I gave up and gave in—and look what it cost me!"

"Mamma," said Tony, "I'm so sorry."

"No, you are not sorry!" his mother exploded. "Even now, all you can think of is Diana! Just like your father, may he burn in hell."

"Cordelia!" Duncaster stirred irascibly. "My dear, that will do!"

Napier had been sitting quietly, hands clasped loosely together, his elbows on his knees in that way Lisette had come to love so well. It was the posture he took on when he was trying to puzzle something out, or decide what was best done. He was a hard man, Lisette knew, but not an unfeeling one.

He sat up straight, signaling that his decision was made. "Has no one ever considered," he said very quietly, "that perhaps Diana Jeffers deserved to *know* who her father was? And that perhaps, had she been told, we might all of us been spared this tragedy?"

"But her father is Edgar Jeffers," said Gwyneth innocently, "Hepplewood's cousin."

Napier slowly shook his head. "I think not," he said quietly. "I think the late Lord Hepplewood impregnated his mistress—whose name, I suspect, was Jane?—then pressed her on his own cousin. Perhaps in exchange for a position as Loughford's steward."

A cold smile was curling Lady Hepplewood's mouth, and she looked beyond crying now. "Congratulations, Assistant Police Commissioner Napier," she said softly. "You're far quicker—and more suspicious—than I. Indeed, no woman was ever caught more unaware by a faithless husband. A man with more loyalty to his valet than his wife. A man I'd loved with all my heart since the day I laid eyes on him."

"And he thanked you by bedding your young son's governess," said Napier, "then sticking her in a house right under your nose, and asking you to practically raise their child. A bitter pill, ma'am, I will not deny."

"Jane Jeffers was a whore, not a governess," said Lady Hepplewood.

Napier shrugged. "There's many a nobleman who still believes in the *droit du seigneur*," he said evenly. "And two sides to every story."

Lady Hepplewood drew herself up, literally shaking her stick at Napier. "My husband never forced himself on *any* woman," she said, her voice chilling. "He had no need. She seduced him."

"And then he called his young cousin back to Loughford, and offered him the assistance he'd so desperately sought," said Napier. "He offered him a position and a wife he couldn't refuse. I do not pass judgment, madam. I've learnt the hard way I've no right. I merely state the facts."

But Gwyneth was sitting stunned on the sofa. "Dear heaven," she whispered. "So Diana is . . . *Tony's sister?* And none of you told her? That—my word, but that *is* cold."

But it was all making sense now to Lisette. Diana's desperate longing for home. Her diffidence. Her quarrel in the colonnade with Tony . . .

"I think Diana felt cast aside—resented, even—and she's unhinged with grief," she said. "That's all, I think, it would have taken: an explanation why they could not marry. Diana accounts Loughford her home—and Tony and his late father the only people who ever loved her. Her father Mr. Jeffers likely just resents her. She needed to know the truth."

"And I shall tell her before the day's out." Tony had hung his head. "I should have done, the moment I learnt the truth."

Instead, he'd clearly given in to his mother's entreaties not to share what he'd been told—and what son would not have been tempted? But at what price? The price of Diana's sanity?

Dr. Underwood, apparently, feared the worst. "With all respect, Lord Hepplewood, it may be too late," he gently cautioned. "Once a fragile mind has broken—a psychosis they call it nowadays—there is oftentimes no returning to reality."

Lady Hepplewood had turned her back, and returned to the French windows to stare out into the gardens. Duncaster was shaking his head.

"I never would have dreamt such a thing," said the old man sorrowfully. "But still, Cordelia, all husbands have their flings."

She turned from the window, wrath blazing again. "You, Henry, *did not*," she said. "Our father *did not*. And my husband did not—not until Jane Jeffers seduced him. It is the worst sort of hypocrisy imaginable, this—this utter *acceptance* of adultery as some small vice to be tolerated. It is ruinous. It destroys every loving marriage it touches."

"I cannot disagree," said Napier quietly. "Which brings us to another sad circumstance."

Tony gave a sharp laugh. "My word! Can there be another?"

Napier shot Lisette a sidelong glance. "I fear there may be," he said, "though I've been unable to puzzle it out. Lisette, my dear, have you anything you'd care to explain?"

Heavens! She'd forgotten the arsenic!

In all the turmoil, Lisette had had time to tell Napier of little more than her suspicions. Now she looked at Gwyneth, hating what had to be said. But she drew a deep breath and began it anyway. "Diana's grandfather owned a cotton mill," she blurted. "Diana's uncle still owns it. She's very knowledgeable about milling processes and fabrics."

"Yes, she's forever rattling on about such things—or used to." Tony was looking askance at Lisette. "But what's that to do with anything?"

"There are some fabric dyes—chemicals, actually—called Paris Green and Scheele's Green," she said. "The latter is not much used nowadays, but both can be quite dangerous."

"I've heard of them," Tony snapped. "They have a little copper arsenite in them to hold the color, I think. But they're accounted safe. What is it you're trying to make out here?"

"They are safe under most circumstances," Lisette acknowledged, looking around him at his mother. "Lady Hepplewood, you brought Diana to Burlingame to separate her from Tony, did you not? And somewhat against your husband's wishes?"

She turned from the window, her face emotionless now. "I could not let them go back to Loughford, living in one another's pockets," she said. "Not after Hepplewood confessed the truth. I begged Edgar Jeffers, of course, to send the girl away, but he just shrugged. So yes, I brought her here. I knew Saint-Bryce would soon be widowed, and if it was money and status Diana wanted—well, rank aside, this estate's worth thrice what Loughford is."

"And Tony?"

Her eyes narrowed. "And I told Tony in no uncertain terms *to go and find a wife*—and to stay away from Diana until he'd done so," she said bitterly. "Loughford or London, it little mattered to me, but he wasn't coming around her again until he found someone suitable. Instead he wasted better than a year gadding about the gaming hells—and worse places, too, I daresay."

"It certainly was an all-encompassing plan," said Napier evenly. "Still, I doubt the idea of removing in a semipermanent state to Burlingame was met with much enthusiasm by your husband."

"Because *he had no plan*," she gritted. "It was left to me to clean up the mess he'd made—just as it was left to me, in utter ignorance, to practically raise my husband's bastard."

"But Diana was miserable here," said Lisette. "When she realized your intentions, she became distraught, and played upon Hepplewood's emotions. She begged him to go home. And since you'd forbidden him to tell her the truth, he tried to placate her."

"Yes," returned Lady Hepplewood. "What of it? He doted on her."

"So he told her to refit all the rooms as a sort of amusement," said Lisette, "and she did—using neutral colors everywhere, save for one place. In his room, where every element was fitted out in rich, regal green."

At that, Tony jolted. "The devil!" he whispered. "What are you saying?"

"That Diana poisoned him," said Napier grimly. "Is that right, my dear?"

It was the third time, Lisette realized, he'd called her that. But she squashed her hope, and forged on with the business at hand. "I think Diana meant merely to make him feel unwell," she answered. "It was in the wallpaper, you see, along with the draperies and bed-hangings."

Tony lost what little color he had left. "You cannot mean . . . copper arsenite?"

"Or perhaps a blend of arsenic trioxide," said Lisette. "I'm not perfectly sure, but it's all stable when dry. In damp climates, however—or if deliberately dampened—it can prove debilitating, or with direct contact, often deadly. It breaks down into arsenic. Diana knew this. And it's why she became so distraught when she realized you'd slept there."

Dr. Underwood stirred from his fascination. "That must be how the footmen fell ill!"

Lisette nodded. "They wet it, tore it down. Breathed it in and carried it out. Even burnt it."

"My word!" said the doctor. "We're lucky they lived."

"But someone did die," said Lisette quietly. "Gwyneth found some of the green velvet. She soaked it and used it as cool compresses on her uncle's forehead for a time. Until Diana realized it, and snatched it away. That's why you felt ill for a few days, Gwen."

"Oh!" Gwyneth laid a hand over her heart, half rising from the sofa. "Oh, no! I could not have—! I—I just found the fabric. It looked so soft. And Diana said moisture was good for his lungs. She—why, she kept that little steaming contraption in the hearth."

"Yes, deliberately, I think," said Lisette. "She just wanted Lord Hepplewood to feel a little unwell. To want to go home. Because 'everyone,' she once told me, 'wants to die at home in their own beds.'"

"Very true! Very true!" said Underwood sagely.

"But once he'd got home—probably summoning his son home, as well—then he'd have had a miraculous recovery," said Napier dryly. "Or that, at least, was Diana's fantasy. For the family to be reunited at Loughford. For things to go on as they had been."

"But still, you're saying . . . *that I killed him*?" Gwyneth clapped a hand to her heart, color draining from her face. "Oh, God! I p-poisoned Uncle Hepplewood?" She bolted from the room, leaving the thick door open behind her.

"Well," said Lady Hepplewood nastily, "I hope you're all happy now. Our lives are ruined."

"As is Felicity Willet's, or nearly so," said Napier. "Two footmen nearly died, and even Gwyneth was briefly ill. This is not just about this—about *our*—family, ma'am. It is about what we owe to our state and station. About our sense of what's right, and perhaps our capacity for forgiveness."

Napier rose at last from the dragon chair, his ruined coat sleeve flapping impotently, his lacerated arm held to his side looking rather like a broken bird's wing. "And now, if you'll forgive me," he added, "I think it best we leave you."

Turning, he offered his good hand down to Lisette.

Lisette took it, and rose to her feet. "I shall help you up the stairs to bed."

Napier's gaze caught hers: wan, exhausted, and—unless she misinterpreted—very fond. "Thank you, my dear."

"But wait!" cried Duncaster after them. "What are we to do?"

Napier turned and shrugged his uninjured side. "I have no idea," he said quietly.

"But you—why, you are the police," said Duncaster fretfully. "We've explanations to make that poor girl, Miss Willet. And Diana to be dealt with."

Oh, now, when it was convenient, he was *the police*, thought Lisette sourly.

But Napier did not snap back as she feared he might. "It strikes me," he said quietly, "that it's Lord Hepplewood's place to go and make the appropriate explanations to his fiancée. Forgive me if I'm less than certain, but I believe that's what is expected of a gentleman?"

"Of course it is," Tony swiftly acknowledged. "And yes, I shall. I—why, I shall tell her everything, and beg her forgiveness."

And her secrecy, Lisette silently added, *if you can get it.*

"And Diana?" said Duncaster tentatively. "What do you suggest?"

For the first time since meeting him, Lisette realized the viscount looked deeply uncertain. It was not just that Napier was the police, she realized; the old man was relying upon Napier's guidance. Yearning for it, perhaps. She forced her hackles down, and joined the others in looking at him expectantly.

"A discreet, quiet confinement to an asylum might be prudent," Napier suggested. "France, I believe, has some excellent private facilities, though they come dear indeed. Dr. Underwood can best guide us."

"But mustn't we arrest her?" Duncaster's bushy eyebrows elevated sharply.

"I've no intention of it," said Napier evenly. "Call the local magistrate if you wish her tried. But think long and hard about it first. Consider if perhaps, on some level, this family didn't fail Diana. Consider whether you can prove intent, and how much scandal this family and poor Miss Willet will bear in the doing of it. She's already facing the embarrassment of a broken betrothal; I rather doubt she'll wish her name attached to a criminal case. For my part, I've recently learnt—and much good it has done me—that there are a great many things in life best swept under the carpet."

"But what about you, my lord?" said Underwood. "Miss Jeffers attacked you."

"Oh, I'll heal up before the month's out," he said, "which is just about how long it will take for our banns to be called. As you heard, Duncaster's keen for me to get on with my life—and my duties to the viscountcy—before the next little family contretemps breaks out."

"Banns?" said Lord Duncaster. "Nonsense! You'll get a special license."

"Well, we shall see," said Napier, cutting a glance down at Lisette.

"Good heavens!" said Dr. Underwood, rising abruptly. "I forgot to bandage your arm!"

But a rush of relief tinged with hope had just passed over Lisette. She thrust a hand at the doctor.

"Give the bandaging to me," she said. "Perhaps I shall try to look after him from here out."

Napier was more relieved than he wished to admit to see the back of his family, and escape to the quiet confines of his own room—to step into that cool, sunlit space with Lisette at his side—even as he inwardly dared anyone to disturb them.

He did not even tell her she oughtn't come in; she was not a child, and he was not a saint.

Moreover, he'd had the living hell scared out of himself this morning, and he was not ashamed to admit it. For an entire six or seven seconds—an eternity, really—he'd faced the very real possibility of a life without her. And in those few seconds, he'd realized without a doubt that it would not have been a life worth living.

So he shut the door, and dragged her hard against him with his good arm, then kissed her long and very, very thoroughly. And when he was finished, he held her tighter still, and set his forehead lightly against hers.

"Good Lord," he said, dragging in the comfort of her scent. "I cannot ever live through that again. Do you hear me, Lisette? Not *ever.*"

She made him no answer, but she kissed him again, a light brush of the lips. A kiss, he hoped, of promise. "Sit down on the bed," she said.

"Just *sit* down?" he echoed incredulously. "A beautiful woman barges her way in my bedchamber, and orders me to merely *sit* on the bed? I must not be a lover worth my salt, Lisette, if that's all you can think to ask."

She smiled up at him—well, not quite a smile, but a curious little quirk—and pushed him toward the bed. "Sit down," she said again, "because I'm going to wrap that arm. There's a very real danger of infection still, so don't be so bloody cavalier."

"I love it when you curse," he said.

But he did sit down, and watched with an intense, almost

heart-wrenching love as she pulled his desk chair to the bed, then tenderly bandaged his wounds. It took some time, and she worked with care. When she was done, she tore the ends of the cloth, wrapped one end around, and tied it in a tidy knot at his wrist.

"There," she said, clutching the roll of bandaging in her lap, her chin lowered.

Napier reached out with his good hand, and tipped her chin up. Her eyes were swimming with tears. "Oh, love," he whispered. "Oh, *don't*."

Her shoulders seemed to draw in, even as her face crumpled a little. "Don't *don't* me!" she cried. "That knife could have killed you! I can bear a great many things, Royden. I can. But that? Better Diana should cut out my heart."

"Ah, could you not live without me, then?" he asked, holding her watery gaze. "I only ask because—well, I'd as soon there were two of us in that miserable state of existence."

She dashed a hand beneath one eye. "I can live without you if I must," she said. "But I could not bear it if anything happened *to* you. You are the most alive, the strongest, most physically *real* person I've ever known. To me you are . . . invincible, really. But that *knife*—oh, God!"

He caught her tear-dampened hand and lifted it to his lips, saying nothing. He hardly knew where to begin. There was so much, really, that wanted un-saying.

Lisette saved him from his introspection.

"Thank you," she said on a snuffle. "Thank you for saving me."

"I was terrified," he said.

"I was not," she answered. "I knew you would save me. But then I saw the blood. Oh, you were bleeding *so much*."

The silence fell around them again. Not awkwardly, no. So often with her, he had no wish to fill the void with unnecessary conversation. And she—well, she was weighing her next words. He knew it, for he *knew her*. And this time, he would wait.

He still held her hand, small and warm, in his own. He wanted to kiss it again, to press his lips to the back of it and swear his undying devotion. But he did not.

"How long were you standing behind me?" she finally asked.

"Long enough," he said.

"Ah. Well." She made a little sound in the back of her throat. "So you know."

"And so I do." He did kiss her hand then, holding her gaze as he did so.

She gave a faint, thready laugh. "And so you're destined to let two murderous criminals waltz away today, I gather?" she said with feigned lightness. "I confess, you're not quite as advertised, Roughshod Roy."

He shrugged. "You killed a man who deserved it," he said. "I know I ought to be more troubled by it. And yet I seem unable to summon any moral outrage. And I think, my dear, you've suffered enough remorse."

"I think of it every day," she whispered, her gaze falling.

Napier didn't understand. "I hate to pry," he said, "since it's thus far netted me nothing but heartache. But do you want to tell me *how* you came to shoot him?"

"Well, I meant to shoot Lord Lazonby," she said.

"Oh, well," he said. "I'm not sure I'd have stopped you."

She gave a feeble laugh. "Of course you would have," she said. "You have a frightful temper, but you never let it best you."

"Well, thank you for that," he said.

"As to *how* it happened—well, I daresay it was because I'd got in the habit of carrying Papa's pocket pistol," she said, her brow knotted. "I wanted to shoot Lazonby, true. But I carried it because . . . well, at the *Chronicle*, one had to frequent some vile places . . . and I was . . ." Her breath had caught oddly.

"Lisette," he whispered, "forget about it. All of it. Because it just doesn't matter."

She shook her head, shut her eyes, and set a finger to his lips. "*And I was Jack,*" she finally said. "There, it's said. I was Jack Coldwater. It was just . . . a name. A name I'd used over the years."

He squeezed her hand. "I know that," he said. "But someday, if you feel like it, I should like to hear how it happened."

Lisette drew a deep breath. "It just . . . happened," she said. "I had a knack for writing, I suppose."

"It's never so simple as that," he countered. "You clearly have a classical education."

"I just read a lot," she said. "And helped out in the shop. Then Uncle's drinking worsened. One night there was a terrible accident in the harbor. A ship caught fire."

"Is that what you and Sir Philip were talking about over dinner?" he asked. "Did you write that article?"

She lifted her gaze to his. "There was no one else," she said simply. "Ashton was drunk as a lord, and hadn't paid the staff. I'd written up other people's notes before. So Aunt begged me, and I just . . . well, I pulled on a cap and some breeches and went down to the harbor to see what might be done. That's where I learned about arsenic, you see."

"Was it?" he said, surprised.

"One of the passengers was just dripping in green worsted," said Lisette. "She was pulled from the water early on, perfectly safe. But she refused to get out of her wet things until they found her husband, and it took hours to row everyone ashore. By then, however, the damage was done."

"And after that," said Napier grimly, "your uncle piled more responsibilities on good old Jack, I don't doubt."

Her only response was a short nod, and her hands thrown up as if in surrender.

A part of Napier was deeply angry, though he tried not to show it. Angry she'd had to face such an awful situation. Angry she'd been forced to carry too many burdens at too young an age—and carry them more or less alone.

It was just as he'd always suspected. There had been no one in Lisette's life that she could trust, or even depend on. Instead she'd been stuck with a scoundrel of a father and an inebriate of an uncle, while quietly going on about the business of keeping life afloat.

"It was not right that your uncle put you in such a grim and dangerous position," he said honestly. "By comparison, it must have made you miss your father all the more."

Her eyes widened. "I missed my entire family," she said. "Yes, of course I miss my father. What child would not?"

He leaned over and set his lips to her forehead. "I know you loved him," he said. "I know you did. But a part of him failed you, Lisette, and it is not wrong to resent that fact."

She was silent so long he feared she might not answer.

"Well," she said after a time, her shoulders falling. "We have got off our subject, haven't we? I was explaining about Sir Wilfred. But save for the truth about Jack, it happened pretty much as Lazonby told you. Even in that, the man did not lie. It pains me to admit how honest he is, really."

But one thing had never made sense to Napier. "And were you following Anisha?"

"Oh, yes. Because I saw her from a distance slipping around to the back gardens, and got this odd notion she meant to meet Lazonby."

"A logical assumption," he acknowledged.

"But when I caught sight of Sir Wilfred dragging her through that door, I knew something terrible had happened," she went on. "I crept up by the open window, and saw she was injured. And when I heard what he said about having framed Lazonby, and wanting rid of Papa, something inside me . . . it just *snapped*."

"Anyone would have been distraught," said Napier soothingly.

"But *I* leapt down the stairs and told him I was going to kill him," she said. "I was not distraught. I was crazed. And Royden, *I meant it.* I made him get on his knees and put his hands behind his head."

"Let me guess," said Napier. "That's when Lazonby turned up?"

Lisette nodded. "He tried to talk me out of it at first," she said, "but after a while, he said—cool as could be—that I should just go ahead and shoot Sir Wilfred. He just wanted to come down the steps and get Lady Anisha out first, in case my shot went wild."

"Very wise," remarked Napier dryly.

"So I stepped back, you know, to let Lazonby pass between us," she whispered, "and somehow—somehow, just as Lazonby scooped her off the floor and turned, Sir Wilfred leapt up and attacked me. I slammed into that marble counter. And the gun just . . . went off. But I killed him. I did. And I meant to."

"Lisette," said Napier firmly, "that is called *an accident*—or self-defense, at the very least."

"That's what Lazonby kept saying," she whispered, staring down at her open hand. "But I knew the truth. I knew what was in my heart. And I knew I had only Lazonby—a man I'd made my mortal enemy—to defend me."

"Not Anisha?"

Lisette shook her head. "She'd been struck nearly insensible. And her face—it was buried against Lazonby's coat. She couldn't have seen. And that's when I think I started screaming . . . and screaming. I couldn't stop. It was as if the gun—even my own hand—didn't belong to me anymore."

"Because it was an accident," he said again, more emphatically.

"Only by chance," she said, lifting an abject gaze to his. "Royden, I wanted to kill him. I truly did. And I think . . . I still think I would have done it. I think, in that moment, I was utterly mad. No better, really, than Diana today. And I wonder—*how* does that happen? How does life turn you into that sort of person? And are you that person ever after?"

Even now, however, she looked frightened. Frightened, he realized, of herself. Of what she could be capable of.

But all people had it in them to do brutal things, under certain—and usually horrific—circumstances. He'd learned that much from his police work.

"Lisette, come here."

He shifted around on the bed, and patted the spot beside him. With a withering smile, she joined him, tucking her slender length along his, and nestling her head in the crook of his arm.

Bending his head, he pressed his lips to her temple. "Lisette, I think it likely you *wouldn't* have killed him," he said. "That in the end, you'd have broken down like Diana. But *I don't care.*"

"But Royden, you are—"

"*I don't care,*" he repeated. "Do you understand? I know you've feared I would—that I would judge you. That I'd keep silent because I love you, then live to regret that silence. But I meant what I said to Duncaster. There's no black and white in life, and more's the pity."

"But I really meant to—"

"Besides, am I any better?" he interjected. "I'm keeping silent to protect my father's legacy and my family's good name. Is that right? Perhaps not. But unless I see a harm I can undo—something I can somehow set to rights—then I'll go to my grave with my lips sealed. As to Sir Wilfred, he was evil and venal and patently cruel, and if you hadn't shot him, he would surely have been hanged."

"Well," she said in a small voice, "I have not grieved him. But I'm sorry to have been the instrument of his death."

He realized Lisette had been through a terror, and it was little wonder she didn't want to relive it. "Sir Wilfred sealed his own fate," he said grimly. "And it makes me angry you were ever left alone and unprotected. You should never have been placed in such a position."

He was still irrationally angry with her father, he realized—and she was not. But so it often went with handsome scoundrels, Napier knew. They eschewed duty, died young, and were then practically canonized, the family wishing to believe that, if only their beloved had lived, he would have turned his life around. But it would never have happened with Sir Arthur Colburne, and Lisette had paid the price for his weaknesses.

As usual, it was as if she read his very thoughts. "Don't feel sorry for me, Royden," she warned, her voice grim. "I'm not a fool. I know that, had Papa lived, I'd have been more parent than child in the end. Ellie would have ended up Lady Percy, diamond of society, and I'd have ended my days rowing Papa's boat and bailing out the water."

"It's called the curse of the competent, Lisette," he said. "Those that can do are ever called upon by those who cannot—or will not."

She gave a little shrug. "No, the curse, Royden, is that we do it and yet we cannot resent them for it," she said. "I loved my father, even knowing his shortcomings. Don't you? Even knowing—?"

"Knowing what Sir Wilfred accused him of?" He sighed. "Yes. A part of me does."

Though in his case, Napier considered, he'd at least had the luxury of being a man grown when the scales had fallen from his eyes. Even now, he had little more than a mere suspicion of what Nicholas Napier had been.

But in his heart, he knew the truth.

"Perhaps I suspected what my father was even before Sir Wilfred's ugly accusation." It was the first time he'd been able to say the words aloud. "For much of my life, Lisette, I worshipped him—despite the fact that he was distant, even forbidding at times. He was, for good or ill, my idol. My understanding of all a man should be."

"It is an admirable thing to idolize one's father," she said. "To wish to be like him."

"And I succeeded," said Napier. "Even to the point of taking my father's old post. And I wonder . . . I wonder if I began to suspect the truth? And Lazonby—so bloody vehement!—even after his conviction was overturned, the bastard wouldn't back down. So if you want to talk about the black pit of human nature, Lisette, how's this? What if part of the reason I refused to listen to Lazonby is that, somewhere deep in my soul, I feared facing the truth?"

She shook her head, her mass of red curls shimmering in the afternoon light. "I don't believe that," she said. "You are a better man than that."

He shrugged. "I think my father was bought, Lisette, and not just once or twice. Oh, he did his job—did it well enough to win accolades aplenty. But when it suited him—for whatever reason—yes, I think he let criminals go. And once—*just* once, I pray—he let an innocent man be convicted. That should be unforgivable."

When he fell quiet a few moments, Lisette spoke again. "And yet it isn't, quite, is it?" she suggested. "Unforgivable, I mean. Don't you see, Royden, that perhaps it's a part of what's brought us close? These past few weeks—ever since Sir Wilfred's death—we've had to face the truth of what our fathers were. And face the fact that we love them still. That we always will love them."

"I wish that I could believe that," he said grimly.

"It is true," she said. "Whatever else he was, Nicholas Napier was your father. He held you as a child, and picked you up when you fell. He berated you, perhaps, but he also challenged you to better yourself." Here, she smiled, and cupped his face with her hand. "And he protected you from the frightful . . . what was her name again?"

He managed a smile. "Minter," he said. "The bounteous Mrs. Minter—though really, a gentleman ought not kiss and tell."

Lisette looked up, and shot him a little wink. "Your secret is safe with me."

He turned on his side then, and let his gaze drift over the perfect oval of face. Those wide, blue-green eyes now soft with affection, those extraordinary cheekbones. And that full Cupid's-bow mouth that begged a man to suck and nibble for hours on end.

But it all paled in comparison to what lay beneath that porcelain-pale skin: a heart that had sustained a world of disillusionment, and yet remained stalwart, pure, and perfect.

"Lisette, I don't think we have any secrets left," he said quietly. "Now, are you going to make me—and, apparently, my grandfather—the happiest of men? Are you going to marry me? Or must I chase you to the ends of the earth?"

She looked up at him in shock. "Marry you?" she said. "Oh, Royden! Have you fully considered—"

This time, it was his turn to set a finger to her lips. "I have fully considered how empty my life will be if I cannot win you," he said firmly. "I considered it very thoroughly this morning whilst you were hanging off that bloody ledge. Indeed, I've been considering it ever since we left London— and for a good deal longer than that, perhaps."

She blinked innocently. "What do you mean, 'a good deal longer than that?'"

He tapped her lips with his finger. "All I need from you now, Lisette, is a yes or a . . . well, a yes. I'm afraid those are the only alternatives left to you—or I'll be compelled to arrest you for Kissing With the Intent to Defraud a Man of His Heart," he offered, "or perhaps even an outright violation of the Larceny Act of 1827—since you've already succeeded in stealing it."

"I believe I hear your heart beating very firmly in your chest," she countered.

"Well then there's always Teasing With Intent to Cause Grievous Bodily Harm," he said. "I could tie you to the bed for *weeks* on that charge alone."

"Grievous bodily harm?" she said incredulously. "I am not responsible for your arm being sliced up."

"No, but you are responsible for this chronic, throbbing erection I've been suffering ever since you unbuttoned your bodice in my office."

"You are never going to let me forget that, are you?"

"I need a *yes*," he repeated.

"And I am oddly disposed to give you one, and damn the consequences," she admitted. "But I would like to know, I think, how long you've been stewing in this unremitting lust?"

He cursed softly beneath his breath, then reached over her with his bandaged arm to yank open the drawer of his night table.

"Have at it," he said, "if it will get me what I want."

Her brow drawing into a pretty knot, Lisette rolled back onto her elbow, and looked into the drawer. "I see your knife," she said, "and I'll allow as how there may be days ahead when I might be tempted to stab you with it."

"Thank you, but I've had enough of that to do me a while," he murmured. "Just lay it aside."

The knife landed atop the night table with a heavy *thunk!* "Good heavens!" she said, extracting a long piece of cream-and-emerald cording.

"Don't carry it off again," he said darkly. "The next time I have my way with you I'll be needing it."

"Yes, I see," she murmured. "Well! What else have we in here? Someone's been playing finders keepers, haven't they?"

Her tiny satin slippers followed—the ones she'd toed off by his hearth—and then half a dozen hairpins. After that came the white tie that threaded through her drawers—he seemed to recall extracting that one with his teeth. Tangled in it was a gold earbob set with a small red stone.

"My garnet earbob!" she said. "I don't even remember losing that."

"It caught in my cravat," he said a little sheepishly, "the day I ripped off your wig—along with two of those hairpins."

"Ah! Now, *what* is this? Hmm. Might these belong to another lady altogether?" She drew out a pair of gloves, and gave him a little slap across the wrist. "Cream-colored kidskin? I have never owned such a thing."

"I assure you, my love," he said a little awkwardly, "that you did. I am not in the habit of collecting items of a personal nature from other women."

She looked at him with a quizzical smile, and arched one eyebrow.

"Perhaps, my dear, you've forgotten?" he suggested. "You left them in my office the day you came to give me my awful thrashing. I believe they were brand new."

Recognition dawned, and with it came embarrassment. "No, you will never let me forget," she said again. "Indeed, they are mine. I'd owned them for all of a day, I think, having lost mine and bought new ones outside Liverpool Station."

"And now," he said quietly, "they are mine. I show them to you merely as—"

"Trophies of conquest?" she said on a laugh.

"Ah, but a gentleman may not claim a true conquest," he replied, "until the lady says yes, or . . . yes."

"Ah, well then," she said, flinging the gloves aside. "I believe it had better be yes. Those are quite nice gloves, and I think the only way I'll get them back again is through the Section Three, Paragraph Six of the Marital Properties Act."

Napier started to tell her there was no such thing in England—that he knew she was just making up tales again, and that he was going to possess her body and soul until the end of time—but Lisette was already kissing him, and the throbbing pain in his arm was finally subsiding. Or rather, *moving.*

To a location a good deal south of his right arm . . .

EPILOGUE

A Case of Good Champagne

*A*utumn was edging around Mayfair, the trees along Hyde Park merely hinting at the blaze of color to come. The breeze had turned pleasantly crisp, requiring Lisette to laughingly clap a hand to her hat as her husband spun their open carriage around the corner into Belgrave Place.

He cut an affectionate glance down at her, then, as if on impulse, bent his head to kiss her lightly on the cheek. "You look radiant this afternoon," he said.

Hand still on the hat, Lisette turned her face up and felt her breath catch. Napier's eyes today were dark as indigo— and as always, just a little inscrutable.

Then suddenly, he smiled and her heart melted. "By the way," he said, "what did Jolley give you just now?"

"Oh, yes. Some sort of letter." Lisette rummaged in her reticule for the envelope Jolley had pressed into her hand on the way out. "Heavens, it's from Gwyneth!"

Napier cut a swift glance down at the address. "Ah," he said quietly. "Is she still in Bordeaux, then?"

Swiftly, Lisette ran her eyes over the lines. "As of Friday

last, yes," she answered. "The hospital, she writes, is more of a . . . a sort of convalescent facility, run by a group of Carmelite sisters. It is in the country, she says, and very peaceful. And look at this—Diana is learning embroidery and tapestry restoration—that must be a quite valuable skill on the Continent?"

"It does sound hopeful," Napier murmured.

Lisette was still reading. "And—yes, here is the most promising part of all—Diana has begun to talk a little about what happened. She understands about Lord Hepplewood—that he was her father, I mean. Gwen thinks the truth is comforting her a little."

"I gather she loved him very much."

"And he loved her, I think," said Lisette quietly. "Insomuch as a selfish man can love, he provided for her, and tried in some measure to care for her."

They had all agreed, with Dr. Underwood's concurrence, that it was best in the end that Diana leave England. She was still liable to be charged with attempted murder should the truth become known beyond the family. Moreover, it was not expected she would ever be entirely well again. Diana's delicate mind, according to Underwood, had shattered under the strain, the grief, and ultimately, her own guilt.

With Diana's parentage exposed, Mr. Jeffers had bitterly surrendered his post at Loughford and made it plain he wished no further contact with Diana or his cousins.

At the thought of a criminal proceeding, Miss Willet had recoiled with all the horror Napier predicted. Like Hepplewood's departing steward, she wanted nothing more to do with her former fiancé or his family. Lady Hepplewood returned to her son's estate in Northumberland, and Tony resumed his life of debauchery in London, and to a rapidly worsening degree.

Surprisingly, it had been Gwyneth who had stepped up to do the family's duty. She, along with a nurse chosen by

Dr. Underwood, had escorted Diana to France. And there Gwyneth remained.

"She means to return to England next week," said Lisette, carefully refolding the letter. "We must keep them both in our prayers, and trust we've done the right thing."

"We have done the merciful thing," Napier reassured her. "And sometimes, mercy is all one can hope for. At least Diana has a measure of peace—and who knows. Perhaps she will recover someday."

They fell into a comfortable silence as Belgravia became Mayfair, and reached Upper Grosvenor Street shortly thereafter to find the crescent-shaped drive in front of Ruthveyn House empty. The drapes, however, were drawn wide and the front steps appeared freshly swept as if in preparation for morning callers.

"I think they must be at home," said Lisette, giving her husband's thigh a reassuring pat. "Are we ready?"

"Utterly," came the calm reply, followed by the sidelong flash of Napier's smile. It was meant, she knew, to reassure her; to pledge not just his troth, but his strength.

After lifting his wife down, Napier gave instructions to his tiger before going up the stairs to drop the knocker. His steps, she noted, were as ever swift and certain; he was not a man who blanched in the face of duty.

They were admitted by a fresh-faced footman who cheerfully took their cards. Before he could so much as turn around, however, Lady Anisha swept into the entrance hall attired in one of her flowing tunics, her arms outstretched in welcome.

"Napier!" she said, coming forward to kiss his cheek. "And Miss Ashton!" She paused to grin almost mischievously. "But wait—you've altered your name, I think, since last we met?"

"Twice, actually," Lisette admitted, feeling a little heat rise to her cheeks. "How do you do, Lady Lazonby?"

"*Anisha*," she said chidingly, returning her attention to Napier, who had thrust a beribboned bottle of wine at her.

"With our compliments," he said, making her a neat bow, "in belated celebration of your marriage, Anisha—as I believe I promised some months past."

She took it, glancing at the label. "Heavens, *Perrier-Jouët!*" she said. "My, you do take your promises seriously."

"I couldn't bear the thought of Lazonby choking on *cheap* champagne," said Napier dryly. "My tiger is taking the rest of it round back."

"How kind you both are. Please, won't you come back to the conservatory?" She had already set off, speaking over one shoulder as the gossamer scarf floated in her wake. "Lazonby is in the garden with Tom playing ringtaw—and as credibly as any street urchin, I vow. I'll call him in."

"I beg you will not disturb him," said Napier.

"Nonsense," Anisha replied, throwing open a door to a sunny, vaulted room. "But first I'll find us some tea. Do go in and be comfortable."

With Napier at her side, Lisette waded into the lush, cavernous space. Above her head, a green parrot perched, preening his feathers amidst a twining vine that had wrapped around one of the rafters. Below, the room was furnished with deep rattan chairs set amongst fanning palms and feathery ferns. And through the walls of glass one could see a fine vista of the rear gardens.

"What the devil?" Napier uttered.

She turned a little, and caught sight of Lazonby through the glass.

The gentleman crouched on all fours in a patch of lawn, his head cocked at an odd angle, hindquarters aloft, and one eye set low to the ground. Before him, a bit of pavement had been laid and chalked with a large circle. A worthy-looking opponent knelt opposite—a tow-headed lad of perhaps eight years, his arms flung resolutely across his chest.

"Anisha's youngest," Napier murmured.

His line of sight properly assessed, Lazonby shot his taw into the ring with a mighty flick, smacking a second marble and sending both off the patch of pavement and into the lawn. Lazonby thrust a fist in the air. The lad fell back into the grass. Then the bickering broke out, along with a bit of good-natured gesturing.

Lisette cut a sidelong glance up at her husband. "And that," she said wryly, "is the murderous Mr. Evil Incarnate. Funny, he does not look all that wicked shooting marbles."

Napier grunted. "Ah, well!" he said, setting an arm about her shoulders. "There's no one I'd sooner eat crow with, my dear, than you."

Just then Anisha appeared beyond the glass, having apparently gone out the kitchen door. Upon seeing her coming across the garden, Lazonby rose, shook the boy's hand, and followed his wife inside.

"All hail the mighty conqueror," announced Anisha good-naturedly as she returned through the conservatory doors.

Lazonby followed, attired in a disheveled cravat, and no coat at all. "I beg your pardon, Lady Saint-Bryce," he said, bowing elegantly. "One ought not receive a newly minted baroness one's shirtsleeves and dirt. I shall just go and change."

"I beg you will not," she insisted.

"Oh, I think we need not stand on ceremony," said Anisha. "Do draw up a chair, everyone."

Sweeping her skirts neatly around, their hostess settled herself on the rattan chaise. Almost at once, however, a pewter-colored tabby leapt into her lap, pressing down the lady's silk tunic rather tellingly. Lisette's eyes must have widened.

Anisha flashed a smile. "Oh, dear! Satin has given up my secret," she murmured, blushing faintly. "And unless I miss my guess, I'm not alone?"

"I beg your pardon?" Lisette cut a furtive glance at her husband, but he was distracted by situating his chair on the uneven flagstone.

"Quick, give me your hand," Anisha murmured, a trio of thin bracelets jangling as she reached out.

Lisette did so uneasily, remembering what had happened the last time. Anisha turned her hand palm up, and began to study it.

"So," said Lazonby, turning his attention to Napier. "I hear you mean to retire from government service."

"I gather they mean to sack me if I do not," said Napier, his mouth twitching a little.

"Really? Hmm. A pity." Lazonby shifted in his chair. "Well. What do you make of the weather, then?"

"Sunny and breezy out front," said Napier dryly. "Any different out back?"

"Actually . . . no." Lazonby winced. "Aye, dashed awkward, isn't it, old fellow, after all our years at one another's throats? Wait—am I to call you Saint-Bryce now?"

"Lord, I don't care," said Napier wearily. "Look, let's have it right out, Lazonby, shall we? I'm late in saying it. I beg your pardon for repeatedly calling you a liar. And for refusing to listen to your claims of innocence. And for my father's perfidy in—"

Lazonby threw up a hand. "Oh, no, my good fellow! You're no more responsible for that one than I am for . . . well, whatever mischief my wife is making just now." He cut Anisha a suspicious glance, then returned his gaze to Napier. "As to the other, well, I apologize for repeatedly calling you a hatchet-faced bast—well, a great many things one oughtn't repeat in front of ladies."

Napier thrust out his hand.

Lazonby took it, and gave it a firm shake.

Lisette drew her hand from Anisha's grasp, and half turned in her chair to face him. "I, too, owe you an apology," she said quietly. "I treated you abominably, Lazonby. And I regret it."

"And I regret I led you into the rookeries and abandoned you," said Lazonby, giving her a little bow from the neck, "and that I slammed you against the wall—er, twice, I think?—and tried to strangle you."

"You tried to *strangle* her—?" Anisha turned to gape at her husband.

Lazonby shrugged a little witheringly. "Amongst other things," he admitted, "such as rifling her flat a couple of times and trying like the devil to have her sacked at the *Chronicle*."

"And I bribed your footman," Lisette admitted morosely, "and set your curricle afire."

"What?" Lazonby sat up very straight. "Was that fire your doing, by Jove? Well done! I never guessed."

"Remind me," said Napier, turning to Anisha, "never to cross either of them again."

"Yes, it might be best," said Anisha, still glowering at Lazonby.

He was twisting uncomfortably in his chair. "Restraint isn't my strong suit, Nish," he reminded her. "Don't whinge over it now, for you knew it when you married me."

"So I did," she acknowledged, setting her palms serenely together. "And now here is what you—what we *all*—must do. We must seek a state of *kshama*—of peace and forebearance—and show only kindness to one another. In this way we can negate, in some small measure, all our bad actions of the past."

"But you've never done anything bad," said her husband, grinning. "It's just the three of us that are out-and-out rotters."

She looked at him chidingly. "The teachings of the Vedas are somewhat metaphorical," she said. "And bad actions include bad thoughts."

"Do *you* have bad thoughts, old girl?" Lazonby teased.

"Sometimes," she said tightly, "I do."

Just then, the fresh-faced footman reappeared with a tea tray, saving Lazonby a further scold. The next quarter hour passed pleasantly as Anisha poured a strong, dark tea and facilitated an amiable conversation.

Despite the faint dread that had followed Lisette here—dread she'd been loathe to confess to her husband—she knew this meeting was something she needed in order to put the dark days truly behind her.

And they *were* behind her, she realized, instinctively resting a hand on her belly, suddenly grateful for Napier's strength—grateful for the new life his love had given her. Lisette felt as if she had somehow returned to herself—as if she'd become again the ordinary person she had been before everything had gone so terribly awry.

She was stirred from her introspection when laughter broke out in response to something Lazonby had said.

Her worst fears, she saw, were to go unrealized. The gentleman was simply too easygoing—and too happily married—to hold much of a grudge against anyone.

Suddenly, Anisha reached across the table and lifted the cover from a tray of sandwiches. The strong odor of salmon assailed her, and Lisette felt a sudden, barely restrained lurch of nausea.

Anisha's eyes flared wide with understanding. She dropped the lid back at once.

"I beg your pardon," said Lisette abruptly. "I feel we've kept you too long."

"Not at all." But Anisha came at once to her feet. "Still, I know you must be going. Newlyweds always have too many social obligations. Perhaps you might come back for dinner? In a few months, of course."

Lisette shot her a look of undying gratitude, and soon they were standing in the front hall awaiting Napier's carriage.

But on the threshold, Napier turned back to address their host. "I wanted you to know, Lazonby," he said, "that I've spent the last two months sorting through my father's old case files."

"Good God, man!" Lazonby feigned a look of horror. "One hopes a newly married man might have passed the time doing something a good deal more pleasant."

Nerves still a little unsettled, Lisette gave a snort of laughter.

"Ah!" Lazonby's dark brows flew aloft. "The wife makes no complaint, I see. My hat is off to you, old fellow. You've been devilish busy."

"Do *hush*, my dear," said his wife. "Napier is trying to make a point."

Napier smiled. "I am, at that," he said. "And my point is, Lazonby, that so far as I can make out, you were the only victim of a malicious prosecution. I have looked very carefully."

"Ah." The laughter left Lazonby's eyes. "Just me, was it?"

Napier shook his head. "No, for I fear it likely a great many cases were *not* prosecuted that should have been. But there are no files for those sorts of cases—and no way I can make them right."

"Ah, well," said Lazonby. "I shouldn't worry. The guilty rarely sin once. Most of them were likely caught again."

"It is to be hoped," said Napier.

And then Anisha was kissing them—both of them—and everyone was saying their good-byes.

In the drive, Napier helped Lisette back into their carriage, his dark, speculative gaze holding hers. But he said no more until they had drawn up before the house in Eaton Square and gone inside to the blessedly quiet front hall.

"Well, that's done!" she said, pulling the pin from her hat. "I am inordinately relieved."

At that, Napier pulled her a little roughly into his arms.

"I'm glad someone is," he said darkly. He lowered his mouth to Lisette's, kissed her very thoroughly, then set her a little away, dipping his gaze to catch hers.

It was *that look.*

Napier's black glower of interrogation.

"*What—?*" she said.

"Out with it, my dear," he said warningly. "Am I to worry? Or not?"

"Oh, Royden!" She managed to smile. "I don't *know.* But I think . . . yes, I think perhaps you *should* worry."

"Ha!" he said, picking her up by the waist to spin her around. "I knew it."

"And your friend Anisha knew it," said Lisette when he'd set her back down again. "How *does* she do that?"

"I've no idea." Napier grinned hugely, then kissed her again. "Well, get packing, my love."

"Really?" She blinked at him. "Where do we go?"

"Back to Burlingame," he said. "The air is cleaner, the environs more restful, and once again you are about to make me—and perhaps even Duncaster—the happiest of men."

*G*ive in to your Impulses!

These unforgettable stories only take a second to buy and give you hours of reading pleasure!

Go to *www.AvonImpulse.com* and see what we have to offer.

Available wherever e-books are sold.

AVONIMPULSE